THE CATALIN CODE

TREVOR DOUGLAS

ⱱıncı
BOOKS

Vinci Books

vinci-books.com

Published by Vinci Books Ltd in 2026

1

Copyright © Trevor Douglas 2014

The author has asserted their moral right to be identified as the author of this work in accordance with the Copyright, Designs and Patents Act 1988. This work is a work of fiction. Names, characters, places and incidents are the product of the author's imagination or are used fictitiously. Any resemblance to actual persons, living or dead, places and incidents is entirely coincidental.

All rights reserved. No part of this publication may be copied, reproduced, distributed, stored in any retrieval system, or transmitted in any form or by any means, including photocopying, recording, or other electronic or mechanical methods, nor used as a source for any form of machine learning including AI datasets, without the prior written permission of the publisher.

The publisher and the author have made every effort to obtain permissions for any third party material used in this book and to comply with copyright law. Any queries in this respect should be brought to the attention of the publisher and any omissions will be corrected in future editions.

A CIP catalogue record for this book is available from the British Library.

Paperback ISBN: 9781036704049

The EU GPSR authorised representative is Logos Europe, 9 rue Nicolas Poussion, 17000 La Rochelle, France contact@logoseurope.eu

By Trevor Douglas

The Catalin Series

The Catalin Connection

The Catalin Code

The Catalin Crossing

The Bridgette Cash Mystery Thriller Series

Cold Comfort

Cold Trail

Cold Hard Cash

The Cold Light of Day

Out in the Cold

Hot and Cold

Rowan Whitecross Murder Mystery Series

Murder on Stark Street

Standalone Novel

The Final Proposition

*This book is dedicated to family and friends who have supported me on the journey of writing and publishing my first novel.
Without your encouragement, support and honest feedback, this book would not have been possible.*

Introduction

This novel takes place in both Bucharest, Romania and Vancouver, Canada. Astute readers who are familiar with the Vancouver area will notice I have taken a little license with some of the geography. Catalin Mountain is a fictitious mountain within the Cypress Provincial Park area and the township of Cypress Falls has been expanded a little to better fit with the story.

Chapter One

The Priest made the sign of the cross and started the final part of the funeral service as they lowered the casket into the ground. Frustrated by a flight delay, Robbie had arrived a few minutes after the service had begun and had been forced to stand at the back of the assembled group of mourners. As he surveyed the gathered crowd, he saw a number of faces he recognized—some he had not seen since high school. Today, like Robbie, they all wore a look of shock and grief as they paid their respects and said a last goodbye.

Jet lagged from a non-stop flight home from London, the last twenty-four hours had been a giant blur. No sooner had he got off the plane than his phone had started to ring. As a freelance journalist, he was used to wading through dozens of messages while he waited for his baggage after a long-haul flight. The second message this time had been from his mother, asking him to call her as soon as he could. He knew from the tone of her voice that something was wrong. When he returned the call, he could barely believe his mother's words.

"I'm so sorry, Robbie. Aaron has been killed in an accident."

His mother explained that his childhood friend, Aaron MacDonald, had died three nights earlier in a hit-and-run accident near to his apartment in Vancouver. His mother didn't know the details, other than the police believed it was most likely a drunk driver. She apologized for not being able to get the message through sooner and explained the funeral arrangements, but by then, Robbie was no longer listening.

Robbie felt guilty that he had not seen 'Mac' for some time. After collecting his bags, he had sat in an airport lounge for almost two hours, finding it difficult to accept that his oldest and most trusted friend was gone. As Robbie listened to the priest's words, he recalled the day their lives changed forever while they were still in high school.

They had been through a lot together. As he stood with his head bowed, Robbie remembered how much he had relied on Mac in later years following the car accident that had killed his wife Annie and left him requiring months of rehabilitation. Mac had been his rock through his recovery. The doctors healed him physically, but Mac was the one who got him out of his funk and helped him start again.

It didn't seem fair that the anchor in his life since Annie's death was now gone as well. He listened intently to the rest of the service and then said his own prayer at the end. As the mourners dispersed, Robbie worked his way through the crowd to speak to Mac's sister, Laura.

Although he hadn't seen Laura for nearly three years, he knew Mac and his sister had remained close. Robbie knew Laura would be doing it tough.

As he moved through the crowd, a deep gravelly voice called out, "Robbie?"

Turning around, Robbie looked into the face of a tall man who was dressed in a dark suit and wearing sunglasses. Although he was now slightly heavier and had a full head of graying hair, Robbie would have recognized Nick Carney anywhere. Slightly taken aback at seeing Nick amongst the mourners, Robbie reached out and shook Nick's hand.

"It's been a while, Nick."

Nick nodded and replied, "Twenty-five years, Robbie."

Robbie tried to hide his surprise as he thought about what to say in response. He had not seen Nick since the end of high school. He remembered Nick had left their hometown of Cypress Falls on a sporting scholarship to study for a degree in criminology.

After graduating, he had joined the Vancouver Metropolitan Police as a base grade police officer before transferring to the newly formed state Organized Crime Task Force. Robbie had followed Nick's career through the newspapers, as he featured regularly as part of a successful team breaking up crime gangs. He had risen steadily through the ranks and had made Deputy Director of the OCTF in his late thirties.

As tactfully as he could put it, Robbie asked, "I didn't know you and Mac kept in contact after school?"

Nick lowered his voice just slightly and replied, "Let's just say I'm here because one of the four of us honored the promise we made and took what we knew to the grave."

Nick waited for a response and when none was forthcoming, he took off his sunglasses and studied Robbie with a slight look of amusement. "You'd have to be suffering from brain damage, not to remember, Robbie?"

"I remember, Nick. Even though it was at the end of

high school, not a single day goes by that I don't think about it."

Nick nodded and began scanning the crowd as he replied, "You see Jerry here today?"

"My connecting flight into Vancouver was delayed and I arrived late. You're the first person I've spoken to."

"You'd think if the Director General of the OCTF could make the funeral of a former school friend, so could the Mayor?"

Robbie remembered reading about Nick's recent promotion to the Director General role when the incumbent had retired after a protracted battle with Parkinson's disease. It had surprised him that Nick had made it to the top job after surviving a corruption incident several years ago. Several of his senior colleagues were still serving jail time after being found guilty and he wondered whether Nick got the job because of his ability, or because he was the last man standing?

Ignoring Nick's big noting of himself, Robbie replied, "I guess Jerry's schedule keeps him busy."

Nick replied flatly, "I wouldn't know."

Robbie knew Jerry and Nick's friendship had soured in recent years. After high school, they had remained close friends as they built their careers until Jerry had made a run for Mayor. Jerry's electoral campaigning happened at the same time Nick was making the newspapers as one of those allegedly involved in the OCTF scandal. Jerry had been a prominent Vancouver lawyer at the time and had publicly distanced himself from Nick to avoid any collateral damage to his campaign for the Mayor's Office.

Their relationship never recovered after they exonerated Nick, and the two continued to trade the occasional insult at one another when the opportunity arose in the media.

Robbie had no interest in pursuing the conversation and felt the feeling was mutual as he watched Nick put on his sunglasses and scan the crowd.

"Hey, Nick, I'm going to head over and catch up with Laura."

Nick nodded as he kept scanning the crowd. "You do that, Robbie, and if you see the good mayor of Vancouver, remind him that Mac's untimely demise changes nothing."

Before Robbie responded, Nick moved off into the crowd of mourners. Robbie shook his head. Nick had been arrogant and self-serving in high school, and nothing appeared to have changed in the years following.

While monitoring the crowd for Jerry, Robbie waded through the sea of mourners to pass on his condolences to Laura. Mac had never married and most people who attended the funeral seemed to be aware of how close Laura had been to her brother. Robbie waited to see her, almost as if he was in a queue as other groups gathered to offer their condolences as well.

He watched Laura as she spoke to the couple ahead of him. Even though she was close to forty, she had lost none of her beauty. He was worried about how she would cope now that her brother was gone. Laura had worked for many years as a police officer and was serving with the OCTF when the corruption incident broke in the newspapers.

Unlike Nick, who knew how to play the political games, Laura had resigned because of the stress from being hounded by the media, even though she was totally innocent. He recalled how Mac had helped her get back on her feet again as she struggled with a drinking problem and a difficult divorce in the aftermath.

As he watched her say a last farewell to the couple ahead of him, he made a mental note to check on her regularly in the months ahead to make sure she didn't sink into a long-term depression again. Still seated, Laura turned towards Robbie and as soon as she recognized who it was, she rose and came forward. Unable to hide her grief, she wept uncontrollably as Robbie held her tightly. They held each other for a long time, neither embarrassed nor feeling the need to speak.

Finally, Robbie said, "I'm so sorry, Laura."

"I'm sorry for you too, Robbie. I know he meant as much to you as he did to me."

Laura sobbed again, and Robbie squeezed her tighter.

After recovering slightly, Laura let go of Robbie and said, "I'm glad you could make the service, Robbie. Your mother told me you've been in Europe and I was worried you might have missed today."

"Mac was my best friend, Laura. I would never miss this."

"It means a lot to me that you're here. Mac has idolized you since you were teenagers, and I'm glad you got to say goodbye."

Robbie frowned. "It's such a shock, Laura. I'm still having trouble believing he's gone. I spoke to him a few days ago when I was in Europe, but I never expected it would be the last time I would ever talk to him."

"I feel the same way, Robbie. I'm numb all over and just can't believe it's really happened."

"Have the police arrested anyone yet?"

Laura shook her head. "Robbie, I need to talk to you about Mac. But not here and not now. Are you in town for a day or two?"

Robbie had made no plans beyond today. He had to complete a story on white-collar crime syndicates he had been working on, but he had planned to fly back home to the east coast to do that.

"I don't have any actual plans so, sure, I'll fit in with you."

"It might be nothing, but I'd like to talk, anyway. Mac hadn't been himself for the last few weeks and some things don't add up. It's probably nothing, but you know him better than anyone else, Robbie, so if you don't mind?"

Robbie wasn't sure how to respond. He remembered how stressed Mac has seemed on the phone when they had last spoken. It was totally out of character for his friend, who was usually very laid back. Robbie had promised to call as soon as he returned, and he now wondered if it was somehow connected?

He knew now was not the time to talk about it and replied, "Sure, it would be nice to catch up, Laura."

They said their goodbyes and agreed to meet after Robbie had recovered from his jet lag. Robbie looked around the crowd at several familiar faces he knew he should catch up with, but he wasn't in the mood to talk. Instead, he went back to his rental car and sat thinking about the accident.

He watched as the mourners slowly dissipated and the cemetery grounds men came and filled in Mac's grave. When they had finished, Robbie got out of the car and walked back to the graveside. Now alone, he stared down at the fresh mound of earth and still found it difficult to believe his friend was gone.

He did his best to remember some of the good times they had together, but his mood darkened as he thought back to nineteen eighty-nine and what Nick had said earlier. One of the four of them had taken what they knew to the grave as they had all promised.

He wondered whether Jerry ever thought about what had happened? He was disappointed he hadn't come to the funeral. He knew Mac and Jerry had stayed in touch and got together for the occasional meal. Surely nobody was that busy that they couldn't find time to say goodbye to someone they had shared so much with?

He thought about Laura again and wondered again what she meant when she said, 'some things didn't add up.' The more he thought about it, the more uneasy he felt. He pulled his smartphone from his pocket and opened up his email application. Using his finger, he quickly scrolled back to the last message he had received from Mac.

To: robert.mayne@promail.com From: <Mac/>
  Subject: Call ASAP

Robbie,
  Please call me as soon as you get off the plane. It doesn't matter what time of day or night. A lot has happened while you've been away, and we need to talk.
  Mac

Robbie looked down again at the fresh mound of earth. Hit and runs were normally an accident, but he knew he couldn't leave it at that. He would need to make sure.

Robbie wanted to say a few last words out loud to his friend, but knew he wasn't strong enough to get them out coherently. Instead, he silently thanked Mac for his friendship and murmured, "It's not over, Mac", before he turned and walked away.

Chapter Two

Dressed in a charcoal gray Italian designer suit, Richard Stelovak sat at the defense table and cautiously watched the jury file back into the stately wood paneled courtroom. He ignored the murmurings of the sizable crowd in the visitors' gallery and glanced down discretely at his watch. They had only been out for a little over an hour, which he took to be a good sign.

With slim, angular features, manicured nails and a two-hundred-dollar haircut, Stelovak looked every bit the accomplished, middle-aged business executive. He had been attentive throughout the trial, polite to the judge and opposing council attorneys, and had carefully followed the script prepared by his defense team.

His legal team's attention to detail impressed Stelovak, and he was confident the seven-figure sum he had paid to retain them and buy off the judge would be worth it. He had followed their instructions to the letter; no guarded whispers at any point to lawyers during the trial unless scripted, no doodling on notepads, looking at the ceiling, staring at jury members, or anyone else for that matter. He would be judged as much on his demeanor as his testimony as he sat on show in front of the jury.

The contacts had been a nice touch as well. His penetrating blue eyes gave him an aloof, if not cold and calculating look. To the jury, his eyes appeared a warm hazel color that was in keeping with the compassionate, law-abiding image the defense team had been cultivating for him throughout the trial.

Stelovak was as annoyed as he was anxious about the trial. In the middle of finalizing a development deal that would provide Stelecom with over two billion dollars in development and construction revenue over the next five years, the trial was something he did not need. He was glad the trial would be over today and satisfied that everything that could be done had been done to get the right verdict.

Arriving as a seventeen-year-old Romanian immigrant and speaking little English, Stelovak had quickly found his way into the gang culture in Vancouver but was smart enough to realize he would be dead before he was thirty if he didn't get out and make it on his own. Carefully using and exploiting every legal and illegal option at his disposal, he had left nothing to chance as he built Stelecom Industries from a modest earth moving business into a multi-million-dollar construction and development company. Today was no exception.

Besides Randolph Keaton, his twenty-nine-year-old in-house legal counsel, who, for an annual retainer of four hundred thousand dollars was on call twenty-four hours a day, Stelovak had engaged three of the finest from the law firm, Phipps, Babb and Associates, including Michael Phipps, one of their two senior partners.

Stelovak had hired Phipps and his firm not only for their

exceptional legal skills but also for the unique association they had with several judges on the bench who, for a fee, could discretely engineer court room outcomes. Bribes and payoffs were commonplace for Stelovak in his construction business and were always handled by highly trusted associates, using company entities completely separate to Stelecom. He had been careful about the bribe to be paid to the presiding judge, Simpson Hanley, and insisted they covered it under the single flat fee for legal services he paid to Phipps's law firm to make it impossible to trace.

The verdict in favor of Stelovak's company in a lawsuit brought by the widow of a subcontractor who had been crushed to death by a hydraulic lift on a Stelecom construction site had been negotiated weeks earlier. Intermediaries for both Phipps and the judge had brokered the deal by phone without ever meeting. Hanley had a string of gambling debts and found himself in need of money to stop his problem from going public. A discrete one hundred and seventy-five-thousand-dollar cash bonus would be paid if he could deliver a favorable outcome for the defendant. As promised, he made life in his courtroom hell for the plaintiff's team throughout the trial.

Stelovak looked across at their table. The confidence and swagger the lawyers had shown at the beginning of the trial was gone. They had not handled the trial or Judge Hanley at all well. They had given Phipps a lot of latitude and he was able to twist the facts and make a convincing argument that the hydraulic lift collapse had been accidental and the result of a design flaw, that the manufacturer had never reported to Stelecom.

Despite the objections and howls of protest by the plaintiff's lawyers, Phipps was even able to convey to the jury that the plaintiff's lawyers had rejected a one million dollar no liability 'good will' gesture by Stelecom. Phipps went on to accuse the lawyers of seeking a settlement against Stelecom rather than the lift manufacturer based on each company's net worth. Judge Hanley had feigned outrage, but not before he let Phipps get his message across to the jury.

Stelovak ignored the whispered commentary from his defense team and focused on the widow as she sat in the middle of her group of lawyers at the plaintiff's table. She looked bewildered, small, and lost as she listened intently to their fervent discussion. Even though she was now left to raise a young daughter alone, Stelovak didn't feel sorry for her. He husband had gotten in his way and had refused a bribe that would have made him rich. He was confident she was about to also learn the hard way that Richard Stelovak was not someone you crossed.

Stelovak watched the jurors as they took their places in the jury box. Michael Phipps leaned in closer and whispered, "They've reached a verdict quickly and they're not making eye contact with her as they come in. That's a good sign for us."

Stelovak subtly nodded but said nothing in response—he would hold his enthusiasm until he heard the formal verdict. Phipps pretended to write something on a notepad in front of Stelovak and continued in a low voice, "There's a guy in the second row of the gallery directly behind the defense table. Looks to be about thirty and is wearing a dark gray off the rack suit. He's been taking a lot of notes this morning and keeps staring at you. Have you—."

Stelovak cut him off and whispered, "His name is Westcott. He's a detective with Vancouver Metro—works homicide."

Phipps had made his fortune as a defense lawyer for

high-profile criminals and was held in high regard within the criminal underworld. Now in his mid-fifties, he was wise enough to know when to exercise discretion, and after representing Richard Stelovak in three separate murder investigations, he knew this was one of those moments.

In response, Phipps tactfully replied, "If you observe him tailing you later, let me know and I'll lodge a formal complaint with his superiors. I'll find out exactly what he's up to."

Stelovak nodded.

After the jurors had settled, Judge Hanley, in an earnest voice any Hollywood director would be proud of, inquired of the chief juror, "Has the jury reached a verdict?"

"Yes, your honor, we have."

Judge Hanley nodded at the chief juror, who passed across the folded paper copy of the verdict. Judge Hanley showed no reaction as he read the decision, nodded and passed the verdict back. Stelovak thought, if he was now one hundred and seventy-five thousand dollars richer, he wasn't showing it.

"In the matter of Wright versus Stelecom Industries, in relation to the wrongful death charges, how find you?"

"Your honor, in the matter of Wright versus Stelecom Industries, we find for the defendant and determine there is no liability on its behalf to pay damages."

Above the roar from the gallery, Judge Hanley banged his gavel multiple times to restore order. He rapidly issued a few brief words of thanks and closing instructions as the courtroom began to clear.

Phipps reached across and shook Stelovak's hand and offered his congratulations. His two associates did the same before joining their boss at the plaintiff's table to shake hands and engage in the usual post trial lawyer small talk.

Stelovak and Keaton rose to leave. Keaton, having no desire to be photographed by the press or to be seen as a side act to his boss on the six o'clock news, placed a gentle hand on Stelovak's shoulder. "I'll see you out front after the press conference."

Stelovak nodded and headed for the front door. He normally shied away from cameras and TV crews, but today was different. Although Stelecom had been successful in its bid as the prime developer for Southwest Industrial, final contracts were not due to be signed for another four days. Stelovak knew from his previous experience dealing with planning and development authorities that until they had the final ink on the contracts, things could still go wrong.

He needed to get on the front foot and do some PR around the court case outcome. Keeping the lawyers and key decision makers in Vancouver Planning and Development happy was important. They would be monitoring the outcome. A bad result for Stelecom would bring their decision on the two billion dollars development deal under enormous scrutiny from the press. He had seen deals fall over at the last minute for far less.

Pushing through the front glass doors, a swirling throng of cameras, questions, and microphones greeted Stelovak. Putting on a practiced smile, designed to be confident without appearing arrogant, Stelovak stopped at the top of the courthouse steps and paused to allow the media a moment to assemble.

"Fourteen months ago, I received a phone call informing me of a tragic accident which claimed the life of one of Stelecom's most dedicated employees. The time since then has been very hard on the family, and once again, I offer them my sincere condolences. During this trial, a jury of your peers has heard all available evidence and has determined that Stelecom is in no way responsible for this tragic and untimely death. I want to say on both a company and a personal level we will continue to fully co-operate with the authorities and legal representatives for Mrs. Wright, should she choose to explore other avenues for compensation. Thank you for your time today."

Stelovak feigned to leave, as he was hit by a barrage of questions.

"Will you be offering Mrs. Wright another no liability settlement?"

"Mrs. Wright still has legal avenues open to her. I would encourage her to fully explore those with her legal counsel."

"So, the money is off the table then?"

"Again, my advice to Mrs. Wright would be to look at her legal options. She is now a widow and left to raise a young child on her own without her husband. Next question."

"Do you believe the lift manufacturer is responsible?"

"It's on the public record that there was a design flaw with that model of lift. Beyond that, I'm not a lawyer and don't believe it is appropriate to comment further. One more question."

"There have been reports that Judge Hanley was very lenient to the Defense in this trial. How do you respond to that?"

Stelovak feigned a look somewhere between surprised and perplexed as he responded, "I thought he ran a very efficient trial. I don't know him personally, but I thought he did a good job in difficult and emotional circumstances. Thank you for your time today."

As Stelovak made his way down the courthouse steps through the crowd of reporters and photographers, the questions kept coming. Some wanting to know if he felt sorry for Mrs. Wright, others challenging him to pay her compensation as a goodwill gesture. There was even one muffled question about Hanley taking a bribe. He timed his exit well, he thought, getting his message out without getting into messy questions and answers that would make him look cruel and heartless.

Keaton was standing alongside the limousine, waiting with Stelovak's driver as he emerged from the throng. He nodded once at his boss and said, "Nice show."

Stelovak mumbled a thank you as he looked down at a legal-size manila envelope Keaton was withdrawing from his Attache case.

Keaton lowered his voice slightly, "We have the photographs. There may be a problem, however."

In the time Keaton had worked for Stelovak, 'problem' was a word he did not use often or lightly. Stelovak looked around. There were still a lot of press and photographers close by. He was looking forward to celebrating tonight. The look on Keaton's face suggested otherwise.

"Ride with me back to the office. We can talk on the way."

Chapter Three

Stelovak thumbed through the eight by ten glossies as his limousine headed back to the Stelecom building after the press conference. There were seven pictures of Leon Blackwell and his temporary secretary. In all photos, Blackwell's trousers were down around his ankles and his secretary's skirt up around her waist. The photographs were not particularly pornographic, but suitable for his purposes. Their faces, state of undress and what they were doing on an office desk were perfectly captured.

Stelovak had used a string of shelf companies operated by Blackwell for the past four years to launder money from his various business interests. Blackwell was the best at what he did and was normally reliable and trustworthy. Recently, Blackwell had been interviewed by police in connection with a raid on another client whose profits he had discreetly moved offshore through a complex series of dividend payments. Blackwell was now very wealthy, and rumors had circulated that he was looking to 'get out of the business' while he still could.

He had been worried about Blackwell for some time. Stelovak was using Blackwell's organization to manage bribes and illegal bonuses, some worth over a million dollars to get the Southwest Development deal over the line. The last thing he needed was for Blackwell to get cold feet and disappear or worse, turn police informant.

While there were no guarantees, Stelovak was confident the photos would give him the leverage he needed. Blackwell was a happily married man with two children and well respected in his community. He would want it to stay that way.

He looked across at Keaton, who sat opposite him and said, "This is good work, Randolph. Make a clean set and pay Blackwell a visit. I think we can make a persuasive argument that if he continues to look after us, we can ensure these pictures never see the light of day."

Returning the photos, Stelovak continued. "Now, what's the problem?"

"The problem is one Eugene Brennan. Our normal photographer for this sort of work is still laid up from his appendix operation. Eugene is his partner and comes highly recommended. He's very good at surveillance photography, as you can see. But he did some research on Blackwell and discovered seventy percent of his work comes from us. I got a call from Eugene saying the price has gone up. Of course, I told him I did not know what he was talking about, but he insisted we were the client and could pay more. He was bluffing of course, but it was a good educated guess."

"Did he make a threat, or is he just pumping us for money?"

"He's pumping us for money. He thinks Stelecom can and should pay more than ten thousand. But he made a veiled threat to the effect that other parties might be interested in knowing more about the photos."

"What other parties?"

"He didn't say, and I didn't show any interest. I didn't want him to get any idea his fishing expedition might be right."

Stelovak thought for a moment. "We can't have this guy running around mouthing off. Even rumors can make it difficult for us. Southwest is not a done deal yet."

"What do you want to do?"

"Who's available?"

Keaton knew immediately what was meant by the question. "I'm sure either Vince or Rudy would be."

Vincent Franco and Rudy Henning were associates with a special skill set that Stelovak occasionally made use of. They were professional, discrete and for an additional fee would take the extra time required to make it look like an accident.

"Both. They meet Brennan with the ten K in cash, like we agreed. He gets one chance and one chance only to accept. If he makes any threat or tries to boost the price, it's over. Does he live alone?"

"I believe so."

"Get them to follow him. Have them call to make the payment when he's at home. That way, if we need to use plan B, we can check to make sure he's got nothing else incriminating lying around."

"What about his business partner?"

"He'll figure it out. He's smart and does well out of us. I'm sure he'd prefer more business and a long life than the alternative."

The limousine pulled up out front of the glass office

block that was Stelecom's head office. Without another word, Stelovak was out of the vehicle and heading for the front doors. Keaton had a few phone calls to make. He was not a betting man, but he did not like Eugene Brennan's odds for living much longer.

Chapter Four

Robbie sat in the rental car sipping a cup of coffee as he looked down the hill at the white Tudor style two-story building. Going under the name of Irish's Tavern, it was three blocks from where Mac had lived and, according to the newspaper reports, the place where Mac had been run down. He remembered Mac had taken him there one night on one of his stopovers. Robbie recalled the food being terrible, but the atmosphere and people more than made up for it.

The jet lag and emotional toll of Saturday's funeral had finally caught up with Robbie. He had slept through most of Sunday, and awoke on Monday morning, still not feeling rested. Laura's concerns and his own doubts about the accident were the perfect cocktail for restless sleep. He was looking forward to seeing her that evening and after getting up early and spending an hour in the hotel gym; he had decided this was as good a place as any to try to find answers.

Robbie studied the stretch of roadway where Mac had

been killed. The road was divided by a six-foot high concrete block retaining wall to accommodate the slope of the land. South bound traffic coming into the largely residential area past Irish's and several other shops used the top side, while north bound traffic leaving the area used the lower side. A purpose-built break in the wall complete with steps and road crossing markers allowed lower side residents to cross to and from the shops.

Robbie got out of the rental and walked across the crossing and up to Irish's. Walking in through the heavy front doors, Robbie's eyes took a moment to adjust to the dim light. The main bar area was on the right-hand side of a large wood paneled room. Apart from Robbie and the man behind the bar cleaning glasses, there were only five patrons who were seated in two groups. Robbie guessed the bartender was in his mid-forties, but it was hard to tell. He was slightly taller than Robbie; he guessed at least six three and weighed somewhere over two hundred and fifty pounds. His hair had the appearance of a salt and pepper mane and extended well below his shoulders and out at an angle that seemed to defy gravity. His matching long goatee and unshaven face gave him a menacing look and hid most of his facial features.

Robbie was surprised by the man's soft tenor voice and slight Irish lilt that greeted him. "What can I get for you?"

"Just a coke. With ice please."

Robbie leaned on the bar and watched as the man fixed his drink. Not sure where to begin, he decided the direct approach was probably best.

"Are you Irish?"

With a wry smile, the man replied. "Both."

"Both?"

"Irish by name and by birth."

Robbie smiled. He already liked the man. "I'm a friend of Mac. We've been friends since junior high. I'm trying to understand what happened... the accident."

The man's features turned sullen. Without a word, Irish extended a huge index finger and pointed at a table near the back wall next to the bar.

Robbie made his way to the table and watched as Irish fixed his own drink. It looked a lot stronger than his coke. Irish then yelled at someone out back to come and take over as he made his way over to Robbie.

After settling into a chair that creaked loudly under his weight, Irish said. "I recognize you now. You were at the funeral."

"Yes. I was."

Irish pulled at his beard for a moment and then said, "You know, Mac was probably the most infuriating man I've ever known. He could talk the leg off a chair, he was unbelievably opinionated and irritating, yet he would give you the shirt off his back in a heartbeat if he thought you needed it. He was a one of a kind. I'm going to miss him."

They were both quiet for a moment before Robbie asked, "How well did you know him?"

"He's been coming in here once or twice a week for about two years. More for the company than anything else. He was smart, but he never threw it in anyone's face. Everybody here loved him."

Irish then cocked his head. "Somehow I get the feeling none of this is news to you. Where are we going with this?"

"I'm not sure Irish. I flew in from an overseas business trip two days ago to be told Mac had been killed in a hit-and-run. I'm just trying to put it all together. It's been a shock. The paper says he was knocked down out front?"

Irish shifted in his chair and then responded in a quiet

voice, "That's what they tell me. I park my car out back and come in through the rear entrance. I'm getting ready to open and next thing I know, there's a cop banging on my front door. When he told me Mac had been killed, I couldn't believe it. I had to sit for a while. The cop tells me it's a hit and run and wants to know how much Mac had been drinking, who he'd been talking to, how often he comes in here. I answer as best I could, but to be honest, I was numb."

Irish took a sip of his drink and added, "Mac was larger than life. It's hard for me to get my head around it. Anyway, the cop, a detective, spends a couple of hours canvassing the neighborhood and then comes back in to see if I remember anything else. I said I didn't, so he leaves his card and tells me to call him if I remember anything. That's it really."

"Did he show you where it happened?"

"I haven't stepped foot outside that front door since that cop visited. Exactly where it happened, I'm not sure. I believe it was somewhere on the lower side, heading north. Mac only lived a couple of blocks from here and would walk home, mostly. He'd use the crossing out front. The cop said they found him up against the retaining wall."

"He got hit on the crossing?"

"No. The road is fairly wide there and some locals walk next to the retaining wall for shelter if it's windy and raining as it was that night."

"Could anyone else here point out where it happened?"

"Gary, one of my bartenders was out there helping the cops, but he's off for two days. I don't think he can tell you a whole lot more anyway. You could maybe ask some locals that live on the lower side. They would have a much better idea than we would here."

"Okay."

"Robbie, I know this is hard, but seriously, I don't think there's much more to know."

"I need some closure, Irish, that's all. The paper implied Mac might have been drunk and basically walked out into traffic?"

"Papers are full of lies, Robbie. Don't believe a word of it. Mac was as sober as a judge. He had a meeting here around eight thirty and sat on a coke while he was waiting. The guy he met was only here about fifteen minutes and left. First time I've ever seen Mac get angry at someone. He didn't look happy afterward and didn't want to talk about it. He made a couple of phone calls and hung around till closing. Strongest thing he drank all night was what you've got in front of you."

Robbie looked down at his glass of coke as he thought about what Irish had said and then asked, "The guy he met. Was he a regular?"

"Never seen him before. He was probably mid-forties, about my height but lean, underweight really. Wore a suit. Looked a bit like an undertaker with a shaved head."

"The paper also mentioned Mac might have been having personal problems?"

"As I said, Robbie, don't believe what you read in the papers. I've been in this business almost twenty years and I've learned more about people than anything else. Whether they come in here in rags or suits, I talk to them for a few minutes and I know who's got problems—who's doing drugs, who's got gambling or drinking problems, who's got marriage problems and money problems. I can tell you who's got it together and who doesn't. Mac had it together."

Irish drained the rest of his glass in one gulp and wiped his mouth. "I have to get back to work. You know where I am if you need anything."

"Thanks Irish."

As they walked to the door, Irish said, "Hold one second."

He retrieved a business card from behind the bar and gave it to, Robbie.

"This is the detective who is looking after the investigation. Can't hurt to call him."

They shook hands and Robbie stepped outside. After walking through the crossing to the lower side of the road, he decided it would be worth his while door knocking and canvassing some of the locals.

Robbie pulled the detective's card out. He decided it couldn't hurt to call him and see if he had made any progress. Using his mobile phone, Robbie dialed the detective's number, expecting to leave a message.

"Westcott."

"Hello, my name's Robbie Mayne, and I'm a friend… was a friend of Aaron MacDonald. I was just wondering if you could answer a couple of questions about the accident?"

"I'm sorry, but you normally have to go through Police Liaison unless you have something specific that can help with the investigation."

"I appreciate you're busy, but he was my oldest friend. We went through school together and have been close ever since. I just want to know if the police think it was an accident?"

"I'm sorry, what was your name?"

"Robbie—Robbie Mayne."

"Look, Robbie, most of these situations, in fact almost all of them, are accidents. Speed, a drunk driver, poor weather—you name it. I canvassed the area for a couple of hours the day after it happened, but didn't find any witnesses. We will try our best to solve it, but truth be told, it looks like an accident. There's not a lot more I can do for now except wait. No vehicle ID, no security camera footage, no witnesses—there's not a lot to go on."

"I see."

"Often these things have a way of resolving themselves within a few weeks. We get a report of blood on a bumper from someone at a body shop doing a repair, someone gets pulled over for a traffic violation and a cop notices damage on the front of the car and starts asking questions. It's surprising how often, with time, we get the driver."

"You noticed nothing suspicious about Aaron's accident? Something different that would show it was deliberate?"

"No, nothing like that."

They were silent for a moment before Westcott asked. "Robbie, is there anything I should know? Did Aaron have any enemies, for example? Is there anyone specific we should talk to? You give me something to go on and I'll make sure it's fully investigated."

"No. Nothing specific, Detective."

"Robbie, I'm sorry for your loss. I don't want to blow you off here, but frankly, there's not much more I can do unless something breaks. It's an open file and an ongoing investigation, but it's one of several cases I'm on at present."

"Okay."

"If you think of anything, by all means, call me back and I'll look into it."

"Just one more question, Detective. Did he suffer?"

The phone was silent for a moment. "Robbie, I'm no doctor and I shouldn't be telling you this, but the autopsy listed a broken neck in addition to substantial head and body injuries. Death would have been almost instantaneous."

Robbie thanked the detective for his time and hung up. He decided to keep the card. The guy seemed overworked, but genuine. He might help if he found something.

Feeling positive that someone must have seen something, Robbie walked back to the rental to grab a pen and notebook.

Parked up a side street, the man watched Robbie return to his car and then leave again. He hit speed dial on his phone and waited several seconds.

"He's still here. Got a notebook from his car. Looks like he's going door to door."

The man listened for a few seconds and then disconnected. He kept his gaze on Robbie as he adjusted his sunglasses and settled in for the wait.

Chapter Five

Bucharest, Romania

Petru glanced at his laptop's digital clock. It was 1:47 a.m. but he was wide awake. He felt a sickening feeling in his stomach as he returned his gaze to the images from the security cameras.

He watched the feed from a camera concealed just above the entrance to his apartment block, as the grainy image of a man walked by the building again. He grimaced. The same man had walked past his apartment block six times in the last hour. His friend Nicolai had been missing for twenty-four hours, and he hoped he was dead. He knew what they were capable of. If he was being held captive and tortured for information, the sweet mercy of death could be days away.

He knew he was next on the list and if his plan did not work, he would be dead within the hour. After taking several deep breaths, switched off the camera feeds and opened another program on his laptop. He spent a few seconds adjusting the laptop until the device's webcam captured most of the left-hand side of his apartment. He then pulled out his smartphone and opened an app that connected to his laptop webcam. Petru adjusted the contrast until he was happy with the live feed he had of his apartment, and then he pushed back from the desk in his wheelchair.

As he wheeled across the darkened living room of his small, drab apartment, he told himself now was not the time to panic. He had made all the preparations he could and hoped the planning would pay off.

Petru estimated he had about ninety seconds before the man would be at his front door. The elevators were slow and unreliable in the old run-down apartment complex, and he knew the man would take the stairs. He had timed some of his fourth-floor neighbors, who preferred stairs over the two ancient elevators. Watching them come in the entranceway on his security camera, he had timed how long it had taken them to climb four floors and walk along the hallway to their apartment doors.

The fourteen-year-old boy who lived with his mother in the apartment next door had set the best time at one minute forty-two seconds. The average time had been well over two minutes. He figured whoever they sent would climb the stairs quickly, but not so fast as to attract attention, even at this late hour. Petru maneuvered his wheelchair into the only bedroom of his apartment to check everything carefully one last time.

The mound he had fashioned in the bed from spare blankets to represent his body did not need any final adjustments. Petru pulled a small digital voice recorder from his pocket, which he had used to record himself while sleeping. The recording went for close to twenty minutes, which he guessed would be more than adequate for his purposes. He pressed the play button on the recorder and adjusted the volume to a level he thought was equivalent to that of someone in a deep sleep. He gently slid the device under the pillow and pulled up the top sheet to cover most of a dark-gray blanket he had fashioned into the shape of his head. Petru studied the ruse, hoping that whoever they sent wouldn't bother to switch the light on first.

Satisfied he had done all he could, he wheeled back into the main living area. On a rare trip out of the apartment, he had sourced several industrial grade springs from a local car mechanic. He had secured them behind the bedroom door and fashioned a locking mechanism that, when released, would snap the bedroom door shut and automatically lock it. He was satisfied that provided his attacker was fully in the bedroom when he released the clip, it would lock him in with no quick way out except by breaking down the door. Conscious that valuable seconds were now ticking away, he reversed his wheelchair into the small bathroom and closed the door.

Petru had never liked the apartment. The building was over forty years old and its cheap concrete and steel construction made it a cold and depressing place to live. It was a long way removed from the luxurious apartment he rented before the shooting. Now, permanently paralyzed from the waist down and with only a meager income, he had initially resented having to stoop so low as to live in such a squalid part of the city. As he contemplated what was likely to unfold in the next few minutes, the concrete walls and steel doors he had disliked for so long, he now hoped would save his life.

As he sat in the darkness, Petru could feel his heart beating loudly in his chest. He breathed deeply and admonished himself to stay calm. He had practiced the routine enough times now so that it became automatic. Now was the moment of truth. Petru picked up his phone and studied the video feed from his laptop. The screen showed his living room, but the image was grainy and lacked sufficient contrast. He made a few adjustments until the furniture in the living room appeared as silhouettes on the screen. He nodded to himself, confident enough he would see the outline of anyone who entered his apartment.

Petru transferred the phone to his right hand and then gingerly lifted a metal ring off a hook with his left. He delicately slid the ring onto his index finger. The metal ring was attached to a thin wire that went through a tiny hole he had drilled through the wall to his bedroom. The wire was connected to a release latch he had installed behind his bedroom door.

He had modeled the latch on the humble mousetrap. It had required some patient trial and error, but he was now confident a slight tug on the wire would snap the bedroom door shut, provided his adversary was fully inside the room. His system would briefly entrap whoever the syndicate sent to kill him and hopefully give him sufficient time to escape.

Within seconds, Petru heard a small but distinctive clinking metallic sound. He knew someone had picked the lock to his front door as his phone screen showed the front door swing slowly open.

At first, the doorway appeared empty, before the silhouette of a man carrying a silenced pistol appeared on the screen. The man appeared to be in no hurry and stood in the doorway with his gun raised—watching and listening. Cautiously, the man took two steps into the apartment and scanned for signs of danger. Satisfied there were no imminent threats, the man silently closed the front door behind him.

Petru watched the silhouette of the man as he walked several steps forward before stopping directly outside the bathroom door and tilting his head slightly as if listening for sounds that would point to the location of his quarry. The apartment was silent except for the sound of Petru's rhythmic breathing emanating softly from the recorder in the bedroom. Petru had not stepped foot inside a church since he was a young boy, but he prayed with the zeal of a monk in divine service that the man would go to the bedroom first. The facts were simple. If the man checked the bathroom first, he knew he was as good as dead.

The man stood still and turned his head slowly from side to side. Although it was difficult to tell from the camera angle, the man did not appear to be wearing any night vision goggles. Petru figured he was probably waiting while his eyes adjusted to the darkness before moving any further into the apartment. The stress of waiting made Petru sweat. He feared losing even a slight grip on the metal ring. The slightest movement could give his position away.

After what seemed like an eternity, the man took one step forward and then another toward the bedroom. The man moved forward and stood at the entrance to the bedroom with the gun raised in a firing position. Without warning, he disappeared into the bedroom and, almost simultaneously, Petru heard the muffled sound of the silenced pistol as it discharged three times in quick succession.

Petru pulled hard on the ring for the release latch. He felt the wire go taught before the bathroom reverberated to the sound of the bedroom door slamming shut. Before Petru registered what had happened, he heard the unmistakable sound of several more muffled gunshots being fired at the cheap metal bedroom door.

Petru grabbed a length of piano wire and his travel bag that he left permanently on a shelf in the bathroom in preparation for this day. Opening the door, he quickly maneuvered his wheelchair to the front door. The noise coming from the bedroom was loud and persistent. The man was obviously throwing his entire weight at the door in an effort to break the lock. Petru estimated he needed two minutes to be ready for what he needed to do next. Judging by the amount of effort the man was putting into the door, he was not sure the lock would hold that long.

Petru opened the front door and quickly wheeled down the hallway to the building elevators. He pressed the call button for the elevator before sliding out of his wheelchair. The stairwell for the apartment block was located next to the elevators, and in preparation for this day, Petru had screwed two small unobtrusive steel hooks into the banister support posts just below shin height. Deftly slipping out of his wheelchair, he used his hands to slide from one post to the other to quickly fasten the wire between the two hooks before pulling it taught and tying it off. Petru barely heard the bell that signaled his elevator had arrived over the din coming from his apartment. Just a few seconds more, he prayed, as he got back into his wheelchair and wheeled to the open elevator doors.

Petru reached in and pressed the ground floor button and then the close button, before reversing his wheelchair back several steps. The sound coming from his apartment had changed subtly in the last twenty seconds. Petru knew the lock on his bedroom door had almost broken and his time was up. As Petru wheeled down the corridor towards a small alcove where he planned to hide, he heard a crashing sound from his apartment as the lock finally gave way and the bedroom door burst open.

Petru barely reached the alcove before he heard his front door open and the sound of running footsteps. Petru did not have time to turn his wheelchair around to see what was happening. As he sat in the alcove's darkness, catching his breath, he listened to the sound of the man's running footsteps and pictured him running past the elevator to the stairs. The footsteps were replaced almost immediately by the muffled thumping sound of a body tumbling down the stairs before the apartment block once again became quiet.

There was no time for Petru to celebrate as he pulled a two-feet wooden stick from his carry bag and wheeled quickly back to the stairwell. Looking down into the dimly lit stairwell, Petru could see the man lying on his side on the landing below. He was not unconscious as Petru had hoped, but he was nursing his left wrist, which was pointing at an odd angle. Petru locked the wheels on his wheelchair before easing out of the chair and onto the floor in front of the stairs. The man did not seem to notice as Petru released the trip wire. Petru knew he needed to move quickly and twisted his body around and pulled himself down the stairs headfirst.

The man writhed in pain and did not notice his presence until he was only three stairs above him. As the man reached down for his gun with his good hand, Petru clubbed the man across the head with his wooden stick. He used measured force; enough to disable him, but not enough to break his skull or cause permanent injury.

The man instantly let go of the gun and collapsed on the floor. Petru slid down the remaining steps and retrieved the gun. Before climbing the stairs again, he studied the man's face. The man was in his early thirties with short, almost crew cut blonde hair. He had sharp features and a familiar cruel look, even though he was unconscious. Petru was positive he had never seen him before. The man groaned and his eyelids fluttered as he tried to turn his head. Petru knew he would not be unconscious for long and quickly searched the man's pockets for some form of ID, but found nothing.

Even though Petru had worked for the syndicate, he had never used a gun. Turning the gun over in his hands now, he found what looked like the safety catch. Next to the safety slide was a small red dot, which he presumed meant the safety lock was off and the gun was ready to fire. As Petru gripped the gun in the firing position, he thought about what the syndicate had done to Afina.

Petru pointed the gun at the man's head and put his finger around the trigger. He paused as a numb feeling spread over him. Despite his hatred for the man and the organization he represented, something inside prevented him from pulling the trigger. He frowned. Clearly, the man came to kill him. He sighed as he re-engaged the gun's safety switch. He was not a killer and never would be. The man stirred again and Petru knew it was time to leave the apartment block for good. Using his hands, he crawled back up the stairs.

After clambering back into his wheelchair, he placed the gun and his travel bag in his lap. Petru hoped not to meet anyone at this hour of the night, but he did not want to take any chances. He wheeled back to the elevator and pressed the call button, conscious that the man would recover shortly. While he waited for the elevator to arrive, he thought about what had just happened and contemplated his future. He was lucky to be alive. With little money and being confined to a wheelchair, he knew he was still an easy target, even with a gun.

The elevator doors opened and Petru wheeled himself in and pressed the button for the ground floor. As the elevator doors closed, he knew the odds were stacked against him and it would be a miracle if he were still alive in a month's time.

Chapter Six

Robbie spent the next two hours asking locals about the Mac's accident without success. So far, no one had seen or heard anything. Not deterred, he had pressed on and started door knocking in the apartment block directly opposite Irish's.

No one had been home on the ground floor. Robbie continued his door knocking on the first floor and was rewarded when an older man, with graying curly red hair, opened the door to apartment seven. He was slightly stooped and overweight, but he had a cheery smile. "Can I help you?"

Robbie introduced himself and then asked the man if he was aware of Mac's hit-and-run accident.

The man immediately became wary and said, "You don't look like you're from the police?"

Robbie answered, "No, the man who died was my friend and I'm just trying to figure out what happened."

The man softened. "I'm sorry for your loss. I don't think I can help much, but come in."

As the man led Robbie down a short hallway to a small living room, he explained, "This place gets hot and my AC is a lot like me—old and doesn't work so good. Can't talk out in the hallway with the door open. It lets in too much hot air."

When they reached the small living room, the man put out his hand to shake Robbie's. "The name's Harry."

After they shook hands and Robbie had introduced himself, Harry gestured for Robbie to sit in one of the two well-worn lounge chairs. After he was seated, Harry lowered his eyes and looked at the floor rather than at Robbie.

In a quiet, almost confessional voice, he said, "I'm not sure I can help you. I didn't actually see anything, but I think I heard it. I read in the paper it happened sometime after ten thirty. I was in bed but couldn't get to sleep. I'm on dialysis and overheat easy. Anyway, I sleep with the widow open and about eleven o'clock I hear an awful bang —really loud. It sounded like maybe a car, but not metal on metal, like one car hitting another. Everything went quiet, no sirens, no nothing, so I assumed everything was okay."

Robbie felt sick in the stomach as Harry added, "I'm pretty sure it was your friend… I should have checked. Maybe I could have called an ambulance? Maybe your friend might still be alive? I've been feeling bad; I didn't at least try… I'm sorry."

Robbie put on an encouraging voice in response as he realized he might have finally found someone who had at least heard something. "Don't feel bad, Harry, this is very helpful. The police tell me the impact was significant and he would have died almost instantly."

Harry nodded and slowly raised his head. "Hopefully it

was all over before he realized anything. I'd hate to think he was lying there suffering. Again, I'm sorry for your loss."

"I guess I'm just trying to understand why it happened—how it happened. The street is straight and reasonably well lit. And the traffic comes down off that rise, at least one hundred yards before the spot, so pedestrians should be easy to see."

Harry thought for a moment. "It was raining lightly on and off throughout the night, as I recall. Maybe that made it hard for him to be seen?"

"Maybe?"

Robbie paused and let out a breath. "Harry, my friend's name was Aaron MacDonald. A long time ago, we were caught up in something that's haunted us ever since. I'm hoping this is just a tragic accident, but I need to be sure. If there's anything else you can remember, it could be a big help."

Harry looked puzzled. "You mean maybe someone meant to run him down?"

Robbie held Harry's gaze. "Hopefully not. But I need to make sure."

In an alarmed voice, Harry replied, "Robbie, you need to be talking to the police."

"I have been Harry, but at present it's just another hit and run to them. Without an eyewitness who can ID the offender, swear it looked deliberate or at least provide a vehicle description, there's not much they can do."

"I'm sorry, I wish there was something I could do. Perhaps I should call the police?"

"I think you should, Harry."

Harry paused a moment as he recalled what had happened. "You know it was a quiet night, not much traffic at all really until it happened. I remember shortly after it happened, maybe two or three minutes, another car came screeching to a halt out there. No bang this time, and then it sped away. I remember thinking, 'it's going to be one of those nights', but it all went quiet again and I heard nothing else."

Sitting forward, Robbie replied, "Perhaps someone saw Mac's body on the road and stopped to check?"

Harry thought for a moment. "No. The car sped up almost immediately after the braking stopped. I remember that clearly. The driver didn't have time to get out and check."

Robbie found this puzzling. He would need to think it through to see if it meant anything. It was perhaps another potential witness, if nothing else. Robbie wanted to keep Harry talking in the hope he might remember something else. "Harry, would you be able to show me where it happened?"

Harry looked apprehensive. "Robbie, I'm not sure that's going to help?"

Robbie replied, "You're probably right, but right now I don't have closure. You would be doing me a big favor?"

Harry looked at his watch. "Well, I don't have long. My sister will be here shortly to take me to the doctor to review my latest tests, but I guess it can't hurt to take a look."

Harry got up and led Robbie out of the apartment block and back across the road and down to where Mac had been found. It surprised Robbie how sick he felt looking over the scene. As if sensing this, Harry gave Robbie a moment to collect his thoughts.

When Robbie had composed himself, he said a quiet, "Okay."

Harry took this as his cue, and after checking for traffic,

walked out onto the road and pointed to the skid marks, which were still clearly visible.

"Here are the skid marks, no question. No other skid marks around here, not even old ones."

Robbie nodded. Harry then walked quickly back off the road and pointed to the ground. "And this is where the body was found. You can even still see some of the yellow chalk marks they used to outline the position of the body."

Robbie walked up and stood beside Harry and looked down at the faint outline of yellow chalk. Robbie stared at the spot and then looked back at the road. Something bothered him. "You said the second car skidded to a halt. So there should be two sets of skid marks—right?"

Harry scratched his chin as he replayed what he had heard over in his mind. "Actually, no. There was no skidding or breaking when it happened, just the bang. The skidding sound was the second car—minutes later. I guess that accounts for why there was only one set of marks."

"Do the police know this?"

Harry shrugged. "I don't know. No one's spoken to me, although I'm at the hospital so much if the police came, they could easily have missed me."

Walking out on the road, Robbie stood over the skid marks. He was no expert, but as he studied the marks, he could not see any sign that two cars had braked in the one place. Robbie looked up and down the road, searching for any other signs of a car swerving or breaking to avoid a pedestrian. Harry had been right; the rest of the road was clear. The lack of any visible evidence that the car that struck Mac had tried to brake or swerve played on his mind. As he walked back off the road, his doubts about it being an accident grew.

The Catalin Code

Harry sensed what Robbie was thinking. "You know, it changes everything, Robbie."

"What does?"

"How they died. My older brother was in Vietnam—he never came back. We got word he was killed in a firefight. We all took it pretty hard. Of course, I was only young then, but I got over it in time. I still missed him. Wasn't a day would go by that I didn't think of him, but I moved on. Got on with my life. I know that's what he would have wanted."

Robbie nodded.

Harry added, "Five years later, we get a call out of the blue from the Army. Some military police officer. My brother hadn't been killed in the line of duty after all. He had been murdered, along with someone else from his platoon. They made it look like he was killed in action, but didn't cover their tracks properly. Drugs, they said. My brother and his friend were reporting it up the chain of command, but it leaked out."

"I'm sorry, Harry."

"It was a long time ago. We were all so confused—so angry. It's one thing to be killed by Vietcong in a war, but quite another when it's murder in cold blood, by one of your own. It's played on my mind ever since. I've never been able to fully accept it or deal with it. Like a sore that won't heal. I hope this is just an accident, Robbie. You seem like a nice guy. Much easier to move on if it's an accident."

Harry looked at his watch and said, "I gotta go. My sister will be here soon, and I need to get my results from my apartment. I'm not sure this has been much help, but hopefully it's a piece of the puzzle, at least."

Robbie said, "Harry, you've been very helpful, admittedly more questions than answers, but it gives me something more to think about. Can I get your phone number? I might need to talk to you again if that's okay?"

They exchanged phone numbers and shook hands. Robbie watched as Harry waddled across the road and disappeared into his apartment block. He stood for a long time looking at the road and the spot where Mac had been killed. He began to wonder whether Harry had the events backwards. Perhaps there was only one set of noises and Harry was confused? Or maybe the two incidents weren't related? Just a coincidence of timing? Harry had certainly raised more questions than he answered.

For now, he would continue canvassing the area to see if anyone else could provide him with some answers.

After another two more hours of door knocking and questioning all the locals he could find, Robbie had no further leads. Feeling flat, he returned to the rental car and sat behind the wheel, thinking. He was not sure what to do next. Maybe Mac's death was an accident? Maybe he was building something out of nothing? Robbie couldn't get over the last phone call he had with Mac. He knew Mac was holding back, wanting to say something, but couldn't or wouldn't. He remembered how insistent Mac had been that they should meet as soon as he got back into the country.

Robbie wondered whether Mac had shared some of his concerns with Laura. After they had cleared her of the corruption charges, he knew Mac had been the one that provided her with the most support as she came to terms with both the end of her career and her marriage.

As Robbie started the car, his phone rang. He checked

the screen as he pressed the answer button, but it was an unlisted number.

"Hi, Robbie, it's Jerry. How are you?"

Chapter Seven

Robbie arrived at the restaurant a few minutes early. It had been a favorite dining haunt of Mac's, and he was pleased Laura had suggested it. Located on the top floor of a building that sat on the river's edge, the restaurant offered its diners breath-taking views of both the Fraser River and the city itself. The building had at one time been Vancouver's only power station and Robbie was thankful the developers had kept much of the building's character and rustic charm when it had been converted into a theater and several restaurants and cafes.

After being seated by the server, he looked across the city skyline under lights and reflected on how much the city had changed in recent years. With a population now approaching a million people, Vancouver had grown up a lot. The city that had been almost entirely economically dependent on its seaport when he had left in his early twenties had become a vibrant, multicultural place to live and work, thanks to booming technology and tourism industries.

As Robbie watched several boats motoring down the

river, he reflected on the day while he waited for Laura. So far, his gut was telling him to continue to be suspicious. His conversation with Irish about Mac being involved in an argument on the night of his death and Harry's recollection of the accident had only confirmed he needed to be patient and keep investigating. He was hoping Laura would bring a different perspective to help focus his investigation.

The phone call from Jerry had been unexpected. Robbie had seen very little of Jerry since nineteen eighty-nine. They had gone in different directions after school and had not really kept in touch. Jerry had ostensibly called to apologize for not getting to Mac's funeral.

A familiar voice broke Robbie's thoughts. "Hey stranger, you look a million miles away."

Laura kissed Robbie on the cheek and then sat down opposite. She was wearing a black evening dress and had her long auburn hair pinned back. She looked stunning and Robbie was now glad he had taken the time to dress up a little for the dinner.

He found himself staring and could see the bemused smile on Laura's face. One of those 'he knew she knew' moments. He smiled to himself, hoping to divert her attention as he felt himself flushing. "You look amazing, Laura. How are you?"

"I'm doing okay, Robbie. I hope you like the restaurant. It was one of Mac's favorites."

"I came here with Mac one night when I was in town about a year ago. It was a great night... I'm going to miss those dinners."

A server appeared and, after greeting them, placed wine menus in front of Robbie and Laura.

"I'm sorry, Robbie, you'll have to fly solo on the wine."

Robbie remembered Laura had battled a drinking

problem when she was going through the OCTF corruption scandal and kicked himself for not remembering this earlier. Looking at the server, Robbie said, "Got a big day tomorrow. I'll just stick with a coke, thanks."

Laura added, "Sparkling mineral water with ice for me, please."

After the server left, Laura continued. "You know, Robbie, it's not an issue anymore. I've been sober for over two years now and it doesn't bother me if other people around me still drink. I'm happy with my mineral water."

"I need to be sharp for tomorrow, so coke is fine."

"Just as long as I'm not holding you back."

Robbie smiled. "No."

The server returned with the meal menus, saving Robbie from an awkward moment. It did not surprise him when Laura ordered a salmon salad. You could not keep a figure like she had dining on steak and fries, he thought.

Robbie ordered Moroccan Lamb. After the server left, Laura said, "Moroccan Lamb was one of his favorites."

"For old times' sake. This is what we had last time we were here."

Laura welled up a little. "Before we talk about Mac, tell me about you? I haven't seen you in ages."

Robbie had barely seen Laura in the years since her divorce and replied, "Well, not much to tell, really. The freelance work is going well. It's a while between paychecks, but they're usually pretty good, so I can't complain."

Laura gave a small, almost shy, laugh.

"You know, I almost feel like a stalker. I've been following your work for years. Some very impressive pieces. Let's see, the expose on government health fraud was big, and those pieces on the construction industry mafia caused a real stir. Syndicated coverage if I'm not mistaken. You have come a long way from the days of being a local crime reporter here in Vancouver."

Robbie did his best to suppress a smile. "Thanks. I travel a lot, but it's been fun. Right now, I'm working on a cyber crime piece. Looks like it's going to be a three-part series now with the first article focusing on identity theft. I'm just back from two weeks in Eastern Europe. There are some big links between cyber crime here and what's going on in the eastern bloc. A lot of our stolen money is winding up over there."

Laura was a picture of concentration. Robbie could see she was genuinely interested.

"Interesting, Robbie. So how soon until I can read the next piece?"

"Well, I was hoping to have it published by the end of the month. I met up with a couple of former hackers in Romania that have gone straight. One even does work for Interpol now. They gave me names of some suspects over here to run down. The evidence is solid, and I need to carefully consider how it's all presented. I've given the data to a financial analyst connected to my publisher's law firm by the name of Will Sherlock. Like his namesake, he's an exceptional investigator, except his specialty is money, not murder. Once he's finished his analysis, we'll sort through what we can and can't publish without being sued. It could be big."

Robbie shifted in his chair. He had always been uncomfortable talking about himself. "Enough about me. What about you?"

"Nothing that exciting, Robbie. I have a small OCTF pension. At least they didn't take that from me, and I have been doing some consulting work, mainly physical security audits. It's rather dry, but it pays the bills. And after what I've been through, it's actually excellent therapy."

Robbie nodded. He knew from long conversations with Mac how difficult it had been for Laura and several other members of the OCTF who had been innocent victims of the scandal.

"When Annie died, work really helped. It still hurt like crazy, of course, but it distracted me and gave me something else to focus on." Robbie was silent for a moment and then added, "Mac also got me through."

"He helped me too, Robbie. He's the reason I'm still here and sober." As tears welled in her eyes, she added, "He stood by me when just about everyone else abandoned me. They labeled me as corrupt on rumor only and condemned me without a trial. It was incredibly tough with the media camped on my doorstep and it was what ultimately ended my marriage. When I was finally exonerated, nobody wanted to hear about it. Nobody wanted to print my story. Yesterday's news, they said. They were so cruel."

"I'm glad you've come through it, Laura. I can't imagine what it must have been like."

"It was awful, but I'm moving on. Bitterness gets you nowhere." Laura paused to wipe the tears from her eyes. She smiled and then added, "So… are you seeing anyone?"

Robbie laughed. "Well, that's a subtle way to change the subject."

Laura nodded. "You know me, Robbie. As subtle as a brick."

Robbie shook his head, feigning disappointment. "Some things never change."

Laura laughed and raised an eyebrow. "You haven't answered my question."

Robbie held both hands up in submission. "No. Hardly

even a date, really. Work has kept me busy and... How about yourself?"

Laura shook her head. "I think I'm still in that space of getting my head together. Life has been complicated enough. I ditched my shrink about nine months ago and don't want to go back. So, a relationship is a complication I'm not ready for yet." She smiled and added, "Besides, it's been so long, I wouldn't know where to start. Apparently, you need to be on RSVP or some other dating website to start with these days, and I don't even do Facebook."

Robbie nodded. "You're right, it can get pretty complicated."

They were silent for a moment, enjoying each other's company and the ambiance of the restaurant. The server bought their meals and Robbie realized he was starving when he smelled the steaming aroma of his Moroccan Lamb.

"Bon appetite, Robbie," said Laura as she picked up her fork.

"Bon appetite, Laura."

After Robbie had made some inroads into his meal, he said, "I had a call from Jerry today."

"Jerry, as in our Mayor, who you and Mac went to school with?"

"Yes, he was sorry he couldn't get to the funeral on Saturday and wants to go to the grave tomorrow and pay his respects. He wanted to know if I would come with him."

"Well, it's nice he wants to stop and remember."

"I've known Jerry a long time. Jerry's mostly interested in Jerry. I was going to tell him no, but realized I needed to say yes. If he's genuine, then it's good to do this together."

Laura nodded in agreement as she continued to eat. Robbie decided it was time to ask a more in-depth question.

It came out slightly blunter than he had expected. "Laura, I'm not convinced Mac's death was an accident."

Laura frowned. In a slightly guarded voice, she replied, "You think Jerry was involved?"

"I don't have enough pieces of the puzzle yet to know if it was an accident or not, let alone start accusing anyone. I'm hoping it was just an accident, but I don't intend to walk away until I know for sure."

Laura put down her fork and then said, "Robbie, I mentioned on Saturday that some things with Mac had been concerning me. Mac hadn't been himself for some time. Three weeks ago, I came down with a bad flu. I was bedridden for a week. My mother would normally come to take care of me, but she was on holiday in Europe with my sister. Mac called me to say hi, just as I got sick. He was concerned no one was looking after me, so he came over every day to check up on me until I was better. He would often just sit and work for hours on his laptop while I slept."

"That sounds like Mac."

"The thing was, he wasn't himself. He was on edge, anxious almost all the time. I was pretty sick, but I could still tell."

"That's not like Mac at all."

"No, it's not. On the last day he came, I was feeling much better, and we sat together and talked for a while. I asked him what was going on. At first, he said everything was okay. But I pressed him, and he said he thought he was being followed. Something to do with his consulting work, but he wouldn't elaborate."

"Did he say what he was working on?"

"No. He was deliberately vague. He didn't mention a client or exactly what he was up to, although he had three laptops all setup on my dining room table. One of them was my Toshiba with a cell phone attached."

"Connected to the internet?"

"I guess."

"You have internet at home, don't you?"

"Internet with Wi-Fi. I asked him what he was doing, and he mumbled 'precautions'. I was still a bit bombed by the drugs, so I didn't push it. I thought I would ask him more about it when I was better."

Robbie thought about this for a moment. "Mac is a genius, period; but with computers and security, he's as good as it gets. He spends so much of his time online that maybe when he said he was being followed, he meant online rather than in the physical sense?"

"Maybe. I wouldn't have a clue if someone was following me online, but Mac would. He may have started out as a computer programmer, but that's how he made his living mostly—showing companies how to keep their information secure online. He didn't give any other clue. He just said he thought he was being followed."

Laura thought for a moment. "He was really keen to talk to you, Robbie. He wouldn't say about what exactly, but I'm wondering now if this is somehow connected?"

Robbie frowned. "I got a call from him about a week ago, while I was still in Europe. He was definitely not himself. He tried to hide it, but I could tell. I asked him several times about it, but he wouldn't open up. He was keen to catch up with me as soon as I got back—insisted on it, in fact. I got the impression he didn't want to talk on the phone. At first, I just dismissed it as a guy thing. You know, easier to open up face to face than over a telephone when you're in different countries. Maybe…"

"Maybe what?"

"I'm not sure, Laura. We're piling up the questions here, good questions, but no answers. We have to start answering some of the questions sooner rather than later if we're to get to the truth."

"Okay, so where do we start?"

"Well, today I went and talked to two guys over where Mac lived. Harry, a guy who lives across the road near to where the accident happened, was very helpful. He heard a noise from out on the road around the time of the accident he thinks was the car hitting Mac, but no sound of brakes. Like it was either deliberate or the driver didn't see Mac at all and just kept going."

Laura's jaw dropped slightly.

Robbie continued. "I also talked to the owner of the bar and grill where Mac used to hangout."

"Irish's?"

"That's the one. Irish tells me Mac was in there on the night he died for a meeting. The guy he met was only there for fifteen minutes. They had an argument, and he leaves. Mac looked upset but didn't want to talk about it and the next thing... he's dead."

"Did Irish know who Mac was talking to? Was he a regular?"

"No. I asked Irish, and he said he'd never seen him before. Got a vague description of a guy who was mid-forties, tall—about six foot three—but skinny with a shaved head and wearing a suit. Irish said he looked like an undertaker."

Laura frowned. "Did you say 'undertaker'?"

"That's what he said."

Laura reached into her bag and pulled out her smart phone. Robbie watched in silence for a moment.

"Laura, what are you..."

The Catalin Code

Laura held up an index finger. Robbie got the message and waited.

A minute later, Laura handed her smart phone across to Robbie. She had her smart phone browser application open and had navigated to the website for a consulting firm. The page showed a bio of its managing director. Robbie's attention was immediately drawn to the photo. Although it was hard to tell his height, the man was in his mid-forties, lean, immaculately dressed, and had a totally shaved head. He could easily pass as an undertaker, Robbie thought.

"Okay. You have my complete attention, Laura. Who is he?"

"He's nobody unless Irish thinks he's the man Mac met."

"We need to get that photo to Irish. Do you have email on your phone?"

Laura nodded. Robbie dialed a number on his phone and waited for the connection.

"Hello, Irish? It's Robbie Mayne. I was in... Yes, that's me. Look, I know you're busy—can you hear me over the noise?"

Robbie pulled away from his phone and said to Laura, "He's going out back, away from the noise in the bar."

Robbie waited a moment. "Yes, that's much better, Irish, thanks. Sorry to trouble you on a working night, but I might have a lead on the guy Mac was having an argument with on the night someone knocked him down. Do you have email?"

Robbie pulled away from his phone again and said to Laura, "He's got email on his iPad which is right in front of him. Can you send the picture from your smart phone?"

"Yes, I just need an address."

"Hey, Irish, what's your email address?"

Robbie relayed the address to Laura, who in turn keyed it into her smart phone. After pushing send, she gave Robbie a thumbs up signal.

"It's on its way now, Irish."

Robbie only had to wait a few seconds for Irish to receive the email and open the photo attachment.

"You're sure? Positive?"

Looking at Laura, he continued his conversation with Irish. "I had some help, Irish. I don't know who it is either, but I'm looking at the person who has the answers. I'll call you tomorrow with an update. Thanks again for your help."

Robbie disconnected. "It's a match. That's definitely the person who was arguing with Mac."

Laura nodded, but looked confused.

"Who is he, Laura?"

"His name is Peter Trelor. He used to be my supervisor at the OCTF." She frowned and added, "Why on earth would Mac be talking to him?"

Chapter Eight

Vincent Franco and Rudy Henning sat in the car outside Eugene Brennan's apartment block. It had been a long night. They had watched the photographer eat a meal in a small diner at six thirty p.m. and were hopeful he would head straight home afterward. Brennan had other ideas and wound up in a bar four blocks from where he lived. He had made four separate attempts to pick up women but, to Franco and Henning's relief, had struck out on each occasion and had headed home alone around nine forty-five p.m.

They allowed him a few minutes to settle in after seeing the lights come on in his fourth-floor apartment.

The two men had agreed Henning would take the lead on this job.

Using one of several disposable cell phones they always carried, Henning made the call. After a few seconds, an irritated voice answered the call.

"Hello."

"Hi, Eugene, the name's Rudy and I'm an associate of

the company that hired you for that special photo shoot you did recently."

"It's late man. Why are you ringing me now?"

"The boss says we owe you money. I've got an envelope full of cash for you."

"How much? The price has gone up. Twenty not ten."

"Eugene, to be honest, I didn't check the contents. The envelope's sealed. Tell you what, I'll drop it over, you count it and if it's not right you can call the boss on my phone and discuss it with him? Can't be fairer than that?"

"What. Now?"

"Like I said, the boss has given me the cash to pass on. I'm just following orders."

"I'm in Holbrook, Ridge Street, just south of the River. You close by? I'm tired and don't want to be up waiting half the night."

Henning smiled as he stared up at the fourth-floor apartment. "I'm not far away at all, really. I'll see you in ten. I just need your full address."

Brennan gave his details, and Henning disconnected. He smiled at Franco. "Looks like it won't be too late a night after all."

Franco nodded. "Better call Keaton and tell him it's on. Just make sure there are no last-minute changes of plan."

Henning made the call and got his final instructions. Franco stayed in the car to act as a lookout. The neighborhood was currently quiet, but it paid to be vigilant.

Henning knocked on the door of apartment 4F. A small, slightly built man opened it. He had dark hair and a mood to match.

"Are you, Rudy?"

"Hi, Eugene, yes I am."

"Come in, let's get this over with. I'm tired."

Eugene's apartment looked more like a disorganized photo lab than a place where anyone actually lived. The only couch visible was covered in camera gear, and there was no place to sit. That was fine with Henning. He needed to stay on his feet, anyway.

"Let's see what you got."

Henning reached into his pocket and pulled out a sealed envelope. He handed it to Brennan without a word. Brennan opened the envelope and started quickly thumbing through the bills. He had clearly done this before, Henning thought.

"You guys don't listen. I said twenty, not ten."

"Eugene, I'm just the delivery guy, as I explained on the phone. You got a problem—we call the boss and get it sorted out. Okay?"

Before Brennan could respond, Henning had the disposable phone out and was speed dialing a number that would connect through to Keaton. When the phone was answered, Henning handed the phone to Brennan.

"I don't need to listen to your conversation with the boss. You mind if I smoke on your balcony while I wait?"

"Help yourself."

Brennan waited until Henning was outside. "Hello."

"Eugene."

"Hello, Keaton. I see my assumption about the real client for the job was on the money. Speaking of which, your guy here only has half of it."

"No. In fact, he has the correct money. It was what we agreed through the broker."

"The broker didn't tell me who the client was. Stelecom is worth over two hundred million. Now, you guys don't need any bad press. The extra ten thousand buys my silence. You got some nice photos. I get a nice bonus. Everyone's happy."

"We had a deal, Eugene."

"And I had additional expenses. That secretary sure took her time getting Blackwell's trousers down. I was camped in situ for three days, waiting for that opportunity. You got some great photos."

"Tell you what, Eugene, let's make it an extra five. We can finish it up tonight; fifteen thousand cash."

"Split the difference. Seventeen five."

"Okay, Eugene, you drive a hard bargain. Tell Rudy to give you the other envelope."

Eugene smiled. "Now you're talking. See, that wasn't so hard." He turned to the balcony. "Hey guy, sorry forgot your name. Keaton says you got a second envelope."

Henning stubbed out his cigarette in the ashtray on the small balcony table. It was now one of four butts. He would collect all four of them in a moment.

Walking in through the glass sliding door towards Brennan, he withdrew the second Manila envelope. It looked roughly the same shape as the first one, only thicker and heavier. Not the perfect disguise for a cut down paving stone, but good enough not to arouse too much suspicion for a short period.

Henning began to hand the envelope over, but with a practiced movement, deftly turned the envelope sideways and struck Brennan flat against his left temple. The blow was delivered with precision. Enough force to stun Brennan, but not enough to cause any lasting injury beyond several weeks of bruising.

Henning caught Brennan as he collapsed. He quickly shuffled him out onto the balcony. Grabbing his belt in one hand and his shirtfront in the other, he lifted Brennan off the ground. Brennan came to and struggled as Henning maneuvered him towards the balcony rail. He briefly kicked out, knocking the table before Henning had him in position and let him go. He watched as he tumbled to an abrupt halt on the driveway below.

Brennan's lifeless body remained largely intact, albeit in a small growing pool of blood and internal body fluids. Even from four floors up, Henning could see that Brennan's head was a mess and the injuries he sustained from the impact to the pavement would conceal any injury from the initial head blow.

Henning's phone rang. It was Franco. "All clear down here. We're lucky his balcony's not out front. As long as we don't get any residents driving into the rear parking lot you should have enough time. How did it go?"

"Okay. Knocked a table on the balcony getting him out. Other than that, all good."

"Okay. Run the checks and keep your phone close by. I see anything I'll call immediately. We call Keaton once you're clear."

"Got it."

Henning shut off his phone. He would spend the next half hour or more making sure there was no information connecting Brennan directly to Stelecom or its principals. Keaton had instructed him to search all documents and digital files in the apartment and remove anything that police could use as a link back.

His last instructions had been to download a copy of Brennan's laptop computer but to leave it behind if possible. He was instructed to look for files containing the words Stelecom or Stelovak. If there was nothing too incriminating, leave the laptop behind. Keaton had been clear; 'Cops are more likely to leave the suicide option on the table if his computer isn't missing.'

After putting on gloves and a hairnet to limit the chances of leaving evidence, Henning located Brennan's laptop. He was relieved it was not password protected as this saved him from spending precious minutes overriding password codes to gain access. He plugged in a high-speed USB hard drive and started the download program.

Henning then checked all five cameras. Fortunately, Brennan was not old school. They were all digital, which made the process much simpler. He quickly cycled through the images on the small viewing screen on each camera. Lots of images that would make a grandmother blush, but no pictures of Blackwell. Once the laptop download was complete, he started the keyword scan of files and directories. While the search was running, he checked through all the paper files on the desk that served as Brennan's office.

Henning then checked the rest of the apartment. It didn't take long. Apart from the camera gear, Brennan had traveled light. After finishing the search, Henning called Franco.

"All clear. Got a copy of the laptop. Nothing to connect us that I could find. Couple of joints and some coke in the bedroom, though."

"OK, that can't hurt. When the cops investigate, hopefully he'll come across as some druggy that got a little too psychotic and jumped. Lockup and come on down. Nobody has walked by yet, so you have time to double check everything before you leave."

Henning disconnected and spent a good five minutes rechecking that nothing had been left behind. He straightened the table on the balcony that Brennan kicked in the struggle and picked up the ashtray and four cigarette butts from the concrete floor. He pocketed the butts and put the ashtray back in the center of the table.

Satisfied after one last check, he left the balcony sliding door open, as instructed by Keaton. 'Jumpers don't normally bother to shut doors behind them, so if it comes to that, leave it open.' He locked the front door of the apartment on his way out and removed the gloves and hairnet before he got to the elevator.

The apartment was now quiet and still. A small breeze wafted up from the street and across the balcony. Although barely detectable, it caused the curtains to sway momentarily in the balcony doorway. Nestled behind a small terracotta pot, a partially extinguished cigarette butt glowed briefly.

Chapter Nine

After learning that the man Mac had met on the night of his death was Laura's old boss, Robbie and Laura decided the restaurant was not the place to continue the conversation. After paying for their meal, Robbie followed Laura back to her apartment in the rental.

Car parking around Laura's apartment was at a premium and Robbie had to park on the street a block away. After walking back and up the two flights of stairs, Laura opened the door to her apartment on the second knock. She had changed into jeans and a comfortable knitted top. She still looked stunning, but Robbie knew now was not the time for compliments.

Laura's apartment had a nice open plan layout and was beautifully decorated. Unlike Robbie, who could barely distinguish anything beyond primary colors, Laura had a flair for decorating and had used an array of earthy tones mixed with orange, purple and gray accents for the soft furnishings.

She made coffee for both of them and invited Robbie to sit on the lounge with her.

"You know, Robbie, I'm not sure where to start. I have no idea why Mac would have met with Peter Trelor."

"You said he used to be your boss. Why not start there?"

Laura thought for a moment. "Okay. Going back a few years, a number of detectives moved from Vancouver Metro to the new Organized Crime Task Force. The OCTF started off small and quickly grew to around eighty detectives, criminologists, and analysts. Nick Carney also transferred across from Vancouver Metro shortly before I did. We were all specially trained to take on major investigations. Organized crime, breaking major drug rings, assisting federal law enforcement agencies, that kind of thing. Peter Trelor was a senior detective at the OCTF and my direct boss. We could all see that both Nick and Trelor were very good at what they did. They earned reputations for being able to get the job done and were extremely competitive. They were both on the fast track for senior promotion. Nick, however, was a little better at the political games. He knew exactly which butts to kiss and was promoted ahead of Trelor."

"Politics," said Robbie with a shake of his head.

Laura nodded. "Even after Nick's promotion, there was still intense competition between the two of them that went on for several years. It all blew up one summer, after you had left town, when the OCTF got caught up in a corruption scandal."

"I followed that fairly closely in the papers."

Laura continued, "You don't know the half of it, Robbie. Regardless of what the papers said, it all boiled down to two major crime gangs at war in Vancouver to control the drug trade. Unbeknownst to us, several members of the OCTF were taking huge bribes from one gang to focus the investigation and resulting prosecutions on the other gang only."

Robbie nodded. "Use the OCTF to put the competitor out of business."

"Right. The gang, which the press called the Syndicate, had strong ties to the Mafia and was well renowned for attempts to bribe law enforcement officers. The OCTF didn't realize it, but Vancouver Metro's own internal investigations team were keeping a very close eye on us. When it became apparent that bribes were being accepted, all hell broke loose. We were all suspended and treated more or less as criminals. They investigated all of our personal affairs and finances. Three members of the OCTF had hidden bank accounts with upwards of half a million dollars in them. They were immediately charged with accepting bribes and all got significant jail time."

Robbie responded, "I remember the press thought you were all guilty, and it was just a matter of time before the rest of you would be prosecuted as well."

Laura sighed. "That's when the fun really started. The press hounded us all for the next year or more. They were relentless. One of the young guys I worked with couldn't handle it and committed suicide. It affected us all in different ways…"

She looked at Robbie on the verge of tears, "That's when I really started drinking—it was all I could do Robbie, it was a nightmare."

Robbie put his arms around Laura and held her tight. "I'm sorry we had to drag this up again, Laura. I can't imagine how hard it must have been."

They stayed in the embrace for several minutes. Laura

finally let go and said, "Thank you, Robbie. I am a lot stronger now. But some wounds I doubt will ever fully heal. It cost me my marriage, and I was on the verge of becoming an alcoholic. I never want to be in that place again."

"I think we've talked about this enough for tonight. Can I ask you just two last questions before I go?"

"Sure."

"Was anybody else ever found guilty?"

"No. There were lots of rumors floating around that Nick was the mastermind—that he was the one with the links to the Syndicate. But they exonerated him. Because of his promotion, he was now management and didn't work with the squads on a day-to-day basis anymore. Although we could never prove it, we believe he got wind of what Metro Internal Affairs was up to and set up the three that took the fall. He made it look like it was his idea to start an inquiry and that impressed senior management and, rather than being prosecuted, they promoted him."

"And now he's OCTF Director."

Laura grimaced. "Justice can sometimes be hard to find."

"Yes, it's often elusive for the people who need it most." Robbie paused. Laura looked wrung out. He kept the last question brief. "Peter Trelor. Did he ever work with Mac?"

"Not that I knew of. I introduced them once at a social function back in the early days of the OCTF. Beyond that, I don't know and Mac certainly never talked about him."

"I think that's enough for tonight. Can I come back tomorrow?"

Laura nodded. "Robbie, would you mind staying over? I know it sounds silly, but after what's happened, I would rather not be alone tonight, and the couch is quite comfy."

"Do you have a spare toothbrush?"

"Still in a box."

"Deal."

Laura kissed Robbie on the cheek and as she got up from the couch. "I'll get you some blankets."

"And the toothbrush."

Laura called back over her shoulder, "And the toothbrush!"

Silhouetted in another rental, four cars further up the hill from Robbie's car, the man put down his binoculars and picked up his phone. He hit redial and waited patiently for the connection.

"Mayne is still here. Lights went out ten minutes ago, so I think that's it for the night."

"Is it safe?"

The man briefly scanned out the car windows into the night as best he could.

"Safe enough. I checked his car earlier; the entire job shouldn't take more than a few minutes."

"OK. Call me if there are any problems, otherwise we can talk tomorrow."

"Will do."

The man disconnected and blew a sigh of relief. It had been a very long day, and he was looking forward to his hotel room and a drink.

He picked up a small bag of cocaine and a vehicle-tracking device from the passenger seat and put them in his jacket pocket. He then reached into a bag on the back seat and withdrew several tools for breaking into cars, which he had made himself.

He set the interior car light switch to the off position and got out of the car into the darkness. As he approached Robbie's car, he made one final three hundred and sixty degree sweep to make sure he was alone.

He figured he would be done here and on his way in less than five minutes.

Chapter Ten

Stelovak normally carried three mobile phones. The first was for legitimate and legal business purposes. The second, replaced fortnightly, had a disposable number and was used for managing much of his illegal business network. The third had a number known only to seven other members of his trusted inner circle.

The third phone was always within arm's reach, day and night. It currently sat on a ledge next to his Jacuzzi. As it rang, he checked the incoming call ID, which displayed one word—Keaton. Stelovak had been expecting the call. As he answered, he turned to the woman who sat opposite and said, "This shouldn't take long."

Without a word, she emerged naked from the tub and put on a full-length white bathrobe. Stelovak watched as she padded across the tiled floor into an adjoining room.

After hearing the click as she softly closed the door behind her, he said, "Yes?"

"Just ringing to let you know the photography issue has been sorted."

"Good. What was the outcome?"

"The price couldn't be negotiated. And our risk exposure was high, so we went with Plan B."

Stelovak insisted they used this form of coded conversation on all telephone calls. Stelovak knew Plan B meant Brennan was now lying on the concrete below his apartment.

"Recovery?"

"Nothing of note recovered."

"So, we can consider the issue closed?"

"We can."

A smile spread across Stelovak's face as he said, "Then I'll see you tomorrow."

Stelovak disconnected and set his phone back down on the ledge again. As the water swirled around him, he called out softly. Plan B had been the best outcome, he thought. No loose ends.

The door opened and the woman, now naked again, made her way back to the Jacuzzi. Stelovak smiled again. Tonight, he was in the mood to celebrate. Tomorrow, he would arrange a special meeting with Leon Blackwell.

Chapter Eleven

Westcott sipped coffee from a Styrofoam cup. It was his second for the day and it was only six thirty a.m. He did not know how many he would get through before the day was over, but it would be way above his average.

He had been woken shortly after four a.m. by a call from the Vancouver Metro Operations Center. The report was brief. They had discovered a body on the driveway of an apartment block in the suburb of Holbrook. White, male, no witnesses and a probable suicide.

He had groaned at the thought of another potential murder case as he rolled out of bed. Vancouver Metro investigated every death that looked like suicide before making a determination, and this would be no different.

Westcott had been at the crime scene along with several police forensic specialists for almost two hours. Delray would be here shortly. He would have to talk to him about his current workload. There were too many cases and not enough time to make real headway on any of them at present.

Westcott watched as the Police photographer took the final pictures of the body of Eugene Carter. He gave Westcott the thumbs up to show he had finished.

The forensic technicians were now upstairs in the apartment collecting evidence. They had already finished outside on the driveway and surrounding perimeter. The coroner came over to ask if the body could be released for transport back to the lab for further examination. Westcott wanted one last look.

After stepping over the police tape that signified the exclusion zone, Westcott got as close as he could without actually stepping into the pool of blood and other fluids that surrounded Carter's body. Squatting, he lifted the white sheet to take a final look before the coroner removed the body.

Carter lay face down with his head twisted at an angle not possible for anyone still living. One eye remained partially open. It was now opaque in death and, like the rest of the body, no longer looked natural. Because of the amount of visible damage to his head, Westcott was sure death would have been instant. It was impossible to tell whether the man had jumped or had been thrown from the balcony. That would require some careful investigation, he thought.

"What a mess."

Westcott looked up to see Felix Delray staring down at the body.

He replied, "Jumpers are never pretty."

Delray took a step back. "You got that right. Where are we at?"

"Preliminary ID is Eugene Carter. Lived in apartment 4F. Occupation appears to be a photographer. No sign of forced entry to his apartment, no sign of a struggle, and nothing appears to have been taken. His balcony window was open. It looks like it happened after ten p.m. last night. It was called in by a resident returning home from shift work at the local hospital. None of the residents interviewed, so far, saw or heard anything."

Felix Delray was a veteran with over thirty years on the force. At twenty-six, Westcott was one of the youngest detectives in Delray's team and he knew he still had a lot to learn. But Delray seemed to like the way he got results and always asked his opinion. "What do you think, Danny?"

Westcott looked up at Carter's balcony. "I'm not sure, boss. It looks like a suicide, but that means nothing. There were small quantities of cocaine and cannabis in the bedroom, but no suicide note. We have located five digital cameras that all appear to be owned by the deceased. The techs had a quick scroll through the images. Looks like the guy did surveillance work, and not all of it legal. It's too early to make a call, but this guy doesn't come across as an upstanding citizen, which makes me wonder what else he was involved in. It's smelling more like murder than suicide."

Delray nodded. "We'll know more once the autopsy is complete and we can positively ID the body. Then we can run some official background checks."

Westcott looked at his boss again. "I also ran Carter's name through the car computer as a starting point and got some hits."

"Such as?"

"Two for drug possession, one DUI, one fraud, and one for receiving stolen goods."

Delray grimaced. "Not exactly an upstanding citizen. It's easy to imagine half a dozen scenarios from that record where someone might want him to take a shortcut to the pavement."

Westcott yawned as he stood. "I think I need another coffee."

Delray put his hand on Westcott's shoulder. "We can't have you permanently running on caffeine, Danny. You've been putting in long hours recently, and it's appreciated. However, you're no good to me, burnt out. Spend today on this and come see me tomorrow morning. We should have a pretty good idea by then on this one. If it's murder, I'll need to hand some of your other case load off to other members of the team."

"Thanks, boss."

"No problem. By the way—I think you're right."

"Murder?"

Delray looked up at the balcony. "I've been doing this a long time. This one feels off. We dig enough, I think we'll find someone with a reason to want him dead."

Westcott watched Delray as he walked back to his car. Delray was old school. He did not have a degree and was not up to date with the latest forensic investigation techniques. But what he did have, even more than just his years of experience, was a nose for crime. Westcott had enormous respect for the man and was quickly learning his degree in criminology helped little in the real world.

Westcott had a feeling there was a lot more to learn about the man who lay dead under the white sheet less than six feet from where he stood.

Chapter Twelve

Robbie stirred as the smell of freshly brewed coffee penetrated his sleep.

"Wake up, sleepyhead."

Robbie opened his eyes. As they focused, he could see a steaming cup of coffee being held in front of him. He was slightly confused and not entirely sure where he was until he saw Laura come into focus.

"Good morning. Have I overslept?"

Handing him the coffee, Laura said, "Not really. It's early, and this is a workday for me."

Taking the coffee, Robbie yawned and said thank you at the same time.

Laura sat on the edge of the couch. "Thanks for staying last night. I normally don't have problems sleeping anymore, but I knew last night would be a struggle."

Robbie rubbed his eyes. "Did I snore?"

"Let's call it some minor rhythmic breathing," said Laura with a laugh.

"I snored. Sorry."

"Robbie, it was fine. Kind of reassuring, really. I think it helped me get to sleep rather than the opposite."

Looking across at the clock in the kitchen, She said, "I have to be out of here soon."

"Okay. I should get going as well."

"No, take your time. I've left a muffin on the kitchen bench for you. Have a shower. No need to rush."

"Thanks."

Laura grimaced. "Robbie, it's important that we finish what we talked about last night. Sorry I wasn't up for it then."

"That's okay. How about tonight?"

Laura nodded. "I would like that, only not another restaurant. I don't feel comfortable discussing this where other people can hear."

"Okay. Where do you have in mind?"

"Why don't you come back here? Do you like Laksa? My mother has a recipe made from coconut milk that's to die for."

"Sounds great."

"Work wise, it's not a big day today, so I should be home around five, if that's good for you?"

"Five is great. I'm visiting Mac's grave with Jerry this morning. And this afternoon I want to go back to the scene of the accident. I need to make sense of it. There are too many loose ends at present."

"Be careful, Robbie. The idea of Mac being followed, whether physically or in cyberspace, concerns me. We still don't know where this is all going, if anywhere."

"Let's hope it's nothing, but I will be careful. I promise."

Laura reached over and gave Robbie a firm hug. "See you tonight."

"Tonight."

After Laura had closed the front door, Robbie sat up properly on the couch. Still draped in blankets, he sipped his coffee and thought about the day ahead. Identifying Peter Trelor as the man Mac had argued with was a good starting point. He would go online later and do some background research on him for the second part of the conversion with Laura.

He smiled as he thought about Laura. Her strength, vulnerability, humor, and intellect were an addictive combination. That she was stunningly beautiful didn't hurt, either.

He thought about Jerry as he headed for the shower. What happened back in nineteen eighty-nine would need to be talked about, he decided. Today would be an excellent opportunity for that. Was he a friend or an enemy? Robbie didn't know, but saw the wisdom of Laura's advice to be careful.

Chapter Thirteen

It was late morning and Westcott had just started on his fifth cup of coffee for the day. He and Brody Adams were the only two from Vancouver Metro left on the scene at Carter's apartment.

As the technician came back in from the balcony, he said, "That's a wrap out there."

"Good work, Brody."

The technician replied, "I figure ten more minutes cataloging evidence and I'll be done."

Westcott looked at the three large plastic evidence containers, all of which were now full. "Lots of evidence to analyze back at the office. Delray wants a brief tomorrow morning. It's going to be a long day."

"Good luck with that."

Westcott watched as Brody put two more small evidence bags into one of the evidence containers. "Balcony?"

"Yes. Only two butts. Quite a breeze last night. Any other evidence has long since vanished. Still, these are worth checking. The first butt is the same brand as those we recovered from inside the apartment. It's been walked on a couple of times and appears to have been there for some time. The second one I discovered was behind the pot plant. It hasn't been there long at all, and it's a different brand. So who knows? I'll complete the evidence log and be on my way. Where are you going to start?"

Westcott stroked his chin. He had a lot of evidence to get through. It would not be possible to process it all before he met with Delray tomorrow. "Finger prints on the two small bags of drugs. We get any prints other than Carter's that we can match on the database—they'll be hauled in for an interview straight away. Next is the laptop—the photos and all the other files. We need to sift through it quickly and see what we can find that may have gotten him killed. We've got Anton, one of our best analysts, on it as we speak."

"You're pretty sure he didn't jump?"

"I'm not positive. But, because of his record and what he does for a living, murder looks a more likely cause of death than suicide. Also, jumping doesn't always work. If you don't land right, you wind up either a quadriplegic or a vegetable, but still alive. Guns are much more efficient. He seems the type that could get a gun easily enough."

Westcott's phone rang. He answered and listening intently for about a minute to an update from Anton Jansen on Carter's laptop. He had only had the computer back in the lab for half an hour, but was already very positive.

Westcott replied, "I'll be back in the office within the hour. This could be the break we need. Good work Anton."

Westcott disconnected and turned to Brody. "We might have our first real break. Anton recovered some files from Carter's laptop drive that have been recently deleted but were still recoverable. They include five surveillance photos of a man and a woman caught in the act on an office table."

"Blackmail?"

"If we can identify and locate them, it's going to make for a very interesting interview."

Chapter Fourteen

Robbie stood by Mac's graveside and checked his watch. It was now five minutes past ten, and Jerry was running late. While he waited, he tried to recall how long it had been since they had last seen each other. Since moving permanently to the east coast, he had lost touch with most of his friends who lived on the west coast, Mac being one of the few exceptions.

The sight of a large, dark limousine interrupted his thoughts. He watched as the vehicle made its way slowly towards him on one of the tree lined service roads. Robbie watched as the vehicle pulled to a halt and a man in his early forties, holding a small wreath of flowers, got out of the vehicle. As the limousine slowly drove away, Robbie realized it was Jerry as he watched him take his time buttoning his double-breasted suit jacket before donning a pair of designer sunglasses.

Robbie remembered how Jerry had a flair for theatrical entrances when they had been at school and thought some things would never change as he watched him stride confidently across the lawn. When he reached the graveside, Jerry reached out his right hand and shook Robbie's hand with a grip that was firm and practiced.

"Robbie, it's good to see you."

Even though Jerry had put on a few pounds and his sandy hairline had grayed and receded a little since they had last met, Robbie thought the years had been kind to him.

"It's good to see you too, Jerry."

"How long has it been?"

"At least ten years—Mac's thirtieth birthday, as I recall."

Jerry nodded and then turned and looked down at the grave. His smile vanished and Robbie gave him a moment to collect his thoughts.

Without looking back, Jerry said, "I wanted to be here for the funeral, but my life's not my own anymore. It's difficult to get away, even for an hour."

Robbie nodded and replied, "Well, it's good that you came to pay your respects. Mac deserves no less."

As Jerry bent down to place the flowers on the grave, he replied, "I couldn't agree more."

Robbie moved back from the edge of the grave to give Jerry some space. Jerry rose to his full height and stood almost at attention with his head bowed for a good minute. He then made the sign of the cross and moved back from the grave's edge to where Robbie was standing.

"They say only the good die young, Robbie. In Mac's case, that was certainly true."

"I'm going to miss him."

Jerry nodded and replied, "Me too. He was the only one of the four of us from high school who I still caught up with on a regular basis."

"Kind of the glue that held us together."

"Yes."

They were quiet for a moment before Robbie said, "I'm surprised you don't see much of Nick anymore? You guys were pretty tight in high school."

"Yes, we were. It's mostly my fault, but when Nick got caught up in that OCTF corruption thing, I had to back right off. In politics, you can't afford to be associated with anyone where there is even just a whiff of corruption. It's shallow, I know, but that's the life of a politician. I tried to patch it up with him after they exonerated him, but he wasn't interested. Said he'd moved on and it taught him who his real friends were."

Robbie nodded. "You're right, you can't blame him for that. I don't envy you Jerry. It must be very hard to stay true to yourself."

"As mayor of Vancouver, I answer to over a million voters, most of whom think they know better than me. I love the challenge, Robbie, but there are days I could easily walk away."

Robbie decided it was time to change tack.

"So, what do you know about Mac's death?"

"Only what I've read in the papers. Hit and run with no witnesses. Vancouver Metro is still trying to locate the driver. It's been such a shock. I never would have thought anything like this would have happened to Mac…"

Robbie thought for a moment and then said, "I'm not sure it was an accident."

"What?"

"Some things don't add up, Jerry. Vancouver Metro is overworked and can't put much time into it, so I'm doing my own investigation."

"Okay, but what things?"

"I'm still digging. I made a promise to Mac in nineteen

eighty-nine that I would always have his back. I can't undo what's happened, but I intend to find out what happened and why. It's the least I can do for him."

"You don't think this is connected to nineteen eighty-nine, surely?"

"Right now, I'm just looking at all the reasons someone might want Mac dead."

"You can't be serious, Robbie. That was well over twenty years ago. We've all moved on. If you'll excuse the pun, it's dead and buried."

"I need to make sure, Jerry. You said it yourself, sometimes you don't have a choice. Mac was my friend and I have to do what I think is right."

"If I didn't know better, Robbie, it sounds like you're even treating me as a suspect?"

"I'm just keeping an open mind, Jerry. That's what they teach us journalists to do."

In a slightly exasperated voice, Jerry replied, "You're talking about something that happened when we were teenagers. Since then you've become a successful journalist. Nick has become head of the OCTF and I'm now the mayor of Vancouver, for God's sake. We're all respected, law-abiding citizens. Don't you think this is just a little paranoid?"

Robbie replied evenly, "I hope so, Jerry. But it wasn't a heart attack or a stroke that killed him. Hit and runs aren't always accidents and for my own peace of mind, I need to be sure."

Jerry shook his head in disgust and said, "Do what you need to do, Robbie."

Without another word, Jerry turned around and walked back to the road. He pulled out his phone and made a ten second call. Moments later, his limousine appeared, and he was gone.

Robbie watched as the limousine left the cemetery. He was not sure exactly what to make of his brief meeting with Jerry. Was Jerry being over sensitive because of his position as mayor? He needed to wait and see if Jerry had a next move.

Chapter Fifteen

Leon Blackwell tentatively pressed the button for the top floor. The elevator trip to the executive level of Stelecom Tower was something he never enjoyed. It was rare that he ever got to meet with Richard Stelovak personally. Stelovak normally used his underlings, usually Randolph Keaton and a trusted finance manager, to handle the financial matters that Blackwell managed on his behalf.

Keaton had summoned him to 'provide a financial status briefing to Richard on current business activities'. He wondered what Keaton meant. Blackwell had nothing to do with the day-to-day financial management of Stelecom. Stelovak used him only for what he was good at—laundering money.

He was the best in the business, and Stelovak knew it. He had meticulously built a reputation for being able to siphon money out of an organization and redistribute it without ever raising suspicion or leaving a trail back to the source. He didn't make mistakes, and no money was ever unaccounted for. The current deal for the Southwest development was big and if all the contracts were signed next Friday as planned, Stelovak would go close to being a billionaire, on paper at least.

While there was a lot riding on this, from Blackwell's point of view, everything was ready. The final secret commissions and bonus payments were locked away in offshore escrow accounts and would be released immediately after the contracts were signed. His work was done, he thought. But with Richard Stelovak, you could assume nothing.

As the elevator opened and Blackwell stepped out into the marble lobby, Stelovak's receptionist picked up the phone and simply said, "He's here."

Blackwell expected a long wait, but Keaton opened the double doors to Stelovak's inner sanctum almost immediately. With a condescending smile, Keaton said, "Good that you could join us on such short notice, Leon. Please come on in."

Stelovak was sitting behind an enormous mahogany desk, back dropped by a large floor to ceiling glass window that provided a breathtaking panoramic view of the bay. His office suite was bigger than most small houses. Blackwell scanned the room as he made his way across the office towards Stelovak's desk. He could see no one else here for the meeting, which made him even more nervous. Meetings with just Stelovak and Keaton invariably turned ugly quickly.

Stelovak smiled and pointed at one of the two chairs in front of his desk. "Have a seat, Leon. It's good to see you."

There was no handshake, but that didn't surprise Blackwell. He knew Stelovak shunned physical contact, anyway. Keaton sat down in the chair alongside Blackwell, facing Stelovak's desk.

Stelovak smiled again. "So Leon, at the end of the week, we will have the final contract signatures on Southwest. How is everything looking from your end?"

"Everything is fine, Richard. The accounts are all in place, and we have transferred the money. I have double and triple checked everything. There is no way the funds can be traced back here. It's a dead end in Romania, as planned. All that is needed is your approval. Your voice authorization to release the payments has all been setup as requested."

Blackwell let out a nervous little laugh as he continued, "My work is done. I'm quite redundant at this point."

Stelovak and Keaton also laughed softly, but with a slightly condescending tone. Blackwell thought to himself, here it comes.

Using a Mont Blanc pen that cost more than most compact cars, Stelovak started writing on a pad in front of him. With his head down, apparently concentrating on what was in front of him, he said, "Leon, you will never be redundant to this organization. We value what you do enormously and will do everything we can to protect you."

Stelovak looked up, clearly expecting a response.

"Well, thank you, Richard, I appreciate that."

"Don't mention it. We all look after each other here. Speaking of which, does the name Eugene Carter mean anything to you?"

"No."

Stelovak nodded. "I thought that might be the case. Never mind, it's good your friends here are keeping an eye out for you."

Stelovak picked up a Manila envelope and slowly slid it across the desk to Blackwell. "One of our associates brought this to me this morning. It appears Eugene Carter is, or should I say was, a photographer."

As Stelovak left the sentence hang in the air, Blackwell knew without even looking what was in the envelope.

"Please Leon, check for yourself, just in case there has been some misunderstanding."

Blackwell looked from Stelovak to Keaton and back to Stelovak again. Both wore looks totally devoid of expression. Drawing in a long breath, Blackwell picked up the envelope. He knew before opening the envelope that this was going to lead to trouble.

Blackwell grimaced as he looked down at the envelope in his hands. He may as well be opening a letter bomb, he thought. He sighed and lifted the flap. Reaching in, he gripped what appeared to be five or six glossy ten by eight photos and slowly slid them out. His heart sank even further when he had the first photo half revealed. There was no doubt it was him and no doubt what he was doing.

As Blackwell slid the photos back into the envelope, Stelovak held up an index finger. "No, please, Leon. You need to check them all."

Blackwell looked across at Keaton, who gave a subtle nod. He reluctantly removed all the photos and quickly thumbed through each one. All variations of the first photo of him—pants down and entangled with his temporary secretary. He had never felt so humiliated in his life.

He returned the photos to the envelope and waited.

"So, Leon, we have a rather delicate situation here. Like you, I'm very concerned that these photographs remain confidential. Not only would they be embarrassing for you if they got out, but they might affect your judgment as well. You do such great work for our organization, we wouldn't want to see anything get in your way. So, I'll tell you what I'm going to do for you, Leon."

Stelovak got up from behind his desk and came around to where Blackwell was sitting. Picking up the Manila envelope he said, "I'm going to look after these for you."

Making his way over to a large modern art painting that cost well into six figures, he continued. "The combination to my safe is only known by Randolph, my secretary, and myself. They will be quite safe here. You needn't worry."

Sliding back the painting, Stelovak revealed a large high-tech steel wall safe that Blackwell thought probably cost more than the painting that sat in front of it. Everyone was silent as they watched Stelovak open the safe. He carefully placed the envelope on the top shelf and then re-locked the safe. After repositioning the painting, he silently returned to his desk.

"Well, that's all the business I had to discuss today. Is there anything else?"

Both Keaton and Blackwell shook their heads.

"Well, let's all hope this next week goes smoothly. I'm looking forward to a big celebration next Friday night. Are you available, Leon?"

Blackwell said the only thing he could say, "I wouldn't miss it, Richard."

"Excellent. I'm sure Randolph will pass on the details of the venue in due course."

Keaton was on his feet now, and Blackwell took this as his cue to leave. Stelovak returned his concentration to writing on his notepad with his Mont Blanc.

The meeting was over, and Blackwell thought so was his life.

Chapter Sixteen

Robbie was not sure what he could achieve by returning to the scene of the hit and run. He knew from long experience as a journalist that the break you needed often came by going over the same evidence multiple times. Sometimes the answer was right in front of you, only not immediately obvious.

He parked the rental just up from Irish's on the opposite side of the road. It had rained on the way over and Robbie sat in the car for a while to see if he could wait it out. As he sat, he watched a man emerge from Irish's and walk across the road and down through the walkway in the retaining wall.

Rather than fully crossing the road, the man turned as he emerged on the lower side of the retaining wall. It suddenly made more sense to Robbie. The man was using the wall as a shelter from the rain, just like Mac had on the night of his death, he thought.

Robbie started the car and pulled back onto the road. The man continued to walk on, seemingly oblivious to

Robbie's car closing in behind him. As he drove past, he looked in the rear-view mirror. Even though he had passed within a feet of the man, he had not flinched at all and had just kept on walking. As he drove on, he realized it was the perfect spot for a hit and run.

Robbie turned up the next side street to head back and park the car again. He went a block and found a street that looked like it ran parallel to the main road. He was not exactly sure where to go and made one wrong turn before he got back to his original parking spot. Robbie parked the car and switched the engine off. As he sat there, he thought about what had just happened. He had proved nothing other than it was surprising more locals had not been killed walking home, particularly when it rained.

Robbie looked at his watch. It was barely five minutes since he had parked here the first time. He frowned and then started the car again. Pulling out onto the road again, Robbie followed the same route he had taken minutes before. He drove past the spot where Mac had been killed and then up the side street and back on the return road to where he had parked before.

After parking his car, he checked his watch again. The elapsed time was just on three minutes. He recalled Harry's words about the accident, and how he had heard the bang of a car hitting Mac and then, minutes later, another car skidding to a halt. It was so obvious now.

"One car, not two," he murmured. He visualized the car waiting in the dark for Mac to emerge from Irish's. As the rain tumbled down, the driver probably did not need to worry too much about his timing. He knew Mac would stay close to the wall for shelter as he walked home. He could see the car pulling onto the northbound lane and picking up speed quickly as it closed in on Mac.

Closing his eyes, Robbie saw the car veering slightly to hit Mac and catapult him into the wall. His eyes remained closed as he saw the car slowing back to normal speed and taking the same streets as Robbie took to come back to where Robbie was now parked.

As he opened his eyes again, Robbie visualized the car turning back onto the road a second time and accelerating towards the spot where Mac lay dead and then braking heavily to ensure it left skid marks on the road.

Robbie murmured, "Easier to pass it off as an accident if it looks like the driver tried to brake."

Robbie sat and stared out the front window for a long time. He did not need to investigate any further here. The first question had been answered. Mac had definitely been murdered. Robbie started the car and pulled out onto the road. Now he needed answers to questions two and three; 'Why?' and 'By whom?'

Chapter Seventeen

It was well after six p.m. when Felix Delray shut off his computer to go home. He had put in close to twelve hours for the day and felt like he had gone backwards. After turning off the lights to his office, he looked in on the detective's room before catching the elevator down to his car in the basement. He expected it to be empty at this time of day and was angry with who he found still there on his own.

"What are you still doing here, Danny? I told you to go home hours ago!"

"Sorry, boss. Got caught up in a fresh development in one case."

"Yeah, well, that all changes tomorrow. You work too hard and I'm reassigning some of your load. Did you get a girlfriend yet, like we talked about?"

"Uh, no, boss."

"Well, get one and that's an order. If I don't see you with a girlfriend by the time of your annual review, I'll mark you down for failing to follow orders."

Westcott smiled.

"And not going home when your boss says so."

Westcott raised his hands in surrender. "Okay, point taken. I promise to go home."

Delray grinned. "And get a girlfriend."

"I'll see what I can do."

"Are you parked in the basement?"

"Yes."

"Switch your computer off and get your coat. I'm officially walking you off the premises."

"Boss, I just need five minutes."

"Five minutes, my ass. Get your coat, we're leaving."

Delray smiled to himself as he watched Westcott reluctantly shut off his computer and clear the files off his desk. If everyone on his squad worked half as hard and was half as smart as Westcott, his job would be easy. Westcott's only flaw was he worked too hard. Delray knew he would probably hit the wall one day and learn the hard way, just as he had. He would make sure he was there to see him through, just as his boss had been for him.

As they got into the elevator, Delray said, "Talk to me."

"Okay. Eugene Carter. I will give you a full briefing tomorrow, but for now we have made good progress. No fingerprints other than Carter's on the plastic bags that the drugs were in and nothing else of note yet from the other physical property."

"Doesn't sound like progress?"

"We did, however, extract some files that had recently been deleted from his computer. Five of them appear to be under surveillance, potentially for blackmail. A man and a woman, pants down, using a desk for other than its intended purpose. No ID on the woman, but the man looks a lot like a guy called Leon Blackwell that we have on file. We should have better confirmation tomorrow once the lab guys finish the facial digital analysis."

"Leon Blackwell. The name rings a bell."

"It should. He's officially an accountant, but he's as dirty as they come. Very cunning and smart. His major client appears to be Richard Stelovak."

"Stelovak again. If I had a dollar for every time that name has come up recently, I could buy both of us a very nice steak. So what is he, Stelovak's laundry man?"

"It's too soon to tell. Blackwell only appears to have a few clients, Stelovak being one of them. Even though he's a qualified accountant, it doesn't appear as though he's done that sort of work for years. I'm hoping to get a positive match against the photos we have of Blackwell on file. If so, we can legitimately haul him in here for questioning."

"Shake his tree real hard. We might even get Stelovak."

"That's my intention. You want to be part of it?"

Delray smiled at Westcott. He didn't normally have the time to help his detectives with interviews. They were all big enough and ugly enough to work on their own, Westcott more than any of the others. He was smart, always had a strategy and great attention to detail. He knew how to give suspects enough rope to hang themselves. Delray didn't think he could do any better but was happy to ride shotgun.

"If you're offering, I'm there."

"I'll keep you posted, boss."

The elevator opened, and they walked towards Delray's car.

"One more thing. The MacDonald hit and run. I got a call from one of his friends, and it looks like we have a lead on the guy who MacDonald had his last drink and argument with. You'll never guess who?"

"Surprise me."

"Peter Trelor."

"The undertaker? What's that sneaky bastard up to, I wonder?"

"Maybe nothing. We officially listed Trelor as missing yesterday."

"This just keeps getting better and better."

Delray glanced at his watch. "I gotta go, Danny. I've been happily married for twenty-eight years and want to make it twenty-nine. I promised Jenny I would be home by seven tonight, so I'm going to need some luck with the lights. I'll see you tomorrow."

Delray got in and started his car. As he reversed out of his car space, he wound down the window.

"Hey, Danny. Good work today and go home now. No sneaking back upstairs after I'm gone."

"I promise, boss. I'm beat. I need to sleep."

"Tomorrow, Danny."

Westcott watched as his boss drove out of the parking lot and then headed for his car. Delray did not need to worry about him working late tonight. He really needed sleep. Westcott got into his car and drove out of the basement. He was looking forward to tomorrow. The opportunity to grill Leon Blackwell about his starring role in the photo shoot on Eugene Carter's camera was going to prove very interesting.

Chapter Eighteen

Robbie was late arriving at Laura's apartment for dinner. After making the breakthrough on Mac's death, he had sat in the rental for over an hour thinking about what he had discovered. He recalled Harry's words, 'It changes everything when you find out they were murdered.'

Harry had been right. It was hard enough to accept Mac's life had been cut short by a tragic accident, but murder took it to a whole new level.

As he headed back to his hotel room, Robbie decided he would spend the rest of the day on the phone and online finding out more about Peter Trelor. He called Westcott first and briefed him on what he had learned. Westcott had been genuinely interested, and they had spoken at length about both the hit and run and Peter Trelor. The research into Trelor that Robbie had done after the call had also been profitable. He now knew a lot more about the man they referred to as the undertaker and why he had an association with Mac.

Just as he was getting ready to leave for dinner, Westcott called back and they spent another twenty minutes on the phone. Westcott expressed his appreciation for the information he had provided, but counseled Robbie not to take the investigation into his own hands. The case would now be officially upgraded to a suspected homicide.

As Robbie got out of the elevator, he could smell an amazing array of oriental spices coming from Laura's apartment, even before he got to the front door.

Laura opened the door shortly after Robbie knocked and greeted him with a big smile. "Perfect timing, Robbie. How was your day?"

Robbie walked in and draped his coat on the back of one of Laura's dining chairs. Half distracted, he murmured, "This smells good," as he sat on the couch.

"It's ready to serve now, or we can leave it simmer for a while?"

Robbie didn't appear to be listening as he stared off into space. Laura turned down the stove and came and sat down next to him.

"Laura, I don't know how to say this gently, but I'm positive now that Mac was murdered."

As her face turned white, Robbie put an arm around her. He felt her crying softly as she rested her head against his shoulder. After several minutes, Laura lifted her head and wiped her eyes. "I think we should eat later."

Robbie watched as she silently went into the kitchen and turned off the stove. When she returned to sit on the couch, Robbie took this as his cue and explained what he had discovered during his investigation that day.

"After visiting the grave with Jerry, I drove back to Irish's. I wasn't entirely sure what I expected to find. Anyway, I parked on one of the lower side streets and planned to go back to the scene of the accident to get a better perspective on what happened. It was raining, and I stayed in the car for a while hoping it would clear. I saw a man come out of Irish's and cross the walkway—I assume to go home. He walked up against the retaining wall for shelter, the same as we think Mac did."

Robbie explained how he had driven past the man and then up a side street and back to where he had parked. He told Laura how he had made a second trip, which he had timed. He grimaced and then declared, "And that's when it hit me. There was only one car, Laura. The first sound Harry heard was Mac being hit. The second was the same car coming back past the scene a few minutes later to brake heavily and leave tire marks on the road near the body."

"To make it look like an accident?"

Robbie nodded. "Yes… to make it look like an accident."

Robbie realized Laura needed some time to process this, just as he had.

They were both quiet for a while until Laura finally looked at Robbie. "So, what do we do now, Robbie?"

"Until an hour ago, I would have said we focus our investigation on Peter Trelor. He was the last person we knew of to have significant contact with Mac, and that they were arguing bothers me. I did a lot of research on him this afternoon, both online and through a few phone calls. Trelor has been very busy since leaving the OCTF. He has his own business doing similar work to what Mac did, only on a larger scale. Defense security consulting and a couple of major companies have his company on the payroll to look after cyber security. It's possible Mac was working with Trelor and that's why they were meeting."

Laura nodded as she tried to take it all in.

Robbie continued, "Anyway, before starting my research, I called Detective Westcott. I didn't see any reason we shouldn't cooperate with the police and let them know what we know. I told him we were sure who Mac met with and my theory that Mac was murdered and how it was made to look like an accident. He thanked me for the information and said he would look into it. He was good to his word. I got a call back from him just before I left the hotel to come here. He told me Trelor lives in a gated estate and got home around ten p.m. on Sunday night. They have a security video and a statement from his live-in girlfriend to say he was home the rest of the evening. So Westcott doesn't think he was the driver, as he had a fairly tight alibi at the time Mac was killed."

Laura frowned. "Could he have somehow faked his arrival at home?"

Robbie shook his head. "I don't think so. And what makes it more interesting is that Trelor left for his office early on Monday morning, but never arrived. Nobody has seen him since, and his bank accounts haven't been touched. According to Westcott, his girlfriend and business associates are extremely concerned, as this is very out of character for him. Vancouver Metro has officially listed him as missing."

Laura went pale. "What on earth are we mixed up in?"

"I'm not sure. I can't see Peter Trelor's argument with Mac and his disappearance the following day, just being a coincidence. We find the answer to why they met and what they talked about, and maybe we get closer to the truth."

"You're right Robbie. Perhaps we should talk to Theo?"

"Theo, as in Mac's business partner?"

"Yes," said Laura with a nod. "If anyone has an idea what Mac was up to, it would be Theo. He was at the funeral, of course, and really upset. He will certainly help wherever he can. We should see him tomorrow if we can."

"Agreed..."

"Robbie, are you okay? You look a million miles away."

Robbie was a million miles away. He had gone back to Catalin Mountain in nineteen eighty-nine. A million questions raced through his mind. How do you tell someone that the two people you suspect most of having a motive to kill your brother are childhood friends? How do you do that without betraying a secret pact you made over twenty years ago? How do you tell someone you increasingly care about that you were part of a cover-up? Robbie got up from the sofa and began to pace.

"Robbie, what's going on here?"

Robbie paused. He realized it would not be possible to keep the secret any longer. Laura was in this as much as he was and also needed to know the truth. "Jerry, Nick, Mac and I were all close friends in high school. As you know, my family has a small farm at Cypress Falls near the base of the Catalin Mountain."

"I remember—Mac used to stay with you sometimes on weekends."

Robbie continued, "In late nineteen eighty-nine, just before we graduated, we went out for some target practice with our bows one afternoon on Catalin Mountain. We had been out there about three hours when we decided to come home. As we were walking out on a fire trail, we came across a man in a small clearing. He was dead. He had an arrow in his back. It was identical to the ones we were using, and we were two short when we packed everything up..."

Robbie looked at Laura, but she had turned away and was now staring at the floor. Robbie had a sinking feeling in his stomach as he continued, "We figured he'd been dead for several hours at most. We debated what to do. Mac and I both thought we should call the police, but Jerry and Nick weren't so sure. We were all fairly sure it was one of our arrows, but Jerry and Nick thought it was too risky to get the police involved. They figured we could all have been charged with manslaughter. They had both won scholarships to study for their degrees and didn't want them jeopardized."

After pausing a moment to collect his thoughts, Robbie added, "To complicate matters, the man was a convicted felon. He'd been to jail twice that I know of for sex offenses in the Cypress Falls area. Jerry's sister was one of his victims. When we realized who he was, Mac and I folded... I'm not proud of it."

Robbie gave Laura an opportunity to respond, but she refused to look at him. He continued, "We found an old abandoned mine-shaft about halfway up the mountain—that's where we disposed of the body. As far as I know, it's still there. We made a promise to each other never to mention what happened again. I've kept that promise until today."

Silence descended on the room. Robbie could hear a clock ticking on the wall. Finally he said, "I don't expect you to understand, Laura. I wouldn't have told you except for what happened to Mac. Right now, I'm wondering whether it's all coming back to haunt us. What happened was supposed to remain a secret. I'm just wondering whether Mac has died for it. In my mind, Jerry and Nick are suspects. I need to find out more and confront them both."

Robbie stood still and waited. The room remained quiet. It had taken him years to come to terms with what happened on that day. In the end, he knew they had done the wrong thing, regardless of what kind of person the dead man had been. He waited another minute. He felt drained and had lost his appetite. There wasn't anything else to say. After grabbing his coat and heading for the door, he called back softly over his shoulder, "I'm sorry, Laura."

"I'm sorry too, Robbie."

Chapter Nineteen

After a restless night at the hotel, Robbie had woken early and spent an hour in the hotel gym doing a mixture of cardio and weights. He had hoped the gym session would clear his mind. Still without an appetite and uneasy about the way he had left Laura's apartment the night before, he decided on a walk to think through what had happened. As he walked along the picturesque boardwalk that followed the twists of the river, Robbie felt normal again. Amongst the throng of walkers, joggers and cyclists that had risen early for fresh air and exercise, he tried to focus on which direction his investigation should take. Despite his surroundings, his thoughts kept returning to Laura's reaction to his confession.

Robbie feared he had permanently damaged their relationship. He also wondered what she now thought of her late brother's involvement in what had happened. As he walked and reflected on what he had said, he was positive he had done the right thing. Keeping what happened on Catalin Mountain a secret any longer would have been dishonest, particularly now he was certain Mac had been murdered.

After walking for almost an hour, his phone rang. It was Laura.

Robbie was not sure what to expect from the call. The call had been brief, with Laura simply asking that they meet to talk as soon as possible. Robbie had suggested breakfast at a restaurant that overlooked the river near to his hotel in forty-five minutes. Laura had agreed and Robbie had just enough time to return to his hotel to shower and change.

As he walked into the restaurant, Robbie figured this would probably be the litmus test of their friendship. Laura sat at a window table with a perfect view of the river below and didn't hear Robbie as he approached.

"Hi."

Laura turned and looked up at Robbie with a frown. "Before you sit down, are there any other secrets?"

Robbie frowned. "Secrets?"

"Is there anything else I need to know about? Because Robbie, after what I went through at the OCTF, there are very few people left in my life I still trust. I want to know if you're one of them."

"No, Laura, no more secrets. There's nothing else. I promise."

Laura looked out the window again as she contemplated Robbie's answer. After an awkward moment of silence, she said, "You better sit down then."

As he sat down, Laura looked at him with a mixture of frustration and confusion.

"Last night. I'm not sure you could have dropped a bigger bombshell on me, even if you tried. I like you Robbie. I like you a lot. But what you told me…"

Laura looked back towards the river again and continued.

"This... secret. It wasn't just you, it was Mac—my own brother! And Jerry, the mayor of Vancouver. And Nick, the commanding officer of the OCTF. Two of Vancouver's supposedly most upstanding citizens. It was all just very... overwhelming."

"You needed to know, Laura."

"You were right, Robbie. You and Mac should have called it in. That's where I was at last night. I'm not saying I'm okay with it now, but I can understand to a degree."

Laura looked back at Robbie and tentatively reached a hand across the table and briefly touched her fingers to Robbie's.

"I appreciate your honesty. I know it couldn't have been easy."

"Thanks for being so understanding."

"I'm not sure I really understand. But I trust you and right now I think that's more important."

Robbie let out a long breath—it had been a rough week. Having someone to share the secret with that he had carried since nineteen eighty-nine was an enormous relief. He had not even shared it with his wife when she was still alive, something he constantly regretted. He was not sure what to say and squeezed Laura's hand tightly. Trust was a commodity in short supply right now, and he was thankful for Laura's friendship.

A server came and stood by the table, but neither Robbie nor Laura seemed to notice him until he coughed loudly and then asked for their order.

When he left, Robbie tried to lighten the mood. "That man's got a nasty cough. He really should have it seen to."

They both laughed. Laura looked at Robbie for a

moment and sighed, "Mayne, I would like nothing more than to banter with you all day, but…"

"There's always a but…"

Laura grew serious again. "Last night after you left, I sat on the couch for a long time trying to process what you had told me. I was angry, very confused, and even felt betrayed. I cried for a while, then I had something to eat and went to bed. I tossed and turned for a long while. I kept thinking about you and Mac and that day on the mountain. Something was nagging me, and I couldn't figure out what it was. It was more than just accepting what had happened and that Mac had kept it a secret. And then I remembered you said it happened in nineteen eighty-nine. Right?"

"Right."

Laura's face showed visible relief as she sat back in her chair. "Mac told me, after all."

Robbie frowned. "I'm not sure I follow?"

"Before I got married, I remember asking Mac who his best friend was. His instant response was you. I asked him why and he gave me a whole host of reasons, but he kept coming back to two qualities."

Robbie smiled. "I tell great jokes and I make great pancakes?"

Laura smiled. "No. He said your word was your bond and he would trust you with his life."

Robbie nodded, but said nothing.

Laura added, "He also said you both shared a burden since late high school you couldn't tell anyone about. He said he made a promise back in nineteen eighty-nine that he couldn't break without asking you."

Laura was silent in reflection for a moment before she continued.

"Mac said he would ask you one day if it was okay to

share it with me. We never talked about it again, and I forgot all about it until last night. When you mentioned it happened in nineteen eighty-nine, I knew the year was significant. I just couldn't remember why."

Laura paused and then softly added, "Even though I never knew what the secret was, I feel better knowing he wanted to tell me."

Robbie pulled out his smart phone from and started tapping the screen.

"Robbie?"

Robbie looked up momentarily. "Sorry, Laura. One of the first phone messages I listened to when I got off the plane was from my mother, who told me to call her urgently. When she broke the news about Mac, I was in shock and didn't really pay much attention to my other phone messages or emails."

Robbie passed his phone to Laura. "This is Mac's last email message to me. I didn't read it until after I heard about his death."

Laura looked at the email message from Mac on Robbie's phone and read it out aloud. "Robbie, please call me as soon as you get off the plane. We need to talk urgently. Mac."

Laura sat back in her chair and said, "Well, that fits with his agitated state?"

Robbie grimaced. "He used an alias for the email address. When it landed in my inbox, it was simply entitled 'Mac'. It was different to all his other messages, which have a full email name. I hadn't thought about it until I got home last night. I discovered an option on my phone to display the full email address for anything sent through with an alias."

Robbie passed his phone across to Laura, who read the email address silently and then out aloud.

"catalin1989@cybamail.com."

Laura looked up at Robbie as she passed his phone back. "Why would Mac be using that event as an email address?"

Robbie replied, "That's an excellent question."

Chapter Twenty

Westcott knocked on Delray's office door.

Delray looked up from some files on his desk and asked, "How did you sleep?"

"Like a baby, boss. Nine hours."

"Good. Come in and take a load off."

As Westcott sat down, he watched Delray straighten what looked like a pile of his case files. Not much of a reprieve coming here, Westcott thought.

"Before we get into anything else, I've looked at your case load. Surprise, you've got way too much on your plate."

Delray pulled two files off the top of the pile and put them on the side of his desk. Pointing at the pile that remained in front of him, Delray continued, "As of now, McKenzie and Jamieson get these. You can brief them and handover later today."

Delray picked up the two files he had placed at the side of his desk and handed them across to Westcott. "You concentrate on these two. The MacDonald hit and run might prove to be nothing, but I want you on it. It's concerning that MacDonald's last conversation was with Peter Trelor, who is now officially missing. I want you to focus on the Trelor angle. You might just solve two for the price of one."

Pointing to the Eugene Carter file, Delray continued. "This one here bothers me. I think you dig hard and fast on the Leon Blackwell angle with those photos, we can pop this one wide open. So that's it unless you have any objections?"

Westcott shook his head. "No, this is great, boss. Thanks."

Delray pushed his chair back from his desk. "All right, what have you got on the Carter case?"

"The photo analysis has come through. The digital facial comparison gives a ninety-seven percent certainty of a match between our file photos and the ones of Blackwell on the desk with the woman."

"Good, we now have justification for an interview. When are you setting that up?"

"As soon as I'm done here."

"Good. Take Jamieson with you and keep me in the loop."

"Also, the lab boys are still doing some DNA analysis. I'm hoping to get the preliminary results back today. Nothing else from physical property yet or from finger print analysis. However, I'm prepared to call it murder, not suicide."

Delray raised an eyebrow. "Do tell."

"There were your typical fingerprints all over the apartment except for the screen door to the balcony. No sign of forced entry, so I'm assuming for the moment Carter knows his killer or has no reason to think he's in danger and lets him in. His killer subdues him and gets him out on the balcony and drops him over the side. He's left fingerprints on the door in the process and needs to wipe it clean. There's no way he can remark the door with a fingerprint or two from Carter because he's now on the pavement four floors below."

Delray thought for a moment. "It works for me, Danny. Good work. So what do we have on file on Blackwell?"

"He's an accountant through and through, just a very dishonest one. I don't believe he's capable of murder. It's possible he sent someone to get the photos back from Carter and it went bad, but I want to explore who else Blackwell is connected to. We know he is well connected to Richard Stelovak, but he has several other high-profile clients. They're all dirty, so any of them might want some additional leverage or insurance. The photos would be a good way to get that. There's a good chance Blackwell doesn't even know about the photos. If that's the case, we can catch him off guard and really apply the pressure."

Pointing to the large pile of files, Delray said, "You see McKenzie and Jamieson, send them my way and I'll give them the good news."

Delray watched Westcott get up and walk out of his office. He had a feeling it would not be long before Westcott got his breakthrough.

Chapter Twenty-One

Laura watched as Robbie sat deep in thought, staring at the email address on his phone screen.

She thought for a moment and said, "Mac used a number of email addresses for his work. Some of them were just for testing at client sites. I used to get emails from him occasionally from random email addresses he was using. Maybe that's what was happening here?"

Robbie shook his head. "I don't think so. Mac wouldn't use that as an email address unless it was significant. It's a pity we can't access it and see what it contains."

Laura thought for a moment. "Maybe we can? I knew some of Mac's password combinations and we could always get help from Theo."

Robbie got up from his chair. "My laptop is in the hotel safe and it's only a two-minute walk from here. If I hurry, I'll be back in five."

"You want me to come with you?"

Robbie smiled. "I'm starved, so someone needs to wait

here for our breakfast. You won't eat my eggs if they arrive before I get back, will you?"

Laura winked. "No guarantees. You'd better hurry."

Laura watched as Robbie walked out of the restaurant. She realized she had learned more about Robbie in the past four days than in all the years she had known him as Mac's best friend. She had understood why Mac liked him so much.

As she sat and waited for his return, she pondered what she had really learned about him since his return to Vancouver. He was easy to be with, and she really enjoyed his company. But it was more than that. It was difficult to put her finger on. Since the scandal and her resignation from the OCTF, she had largely insulated herself from the world.

Laura readily acknowledged she had become bitter and angry and found it almost impossible to trust people anymore. The therapy had helped. She had learned to forgive and let go, but she still could not fully trust anyone except close family. Being able to let go had at least allowed her to get on with her life. She had begun to socialize again and was making friends, although she had not permitted anyone to get close.

Her psychiatrist had wanted her to continue therapy to help her resolve the trust issues, but Laura was tired of the therapy sessions. Learning to trust people would have to wait for another day.

Robbie's revelation about what had happened on Catalin Mountain had floored her at first. But she soon realized that Robbie had shared something of his past that made him incredibly vulnerable. Something he could surely only do with someone he fully trusted. It was a nice feeling to know someone trusted you enough to share like that.

Laura realized that apart from her immediate family, Robbie was the first person she had really trusted in years. She wondered whether he was the breakthrough she needed. Perhaps she could begin trusting others now that she felt Robbie was someone she could rely on? Time would tell. Maybe she wouldn't need to go back to her shrink after all?

Her thoughts drifted back to her brother. Not for the first time since she and Robbie had become certain he had been murdered; did she worry about their safety. Were they safe? Could they become victims like Mac if they dug too deep? She decided it was something she would need to discuss with Robbie right away.

Laura thought about Mac's email again and the reference back to nineteen eighty-nine. She thought about Nick and Jerry. Could they have really been involved in Mac's murder? She could not imagine a situation in which Mac would give away the secret of what happened all those years ago. But she realized there were things about his life that she didn't know. Perhaps circumstances had changed? Perhaps Jerry or Nick now felt Mac was a threat that had to be dealt with?

"Did you eat my eggs?"

Laura jumped. She looked up to see Robbie, with his laptop under his arm, smiling and staring down at her. "Robbie, you've got to stop sneaking up on me like that. That's twice in less than an hour."

"Sorry, but you looked a million miles away. So, did you?"

Laura looked back at him blankly.

Still smiling, Robbie sat down opposite Laura. "My eggs. Did you eat them?"

Laura was about to say no when the server with the 'bad

cough' appeared from the kitchen with their breakfast. Pointing to the server, she said, "As luck would have it, you arrived back in the nick of time."

"Good. I'm starved. How about we eat and then see if we can make sense of this email code, if that's what it is?"

The smell of their breakfast being placed before them made Laura instantly hungry. "No argument from me."

Robbie quickly devoured his bacon and eggs and powered up his laptop as Laura finished the last of her omelet.

"So, while I was walking back to the hotel, I started thinking. I remembered over the years, all the emails I ever got from Mac were all from the one provider. Mac regularly used the same three or four email addresses for business and personal email, but they were all from cybamail.com."

Robbie had his laptop powered up and ready to go. He keyed www.cybamail.com into his browser and hit enter. He looked at Laura and crossed his fingers.

Laura moved her chair around to Robbie's side of the table as they watched the screen refresh. A few seconds passed and the home page for Cyba Cloud Services appeared. Robbie looked at Laura. "This is a good start."

Robbie clicked on the Cyba Email Icon at the top left of the screen. The page quickly refreshed to a Cybamail login screen, which was like those provided by HotMail and Gmail. The page requested both an email identifier and matching password. Robbie keyed in catalin1989@cybamail.com into the email identifier field and then moved the mouse pointer to the password field.

"From here, it's just a guess, Laura. I'm afraid I have no idea what the password is."

Laura sat very still looking at the screen and thinking. Robbie waited patiently and silently while Laura thought.

She reached into her carry bag and withdrew a pen and small notebook. "Mac was a creature of habit. I knew some of the more common passwords he used, but not all of them, of course."

She began to write down some words in the notebook. After about two minutes, she said, "I can't think of any others right now, but this is a start at least."

Robbie looked at the list. Most of the words he knew. 'Winfield' was at the top of the list and was the name of Mac's dog that had been his soul mate throughout his childhood. It did not surprise Robbie to see the word 'Hollier' next on the list. Hollier was Mac's mother's maiden name. The next two passwords were also no surprise: 'Calwell', Laura's surname after she got married and 'Cypress Falls', the name of the high school that Mac and Robbie had both attended. Robbie scanned the rest of the list. The last two words surprised him; 'Robbie' and 'Mayne'.

"Mac used my name in his passwords?"

Laura smiled. "You were his best friend, Robbie. You shouldn't be surprised. In fact, because you are the connection for him to Catalin and nineteen eighty-nine, maybe we should start with password combinations surrounding your name?"

Somewhat embarrassed, Robbie replied, "Okay."

Laura continued, "Mac never used straight forward passwords. He was very particular about ensuring they were complex enough to prevent easy hacking. He would probably spell 'Robbie' with a zero instead of the 'o', a number one instead of the 'i' and a three instead of the 'e'.

Robbie frowned and replied, "I understand the zero looks like an 'o' and the number one looks like an 'i' but the number three?"

"It looks like a capital 'E' reversed."

"Okay, that works."

Laura continued, "He would probably spell 'Mayne' with an '@' symbol instead of the 'a' and a number three at the end instead of the 'e'. He also used straight numbers as well at the end, but they all had meaning. When he used Winfield, he would use 1987."

"That was the year Winfield died."

"Right. When he set up my home Wi-Fi password, he used the code 'W1nf13ld1987'. It looks random until you understand the code, then it's easy to remember without writing it down. He would use our mother's birth year or month and date of birth with any password combination for her name. Unless he's changed his format, any passwords with your name will most likely include your year of birth or month and date of birth in the combination."

"OK, let's start with combinations for 'Robbie'." Robbie keyed in his first name in the format suggested by Laura and his birth year. He looked at Laura and pressed enter. The screen refreshed and displayed a message in red below the login, 'Invalid User ID or password.'

With a smile that looked more like a grimace, Robbie replied, "This could take a while."

Robbie then tried his first name again with 0609 for his birth date and month at the end. The screen refreshed and again displayed the same error message: 'Invalid User ID or Password.'

Laura suggested, "Try your last name instead."

Robbie keyed in his last name using the 'M@yn3' format and added his year of birth to the end. He pressed enter and waited. The screen refreshed and again displayed the same error message: 'Invalid User ID or password.'

Robbie keyed in his last name and substituted his year of birth for his birth date and month. He pressed enter and waited again. The screen refreshed and again displayed the same error message: 'Invalid User ID or password.'

Letting out a long breath, Robbie said, "We're going to have to be patient and persevere."

Laura replied, "Perseverance I'm okay at. Patience, however, is not my strong suit."

They spent the next hour trying various combinations without success. They were both frustrated and disappointed.

Pushing his chair back from the table, Robbie said, "I think it's time for a break. Let's shut this down and go for a walk to clear our heads. If we think about something else for a while, maybe it will come to us?"

Laura sighed. "I feel like we're so close."

Robbie was just about to shut down his laptop and paused. "There's one obvious password we haven't tried. Your old Wi-Fi password. That's one password only you and Mac knew about."

Laura nodded. "Try it, Robbie."

Robbie keyed in the password. Before he hit enter, he turned to Laura. "If this doesn't work, we go for the walk and clear our heads. Agreed?"

"Agreed."

Robbie hit the enter key and waited for the screen to refresh with the familiar 'Invalid User ID or Password' message. He stared, almost in disbelief, as the Inbox for catalin1989@cybamail.com appeared instead.

Chapter Twenty-Two

Robbie and Laura decided the restaurant was not the place to examine Mac's email account. They paid for breakfast and hurried back to Robbie's hotel room. Once inside, they posted the 'Do Not Disturb' sign, locked the door and set up Robbie's laptop on the small writing table.

Robbie opened the mail account again. All were from the one email address; 'codos9009@proteja.bg'.

"I think we should start with the oldest emails first. That way we should fully understand all the history without getting confused."

Laura pointed at a 'View All' option at the top left of the screen. "I think this email system will allow you to view all email, both sent and received in chronological order. That would be useful for us so that we have a real sense of the conversation."

Robbie clicked on the 'View All' option. The web page refreshed and showed all emails in date order.

Robbie looked at the list. "Only seven emails in total.

The Catalin Code

This shouldn't take long. Fingers crossed, we get a real sense of what Mac was caught up in."

They opened the oldest email message, which had been sent by Mac, and began reading.

To: codos9009@proteja.bg From: catalin1989@cybamail.com
Subject: New Address

C

Please use this temporary email address for all future email comms. What I'm doing is illegal here and I can't afford to be seen to be connected. I could get prison time if caught.

Ghost loaded and tested. Laptop was picked up yesterday. I have started monitoring but nothing of importance yet.

Be careful, I don't think he's suspicious yet, but he's very well connected.

M

Laura and Robbie read the message several times each before they spoke.

"What do you think, Robbie?"

"We need to read the other emails, of course, but several things concern me straight away. One, what Mac is doing is illegal. That is totally unlike Mac unless he has a very good reason. Two, Mac is encouraging Codos, whoever that is, to also be careful. Hopefully, the other emails will help us understand whether 'careful' means don't get caught, or danger, or both. Three, the language they use is concise and familiar, like they know each other."

"Codos might be from another country, too. Look at the extension of the email address. It would be useful to know whether the 'bg' is significant."

"Good pickup, Laura. Let's look it up."

Switching to another browser window, Robbie keyed 'country of origin bg' into the search engine and pressed the search key. The screen refreshed to display pages of search results. Robbie did not need to investigate any further than the results on the first page. The summary text for each match was consistent. 'bg' was the country identifier for Bulgaria.

"We'll that's useful to know. Codos uses a Bulgarian email provider. It's a reasonable bet he or she is probably located in Bulgaria, or somewhere else in East Europe at least. Let's read the next email."

To: catalin1989@cybamail.com From: codos9009@proteja.bg
Subject: Re: New Address

OK, will use this email for all future comms.

You need to be very careful yourself. If Ghost is discovered, he will know who installed it. Be ready to remotely remove it if you get suspicious.

Also, contact confirms money has been deposited into the bank accounts detailed in my last email. This is a serious payoff. I don't need to tell you what they're capable of if you're identified, particularly with $3M at stake.

Codos

Robbie let out a long breath. "Three million dollars is more than enough money to get you killed. We need to break this down, piece by piece."

Laura retrieved her notepad and a pen from her bag and began writing. "We need to make notes of the key points as we go. From the first email, we have the temporary email address, the contact we think is in Bulgaria and illegal monitoring of someone presumably here who owns or uses a laptop."

Robbie added, "Ghost is probably some sort of stealth monitoring program that Mac has loaded without the owner being aware. We also can be reasonably sure Mac knows the owner because of what he said about the owner picking up the laptop in the first email and the warning from Codos in the second email."

Laura continued making notes. "There are multiple bank accounts with three million dollars in them, which someone identified by Codos as 'the contact' is monitoring."

Robbie quickly reread the second email. "The money seems to be a payoff for something going on over here. Maybe this is what Mac is trying to find out more about by the Ghost program?"

Laura re-read the last part of the second email. "Mac was given information on the bank accounts, presumably sent to one of his other email accounts that he operates?"

Robbie watched while Laura finished making notes. When she finished, she looked up at the screen again. "Ready."

Robbie opened the third email.

To: catalin1989@cybamail.com From: codos9009@proteja.bg
Subject: Discovered

Contact is having difficulty getting information. Bank appears suspicious and procedures have changed. Email and Internet have been replaced by secure phone communication.

Contact is concerned he has been discovered. My advice is to remove Ghost immediately before you are discovered.

Gathering further evidence now is not worth the risk!
Codos

Robbie watched as Laura continued to make notes. "From the tone and content of this email, it looks like everything is unraveling."

Laura looked up from her notepad. "This is the first mention of a bank, presumably in Bulgaria?"

"Yes. It looks like the contact either works closely with or for 'the bank' to detect changes in procedure like he has described."

"Codos clearly thinks gathering evidence is too risky."

"Yes. The 'gathering information' phrase is interesting. Maybe they're not after the three million dollars, just evidence?"

"You know, Robbie, what I don't understand is why Mac would get involved in something like this? It seems so... covert. That's not Mac. We both knew he was a straight up guy. He would normally report something like this to the police and let them deal with it."

"I agree. Let's keep reading."

To: codos9009@proteja.bg From: catalin1989@cybamail.com
Subject: Re: Discovered

C

No longer have access to laptop. Suspect Ghost already discovered/removed. I am making contingency plans and will notify colleague ASAP.

M

Robbie looked at Laura's notes. "This is the first time Mac has used the word 'colleague'. Codos uses the word 'contact' for the person providing him with information from the bank."

"And from earlier emails, we can assume Codos was used as some sort of go between for the 'contact'."

"Which means the 'colleague' of Mac is another person."

"It would be really helpful if people's real names were used."

"It would, Laura, but Mac was obviously worried about discovery, hence the cryptic messages and temporary email address."

"Let's keep reading."

To: catalin1989@cybamail.com From: codos9009@proteja.bg
Subject: Contact

Contact has been missing for two days. Blood found in his apartment, but no body. I'm going to ground (you need to do the same). Will check email periodically and provide updates as best I can. Take care my friend, this is going bad.
Codos

Robbie pointed at the date of the email. "This was sent after Mac was murdered. Codos doesn't know about Mac when he wrote this."

Robbie closed the email and opened the next email, also sent by Codos.

To: catalin1989@cybamail.com From: codos9009@proteja.bg
Subject: Fwd: Contact

Contact's body found this morning dumped in a storm drain at the edge of the city. Signs of torture. He would have told them everything he knew. Police have no suspects yet.

They have come after me, too. Now in hiding. You need to plan for the worst.

Again, take care.

Robbie and Laura reread the email several times in silence.

"I can't believe what I'm reading, Robbie. Other people being murdered as well, and on the other side of the world. What have we gotten involved in?"

Robbie didn't answer, but clicked on the last email instead.

To: catalin1989@cybamail.com From: codos9009@proteja.bg
  Subject: Please Confirm

It's been days since our last contact. I'm worried. Please respond.
  Call/text my number if you need to.
  If you need anything, let me know.
  Codos

Laura and Robbie sat in silence, processing the content of the emails they had just read.

Finally, Robbie looked at Laura. "I'm not sure what I expected to find in the emails, but it wasn't this."

"I'm worried, Robbie. I was thinking about this at breakfast. We could be next."

Robbie was about to respond when his phone rang. He looked at the caller ID, but it was a number he did not recognize.

Robbie picked up the phone and pressed the answer button. "Hello, this is Robbie."

"Hi, Robbie, it's Jerry."

Chapter Twenty-Three

Leon Blackwell sat at his desk, still unable to concentrate on anything except yesterday's meeting with Richard Stelovak and those photos. He had arrived late to the office and had told his secretary he was not feeling well and instructed her to cancel all his appointments for the day and to take messages if anyone called.

As he reviewed what had happened, he became angry as he realized he had let his guard down completely and had been stupid enough to fall for the setup. The temporary secretary that he hired to cover a short period of staff absence was skilled at a lot of things other than what they normally taught at business college. Easy enough, he thought, for Stelovak or Keaton to bribe the agency to provide a temp secretary who was willing to do far more than just office work.

He cursed himself as he sat alone in his office. How could he not to see through it? She had been coming on to him, virtually, from the time she had first stepped through the front door. He had been taken by surprise late on her third workday with her ruse after everyone had gone home.

He replayed the scene over in his mind again. Her seemingly innocent request for help with the printer. Her pointing out where the paper was jammed. Him bending down with his back to her to remove the jam. Her words that followed, 'I've locked the front door. We're all alone now.'

He remembered turning around in confusion to ask what she meant, but before any words came out of his mouth, he was confronted with her sitting on the desk, legs wide apart and her short dress up around her navel. She had a lithe, perfectly proportioned body and her small black panties hid very little.

He went on autopilot. He did not think about his wife or his two daughters or that this might be a setup. He was caught up in the moment. A primitive instinct to be satisfied.

Even afterward, as he drove home, he still had not considered it might be a setup. What businessman in their right mind allows something like this to happen in their front office? He realized how stupid he had been.

He wondered what Stelovak really wanted. They had worked together for years with never an ounce of trouble. Perhaps he had heard he wanted out of the business? He had been very discreet with his planning. Not even his wife knew many of the details yet. Perhaps he hadn't been discreet enough?

His secretary interrupted his thoughts on the intercom. "Excuse me, Mr. Blackwell. I have two gentlemen to see you."

In an irritated voice, Blackwell responded, "Irene, I told you, no appointments today."

"I'm sorry, sir, but these two gentlemen are detectives from Vancouver Police."

Blackwell sat stunned for a moment. He almost demanded his secretary to ask the reason for the unannounced visit and then thought better of it.

Blackwell put on his game face, "Show them in, please."

The door to his office opened and his secretary allowed two men in suits to come in. She pointed to the two visitor's chairs in front of Blackwell's desk and then closed the door.

Blackwell decided to go on the front foot and call his lawyer in at the first sign of trouble. "Gentlemen, this is unexpected. Please come in and have a seat."

The two detectives were both about six feet tall and of athletic build. The younger one seemed to be the lead.

"Mr. Blackwell, let me introduce us. I'm Detective Westcott, and my partner is Detective Jamieson."

Blackwell nodded, but made no offer to shake hands.

Westcott continued, "Vancouver Police have been investigating the recent apparent suicide of a photographer by the name of Eugene Carter. Did you know Mr. Carter?"

"I've never heard of him."

"Mr. Blackwell, Mr. Carter seemed to know a lot about you... Quite a lot, in fact."

Westcott placed an envelope on the table, not unlike the one Stelovak had produced yesterday. Blackwell suddenly found it very hard to breathe. He knew what was coming.

"I'm sorry, detectives. I won't be continuing this conversation without my lawyer."

"Mr. Blackwell, that's entirely your prerogative. However, I want to point out that at present you're not being treated as a formal suspect. In fact, the case is still officially listed as a suspected suicide. We are here because, potentially, you are a victim. Now, unless you have something to hide, it would be quite unusual for you to be requiring a lawyer at this stage. Do you have anything to hide, Mr. Blackwell?"

"Of course not."

"So, is there any real need for a lawyer?"

Blackwell thought, this young guy is good. He's backed me into a corner in two moves. He knew playing cool and saying he did not need a lawyer might lead him to say something incriminating that he would later regret. On the other hand, requesting a lawyer be present would make him look guilty and put him firmly in their focus. Something he wanted to avoid at all costs.

He tried a different tack. "What's in the envelope?"

"Well, Mr. Blackwell, that's what we're here to discuss. Do you require a lawyer to be present? If so, we would be happy to reconvene down at South-Central and conduct a formally recorded interview. Of course, I can't guarantee you the same discretion as I can here, but that's entirely up to you?"

So, there it was, thought Blackwell. If I go downtown, I'll be seen as a formal suspect and Stelovak will find out within hours. Blackwell knew he had plants everywhere. If I do the interview here, maybe nobody finds out. All I need to do is deny everything and I'll be okay, he thought.

"No, detective, I won't be requiring a lawyer."

Westcott leaned forward. "Mr. Blackwell, I would like to begin our discussion today by getting you to look at the contents of the envelope in front of you."

Blackwell was about to say something in protest, but realized it was a waste of time. These cops had already seen the photos, anyway. He knew he needed to show emotion; he just had to make sure it came across as shock and surprise.

Blackwell picked up the envelope and carefully withdrew the first photograph and placed it on his desk. It was the image Stelovak had shown him yesterday. So much for the photos staying confidential. He stared down at the photo for a long time, trying to compose himself, thinking through what he was going to say. He weighed up whether to ask for his lawyer again, but the idea of his wife finding out about this and him being formally interviewed in connection with what he knew about a murder was untenable.

Without looking up at Westcott and Jamieson, he asked, "Where did you get these, detectives?"

"We found them on the laptop belonging to the now deceased photographer Eugene Carter. Apparently, Mr. Carter has, or should I say, had, quite a reputation for illegal surveillance work. Now, as I said earlier, you're not a suspect in Mr. Carter's death at this point, but clearly, these are compromising pictures of yourself with someone other than your wife."

Westcott let the word 'wife' hang in the air for a moment. A sheen of sweat formed on Blackwell's forehead as he looked down at his desk.

"What we want to know, Mr. Blackwell, is why someone would want to take pictures like this of yourself? You're quite wealthy from all reports, so perhaps it's money? You have, how shall we say it, a small but interesting client base? Perhaps one of them was seeking leverage or insurance?"

Westcott was patient and prepared to wait, but he was already certain he knew the answer.

"I have no idea."

"So you're saying, Mr. Blackwell, that these photographs are a complete surprise to you and that you have never seen them before?"

Blackwell finally looked up and made eye contact with Westcott. "Yes."

Blackwell knew Westcott was not buying it. He had never been a good liar, and now he was being caught out. It was now a game... 'I know he knows that I'm lying'.

Westcott shook his head. "Why do I feel, Mr. Blackwell, that you're not being honest with us?"

Blackwell shifted in his chair. He started to drum his fingers on the desk but realized that made him seem even more nervous, and he quickly stopped. He tried a different tack.

Smiling at the two detectives, he said, "Guys, this has been a real shock. I'm guilty of infidelity, but nothing more. Please don't let my wife find out."

Westcott replied, "Mr. Blackwell, can I call you Leon?"

Blackwell hesitated and then said, "Sure, why not?"

Westcott put both hands on Blackwell's desk and leaned forward slightly. "Leon, I've met some people in my life who are bad liars, some who are downright awful, in fact. But you, Leon, are probably the worst liar I have ever met."

Blackwell looked like a deer caught in the headlights as he looked from Westcott to Jamieson and back again.

"I don't know what to say, detectives."

"Why don't we start with the truth, Leon? It always works best with that as a starting point."

Blackwell could no longer make eye contact. "I've told you the truth."

Westcott replied, "Leon, you have no idea how much trouble you're in and I'm not talking about Vancouver Police. These guys you're mixed up with play for keeps. I don't know exactly what the deal with Carter was. He's obviously not been able to keep his mouth shut, or wanted more money, or was trying a little blackmail of his own on the side, perhaps even with you? Whatever it was, Leon, he crossed the wrong people and now he's in a morgue. Is that what you want? Do you want your wife to come to the morgue to identify what's left of you?"

"Of course not!"

Westcott grimaced. "Well, Leon, only you can change that."

Blackwell became very sullen. It was clear he was terrified of the ramifications. Westcott had been right about whom he should really fear. He decided it was time for a different play and added, "Leon, I need some air for a minute. I'm going to leave you with detective Jamieson, who is going to get some details of the agency you hired the temp secretary through. Okay?"

Blackwell nodded.

Westcott left Blackwell's office and went back out to the reception area. He asked the receptionist if there was a room he could use to make a private call. She pointed to a spiral steel staircase. "Conference room is at the top of the stairs, first room on your left."

Westcott thanked her and pulled out his phone and hit speed dial as he climbed the stairs.

Felix Delray answered just as Westcott was closing the conference room door.

"What have you got?"

"Boss, he did the interview without a lawyer, so I didn't bring him in."

"Okay. So how did it go?"

"He's scared, boss. He knows we know he's lying, but he refuses to talk."

"So, do you want to bring him in and we play a little tag team?"

Westcott thought for a moment. "If he comes in, it will be with a lawyer and we'll probably get nothing."

Delray knew where this was headed but wanted to hear it from Westcott himself. He wanted Westcott to be making the key decisions.

"So, what do you want to do, Danny?"

"Boss, I don't believe he's killed anyone. He's just a dirty accountant who has a lot of secrets about some very high-profile criminals who we would like to see behind bars. I'd like to offer him immunity and put him and his family in witness protection. Give him a day or so to think about it and he might become the card that brings the whole house down."

"Do you think he'll run?"

Westcott tried to put himself in Leon Blackwell's shoes. "His first instinct will be to run, but he knows he will be a fugitive not only from us but also from whoever is behind this. If it's Stelovak, he knows he won't be safe even if he changes his identity and disappears completely. It's not easy to disappear when you're up against someone with almost unlimited resources. I told him right now he should be in fear for his life and he didn't need any convincing. I think if we give him a day to think it through and put him under surveillance as a precaution, he will probably fold."

"I trust your judgment, Danny. Push him hard to take the deal today, even let him ring his wife if he wants. If he says no, give him forty-eight hours and then the deal is off. We'll put him under twenty-four-hour surveillance and put a block on his passport, just in case."

"Okay, boss."

"Good luck, Danny."

After disconnecting from Delray, Westcott made his way down the stairwell for part two of the interview. He would throw Blackwell the lifeline with the conditions Delray had put on the table. He didn't expect Blackwell to take up the offer immediately, but he didn't think he would need to wait long for the answer.

The photos had changed Blackwell's life forever. It was now up to Blackwell to decide how.

Chapter Twenty-Four

The call from Jerry had been a surprise to Robbie. Jerry had apologized for his behavior at the grave and admitted that it was appropriate for Robbie to be investigating further.

'I'm obviously not too thrilled about being included in the investigation, Robbie, but I understand, and I'll do what I can to help.'

After thanking Jerry for the call, Robbie arranged to meet Jerry that evening for dinner.

Robbie and Laura had spent the next hour trying to make sense of the emails between Mac and Codos. They agreed they were going around in circles and needed a break. Laura had suggested they go for a drive to clear their minds.

Robbie thought a moment. "I've been feeling a little nostalgic since returning to Vancouver. I would like to drive over to Cypress Falls while I'm here and visit the place where I grew up. It would only take forty-five minutes on the freeway?"

"Sounds great Robbie. A change of scenery could be just the tonic we need."

They took Laura's Ford Bronco four-wheel drive in preference to Robbie's smaller rental. Affectionately known as 'Big Red', the Bronco was originally owned by Laura's father. When he had died, Laura could not stand the thought of selling it and Big Red had been her daily drive for over eight years.

Laura loved every opportunity she could get to take the vehicle out of the city. Today was no exception and both she and Robbie enjoyed the trip as the traffic thinned and the vista changed to rolling green countryside and farmlands after thirty minutes on the freeway. She occasionally glanced at Robbie as she drove. By now, she was very comfortable with his presence and fond of his many down to earth and even quirky qualities. She found his slightly lopsided smile endearing. It changed his usually handsome, serious features into something caught between vulnerable and comical.

Robbie caught Laura looking and smiling. "What?"

Laura looked straight ahead again, but continued smiling. "Nothing."

"I'm prone to get a little nervous when a woman smiles at me like that and says 'nothing'." Robbie continued, more under his breath than out aloud, "Not that it's happened in a while."

"What?"

It was Robbie's turn to smile. "Nothing."

They both laughed as they drove on, enjoying the view. Vancouver city and the town of Cypress Falls were separated by a large expanse of mainly forested terrain, which included the Catalin Mountain.

The countryside itself had changed very little in the ten

years since Robbie had last been there. He expected a lot of change in his old hometown, of course. The freeway had been in for seven years now and Robbie had heard Cypress Falls had become far more progressive. The staid and aging rural community he had left after graduating from high school was changing. New housing estates were being developed for people who worked in Vancouver and could not afford to purchase in the city or were seeking a quieter place to raise their families.

"You're very quiet, Robbie. What's going on in that head of yours?"

"I was thinking about the farm where I grew up. Everything changes, but hopefully it hasn't changed too much."

"So, how long has it been since you actually lived out here?"

"Close to twenty years now. My mother stayed on for a while. But after my father died, even though it was quite small, we both knew the farm was not a long-term prospect. With me gone, she wanted to move to something smaller and more manageable, which is why it's taken me so long to get out here, I guess."

"Do you miss it?"

"Kind of. I miss the peace and solitude from time to time. I've lived and worked mainly on the east coast since I graduated, but always rented. Annie and I were making plans to buy a house over there. You know, settle down and start a family. But after she passed, I lost interest."

"Sorry, Robbie, I didn't mean to pry."

"It's okay. I don't imagine it will ever be easy to talk about, but I've accepted it and I'm moving on."

Laura was not sure what to say and didn't want to make it any harder on Robbie, so she concentrated on driving.

As they approached the outskirts of his old hometown,

Robbie was surprised at the number of new housing developments that had sprung up. As they pulled off the freeway onto a side road, Robbie asked Laura to stop for a moment. "This all used to be vacant land when I left. The city is really coming to Cypress Falls in a hurry."

Robbie pointed down the side road. "The farm is about five minutes down this road."

Laura smiled at Robbie as she put the Bronco into gear. The view down the road quickly turned from houses into farmland. "I don't think the city will have overtaken your farm just yet."

They drove the rest of the way along the tree lined road at a steady pace, enjoying the scenery. Laura could tell by the smile on Robbie's face that this area had changed little since he had left. They pulled up in front of a long gravel driveway that led from the road up into a tree-lined ridge. Within the trees stood a solid looking white colonial house in need of some repairs. Several horses occupied the fields on either side of the driveway and, after raising their heads to see who had arrived, they had quickly returned to grazing.

Robbie was still smiling as he looked up at the house and the surrounding farmland. The drive out of Vancouver had been a good move, Laura thought.

"That's quite a goofy smile you have going there, Mayne. I take it not much has changed?"

"Not much at all, really. It's quite surprising really when you think about how much has changed just a few minutes' drive from here. Let's drive up to the house."

"You're sure that's okay? No one lives there?"

"Not for about eighteen months. The couple that currently leases it live in Cypress Falls itself and just wanted the land and stables for their horses."

Laura started the Bronco, and they drove slowly up the gravel driveway to the house. The horses completely ignored them this time and kept grazing. Laura was impressed with the view from the front of the house.

"This is really something, Robbie. I can understand why you're getting nostalgic.

"My mother would love me to return here to live. This was just a block of land when my father bought it. He built the house and stables, mostly by himself. You can understand why she doesn't want to let it go."

They spent half an hour walking around the house and stables. Robbie stopped regularly to check the general state of repair.

"It needs some work, but not as much as I would have thought."

Laura looked up beyond the ridge. "What's up beyond there?"

"Our boundary ends at the ridge line. Beyond that, it's all state forest that leads around to the Catalin Mountain."

Robbie and Laura exchanged a look. Robbie was pretty sure he knew what Laura was thinking. "Would you like me to show you where it happened?"

"Robbie, I don't want to push you. It must be…"

"It's okay, Laura. Under the circumstances, it may help for you to see where it happened. The emails still don't make much sense and you're in this as much as I am."

"If you think it will help."

"If you're up to it, I would like to show you. You don't know how much of a relief it is to finally share what happened with someone else. I don't know if it's in any way connected, but Mac's death was no accident."

Laura held Robbie's gaze as she thought about the Catalin email address that Mac had been using. "You're right Robbie. If there is a connection, maybe this will help us understand what it is."

Robbie looked up along the ridge line again. "It will take us at least forty-five minutes to walk from here, and most likely longer given the trails have probably changed and won't be familiar. They put a lookout point in off the freeway when it was being built, which will get us much closer. Hopefully, we can navigate from there without getting lost."

Laura took one more look around before getting back into the Bronco. She had been enjoying the day and would have loved to have spent more time here learning more about the place where Robbie grew up. As they approached the freeway on the drive back from the farm, Robbie pointed to a sign.

"We need to turn here and head back on the freeway towards Vancouver for about five minutes. The lookout should be clearly signposted."

Laura looked towards the houses that formed the outskirts of Cypress Falls; "We technically didn't quite make it to Cypress Falls today, did we?"

"No, but we can come back another day if you like?"

Laura turned onto the entry ramp for the freeway. "Deal. By the way, I have an excellent memory. I don't forget promises."

Robbie started scanning the road signs for the lookout. "Why does that not surprise me?"

It only took three minutes to reach the turnoff. The road from the freeway to the lookout was winding and mostly gravel and not overly well maintained. Laura found she needed to stay in low gear.

"I'm surprised this isn't a sealed road. Isn't this supposed to be a tourist spot?"

"I think that was the original intention. Maybe it was the victim of government funding cutbacks? I've only been up here once before. The view from the top was very good, as I recall."

It took Laura another five minutes to make the drive up to the lookout. Robbie and Laura both agreed the road was hardly inviting and would be difficult to navigate in wet weather in a standard vehicle. The lookout was not what Laura expected or what Robbie remembered. The parking lot could accommodate two dozen cars at most and apart from the lookout platform, the dense trees that surrounded it totally obscured it.

As they made their way out onto the viewing platform, Robbie looked up and around. "These trees used to be all much smaller. I remember there used to be views almost all the way around."

"We'll, not anymore, Robbie. The view is really something from the platform, though."

Robbie walked out onto the steel platform and joined Laura. The platform extended out just far enough to allow them an uninterrupted view of the panoramic mountainside below. Robbie had to agree with Laura—the view was much better from this vantage point. Robbie stood in silence for several minutes, scanning the terrain below.

Finally, he pointed towards the southwest. "The terrain is more overgrown than when we were here all those years ago, but I'm pretty sure it's down there. I think I remember looking up at that rock face as we approached the mine shaft. I think if we go down below that face and look up, I'll be able to get my bearings and know where to look."

"Then that's where we'll start, Robbie. I noticed a small fire trail off the road on the way up that looked as if it headed in that general direction. Even if we can't use the trail, we should save ten or fifteen minutes walking time if we park there?"

Robbie agreed, and they got back in the Bronco and made their way back down and parked at the entrance to the trail. Robbie got out and walked a short way up the fire trail before returning.

"It's drivable, but there are lots of bushes and undergrowth encroaching that will probably scratch your car. Let's take it on foot from here."

They walked up the fire trail for about ten minutes before stopping in a clearing. Robbie looked up the mountain, scanning for landmarks he remembered to get his bearings, and then pointed towards a prominent rock face.

"I'm reasonably confident that's it there. It's probably only another ten minutes from here at the most, although we won't be able to use the fire trail." Robbie grimaced and added, "This can't be easy for you, Laura…"

"None of this is easy, Robbie. But it may help—so we do what we need to do. How are you feeling?"

Robbie shrugged. "Okay for now, but how I feel when we actually get there, I'm not so sure."

They rested for several minutes before continuing. Before long, Robbie found another connecting trail. "This trail I remember. We are close."

They walked for several more minutes and then Robbie stopped and pointed through trees to a bramble thicket. "I think that's it."

They made their way through the trees. The bramble thicket looked no different to Laura than many others she had seen on the way in.

Laura watched as Robbie slowly circled the thicket and came back and stood beside her. It was well over head height and quite dense. She commented, "If there's a mine shaft in there, Robbie, it's well hidden."

Robbie got down on his hands and knees and started pulling up vines to expose some of the ground beneath the thicket. "They covered the shaft with a timber structure to prevent people from falling in. It's long since rotted away, but some of the timber is still here under the vines. If I can find any of..."

Robbie stopped talking and dragged out a short, thick wooden beam. It was sodden, covered in dirt and falling apart, but there was no doubt what it was.

Robbie laid it on the ground and went and sat on a large nearby rock and stared at the thicket. Laura came over and sat beside Robbie.

After taking a moment to compose himself, Robbie said, "This is definitely the place." Robbie went quiet again for a while and then continued, "It feels like it only happened yesterday. I can clearly remember the four of us arguing. Checking his cold stiff hand for a pulse. Carrying the body up here. Clearing the brambles away and... I have that same nauseous feeling in my stomach I had back then. I sat on this very rock feeling confused, very guilty, and angry."

"Don't beat yourself up too much. You were just a kid trying to do the right thing. We all make mistakes and you were a victim of circumstance as much as anything else."

"In some ways, I'm glad I still feel this way. It's good I still feel some regret."

Robbie got up from the rock and walked back over to the thicket. "I'm still not making the connection, though. What on earth does what happened here all those years ago have to do with what Mac was involved in?"

"Do you think it has anything to do with the man buried here?"

Robbie thought for a moment. "Stuart Wilson was a sex offender who had two prison terms that we know of. Mac and I followed the papers for months after this happened. We expected to see headlines about a man missing from Cypress Falls or a body found on Catalin Mountain, but nothing. It's like he just left town, and no one cared."

"No family?"

Robbie shook his head. "A father who he never got on with. We assumed he fell out with most of his relatives and no one ever reported him missing. Maybe they all thought he'd left town or landed back in prison?"

"Kind of sad…"

"I just don't see Wilson as the connection, particularly now we can see this place clearly hasn't been disturbed. If it's not Wilson, it either has to be the place itself or the people."

"Meaning you, or Nick, or Jerry?"

"Or maybe all of us? I can't imagine Mac creating that email account, clearly referencing what happened back here, without it having significance. Maybe we need to re-read those emails and substitute the cryptic references for Jerry, or Nick, or even me?"

"It works for me in jigsaw puzzles. You take a piece and try it in various spots until you find the place it fits."

Robbie looked up at the sky. "It gets dark early on this side of the mountain, so we should head back. Also, I've just realized we totally skipped lunch. I'm sorry."

Laura managed half a smile. "It's okay. This was really important."

"Are you hungry?"

"Starved actually," said Laura with a laugh.

As they started the trip back to where they had parked the car, Robbie said, "There's a diner just off the freeway on the approach to Vancouver. Mac used to rave about their burgers and would sometimes drive out there just to eat one."

"Lead the way."

Robbie and Laura made their way back to the main fire trail and then headed towards the road.

As they continued to walk, Robbie said, "Thanks for coming today. I can only imagine how hard it must be for you to understand."

"Let's hope something comes of it when we re-examine the emails."

"I would love to get started on it as soon as we get back, but I need a shower and a change of clothes before dinner with Jerry."

As they arrived back at Laura's Bronco, Robbie asked, "What are you planning for tonight?"

"I'm not sure. I think I might drive across town and see my sister and mother. I haven't seen them since the day of the funeral and there's legal stuff for Mac's estate that we need to work through. It's at least an hour's drive from my apartment, so I'll probably stay the night and come home in the morning."

Laura's voice trailed off as she took one last look back up at the mountain. "My first preference would have been to have dinner with you…"

Laura looked at Robbie again and gave an awkward smile. "Just putting it out there, Mayne. I thought you should know."

Robbie had never been very good at reading signals from women. As good as he was as an investigative journalist in reading people, Robbie knew he was clueless with romance and signals from the opposite sex. He clearly remembered Annie having to take the lead when they got together. He looked at Laura now, totally unsure of what to say. She was much more than just intelligent and stunningly attractive. He loved her laugh and sense of humor. She was already much more than just a good friend. As clueless as he was, Robbie realized what was happening. Don't blow this, he thought.

Robbie knew the right words would be hard to find. "Laura, I really like you…"

Laura's face registered disappointment and even hurt as she responded, "But…"

Robbie found his feet walking him to stand directly in front of Laura. He gently put his index finger to her lips to stop her from continuing. "No buts."

Robbie put his arms around Laura and gently kissed her. She made no move to pull away and put her arms around Robbie and held him gently. Robbie didn't want the moment to end. He felt this was much more than a simple, if not lingering, kiss.

They finally parted to look at one another, but were still locked in their embrace. "You have no idea how much I've wanted to do that, Robbie."

Robbie's lopsided smile was back. They held each other, enjoying the intimacy in the silence of the forest.

The man briefly diverted his eyes from the road to check caller ID on his phone before answering.

He pressed the button on the steering wheel to answer hands free and said, "Heading back to Vancouver on the southern freeway. We should hit the city limits in about fifteen minutes."

"We agreed you would update me every two hours."

"Since checking in with you this morning, they have spent the rest of the day on Catalin Mountain. First stopping at the lookout and then taking a walk through the forest. There is no phone reception up there, so I've had no way of contacting you."

The caller replied in an irritated voice, "I've been able to contact you?"

"I've had reception for the last ten or fifteen minutes only. Right now, I'm about ten cars behind the four-wheel drive. There is no tracker on her car as requested, so I have to keep visual contact or I'm in danger of losing them."

"Don't let them out of your sight. If they separate, stick with Mayne. This has gone on too long."

"What do you want me to do?"

"Implement the plan as agreed. Tonight, if possible. We need him out of the way."

"And if the opportunity doesn't arise? Shall I use my initiative?"

"No. Call back to discuss options. This guy can't simply wind up dead or missing. It's messy enough as it is. We want no more attention."

The line went dead, which was fine with the man. He returned his focus to the four-wheel drive up ahead. He had what he needed for now. The instructions were clear. Robbie Mayne's life expectancy was now twenty-four hours at best.

Chapter Twenty-Five

Westcott had been at his desk for over two hours waiting on the call from forensics. Waiting was not something he was good at.

He flipped through the coroner's report of Eugene Carter again. The report confirmed the cause of death was significant trauma to the head, consistent with falling from a multi-story building onto a concrete pavement. The head injuries were described in complex medical terms. Westcott had read enough of these reports to understand that Carter's brain had been reduced to pulp when the left side of his skull was severely crushed on impact with the pavement.

Death was instantaneous and was estimated to have occurred between ten p.m. and midnight on the night he had been discovered. The report provided pages of additional information on other injuries Carter had sustained from the fall, including broken ribs, pelvis, spine and tibia.

The report also detailed a significant range of internal

injuries that Carter had suffered as well. A reasonably effective way to guarantee death, Westcott thought.

The report included a toxicology analysis of Carter's blood. It showed Carter had used cocaine in the previous forty-eight hours and had a moderate blood alcohol reading at the time of death. It was interesting, but unsurprising to Westcott.

It was the associated forensics report on Carter's clothing that had provided the first breakthrough. The report was on the whole, unremarkable except for one line, which read, 'belt buckle contains several partial non matching fingerprints'.

Westcott knew this could be vital evidence and was far quicker to process than DNA samples from Carter's apartment that he was still waiting on. After getting the Vancouver Police technicians to develop digital copies of each partial print, he ran them through the fingerprint database in the hope of a match. He got lucky with both prints returning matches. The first, not surprisingly, was Carter himself. The second partial print belonged to a man who, according to the police criminal database, had two known aliases; Rudy Henning and Randall Holland.

He closed the coroner's report and returned his attention to the police record for Rudy Henning, which he had opened on his computer screen. He knew he was close. Henning or Holland was thirty-nine years old and had committed multiple offenses as a juvenile, including burglary, car theft, and minor drug trafficking. He had been caught committing an armed robbery in his early twenties and had spent almost eight years in prison for the crime. He had only been arrested once since but had gotten off on a technicality.

What intrigued Westcott was not only the number of

times police had interviewed Henning without charges being laid in the subsequent years, but also the crimes themselves. Two murders and three missing person cases were at the top of the list. Henning clearly had an excellent lawyer and always had solid alibis, according to the file. Westcott had seen this kind of profile before. He knew Henning was a professional hit man and worked for clients with deep pockets and good lawyers.

He had discussed the breakthrough with his boss. Felix Delray had agreed with Westcott that they would not get a murder conviction against Henning on the strength of a partial fingerprint on a belt buckle. Even though Henning probably made the fingerprint on the belt buckle throwing Carter off the balcony, it would be almost impossible to prove in a trial.

A defense lawyer of the type Henning used would come up with a convincing story. Westcott could imagine a defense being developed around Henning walking by, noticing the victim in the driveway and going to offer help. In determining that the victim was already dead, he inadvertently left a fingerprint. The only thing this good Samaritan had done wrong was flee the scene, rather than get involved. They would hit Henning with not much more than a fine and a caution if they were lucky.

Westcott needed a link to the apartment. A witness, security camera footage or forensic evidence to prove Henning was in the apartment on the night of Carter's death.

Without a hard link that could place Henning inside the apartment, he had nothing.

Westcott's phone rang. He checked caller ID before picking it up. It was Forensics. He had been on the force more than five years now, but he still got an adrenaline rush at times like this. He felt his pulse quicken and his gut tighten. He knew this was the call that would either send him back to square one or break the case wide open. He took a deep breath and picked up the phone.

"Westcott."

"Danny, it's Ross from the lab."

Westcott always thought it bad luck to speak at this point and held his breath.

"We just finished the DNA analysis. You there, Danny?"

"I'm here, Ross."

"Well, I could bore you with a lot of detail, but I'll let you read that for yourself in your own time. Instead, I'll cut to the chase..."

Westcott wanted to scream 'just tell me already' but held his tongue.

"We have a match, Danny. Henning's DNA is on the cigarette recovered from the balcony. Unless cigarettes now float on the breeze, he was on the balcony sometime on the day of Carter's death. Congratulations, Danny. You got what you need for an arrest."

Westcott fist pumped the air as he thanked Ross for giving the case priority. He arranged to go down to the lab shortly and collect the official report. From there, he would process the paperwork to arrest Henning and make formal charges. He got up from his chair to tell Delray the good news. Somehow, he did not think Delray would mind the interruption.

Chapter Twenty-Six

Robbie was running late for dinner with Jerry. He and Laura had stopped at the diner on the way back from Catalin Mountain for burgers as planned. They had then spent well over an hour talking before making the rest of the journey back into Vancouver through peak hour traffic. When Laura finally dropped Robbie back at his hotel, they had arranged to meet at the hotel on her return from visiting her mother and sister in the morning. They planned to devote the following day to analyzing the email messages further and hopefully getting the breakthrough on what they meant.

Robbie had taken a shower before changing into fresh clothes for dinner with Jerry. The shower was relaxing and gave him time to think. He tried to focus on the email messages and the link between Mac and his European contact, but his thoughts kept returning to Laura.

He smiled as he replayed their first kiss over in his mind. It had been a long time since one kiss had meant so much. He felt like an awkward teenager.

He knew it was too early to tell where their relationship was headed, but he felt strongly about Laura and felt the feeling was mutual. Finding out who killed Mac and why would remain their number one priority. He hoped they would both live through it and build a relationship afterward.

Robbie was contemplating what the future might hold when he realized he had spent much longer in the shower than planned. He quickly checked his watch as he towelled off. Forty minutes in the shower—he was going to be late.

As mayor of Vancouver, Jerry frequently dined out and knew most, if not all, the good restaurants in the city. Jerry had picked a small, out of the way Italian restaurant called Giorgio's. Jerry had assured Robbie it would be a meal to remember. 'We'll have a great time, Robbie. I've reserved a booth in the back. We can talk in peace and quiet without being disturbed. And the food's great. What more could you want?'

Robbie had agreed to the meal with an ulterior motive. He wanted to find out more about Jerry's relationship with Mac, and this would be the perfect opportunity. He was under no illusions that Jerry had an agenda as well. It was going to be an interesting evening.

He looked up Giorgio's on a map. It was ten blocks from the hotel and Robbie decided it would be quicker to take a cab than walk.

Hailing a cab had proved challenging and Robbie walked into the restaurant ten minutes late. As Robbie looked around for Jerry, he noticed the restaurant was hardly small, as Jerry had suggested. The tables were well spaced, and all the servers were formally dressed in black. The decor was opulent, with starched white tablecloths, highly polished silver cutlery, and original artwork on the walls. Robbie guessed entrees would start at over thirty dollars, with mains probably more than double. Nice to be on the government payroll, Robbie thought. A server came and welcomed him to Giorgio's and asked if he had a reservation.

"I'm here with Jerry Marsden. I think he's already here. I'm running late."

"The mayor. Certainly sir, if you will follow me, please."

Robbie followed the server towards the rear of the restaurant. The 'booth' turned out to be a small private room. The server showed Robbie in. Jerry got to his feet and shook Robbie's hand.

"Have a seat, Robbie, it's good to see you."

Robbie looked around the room and smiled. "It's hardly a booth, Jerry."

Jerry laughed, "That's what they call it here, Robbie. Maybe 'booth' means something different in Italian?"

"Maybe."

As they sat down, Jerry continued. "I get very little downtime and I'm constantly under the microscope. When you're the elected mayor of a city the size of Vancouver, you always have to be on guard. Careful what you say, careful what you do, who you mix with. One slip and it's on the front page. It's just easier to be out of the spotlight when you're just after a quiet meal."

"No problem, Jerry. I don't photograph well anyway, so the 'booth' is good."

As Robbie took his seat, Jerry leaned forward and lowered his voice. "So Robbie, before we order, I just want to apologize again for yesterday. I was out of line and I'm sorry for that. I've got to level with you. I think these things are best handled by the police, but I respect your decision to do your own investigating. You need to know that as mayor, if the press gets wind of what you're doing and that you, Mac and I were school friends, I'll wind up on the front pages and the nightly news. They aren't balanced, impartial, or interested in the truth. The media try to convict people in my position to sell newspapers and get ratings."

Jerry paused and took a sip of water and then added, "I guess that's why I was so upset. I work really hard at staying clean."

Jerry searched Robbie's eyes for confirmation it was all okay. "I understand Jerry. I am a journalist, but I have my principles and my integrity. I never publish unless I'm sure of my facts."

Jerry smiled, "Good Robbie. That's all I can ask."

Jerry picked up the menu. "How's your Italian, Robbie? I'm sure they get an extra five bucks a meal because it sounds more elegant when everything is written in a foreign language."

Robbie picked up a menu and scanned the choices. He was right about the prices.

They both spent several minutes discussing what to order. When the server returned, Jerry and Robbie gave their menu selections. Jerry then ordered a bottle of Bordeaux.

When the server left, Jerry sat back in his chair and looked at Robbie. "It's been a long time, Robbie. So much has happened since school. Where does the time go?"

Robbie replied, "I'm not sure I know. One minute you're knocking yourself out trying to get decent grades, the next minute you're covering stories as an overseas correspondent or running for mayor."

Jerry's smile dissolved. "You know, Robbie, we were pretty tight in high school. We never really had a falling out, but we definitely drifted apart. I hardly ever saw you after

The Catalin Code

school, even though we both did our degrees here in Vancouver."

Robbie thought for a moment before he responded, "The simple answer would be for me to say that lots of friendships don't last beyond high school and what happened between us was fairly normal."

Jerry leaned forward again and put his elbows on the table. "But you were never one for simple answers. You always gave it to us straight, whether we liked it or not. Kind of the group conscience, as I recall."

"Maybe."

"You haven't answered the question."

Robbie had not expected Jerry to go on the front foot quite so early in the evening. He was definitely controlling, even manipulating the conversation. Robbie decided he could use this to his advantage.

"I think you and I both know why the friendship with both you and Nick didn't survive high school, Jerry."

"Catalin?"

Robbie nodded. He decided not to say anything. They had reached the subject he had wanted to discuss without having to steer the conversation. He was interested in hearing what Jerry had to say.

"You regret what we did, Robbie?"

"Every day, Jerry. Although Wilson was a lowlife and despite what he'd done to your sister, I regret I wasn't stronger."

It surprised Robbie at how quickly his anger arose as he began thinking about it. He took a moment to get his anger in check before continuing. "Before Annie and I were married, we spent a lot of time together getting to know one another. I remember her asking me one day if I had any secrets and I said to her there was nothing worth sharing and have felt guilty ever since. I hoped one day this would somehow resolve itself and I could be honest with her. But the accident changed all that and now I will never get the chance. She deserved better, Jerry. Much better."

"I'm sorry, Robbie. I can't imagine what you've been through. I can understand how this would continue to weigh on your mind. I guess I'm lucky. Catherine has never asked, so I've never had to lie."

Robbie was not sure he believed that last statement from Jerry, but let it slide. He knew Jerry was off balance and decided he should now ask the questions.

"So, Jerry, did you really think we could keep what happened a secret?"

Jerry eyes widened momentarily. "Yes. I still don't think we did anything wrong. We were in a tough situation. Who knows how it might have played out had we called it in? My worst nightmare was doing prison time because that low life got accidentally shot. It's behind us, Robbie. In the past, where it belongs."

Robbie kept on the offensive. "Do you ever worry it will get out?"

"What do you mean?"

"That what happened on Catalin will be made... public?"

Jerry let out a short laugh.

"Robbie, I don't have enough time in the day to worry about what happened last week, let alone something that happened over twenty years ago. Besides, there are only four people who know about it and none of us has anything to gain and a lot to lose."

"Three, Jerry. We don't have Mac, anymore."

Jerry grimaced. "Yes. Three of us."

"What about Nick?"

"What about him?"

"Do you think he is still concerned that what happened might go public?"

Jerry looked away and thought about his question. It was not clear to Robbie whether he was simply thinking it through or whether he was trying to think of a clever politician's answer. After years of fending questions from the media, Jerry was now the consummate professional and didn't telegraph the same telltale signs as normal people.

"Robbie, if you're asking, would he want it going public? The answer is, of course, not. None of us would want to see that happen.

Beyond that, Nick and I have hardly spoken since the OCTF affair. I had to distance myself from him during the inquiry, and he took it personally. Basically, we haven't talked in years."

"I do remember Mac telling me about you and Nick having a rather public slanging match. I assume that's what it was about?"

"It wasn't my finest moment, that's for sure. Everyone at the OCTF was under pressure. It killed relationships and marriages. Ironically, it was Mac who was the one who kept in touch and tried to keep my friendship with Nick alive. He even organized a meal for the three of us at this very restaurant to patch things up."

"How did that go?"

Jerry shrugged. "Nick never showed. He didn't know at first that I was coming. When he found out what Mac was up to, he didn't bother to cancel. Mac and I turned up, but not Nick. Mac continued to stay in touch with Nick and tried again to get us together. But by then, neither of us were interested."

Robbie was not sure he would learn much more from

Jerry tonight. He had one more question he wanted an answer, or at least a reaction to before their meals arrived and the momentum was interrupted.

"I'm positive Mac was murdered."

Jerry's eyes widened. "And what makes you say that?"

Robbie went into the same detailed explanation he had given Laura. He omitted the part about the argument with Peter Trelor, but told him everything else. He was summing up when the server arrived with their meals.

After the server left, Robbie continued, "So there you have it, Jerry. I don't have an eyewitness, but I have someone reliable who heard what happened. The timing between the initial impact and a car circling back to leave bogus brake marks fits with what the witness heard. I don't have an obvious motive yet, but I'm working on it."

Jerry shook his head. "I can't believe it, Robbie. Murder? Why would anyone want to murder Mac?"

"That's what I'm trying to find out. I'm still not convinced that a body at the bottom of a mine shaft on Catalin Mountain, regardless of how long it's been there, is still not a motive."

Jerry nodded, lost in thought. Finally, he said, "Now I'm not accusing anyone, but have you talked to Nick yet?"

"Apart from a quick conversation at Mac's funeral, I haven't talked to Nick since high school."

"Well... you guys are going to have a lot to catch up on."

"Yes, we are."

Jerry was ready to change subjects and lowered his head slightly to smell his seafood marinara. Picking up his fork, he said, "This smells amazing."

Robbie took his cue from Jerry and picked up his fork as

well. He was satisfied that he had gotten all the information he was likely to get from Jerry. It was time to eat.

The rest of the evening proved pleasant enough. It reminded Robbie of many of the nights they had enjoyed when they hung out together as teenagers. Jerry was in vintage form, with lots of jokes and stories that made Robbie laugh. It was almost eleven p.m. when they finally left the restaurant. Jerry insisted he drive Robbie back to his hotel.

"I'm surprised you don't have a limousine and driver, Jerry."

"I do, Robbie. But I prefer to drive myself when I'm not in a hurry—always have."

As they pulled up out the front of Robbie's hotel, Jerry said, "Robbie, I really had a good time tonight. Let's not make it so long next time."

"Sounds good to me, Jerry. I'll be in touch."

As Robbie got out of the car, Jerry added, "And by the way, good luck with Nick."

Robbie watched as Jerry's Lexus pulled away from the curb and out into light traffic. He was not sure what to make of the evening. It had been a long day, and he was tired. He decided he would go for an early walk in the morning before Laura arrived to review what he had learned.

After retrieving his laptop from hotel security and taking the elevator up to his room, Robbie felt a sense of relief when he finally closed the door to his hotel room. As he debated whether to have another shower before heading to bed, his phoned buzzed. He looked down at the screen and smiled. It was a message from Laura.

Hope dinner with Jerry went well. I enjoyed our day, especially the 'moment'. C U tomorrow. Laura xx

Robbie smiled and texted back.

Dinner with Jerry, okay. I too enjoyed the day! Sleep tight. Robbie xx

Robbie put the phone down on his bed, then stretched and yawned. He decided the shower could wait until morning. As he pulled back his bed sheets, he heard a knock on his room door.

Walking to the door, he looked through the spy hole and saw two police officers.

"Who is it?"

"Vancouver Police. We are looking for the owner of a Silver Toyota parked in the basement. Hotel staff have informed us that the car is registered against this hotel room."

Robbie opened the door, thinking the car had been broken into or damaged by another hotel patron.

"It's a rental car officer, currently rented by me. What's the problem?"

The shorter of the two uniformed officers who seemed in charge responded, "We'll have to ask you to accompany us down to the basement to inspect the vehicle, sir."

Robbie thought the answer was a little vague, but let it go. He was not in the mood to argue and would know soon enough. "Okay. Let me get my key."

They rode down the elevator in silence. When the door opened at the basement parking lot, only the shorter officer got out.

"Lead the way, please, sir."

Robbie was becoming increasingly concerned, but tried to remain calm. He led the officers over to his rental car. It did not look damaged in any way.

"So, what's going on here, officers?"

The shorter of the two police officers suddenly became aggressive. "Unlock the vehicle. Now!"

Robbie pointed the remote at the car and pressed unlock. The car lights flashed, and the internal door locks popped. The shorter of the two offices signaled to his colleague, who opened each of the four doors and then began a thorough search of the interior.

"You mind telling me what you're looking for, officer?"

The shorter officer said with a condescending smile, "Why don't you tell us and save us all the trouble?"

Robbie was now angry, but knew better than to let it show.

"I'm sorry, I don't understand."

"Coke, ice, crack, party pills? What's your deal?"

Robbie gave a wry smile and shook his head. "I'm not a drug dealer. You must be mistaken."

"Mistaken am I? We'll see about that. You've been reported for conducting... how shall we say it? 'Two suspicious transactions' from the trunk of your car."

The officer searching the car came around to the rear and started inspecting the cargo area. Apart from a pair of slightly wet runners, it was clear.

"Check the tire well."

The officer searching the car lifted the carpet-covered board that hid the car's spare wheel. He started searching in, around, and under the wheel.

Robbie's gut muscles tightened. He knew he was being setup and there was little he could do about it and said, "You guys have a search warrant?"

The officer reached into his pocket and pulled out a folder document and handed it to Robbie. Robbie was about to protest that this should have happened before the search began when the other officer who had been searching the car yelled out, "Bingo!"

The officer searching the car withdrew a small clear plastic bag containing white powder and brought it over.

The shorter office said, "Well, well. What do we have here?"

He opened the bag and examined the contents, and let out a small whistle.

"High grade Cocaine. Well, Mr. 'I'm-not-a-drug-dealer', seems you're wrong on two accounts. You are a drug dealer and I'm not mistaken."

He pushed Robbie hard up against the car. "You're under arrest."

Chapter Twenty-Seven

Robbie lay on the top bunk in the small cell and looked at his watch. There was just enough light seeping under the heavy steel door to see the time. It was one fifteen in the morning.

He had never been in jail before and had no desire to prolong his stay any longer than necessary. The cell was small, had no windows and very limited ventilation. Its only furnishings were a two-bed bunk and a steel toilet. The place was damp and smelt of urine, sweat, and mold. It still smelt as strong now as it had done an hour ago when Robbie had been shoved inside by the guards. It was going to be a long night.

Robbie was still coming to terms with what had happened. One moment he was preparing for bed and the next he was in handcuffs and on his way to the Vancouver Police inner city holding cells. The arresting police officers told him they wouldn't formally charge him until the morning when the first detectives came on shift at seven thirty a.m.

He had asked when he would get to see his lawyer and was told by the shorter police officer he would get to make the call in the morning. Robbie knew protesting about this being a violation of his human rights would fall on deaf ears and probably only make matters worse. He was thankful for a cell on his own, at least. He doubted he would sleep, but it gave him time to think more about what had happened and why.

Robbie knew this was all connected to Mac. Someone did not want him investigating. He was glad Laura was staying with her mother and sister tonight. They would both need to be extremely careful from here on in if they were to avoid ending up like Mac.

As he thought through what he needed to do in the morning to get bail, Robbie heard footsteps in the corridor and a key being inserted in the lock of his cell door. Robbie cursed silently. He did not want to be sharing the cell with anyone else tonight and wondered how that would work as the lower bunk had no mattress.

Robbie quickly rolled over and faced the wall, pretending to sleep. The door opened and closed again, although there were no sounds of guards talking or footsteps from anyone entering. Robbie lay still on the top bunk, wondering what was happening. Had the guards simply been checking on him? Was he still alone? If they had put someone else into the tiny cell with him, why had not he heard them?

The quiet was eerie. Robbie opened his eyes and looked at the wall to see if he could see any telltale silhouettes or movement in the shadows. Everything looked normal in the darkness, yet Robbie had a strong sense that he was not alone. He concentrated on the sounds he could hear. Even with steel doors and thick concrete walls, a cell block of this size was never perfectly quiet. He could vaguely make out the sounds of men sleeping in other cells. Rhythmic breathing, snoring and the occasional murmur. The building also quietly creaked of its own accord. These were all background and distant noises that he expected. He concentrated on sounds from within his cell. If someone else was in the cell, they were perfectly quiet. Robbie had never felt more vulnerable in his life.

As he contemplated what to do, he heard a very faint sound. He thought it sounded like a small piece of gravel rolling slightly under someone's shoe. Robbie froze, not sure what his next move should be. He continued to strain to hear more sounds, but the cell became quiet again.

In the silence, Robbie detected a slight change in the airflow. The change was so subtle that Robbie questioned whether he was simply imagining it. His sense that he was not alone became even stronger, to the point of being overwhelming. He suddenly realized what the airflow was. Someone breathing. For Robbie to detect this meant they had to be very close.

The breathing stopped. Robbie's world imploded as an excruciating jolt of pain exploded in his spine. As he gasped in agony, he was left seeing a kaleidoscope of white, yellow, and red. The savage force of the massive punch to his kidneys had barely registered before Robbie felt himself falling. The pain from the impact of hitting the concrete floor barely registered against the nauseating shock and pain he still felt from the initial blow.

As he recovered slightly, he found breathing impossible. In the darkness, he realized he had momentarily passed out, and he was now pinned to the floor by an attacker who was exceptionally strong. The searing pain in his lower back had not abated, but had a new companion as Robbie felt his larynx being crushed.

Robbie kicked and flayed in the darkness, but couldn't break the stranglehold of his attacker. Robbie felt his feet kick up against the opposite wall of the cell. He pushed against the wall with all the power his legs could muster to wedge the top part of his body under the bottom bunk. He was not sure it would help, but he hoped it would at least break the hold the man had on his neck. Robbie only partly succeeded. The cell was slightly wider than he expected, and his legs were not long enough to push any more than his head under the bunk. In the darkness, he could faintly make out the outline of the metal steel frame of the side of the bottom bunk above his head. His attacker had to slightly shift his position and weight, but was relentless. Robbie's throat and chest were on fire as the man continued to strangle him. He knew he had only seconds left before it would be all over.

Although it was too dark to see the man's face, Robbie could feel his breath. He tried to swing a punch, but the bed frame made it all but impossible. Instead, Robbie reached up to gauge the man's eyes, but the man kept moving his head.

Robbie felt his strength waning rapidly. Without oxygen, he was going to pass out in seconds, and he knew he would be dead shortly after. In desperation, Robbie grabbed at the man's ears and pushed back with all his strength. The man grunted and momentarily released his grip on Robbie's neck. Robbie gulped one breath of precious oxygen before the vice grip was reapplied to his neck.

Continuing to maintain his grip on the man's ears, Robbie pushed back the man's head as best he could. The man was powerful and used his neck muscles to hold his head steady. He continued to grunt and was obviously in pain.

Robbie knew there was no way he could beat the man with strength. His attacker was physically stronger, and the stalemate would not last much longer. He had one last play. If this did not work, he knew it was over. Now sweating profusely, he hoped his grip on the man's ears would hold a little longer. He had to use the man's strength against him, and his timing had to be perfect.

Robbie gripped the man's ears even tighter and pushed back for all his worth. The man's grunt turned to a muffled screamed as he pushed his head forward to ensure he kept his strangle grip on Robbie's neck for those final few seconds. As the man screamed, Robbie instantly turned the push to a pull and jerked the man's head down and forward with as much force as he could muster. The man's head crunched with a loud bang as it hit the steel bed frame of the bottom bunk. The scream turned to a howl and Robbie felt warm liquid drops land in quick succession on his face. Blood he thought. Hopefully, he had broken the man's nose.

The man's grip loosened momentarily around Robbie's neck, allowing him to breathe. Robbie's grip remained firm on the man's ears, as he lifted the man's head again and brought it crashing down on the side rail of the bunk a second time. The man let go of Robbie's neck and tried to brace against the bed rail, but found it slippery with his own blood. Robbie raised the man's head a third time and brought it down again. The sound was deafening this time and shook the whole bunk frame. Although still in intense pain and now exhausted, Robbie lifted the man's head a fourth and fifth time and slammed it down onto the railing.

Robbie pushed the man, who was now a dead weight,

off of him as best he could. He lay on the concrete floor, panting and exhausted. The pain, which he had forced out of his mind while he fought for his life, returned with a vengeance. He felt a whole new wave of nausea as the room spun. It was the last thing he remembered before he blacked out.

Chapter Twenty-Eight

Keaton poured his first cup of coffee for the day. As he took those first few satisfying sips, he looked out of his top story apartment window across the Vancouver River towards the city. Dawn was still some minutes away and the city still had that magic neon aura as its silhouette reflected off the water.

He would normally still be in bed at this hour, but this morning was different. Stelovak was getting increasingly difficult to deal with and had, on short notice, demanded that Henning and Franco take care of Robbie Mayne, who Stelovak described as that 'loose end.' He was expecting a call shortly that he would then have to relay to Stelovak. He hoped it would be good news. As he waited, he looked out and marveled at the number of people who were up and already out exercising in the pre-dawn on the boardwalk next to the river.

As he stood at the window sipping his coffee, he reflected on his life since graduating law school and wondered how much longer he could work for Richard

Stelovak. Very little of what he did involved the practice of law, either legal or otherwise. Stelovak referred to Keaton as his 'risk manager' and tasked him with ensuring Stelovak was always legally covered in his business dealings, most of which were illegal in some shape or form.

Keaton knew he would never go back to the legal practice of law. The power and money from what he did was too intoxicating. He would live on a natural high for days every time he got the better of police and other legal authorities. The Southwest deal would be over this week and things would return to normal. He might even hit Stelovak up for a few days off. He had certainly earned it. One of his two disposable phones rang. It was Henning.

"How did it go, Rudy?"

There was silence on the line for a moment. Keaton knew silence meant trouble.

"Rudy, talk to me."

Keaton became frustrated by the silence. Silence meant his phone call to Stelovak would convey bad news.

"Okay, what happened to Mayne?"

"It didn't go according to plan. Mayne jumped Vince. Broke his nose and... knocked him out."

Keaton could not believe what he was hearing. Vincent Franco was an enormous man and spent most of his spare time in the gym. "You're telling me Mayne is still alive?"

"Yeah. He's still alive."

Keaton closed his eyes and did his best to control his breathing. Stelovak was going to be livid when he heard this. There would be repercussions for all of them. Right now, he had to get as much information as he could. Stelovak would question him long and hard, and he needed to be fully prepared with all the facts first.

"Okay, Rudy. We need to go through this from start to

finish. Stelovak will want all the details, so don't leave anything out and no lies. You know he'll eventually find out, which will only make it worse."

Henning was silent for a moment and then began detailing everything that had happened at the jail. "After disabling the security camera system, the guard we paid off let Franco in through a rear entrance. They had already moved Mayne from a general holding cell to a two-man cell for the night. Franco went in to strangle Mayne while he slept, and then the guard was going to move his body back to the general cell before they brought in the other prisoners."

Keaton barked, "I know the plan, Rudy. Mayne's body was to be put back in the general cell and set up to look like he was sleeping. Clearly that didn't happen."

"No."

"So, what happened?"

"The guard gave Franco fifteen minutes to complete the job. He was not sure what happened, but there was blood all over Franco and Mayne. Mayne looked dead and Franco was out cold and looked like a truck had backed over his face. The guard panicked and dragged Franco out and re-locked the cell."

"So, what does Franco have to say about all of this? How did he let Mayne get the better of him?"

"I don't know yet, Randolph. Franco is badly concussed and has a broken nose. I took him to a doctor who works for cash and won't ask questions, and got him patched up. Franco has been doing this for close to twenty years and until last night, no one has ever got the better of him."

Keaton was sure Henning was deliberately leaving details out, but he figured he had enough for now to make the call to Stelovak.

"Where are you now?"

"Back at my apartment. Franco is asleep on the couch."

"Don't move until you hear from me."

Keaton disconnected and let out a long breath. They would be lucky to get out of this alive. Keaton rehearsed what he would say to Stelovak and then dialed Stelovak's number.

Stelovak answered after four rings. "I hope you have good news for me."

Keaton had long since learned that Richard Stelovak had a short fuse when it came to people who waffled. Being direct and blunt always seemed the best approach.

"Not today, Richard. Mayne is still alive."

"What do you mean, he's still alive? The instructions were perfectly clear. Vincent Franco was getting paid a lot of…"

"Robbie Mayne broke his nose and knocked him unconscious."

"What? Franco is built like a horse. How does anyone get the better of him?"

"I'm finding out, Richard. Franco and Henning are holed up in Henning's apartment for the time being."

"Was he identified?"

"He left a lot of blood behind, so he won't be able to hang around Vancouver for very long."

The connection went silent for a minute. Keaton thought Stelovak might have disconnected until he came back with instructions in a clipped voice. "I pay you a lot of money, Randolph. Right now, you and those two idiots are a total liability to me. We'll meet in my office this afternoon to discuss what to do with Mayne. You've got until then to figure out how to replace Franco and Henning permanently."

Stelovak disconnected. Keaton went back to looking out the window. Dawn had come and the magic of the city skyline at night had disappeared into the haze of a rising sun.

He did not think he would see too many more sunrises in Vancouver. The writing was on the wall. He had been around Richard Stelovak long enough to know you were either in the inner circle or dead. He would talk it through with Franco and Henning today. Together, they might all just get out of this alive and give Richard Stelovak a parting gift in the process that he so richly deserved.

Chapter Twenty-Nine

Robbie sipped a cup of water as he watched the doctor complete file notes on his medical condition. His throat was still on fire, but according to the doctor, other than some swelling and bruising, no serious damage had been done.

The doctor was more concerned about Robbie's kidneys and wanted Robbie to urinate once more to check for traces of blood. A positive test for blood in his urine would mean a trip to Vancouver General Hospital for specialist treatment.

Hence the cup. Robbie wanted out of the small infirmary and jail as soon as possible. It was well after nine thirty a.m. and he needed to call Laura and a lawyer, but the doctor was not interested. The ultimatum was until he had peed in a cup; he wasn't going anywhere. Robbie was on his third cup of water now. He figured it would not be too much longer before his bladder got the message and he could give the doctor what he wanted.

There was a knock on the door. The doctor, a pleasant man in his early sixties, said, "Come in," without looking up from the report he was writing.

The door opened and a man, who Robbie guessed was in his late twenties, walked in. He wore both a coat and a tie and had intense blue eyes. Either a lawyer or a cop, Robbie figured. He looked intelligent and confident, without appearing arrogant. Robbie guessed cop.

The doctor looked up and in a slightly irritated voice said, "Good morning, Detective Westcott. As I said to you on the phone, you would be the first person I call when I have finished the tests. We're still waiting for another urine sample before we can be sure."

In a croaky voice, Robbie said, "Not for much longer."

The doctor and Westcott turned to look at Robbie. "I'm ready to go. You got a cup?"

The doctor gave Robbie a specimen cup and led him to a small adjoining bathroom. After closing the door to give Robbie some privacy, he turned to Westcott.

"He can't go anywhere. There are no windows. Through this office is the only way out."

"It's okay Doc," said Westcott. "He's going to be released. We're not pressing charges—in fact, we'll be lucky if he doesn't sue the city."

"He's very lucky to be alive."

"Perhaps."

"Perhaps?"

"His attacker underestimated him. I've seen the cell and all the blood. Looks to me like Robbie Mayne is a formidable opponent. I'm not so sure who's luckier."

The door to the bathroom opened, and Robbie emerged with his cup. The doctor took the cup and looked at the sample.

"Can't see any traces of blood, which is a good start. I'll need to run a test to be sure. It won't take long."

Westcott was eager to get started. "Do you mind if I start the interview next door while we wait, Doc?"

The doctor looked at Robbie. "It's up to you, Mr. Mayne. Technically, you remain in my care until I finish the tests and discharge you."

Robbie looked at Westcott. "I hear I'm not being charged. Is that correct?"

Westcott nodded. "That's correct, Mr. Mayne. I'll go into the reasons when we do the interview."

Westcott then stuck out his hand. "Forgive me, I'm Detective Danny Westcott. We talked on the phone the other day."

Robbie shook Westcott's hand. "Call me Robbie."

Robbie frowned as he looked down at his hospital gown. "This thing is pretty drafty. Any chance I can get some clothes, Doctor? Also, I need to call someone. They'll be worried by now."

Westcott said, "Are you referring to Ms. Laura Calwell?"

Robbie's eyes widened. "Yes. How did you...?"

"She came to see you at your hotel early this morning. The hotel staff informed her of your arrest. She's actually waiting downstairs."

Robbie was only wearing a surgical gown at present. He remembered being cleaned up earlier by some sort of nursing orderly, but had no memory of what happened to his clothes. He assumed they would not be in a fit state to wear.

The nightmare of the previous evening was not much more than a blur, but the pain in his lower back and throat was very real and still severe. The doctor had given him a sedative, which had taken the edge off it. Based on the amount of pain he was in, Robbie figured the doctor was right and he would need painkillers for a few more days at least.

"I'd like to see Laura. She'll be worried. But frankly, I don't think she's ready to see me with my butt on public display. I'm happy to be interviewed when I'm in clothes and after I've seen Laura."

Westcott looked at the doctor.

"Okay if I get Robbie some clothes? I can send Laura up with a guard and she can wait next door?"

The doctor nodded. "Nobody needs to be seeing his butt."

After Westcott had left the room, the doctor added, "The test is looking okay, so I'll fill in the release forms and write a script. You're going to need some painkillers."

As Robbie sat and waited for Westcott to return, he felt a little lightheaded. Despite the pain, he was quite hungry.

Westcott returned several minutes later. "You're about my size, Robbie, so I'm pretty sure these will fit. You won't win any fashion contests, but they're clean, at least. I brought your shoes as well."

Robbie quickly got dressed and handed the surgical gown back to the doctor. "Thank you. Hopefully, I won't be needing this again."

The doctor smiled. "Let's hope so."

Westcott led Robbie into the hallway. "I got word Ms. Calwell is on her way up. She's quite upset, actually."

Westcott pointed to the door next to the examination room. "I'll give you a few minutes alone and then we'll start the interview if that's okay?"

Robbie managed a brief smile. "Thanks, Detective."

Robbie opened the door. The room was a small waiting room, presumably for the examination room next door. There were three lounge chairs and a coffee table with a few ancient National Geographic magazines and nothing much else. Robbie stood. He did not have to wait long before there was a faint knock on the door.

"Come in."

The door opened and Laura walked in. She had puffy eyes and her makeup had run a little. It was clear she had been crying. To Robbie, she looked amazing.

Laura walked to Robbie and put her arms around him, and gently hugged him. Finally, still in their embrace, Laura said, "How are you really? The doctor says you're going to be fine, but you look a mess."

"I'm fine."

Laura frowned. "Liar."

"Okay, I'm sore all over. But I'm still here and that's the main thing."

"Yes, it is."

Laura's bottom lip quivered, as she added, "I'm scared. We lost Mac, and we almost lost you."

"We're close, Laura. Another day or two is all we need."

Laura frowned. "Provided we live that long."

Robbie hugged her tight. "I plan on hanging around."

Laura reached up and kissed Robbie. If possible, the kiss was better than yesterday. He would have happily let the moment last a lot longer, but a gentle cough and knock at the open door interrupted them.

A slightly embarrassed Westcott said, "Sorry. Would you prefer I give you some more time?"

Laura looked up at Robbie. "As long as you give him back in one piece and don't take too long, Detective."

Robbie looked at Westcott. "I want Laura to stay. Believe me, she's in this as much as I am."

Laura added, "I would like to stay, if that's okay?"

Westcott motioned to the chairs. "Have a seat, everyone. We've got lots to talk about."

When they had settled in their chairs, Westcott took the lead.

"Okay, first things first. Robbie, you're not being charged. We know you were set up. The call the arresting officers received last night was supposedly from another hotel guest. However, we have investigated further, and the name and room number the caller gave have proved bogus."

In a croaky voice, Robbie asked, "What about the drugs found in my car?"

Westcott grimaced. "The bag of cocaine we recovered from your car had no fingerprints on it. That's very unusual. And considering what happened in your cell last night, someone clearly wanted you dead."

Westcott looked from Laura to Robbie before continuing, "The question is why, Robbie? I'm presuming this has something to do with Aaron MacDonald's death?"

Robbie nodded. "I agree, Detective. I just don't understand why."

"After your call about Aaron the other day, I made a file entry about you on our computer system and linked it to Aaron's case. For active cases, we get alerts on the system for any activity for people associated with them. You could not believe my surprise when I logged on early this morning and your name came up on an alert as being arrested. I tried ringing the lockup shift supervisor but got no answer, so I came down to see for myself. To put it mildly, all hell had broken loose."

Westcott paused for a moment. He obviously had a lot more to say. "I'll get you to explain in your own words what happened in a minute, Robbie, but when I got here, I spoke to the doctor first. I couldn't get any sense out of anyone else. They were all locked in a closed-door meeting. The Doc explained your injuries. You had obviously been attacked and come close to being strangled to death."

Robbie said, "Nothing like this has ever happened to me in my life."

"The Doc then showed me what was left of your clothes. They were saturated with blood, but it wasn't yours. After photographing you, they cleaned you up and re-examined you. Other than signs someone had tried to strangle you, the Doc found no cuts or wounds on your body. The blood belonged to whoever attacked you. You were still drifting in and out of consciousness, so I went and had a look at your cell."

Westcott shook his head. "There was blood everywhere. I'm not even sure whoever attacked you survived."

Robbie frowned. "What do you mean by, you're not sure they survived?"

Westcott continued, "They discovered you unconscious in your cell around four a.m. on a routine check. The blood in the hallway outside your cell alerted the guards. You were alone, Robbie. There was no one else in the cell. That's why all hell has broken loose. Whoever did this has vanished."

Chapter Thirty

Robbie and Laura looked at one another in disbelief and then looked back at Westcott for answers.

Westcott let out a long breath. "I need you to explain what happened last night as best you can. So far, we know for sure there was one shift supervisor and three guards here between midnight and six a.m. Even though they all check out, I'm sure one or more of them were involved in this, but none of them have any injuries that fit with what happened in the cell."

Laura frowned. "None of them?"

There were twelve registered men in the lockup last night, including you. Most of them came in earlier than you for drunk and disorderly conduct. We have examined them. None of them have any injuries that fit with what happened in your cell. The only conclusion we have is that it was someone else who attacked you."

"Someone who's no longer here?"

"It looks that way, Robbie. This isn't my case. I'll take your statement now and then hand it on to whoever it's assigned to.

But I imagine they will want you to do a quick lineup check of the guards and inmates. Just to be absolutely sure."

"You needn't bother, detective. It was too dark. I saw nothing more than a dim profile in the dark. I couldn't tell you if he was white or black or young or old. The only thing I can tell you for sure was he was big and really strong."

Westcott briefly smiled. "I'm interested to hear your story, Robbie. From all the blood in there, it looks like he came off worse."

"I'd call it a draw," croaked Robbie. "We're both still alive but licking our wounds."

Westcott settled in his chair and opened a notebook. "I'm ready when you are."

Robbie spent the next fifteen minutes reliving the night before, from the knock on the hotel door by the police until this morning when he woke up to find the doctor examining him.

He spared no detail in retelling his fight for survival in the small cell and how he finally got the better of his attacker. Laura remained silent throughout and went pale as Robbie recounted how close he had come to dying.

Robbie reached over and squeezed her hand. "I'm okay."

When Robbie had finished, Westcott put down his pen and notebook. As he reviewed what Robbie had told him, he concluded Robbie was lucky to be alive. Westcott looked at Robbie. There were still more questions he wanted to ask.

Laura spoke for the first time, "Detective, I appreciate you probably still have a lot of questions, but frankly, Robbie looks exhausted. I would like to take him home. He really needs to rest."

Westcott replied, "You're right, Laura. I've got plenty to

work though for now, and as I said, this isn't my case. I'll pass this statement on to the detective in charge. But I will need to talk to you again. I want to review the Aaron MacDonald case first. I'm sure that's the connection."

Laura and Robbie both agreed. They gave Westcott their contact details. Westcott apologized for what had happened.

"You know, Robbie, you're quite within your rights to sue the city for what happened. I can't say I would blame you."

Robbie looked at Westcott and shook his head. "I'll mend. I just want justice for Mac."

On their way out, Robbie stopped at the doctor's office and thanked him again for his help.

As they walked to Laura's car, Laura said, "Robbie, I'd like you to come and stay with me until this is over. You could do with some looking after and, frankly, I don't want to be alone."

Robbie readily agreed, and they drove back to his hotel to pack his bags and check out. The drive to Laura's apartment from the hotel was only fifteen minutes, but by the time Laura parked the car in the basement parking of her apartment block, Robbie was already asleep with exhaustion.

After parking, Laura rubbed Robbie's shoulder. "We're here."

Robbie opened his eyes and managed half a sleepy smile. Still with his croaky voice, he replied, "Thanks, Laura. You're the best."

Laura smiled as she got out of the four-wheel drive to collect his bags. "You're not so bad yourself."

Robbie was thankful for the elevator. When they got to

Laura's apartment, Laura motioned Robbie to lie down on the couch.

"I'll put fresh sheets on the bed. Then you can lie down and sleep as long as you need."

"I'm fine out here, Laura, really."

Laura called back over her shoulder as she entered the bedroom, "You will sleep better in here, and besides, I won't have to tippy-toe around you. I can get…"

Laura emerged from the bedroom with a confused look on her face. She walked into the kitchen, looked around, and then came back to the main living area.

"Laura, what's wrong?"

Laura didn't respond. Instead, she opened a small bureau that she kept her stationery and bills in. Laura looked at Robbie. The look of confusion had turned to a look of concern. "My laptop is missing. Someone has been in my apartment, Robbie."

Chapter Thirty-One

Westcott and Delray made the final checks and adjustments as they waited on the signal that the other team was in position. They had done this routine of rechecking guns, bulletproof vests and other supporting equipment many times before. Delray had drummed it into all his men that every piece of equipment should be checked, rechecked and then cross-checked again by another member of your team before going into a potential conflict situation.

Westcott couldn't blame Delray for his caution. He had already seen one detective pensioned out of the force when he had failed to check his gun properly and it misfired in a take-down. The perpetrator got away, leaving the detective with a bullet hole in his stomach, which almost bled out.

After getting word from the surveillance team that Henning had returned home, Delray and Westcott had met late that morning with Jamieson and McKenzie, who formed the other two members of the team to plan the arrest. They had all the correct paperwork in place to make a legal search and arrest and had studied plans of the apartment block.

Westcott knew from Henning's profile that he may be armed and dangerous and a threat to the team. They had worked through a dozen different scenarios of what might happen if Henning refused to go quietly or tried to escape or turned the arrest into a shootout. His boss thought the odds of a shootout were small. Henning's arrest record showed a distinct preference for a showdown in court with lawyers, rather than a battle on the streets with guns. Still, his boss was old enough and wise enough to know you never banked on assumptions and prepared for all possibilities.

The portable two-way radio Westcott held came to life. "We're in position."

It was Jamieson confirming he and McKenzie were now at their designated positions at the back of the apartment complex. Westcott asked, "How does it look?"

"It's all quiet. We've been here for over ten minutes and haven't seen a soul. Everything is where it's listed on the plan. I've got the laneway exit covered and McKenzie is covering the side of the building. Any last-minute instructions?"

Westcott looked at Delray, who said, "Stay calm, stay cool, and stay alive."

Westcott added, "Did you get that?"

"We did. Good luck and stay alive yourself."

Delray looked at Westcott. "You ready, Danny?"

Westcott nodded. He could feel his adrenaline pumping, which he took to be a good thing.

"Same advice to you as the other two, Danny—stay calm, stay cool, and stay alive. Let's go."

They crossed the road and entered the brick apartment by the main entrance, which was on the driveway side of the complex. McKenzie was currently watching this exit from behind a dumpster at the back of the complex. The apartment block was only two levels high, with eight apartments on each floor. Henning lived in one of the two-second level apartments at the rear of the complex. It had a balcony facing the rear courtyard, which was where Jamieson was currently situated, just in case Henning tried to make a run for it, either from the balcony or the rear exit.

Delray and Westcott put on their blue vests, which identified them as Vancouver Police before quickly climbing the stairs. Westcott knocked on the door of apartment 2C. They had decided not to announce their arrival. Westcott and Delray waited.

Westcott knocked on the door a second time.

"Who is it?"

"Detective Westcott and Inspector Delray from Vancouver Police. We're here to speak with Rudy Henning."

"Putting clothes on. Hang on a minute."

"We have a warrant to search the premises. Open the door now or we break it in."

"Coming."

The door stayed closed. Delray gave Westcott the nod to put his foot through it just as Rudy Henning opened the door. He was in his mid-forties with slightly thinning hair. He was about the same height as Westcott and had a solid build. Westcott got the sense that the man was very intelligent and would need to be watched closely.

With an almost knowing smile, he said, "I will need to see some ID and your search papers before we go any further."

Westcott and Delray held up their badges for Henning and then showed the documentation for the search warrant.

Henning took time examining their badges and the warrant. "It all looks in order. I'll need to call my lawyer."

"You can do that from inside. Let's go."

Henning rolled his eyes as if the visit was nothing more than a terrible inconvenience. Delray and Westcott followed Henning into his apartment. The main living area of the apartment was sparsely furnished.

Westcott did a quick scan. No pictures on the walls, just two quality leather sofas and a large plasma TV on an oak cabinet. Henning traveled light, which was not surprising, he thought, if the police files were accurate about his profession.

The kitchen, dining and lounge room were all one open plan space. A small hallway connected this area to what Westcott presumed were two bedrooms, a laundry and a bathroom. All doors to these rooms were currently closed.

Westcott looked at Delray, who nodded. They did not need to exchange words. Delray would cover Henning while Westcott checked the other rooms to make sure no one else was in the apartment. Once cleared, they would contact Jamieson and McKenzie to come and assist with the search.

Henning had conveniently placed himself at the entrance to the hallway as he dialed the number for his lawyer. Westcott immediately became suspicious and went to push past Henning, who blocked his entrance.

"You can't start a search until I contact my lawyer, pal. So back off!"

Westcott was just about to respond when Delray, with his service revolver out and pointing at Henning's chest said, "I've got a search warrant, a loaded gun and a short temper. Now get out of the man's…"

Before Delray could finish his sentence, the two-way

radio clipped to Westcott's belt came to life. It was Jamieson.

"We have an unidentified man on the balcony. He's looking to jump into…"

Delray and Westcott both knew what to do. This was one scenario they had planned for. Westcott produced handcuffs immediately and pushed Henning face down on the floor. While Delray covered him with the gun, Westcott pulled Henning's arms back and handcuffed his hands behind his back.

Delray was just about to yell 'be careful' to Westcott as he ran out of the apartment when he heard the sound that he feared most in this situation—a gunshot and close by. To Delray, it sounded like it had come from behind the apartment block.

Delray had a second pair of cuffs and looked for somewhere to handcuff Henning to. His desperate search revealed nothing suitable. "Son of a bitch!"

Delray shoved Henning down the hallway in front of him. "Open the door that gets us to the balcony."

Henning sauntered, deliberately trying to add seconds to the short journey to the end of the corridor. Delray brought the butt of his pistol down hard on Henning's shoulder, who howled in protest as he staggered forward. "Any more delays and the next one will be behind the ear. Get me on the balcony now!"

Henning opened the door on the right. Apart from a small office table and a laptop, the room was empty. The glass sliding door to the balcony was open. Delray pushed Henning through the bedroom and out onto the balcony. He was in the process of instructing Henning to lie on the balcony floor when he looked over the railing and saw Jamieson lying in a pool of blood on the concrete below.

McKenzie was the first man in position. Situated behind a dumpster at the end of the apartment block's driveway, he had a good visibility of the entrance, which was on the side of the property, but limited visibility to the rear. His main role was to cover anyone trying to exit through either the main entrance or coming around to the driveway from the rear. It was unlikely that he would be required. He hoped that Henning would go quietly and that he would simply be required to come up to the apartment for the search.

McKenzie had been in position for about fifteen minutes when he heard the gunshot at the rear of the apartment complex. His reflex action was to charge around the back, guns blazing. Delray was a meticulous planner and he had been instructed to stay in position for a few seconds to see if anyone emerged from the rear of the complex.

McKenzie counted off ten seconds and then emerged from behind the dumpster with his gun drawn and raised to the firing position. He rushed to the rear of the complex and scanned the area and saw no one except Jamieson lying on the ground close to the brick wall that separated the blind side of the apartment block from its neighbor. McKenzie could hear Jamieson groaning, so he knew he was still alive. He holstered his gun and ran to his partner's side.

McKenzie cursed at the sight of a pool of blood beneath Jamieson that was growing by the second. He reached for the two-way and radioed for an ambulance.

Westcott took the stairs three at a time. His first concern was the safety of Jamieson and McKenzie. With his gun drawn and held in tight to the right side of his body, Westcott paused in the building entryway and looked down the driveway to the rear of the apartment block. It looked clear. Westcott sprinted down the driveway with his gun held up in the firing position. He briefly paused at the rear corner of the building, just in case he was walking into an ambush. As he scanned the rear of the complex, his gut tightened as he saw McKenzie kneeling over Jamieson, who was lying in a pool of blood.

Westcott quickly covered the ground across the back of the apartment block and knelt beside McKenzie. Like McKenzie, Westcott was pleased to hear Jamieson groaning, which meant he was not only alive but also conscious.

McKenzie had taken his jacket off and was using it as a pressure bandage on Jamieson's shoulder. Without taking his eyes off Jamieson, he quickly apprised Westcott of the situation.

"He's taken one high in the shoulder and is losing a lot of blood. I've called the ambulance. ETA is two minutes."

Jamieson opened his eyes and looked at Westcott. Through gritted teeth, he said, "Be careful, Danny, he's a pro. Bastard shot me as I climbed up over the wall to chase him."

Westcott urged Jamieson to be quiet and concentrate on not passing out. Jamieson was a lather of sweat and in extreme pain, which both Westcott and McKenzie took as a good sign. He ignored Westcott and continued talking in raspy breaths.

"He had me cold. A big guy with a busted nose and stitches across his forehead. His gun was pointed at my chest. Then he said, 'this is your lucky day,' and then he moved his aim and shot me in the shoulder."

They heard a siren in the distance.

McKenzie said, "Stay with me, buddy. Ambulance will be here in a minute."

Westcott got up to take off after the shooter. He figured he might have a two-block advantage at most.

Delray was watching everything unfold from the balcony. He currently had his gun pointed at Henning's head, who remained silent on the floor. He knew Westcott would be keen to pursue the shooter.

"Danny!"

Westcott looked up at Delray, who was still on the balcony. "Hey, boss. You get all that."

"I got it," said Delray with a nod. "He's turning blue and shock is setting in. We need that ambulance now!"

Westcott desperately wanted to chase down the man who had shot Jamieson, but as he looked up at Delray, he knew what Delray was thinking was the right call. Jamieson was losing color as well as blood. He needed to be out front to flag down the ambulance and make sure they got to Jamieson in time.

"Boss, I'm going to wait out front to make sure the ambulance doesn't miss the driveway."

Delray watched Westcott jog back around to the driveway. He murmured, "Good call, Danny—we'll get the shooter later."

Delray was thankful that Westcott had his priorities right. As he watched McKenzie comfort Jamieson, he knew there would indeed be another day. After what Westcott had told him about Robbie Mayne's attack in the lockup, and Jamieson's description, he now had a pretty good idea of who the shooter was.

Chapter Thirty-Two

Laura walked slowly around her apartment, examining bookshelves, cupboards and drawers. Robbie remained on the couch, out of her way. He had not been here often enough to be able to tell what was in place, out of place, or missing.

After ten minutes of careful examination, Laura came and sat on the edge of the couch. She looked almost as pale as Robbie.

"Whoever's been here has been very thorough. The only thing missing I think is my laptop, but just about every cupboard and drawer seems to have been touched. I'm very particular about how I store and place things. I know when things have been moved."

"So, whoever has been here has tried to disguise it?"

"I guess. What could I possibly have that someone would be interested in? You think stealing my laptop is connected to the emails?" Robbie shook his head and added, "We're missing something. Probably something big.

Whatever it is, Mac got killed for it and I nearly got killed for it. We have to study those emails again—today."

"Robbie, we do, but you need rest."

Getting up from the couch, Robbie said, "You're right. But not here. I'm not sure we're safe here any longer. We need to go stay somewhere where no one will find us for a few days until we sort this out."

"Where do you suggest?"

"I think a motel. Preferably on the outskirts of the city. Somewhere that takes cash and doesn't ask too many questions."

Robbie thought Laura might object, but she said, "I'll go pack. Give me five minutes."

As Laura walked into her bedroom, Robbie called after her. "There's something else I need to tell you."

Laura came back to the bedroom door. "Okay."

"I'm almost certain we were followed yesterday."

Laura sighed and came into the living room and sat next to Robbie. "This just keeps getting better."

"I think we had a gray Toyota following us out to Cypress Falls yesterday. It was about eight cars behind us. I thought nothing of it. You know, on a freeway, lots of cars follow you. But when we came back from Catalin, it was there again, about eight cars back."

Laura's eyes widened. "You saw the same car?"

Robbie nodded. "At first, I thought it was just a coincidence. It disappeared when we stopped to eat, but it was back following us as we came into the city. It wasn't until you dropped me back at the hotel that I was really sure. It was still there behind us in traffic."

"What have we got ourselves into, Robbie?"

"When you stopped to let me out at the hotel, it immediately turned into a side street. Almost as if the driver didn't want to risk me getting a look at him as he drove by."

Laura looked around her apartment. "We really do need to leave here, don't we?"

"Yes. We need to go somewhere where we are off the grid for a while."

"Five minutes, Robbie."

While Laura was packing, Robbie's phone rang. "Robbie Mayne."

Robbie listened for several minutes without interrupting. "Okay, thanks for the update, detective. You have my number. Keep me posted."

Robbie disconnected. He put his phone down and began rubbing his temples. He needed sleep.

Laura came out of the bedroom with two bags. She said in a quiet voice, "I'm ready. Who was on the phone?"

Robbie, still rubbing his temples, replied, "Westcott. They have finished the forensic examination on the rental. I can collect it anytime I like."

"Okay. Did it show up anything?"

"Yes, and no."

Laura frowned. "Yes, and no?"

"No, to fingerprints and DNA. But… they did a search under the car."

"And?"

Robbie stopped massaging his temples and looked at Laura. "Someone has recently fitted the car with a sophisticated tracking device. It's likely they have followed me since I arrived here on Saturday."

Chapter Thirty-Three

Richard Stelovak drummed his fingers impatiently on the table and glanced at his Louis Vuitton watch for the fourth time in as many minutes. Tired of sitting, he stood up from his desk and paced. Very few things in life unsettled him, but the call he had just received from Keaton had him worried. With the Southwest development deal due to be signed off tomorrow, the last thing he needed now were any more complications. While he was concerned about Robbie Mayne and the incriminating list he was supposedly carrying around, that would now have to wait another day or two.

Keaton's call about Blackwell now made him the number one priority. Blackwell was now not only a threat to the Southwest development deal but also potentially to everything else he had worked for. As he paced, Stelovak was thankful he had taken the precaution of having the bug setup in Blackwell's office six months ago to monitor his conversations.

The Southwest development deal was too important to

him to be relying simply on what Blackwell told him to his face. He had to make sure everything Blackwell was telling him to his face was consistent with what he said behind closed doors. So far, Blackwell had proven to be consistent in everything he said. The monitoring revealed Blackwell had only hidden one thing from Stelovak, and that was his plan to get out of the business.

Keaton had told him over the phone that Vancouver Metro had recovered deleted copies of the Blackwell photos on Brennan's laptop and interviewed Blackwell in connection with the photographer's death. Blackwell was now panicking and making plans to leave in the next twenty-four hours, despite Stelovak's threats. Stelovak had requested a full briefing immediately, including the recording of the conversation with the police in Blackwell's office.

Keaton needed a few minutes to organize a copy of the recording. Stelovak did not want to wait, but he knew it was vital that he heard the conversation for himself. He had a lot riding on this and was not about to make decisions on second or third hand information.

His secretary interrupted his thoughts to let him know Keaton was waiting outside. Returning to his desk, Stelovak instructed his secretary to show Keaton in.

Keaton entered the office holding what looked like a small Dictaphone. "I'm sorry for the delay, Richard. It took the technician longer than expected to make the copy."

With a grim face, Stelovak pointed to a chair in front of his desk and waited for Keaton to be seated. "I want details. Assume nothing and don't leave anything out."

Keaton spent the next hour playing excerpts from the police interview in Blackwell's office. The recording spoke for itself, like a third person in the room. Stelovak's mood got progressively darker the more he heard from the interview. His rage focused more on the Dictaphone than Keaton, which was fine with Keaton.

At the end of the police interview, Keaton stopped the Dictaphone.

"We recorded another five significant conversations. Two with his wife and three to arrange travel, money and new IDs in that order. Rather than playing all of them, I'd like to play just the last conversation with his wife. It sums up all the others pretty well."

Stelovak gave a barely discernible nod. Keaton hit the play button.

"Did you get the girls organized? Okay, good. I've arranged the travel and the new documents. Yes, the money is already there, and I have the one hundred and fifty cash from the safe."

There was silence for about thirty seconds while Blackwell listened to his wife.

"It's all taken care of. You don't need to worry. I'm sending all the staff home at five o'clock. That will give me an hour and a half to shred everything. No, don't come before then. I won't be ready."

Some more silence followed.

"Look, I have to go. I've got a lot to do. I'll see you at six thirty and remember, just one bag. We buy a whole new wardrobe when we get there. And don't forget to park in the alley. The plain-clothes cop is still out front. No no, it's fine. He's waiting for me to come up from the parking lot. And he can't see the alley from where he's parked, anyway."

There was some background noise, before Blackwell continued, "Just ring when you're out back and I'll come down straight away. Six thirty, okay?"

Keaton pressed stop on the Dictaphone. He could not remember a time when Stelovak's mood looked darker. He had other news that Stelovak needed to hear as well. It may as well be now, Keaton thought. Better to get it all on the table at once.

"During all this, Richard, I got a phone call from Vincent. It appears they have arrested Rudy in connection with the Brennan matter. Apparently, Vancouver Metro found his DNA on a cigarette butt at Brennan's apartment."

Stelovak slapped the palm of his right hand down on the desk with such force that Keaton flinched. His boss then launched into a two-minute tirade of profanity and abuse about the incompetence and lack of commitment of everyone around him. Afterward, he pushed back from his desk and walked over to the window.

As silence descended on the office again, Keaton knew better than to speak. Stelovak would say what needed to be said when he was good and ready.

Staring out the window with his back to Keaton, Stelovak continued. "I sign the contracts at four p.m. tomorrow. One more day is all I need. My net worth will go from two hundred to over five hundred million. I'll go from being one of the richest men in this city to one of the richest in the country."

Stelovak turned from the window. His mood was still dark.

"No accountant or incompetent associate is going to get in my way."

Stelovak returned to his desk and sat down to massage his temples.

"Blackwell has told us everything is set for Southwest. That his work is done?"

Keaton nodded. "Correct, Richard. Blackwell has it all arranged. The last three million in commissions have been transferred to the escrow account and will be released upon your voice command as requested. Blackwell has it all arranged with the Roma Bank as instructed. Only your phone call and voice command can authorize the release. I will, of course, be with you through the whole contract signing process tomorrow before we get to that point."

Stelovak thought for a moment in silence.

"I see no need to keep Blackwell around then. If the bribes, or commissions as you politely call them, are ready, what further need do we have of him?"

Keaton knew the question was rhetorical, and the room went quiet again as Stelovak thought through the alternatives and weighed up his options. Stelovak was utterly ruthless and totally without conscience when he needed to be. Keaton knew before he had said anything that Blackwell's fate had been sealed. The only question was how and when?

"It must be tonight. We can't afford for him to run. If the police get a hold of him, he'll take the immunity and witness protection and give us all up. And even if by some miracle he gets out of the country, he'll wind up on an Interpol watch list and remain a ticking time bomb."

Stelovak had regained most of his composure. In a much softer voice, he said, "We could all go to prison for a long, long time, Randolph. Is that what you want?"

"Of course not, Richard."

Stelovak rose from his chair and walked across to the wall safe. He quietly slid aside the picture and deftly entered the safe combination and opened the main safe door. Stelovak then discreetly moved his body to shield the combination he entered to open the inner second compartment from Keaton. Keaton had rarely seen this compartment opened. Stelovak called it 'the holy of holies.'

Keaton knew it contained somewhere between one and

two million in cash, but the real value was in the bearer bonds and international money notes it contained. Keaton had no idea of their value, but knew it was significant.

Stelovak extracted and counted off five pieces of heavy white bond paper. He closed both safe doors and came back to his desk. After he was seated, Stelovak picked up his Mont Blanc fountain pen. As he unscrewed the cap and began to sign each note, he said to Keaton.

"Money notes from the Roma Bank. Acceptable in most banks, Randolph, not just here, but right around the world. Paris, London, Milan, even Baghdad. Each one of these is worth one hundred thousand in our currency. You can do the math for what their worth in your destination city of choice. I will lay out three million in bribe money tomorrow to see this deal go safely through. And considering the stakes, it's money well spent."

Stelovak paused and held Keaton's gaze. "I'm putting another five hundred on the table for you to take care of Blackwell tonight… before he leaves his office." After Stelovak finished signing the notes, he retrieved a large white envelope from his desk. Keaton watched as Stelovak placed the signed notes carefully in the envelope, sealed it and wrote Keaton's name on the front in a neat cursive script.

He walked back to his safe and reopened the main compartment. Keaton watched in silence as Stelovak placed the envelope on the middle shelf.

As Stelovak re-locked the main safe door and returned to his desk, he said, "Randolph, you will have noticed that I have placed the notes, your notes, in the main compartment. You can collect them any time you want on your return."

The office became silent again. Keaton knew Stelovak

was not giving him a choice. He didn't think he would be asked to kill Blackwell personally, but certainly to supervise it and make sure it was done properly.

It was an enormous risk for Keaton. In the entire time he had worked for Stelovak, he had never been directly involved in the murder of anyone. Keaton was the one who gave the order and paid the money to the 'associates' who did the actual work. He thought it ironic that the payments for these murders were made through untraceable subsidiary companies set up by Blackwell, who was now the target.

Keaton weighed up his options. The biggest risk was not the police, or becoming a prime suspect for the crime, but saying 'No' to Richard Stelovak. Keaton figured if he said no, there was a high probability he would be lying in a morgue alongside Leon Blackwell within twenty-four hours.

For now, Keaton would have to say 'Yes' and then think through his options. He had some money set aside. Enough to leave Vancouver on short notice and start again with a new identity. The question was, would he get the opportunity? Time was running short. He figured they only had two hours at most to plan for Blackwell's demise if it was to happen after all Blackwell's employees went home and before six thirty when he left for good.

"What do you have in mind, Richard?"

Stelovak smiled. Keaton had never cared for Stelovak's smile. His brilliant steel-blue eyes gave him a cold and insincere look. Keaton knew he couldn't be trusted. "It's simple. I want you to make sure Blackwell doesn't leave his office alive. You need to team up with Vincent Franco, seeing as his partner is currently unavailable. I don't expect you to get your hands dirty. I want you there to make sure there are no mistakes, unlike last time."

Keaton nodded, but said nothing.

"Also, Blackwell knows you. If he has the front door to his office locked, he will probably let you in if you arrive with some documents. You simply say we need him to quickly review them ahead of tomorrow's contract signing and he will have no choice. Once you're in, it shouldn't be too hard to get Franco in and the rest is easy."

Keaton thought for a moment. "We know Vancouver Metro has a plain clothes guy out the front. Trying to pull off something like this is going to be high risk?"

Stelovak smiled again. Keaton wished he would stop doing that. "The police officer is there to follow Blackwell home from work. He will be planning to report in when he has followed Blackwell safely home. He could sit out front until nine or ten p.m. under the impression Blackwell is working late without raising an alarm. You go in through the back, you come out through the back without incident. And remember Randolph, a bonus of four hundred thousand for you and one hundred for Franco."

Keaton knew he had no options at this point. "Okay, Richard. Whatever you say."

"Also, leave a copy of the photographs with some of his prints on them and make it look like a suicide."

"Okay, although I'm not sure we have enough time to set it up to fool Vancouver Metro?"

"I agree. My intention is to buy us some additional insurance. Hard to prove murder beyond reasonable doubt to a jury if much of the evidence points to suicide and you have a good lawyer."

Keaton cared little for Stelovak's use of the 'you' in his answer, but knew right now there was nothing he could do about it. Keaton reluctantly nodded his agreement.

Stelovak continued, "Good. Now, what about Henning?"

"Phipps is representing him. He doesn't think he is likely to talk."

"Henning can't produce anything that directly links back to me or Stelecom?"

"No."

"Keep me fully appraised. If it looks like it's going south, we may need to make alternate arrangements quickly."

Keaton thought better of saying anything about the mounting body count and the risks they were taking and simply nodded his agreement.

Stelovak opened up the top drawer of his desk and pulled out one of several disposable phones.

"We need to call Franco now. I'm sure he's making plans to leave town. I think we have enough on the table to convince him to delay his exit by a few hours."

Chapter Thirty-Four

Laura watched over Robbie as he lay sleeping on one of the two beds in the motel room. She knew he was lucky to be alive. After the ordeal he had been through and how exhausted he was, she knew he was likely to sleep for several more hours.

She walked to the window and looked out at the view from the first-floor. It was anything but spectacular. They had decided on a budget motel on the outer fringe of the city near a block of a multi-story parking lot.

After being alerted to the tracking device on Robbie's rental by detective Westcott, they had examined Laura's four-wheel drive before leaving her apartment building. Although they had found no trace of anything resembling a tracking device, they decided not to park in the motel's parking lot, just in case. Neither Robbie nor Laura wanted a repeat of what happened last night.

Laura felt they were safe for the moment and decided to start re-examining the Catalin email messages. She powered up Robbie's laptop and entered the password he had written on a scrap of paper for her. While she waited for the laptop to go through the startup routine, she looked at the password. Laura felt uneasy about having anything like this lying around after what had happened in her apartment. She crumpled the paper and went into the small adjoining bathroom and flushed it down the toilet.

Laura looked at Robbie as she returned and was thankful he could sleep. Rest was what he needed more than anything else at present. After sitting down at the small writing table, Laura opened up the web browser on Robbie's laptop and logged into Mac's Catalin email account.

Laura carefully re-read each email message and made notes as she went to discuss with Robbie when he woke. She kept coming back to the first email about the laptop.

To: codos9009@proteja.bg From: catalin1989@cybamail.com
Subject: New Address

C

Please use this temporary email address for all future email comms. What I'm doing is illegal here and I can't afford to be seen to be connected. I could get prison time if caught.

Ghost loaded and tested. Laptop was picked up yesterday. I have started monitoring but nothing of importance yet.

Be careful. I don't think he's suspicious yet, but he's very well connected.

M

The way the email was worded, it was obviously someone Mac knew. She murmured, "You knew thousands of people, Mac. And almost every one of them has a laptop."

If the person had dropped off and picked up the laptop from Mac's apartment, it would be almost impossible to trace who it was unless Mac had mentioned it to a neighbor. That was highly unlikely, she thought. She looked at the date of the email. If the laptop had been dropped at his work, Theo Finland would be the one person who might know. Mac and Theo had been business partners for seven years and had shared office space in the city. Their 'office' was little more than two workrooms, a kitchenette and a drab small common area.

While Mac had specialized in computer security, Theo worked mainly as a software programmer. Mac and Theo did not work on many projects together, and their business alliance was more about sharing the expenses to keep their operating costs down. Laura knew Theo would probably would not know anything about the laptop, but it was worth a call. She crossed her fingers as she dialed the office number, hoping Theo would pick up. Instead, she got the answering machine. Laura recognized Theo's voice.

"Hi, we're not here right now. Leave a message after the beep and we'll get back to you."

"Hi, Theo. It's Laura. Can you please call me when you get this message? I'm trying to track down some information about one of Mac's clients. Thanks."

Laura disconnected. She had barely begun looking at the emails again before her phone rang.

"Hi, Laura, sorry I missed your call. What's up?"

"Hi, Theo. I'm trying to find out some information about one of Mac's clients. It looks like Mac did some repairs on a laptop for them."

"A laptop? Doesn't sound like Mac. He did security work mostly. Repairs to equipment other than the stuff we have here in the office, he would normally palm off. Unless it was for a friend?"

"Theo, I've got to level with you. I'm pretty sure Mac was murdered. The hit and run was no accident."

Theo was silent for a moment. "Murder? Why would anyone want to murder Mac?"

Before Laura could respond, Theo became emotional and began telling Laura how much he missed Mac and how it would never be the same. He had come to the funeral, of course, but it had not really sunk in until he got to the office on Monday and Mac was not there. Laura liked Theo and listened patiently. It was obvious Theo needed to share his grief.

"I'm sorry I unloaded on you like that, Laura. I can't believe he was murdered. Who would want to do that to Mac, of all people?"

"That's what we're trying to find out, Theo. The laptop, or more importantly, who it belongs to, could be the key."

Laura read off the date of the first email to Theo, hoping it would jog his memory.

Theo thought for a moment. "Sorry, Laura, it doesn't ring a bell. I was doing a lot of work on a client site then and wasn't in the office much."

"Okay. If you remember anything, please call me back straight away. It maybe the breakthrough we need."

Theo was silent for a moment. "Hang on a second, Laura."

Laura could hear Theo pounding away furiously at a computer keyboard.

As he crunched the keyboard, Theo said, "Mac and I shared a business calendar. I'm just going to check around the date you gave me, for any mention of a laptop."

Laura waited patiently while Theo searched. She could

The Catalin Code

hear occasional bursts of keyboard activity followed by pauses. "There's no mention of a laptop in any of his appointments, Laura. They're mostly for site visits and conference calls."

Laura started to feel quite deflated. She had hoped to get some sort of clue, at least.

"Okay, Theo. It was worth a try. Thanks anyway."

"I'm really sorry, Laura. He was my friend. I really want to help."

Laura did not hang up. She hated admitting defeat. Her experience at the OCTF taught her to persist even when the odds were stacked against her.

"You still there, Laura?"

"I am, Theo."

"Theo, would you mind reading out the diary entries from the date I gave you? We might have missed something because it's not immediately obvious."

"Okay, let's see. It starts with a conference call at nine a.m. to a bank. That goes for an hour. From ten thirty a.m. to three p.m. he was actually on site with me. Four p.m. he had another conference call to discuss a new project. That was with an online publishing company. At five p.m. it looks like he double booked. He's got a 'dry cleaning pickup' and a 'Nick.' That's it."

Laura felt a slight tingle of hope. "Theo, the last entry at five p.m. Is that one entry as in pickup cleaning from Nick or…"

"No. Two separate entries. Hang on."

Laura heard Theo pounding on the keyboard again. "Okay, he made the diary entry for dry cleaning three days prior to the appointment day. That fits as a reminder. Now let's see…"

Laura heard more keystrokes. "The appointment for

'Nick' was made at eight fifty-four a.m. on the actual day of the appointment."

Laura whispered, 'Nick Carney,' more to herself than Theo.

Theo said, "Mr. OCTF himself. Now that you mention it, that fits. I remember he came stomping in here a couple of days after this date demanding to see Mac."

"Was it to pick up a laptop?"

"I don't know what he wanted. The guy was really rude. Mac was out at the time and I couldn't get rid of him quick enough."

Laura felt a tingle of excitement. Maybe this was the breakthrough they were looking for. "Theo, you've been very helpful. If I need more information, do you mind if I call you back?"

"Any time, Laura. I'm glad to help."

"Just one more thing. Don't mention the diary or Nick to anyone unless it's the police. And by police, I mean Vancouver Metro, not OCTF."

"Got it. Laura, be careful, okay?"

Laura looked at Robbie, who was still fast asleep. "I will, Theo, I will."

Chapter Thirty-Five

Westcott stood and watched through the one-way glass mirror as Michael Phipps conferred in fervent whispers with his client. It surprised Westcott that Henning could afford a lawyer of the caliber of Phipps. Someone with deep pockets was clearly financing this. He was becoming increasingly confident he knew who.

The door to the observation room opened. Westcott turned to see Felix Delray walk in. "I just got off the phone to the hospital. Looks like McKenzie's going to be okay. He's out of surgery and stable. He's lost a lot of blood and needs at least one more operation, but the doctor is happy for now. I'm planning to head across and see him as soon as we finish here."

Delray paused and looked through the observation window. "Well, well. Michael Phipps. He's way above Henning's pay grade. Who's financing this?"

Westcott returned his gaze to the window and watched Henning and Phipps converse before replying to Delray. "Phipps works for some heavy hitters. The heaviest being

Richard Stelovak. It's no secret Stelovak used Leon Blackwell to launder his money. We just haven't been able to prove it. My guess is Stelovak is concerned we can tie Henning's involvement in Eugene Brennan's murder back to the photographs Brennan took of Blackwell."

Delray added, "And ultimately, back to him."

Westcott nodded.

Delray looked back through the glass. Phipps and Henning were still talking, but not huddled as closely anymore. He figured they had their story straight. "It fits. Stelovak's got that land development thing going through. He can't afford any bad press right now and certainly doesn't want Henning doing a deal with us."

"Who better to convince him he can beat the charges than Michael Phipps?"

Delray looked back at Westcott. "You ready?"

Westcott was still looking through the window and focused on Henning and Phipps. They had fast tracked the DNA analysis of the blood left behind in the holding cell where Robbie Mayne and been attacked and got a match for Vincent Franco. It surprised neither of them when the Vancouver Metro police database showed Henning as a known associate of Franco. McKenzie's description of the man who shot him while fleeing from Henning's apartment was also damning.

Delray's analysis had been straight and to the point. 'Not too many scumbags running around with a broken nose and dozens of fresh stitches on their forehead. This is no coincidence.'

Westcott was eager to get this done. While he wanted justice for Eugene Brennan's murder, his thoughts kept returning to Aaron MacDonald and Robbie Mayne. Both decent men. One was dead, and the other was extremely lucky to still be alive. This had gone on for too long. Westcott felt they had enough evidence now to get criminal convictions.

"Ready, boss."

Both men implicitly knew the role they would play in the interview. They had done this before and would do it again. Delray had full confidence in Westcott and, as usual, was keen for him to take the lead.

Westcott paused before opening the door to the interview room. He wanted to make sure his boss was right behind him when they entered. He burst into the interview room and began his rapid-fire introduction to the interrogation. His strategy was always to get the witness off balance and keep them there if possible until he got what he needed. It was often mentally exhausting, but a uniquely effective way of getting the truth.

"This interview is being recorded by both a video recorder and a separate voice recording system. This is in line with Vancouver Police procedure. You have no right of appeal against this procedure, gentlemen."

Westcott detailed the date and time of the interview for the recording and again appraised both Henning and his lawyer of his rights and the charges. The entire process took several minutes. Delray sat down and watched with some pride as Westcott delivered the monologue with strong and confident precision.

While Henning looked slightly overwhelmed, Phipps sat impassive with a slightly bemused look on his face. When Westcott had finished, Phipps softly clapped. "Bravo, Detective Westcott. Let the record reflect that Vancouver Metro has at least one police officer that can string two sentences together coherently. Should you ever wish to change professions, I have several contacts in the theater. I'm sure they would be keen to see your talents put to better use than they are here."

Phipps adjusted his bow tie as Westcott continued, undeterred. Delray marveled at how Westcott's tone shifted from aggression to almost boredom.

"Rudy, do you know why you're here?"

Phipps shot back, "Of course my client knows why he's here?"

Westcott came and stood on the opposite side of the table to Henning and Phipps. Leaning down and in with his hands pressed to the table, he locked eyes on Henning and continued in a quiet voice.

"Let me break it down for you, Rudi. You're here on one murder charge already and because a cop was shot by an associate during your arrest…"

Phipps shot back, "There is no evidence my client knew the person who discharged a firearm at a police officer. He was as surprised as you."

Delray chuckled. "Give us a break. No one's buying your client did not know someone was hiding in his spare bedroom!"

"No idea at all, inspector. The crime rate is exceptionally high in the neighborhood my client lives in. Break and enters occur all the time."

Westcott kept his hands pressed to the table and his focus on Henning.

"What do you think, Rudy? Is the judge going to buy that? Would you?"

Phipps quickly answered, "Don't answer that, Rudy."

Westcott pulled away from the table and went and sat at the far end of the table with Delray. He drummed his fingers on the table and let a few seconds pass before he continued.

"A cop was shot during your arrest, Rudy. Whether or not you pulled the trigger is irrelevant. Doesn't matter what the man in the fancy suit sitting next to you says, you're not getting bail. We've got a fingerprint on Eugene Brennan's belt buckle that matches yours and a cigarette butt from his balcony with your DNA."

Westcott got up from his chair and began pacing slowly. "You know, Rudy, they also have these new tests for cigarettes now. Saliva tests. We not only know who smoked the cigarette, we also know it was within twelve hours of Brennan's death."

Westcott stopped pacing and looked at Henning. "A six-year-old that can barely spell 'law' could convince a jury you're guilty."

Henning shifted in his seat and would not make eye contact with Westcott. "I've got nothing to say."

Westcott sat down again. "You know, Rudy, it seems to me like you're sitting at the wrong end of the table. You're going down for a long time. Right now, you need friends and looking around this room, we're the closest thing you've got."

Westcott pointed at Phipps. "Your counselor here isn't your friend…"

Phipps was doing his best to look bored and totally disinterested. "Detective, you're wasting our time here. I'm going to have to insist you actually ask some questions, preferably intelligent ones, otherwise we can discuss this at the bail hearing with the judge."

"You see, Rudy, I'm not sure who's funding your legal bill. I know it's not you.

Phipps put his legal notepad back in his leather satchel. "We're done here for today."

"I got a feeling it might be Richard Stelovak."

Westcott and Delray watched both men intensely as Westcott used the word 'Stelovak'. Phipps' face remained impassive, but there was a slight stutter in the motion he used to place his notebook in the satchel. Henning was, by comparison, an open book. While he tried to remain passive, his eyes widened momentarily. It was clear it was a name he knew.

Phipps removed his spectacles. As he began putting them in a leather case, he smiled. "Detective, you're on a fishing expedition and nothing more. This is all getting terribly tedious. The interview is over. We'll see you at the bail hearing and not before. Now, if you don't mind, I'd like to confer with my client in private before I leave."

Delray nodded at Westcott. Westcott looked at Henning. "We'd like to put an offer on the table, Rudy. You sign a full confession and cooperate with our investigation; we'll get your sentence down to fifteen years' and then parole and we'll wave all other charges. You won't be a young man when you get out, but fifteen years for your role in this is a good deal."

Phipps roared with laughter. "I've heard nothing so ridiculous in all my life. We're done here."

Westcott shut off the recording equipment. As he and Delray left the room, Delray turned at the doorway and said, "The offer will not be on the table long, Rudy. We will arrest Vincent Franco shortly. Every cop in the city's looking for him. I'll offer him the same deal. First one to cooperate gets it. No prizes for coming second except an extra ten to fifteen behind bars. You need to think about that."

They closed the door and returned to the observation room to watch the exchange between Phipps and Henning. Neither Westcott nor Delray expected to close the deal today. It was more about planting a seed and getting

Henning thinking. As they looked through the glass, they could see that Phipps was becoming quite animated. They would encourage Henning to waive his right to a lawyer tomorrow.

Delray smiled, "He's thinking. Good work in there, Danny."

Chapter Thirty-Six

Robbie slept solidly for three hours. When he awoke, his throat was still on fire, but his back pain had eased. He decided not to take any more painkillers. He needed to be alert.

He had barely rubbed the sleep out of his eyes before Laura was sitting on his bed and telling him about her conversation with Theo and the discovery that Nick Carney owned the laptop. It did not surprise Robbie that she had made the breakthrough. The years of analysis and investigation she had done at the OCTF were making her invaluable.

It surprised Robbie that Nick was the owner. His first question had been, why? 'Why would he be giving the laptop to Mac to look at?'

Laura and Robbie had discussed this at length. Nick would have access to a number of specialist technical staff at OCTF who would be more than capable of fixing a laptop. They had both agreed it probably contained personal or sensitive information he did not want anyone at OCTF seeing.

Robbie had taken a quick shower to fully wake up. When he emerged from the tiny adjoining bathroom, Laura had his laptop powered up again and reconnected to the Catalin email account.

Robbie shook his head as he pulled up a chair to sit next to Laura. "What are the odds? Nick gets his laptop repaired by the one guy who really knows he's crooked."

"Maybe Nick's not as smart as I thought he was?"

Robbie nodded. "Nick should have known better. Mac was as honest as the day is long."

They opened the first email message again and read it with Nick Carney as the laptop owner.

To: codos9009@proteja.bg From: catalin1989@cybamail.com
Subject: New Address

C

Please use this temporary email address for all future email comms. What I'm doing is illegal here and I can't afford to be seen to be connected. I could get prison time if caught.

Ghost loaded and tested. Laptop was picked up yesterday. I have monitored but nothing of importance yet.

Be careful. I don't think he's suspicious yet, but he's very well connected.

M

Robbie got a pen and started adding to the notes Laura had already made. "So, we now know it was Nick's laptop that Mac was monitoring. Nick was his friend, so he wouldn't do that without good reason."

Laura added, "The email suggests something is going to happen that Nick himself is involved in."

Robbie got up from his chair and paced. "Normally, Mac would go straight to the police."

"Kind of difficult to know who to trust in this situation because Nick is the police, or at least an arm of the police as chief of the OCTF."

Robbie came back and sat beside Laura again and reread the email again. "Look at the last line of the email. Nick is definitely not on his own and Mac is concerned Codos could also be in danger."

Laura frowned. "I wonder if Codos met a similar fate to Mac?"

Robbie swung the laptop around to face him directly and said, "Let's see if we can find out," as he typed a reply.

To: codos9009@proteja.bg From: catalin1989@cybamail.com
Subject: Help?

Codos

I was a close friend of Mac. I'm not sure if you have heard yet, but he was killed in a motor vehicle hit-and-run accident last week. We know it was murder and we are trying to find out who is responsible.

A friend and I stumbled upon this email address and figured out the password. We are positive this is all connected.

Sorry to be telling you like this, but can you help?
Sincerely, Robbie

Robbie looked at Laura. "We may never get a reply. Codos might be long gone if he's heard about Mac or worse, he might also have been murdered. Let's keep going through the emails."

Laura opened up the next email in the sequence.

To: catalin1989@cybamail.com From: codos9009@proteja.bg
Subject: Re: New Address

OK, will use this email for all future comms.

You need to be very careful yourself. If Ghost is discovered, he will know who installed it. Be ready to remotely wipe it if you get suspicious.

Also, contact confirms money has been deposited into the bank accounts detailed in my last email. This is some serious payoff. I needn't tell you what they're capable of if you're identified, particularly with $3M at stake.

Codos

Robbie and Laura were both silent for a while. Laura spoke first. "Nick is involved in something very ugly. Three million dollars in payoffs is a lot of dirty money."

"Mac was taking an enormous risk trying to find out what was going on."

Robbie got up and returned to his pacing. Laura said, "What are you thinking, Robbie?"

"I'm thinking of how I organize a meeting with Nick Carney. My first question to him will be why he felt it necessary to kill my best friend."

Laura refocused her attention on the laptop. She clicked the mouse pad once and then stared almost in disbelief at the screen. "You need to come here, Robbie."

Robbie came and stood behind Laura and looked at the laptop. Laura had closed the message they had been looking at and returned to the main screen for the Catalin email account. There was one new message in the Inbox. It was from Codos.

Chapter Thirty-Seven

Keaton and Franco drove slowly up the laneway behind Blackwell's building. It was just after five thirty p.m. They found a parking spot three buildings down from the rear entrance to where Blackwell had his office. Franco wore a baseball cap pulled low to hide his broken nose and the patchwork of stitches on his forehead.

They had discussed the job on the drive into the city. Neither man was happy with the setup. It was short notice, and they had little time to plan. Franco had not wavered when asked to do the job. The fee was more than double what he normally got and after what happened last night with the Mayne job; he knew he needed to leave town before Vancouver Metro caught up with him. He had barely escaped from Henning's apartment after shooting the cop and knew he wouldn't be so lucky next time. The extra money he earned tonight would allow him to relocate, get a new identity, and live well for many months while he contemplated what he would do next.

For Keaton, what he was about to do was something he would have never thought possible when he first left law school. But times change, he reflected. After the debacle with the Mayne job and Henning getting arrested, he knew he had little choice. He had a feeling he had reached a crossroad in his association with Richard Stelovak. The next week would be very interesting. One more slip and he figured he would be gone one way or another.

Franco parked the car, and they sat and watched the traffic that used the lane way for a few minutes. It was important to get a feel for whether the laneway was likely to be busy or not at this time of day. The last thing they needed was to be blocked in by a delivery truck or some other unexpected event that would delay their departure. It remained quiet, which made Keaton and Franco both breathe a little easier.

They were still concerned about the plain-clothes cop who was stationed out front to monitor Blackwell's movements. They had cruised by his car before coming up the laneway. The cop was still there and looked bored, which suited them fine.

Franco had brought along a portable monitoring device for the bug Stelovak had placed in Blackwell's office. As they sat in the car and listened, so far all they had heard was Blackwell shuffling around and the sound of a shredder working away in the background. They listened for another ten minutes but did not hear any other voices.

Confident that Blackwell was now on his own, Keaton and Franco reviewed the plan one more time. Franco knew this was Keaton's first time being there for the actual hit. Organizing and planning a hit was one thing, but actually carrying it out was quite another. Franco had seen men killed on their first assignment because they had hesitated when it came to actually killing someone in cold blood. Any doubts about what you were doing affected your judgment and response time and typically impacted upon your ability to make the right decision quickly.

Jobs like this rarely went according to plan, and you needed to react quickly and decisively. Franco had observed Keaton in many varied situations. He was almost as cold and calculating as Stelovak. Franco was reasonably sure he could carry out his role.

Franco looked at his watch. "It's almost six. Front and back doors automatically lock at six, so we need to get going. You ready?"

Keaton picked up the document wallet he would use as a ruse to get him in the front door.

"Ready."

They locked the car and walked up to the glass door at the rear entrance of Blackwell's building. Keaton and Franco walked in as if they owned the place. Keaton had changed out of his suit into casual clothes, which allowed him to wear a baseball cap without attracting too much attention. Both men kept their heads down to avoid giving the security cameras anything more than a baseball cap as a facial identifier. They were confident that these precautions would keep their identities hidden.

As they turned to walk into the main foyer of the building, Franco turned left and went into the men's bathroom to wait for Keaton's signal. Keaton continued straight ahead and stopped at the glass door to Blackwell's office. The blinds were only partially closed, and he could see through to the reception area. It was deserted and only lit by one utility light. This was a good start, he thought. Using a handkerchief to prevent leaving fingerprints, Keaton attempted to open the door, but it was locked.

Keaton looked down at his phone and hit refresh on the screen to stop the screen lock engaging. He had a text message ready to send to Franco's phone with a single word message. If the door had been open, he would have pressed send now. Franco would have come in with him straight away. Instead, Keaton removed his cap and knocked quietly on the door. He waited, but no one came. Keaton knocked again, this time louder and longer.

Keaton was just about to knock a third time when Leon Blackwell appeared in the doorway that separated the reception area from the main office. He looked worried and stood his ground. Keaton put on his best smile; pointed at the document wallet he carried and shrugged his shoulders.

"Hey Leon, Richard wants your opinion on these before the contract signing tomorrow."

Leon Blackwell looked worried. Very worried. It was clear to Keaton that arriving here at this time of day dressed in casual clothes and without an appointment was making Blackwell extremely suspicious. As Blackwell stood in the doorway, Keaton could see he was weighing up what to do. Keaton was not sure how Blackwell would react. His worst nightmare was Blackwell refusing him entry and calling the police.

Keaton kept the smile on his face and was relieved when Blackwell started walking towards the front door. Blackwell stopped short of the front door and carefully scanned the building foyer behind Keaton, looking for signs that Keaton was not alone.

Keaton kept the most relaxed smile on his face that he could as Blackwell opened the door. It was important that he gain Blackwell's trust immediately. He needed Blackwell to leave the door open for Franco to get in; otherwise, it was going to be very hard to make it look like a suicide.

"Randolph, I didn't know we had an appointment?"

"Hi Leon. No, we don't. I'm really sorry, but Richard wanted you to take a quick look over these documents ahead of tomorrow's contract signing for Southwest. There are a couple of companies listed he wants some background on and he thought you might be able to help."

Blackwell was not buying Keaton's story. "Couldn't he have just called?"

Keaton chuckled. "Well, Richard has a lot on his mind right now. I've got a date tonight, and it looked like I was going to be stuck there with him until late in the evening. So, between you and me, I volunteered for this to get me out of the office. I'll phone him with an update shortly and have the rest of the night to myself."

Keaton noticed Blackwell relax slightly. He was halfway there. He made a move into the center of the reception area as he said, "So, Leon, the office is awfully quiet. Everyone gone already?"

Blackwell's eyes widened a little, and he stammered as he tried to regain his composure. "I sent them home at five o'clock. I've got carpet cleaners coming in. They should be here any minute."

Keaton smiled. He knew he had Blackwell where he wanted him. "Well, let's get this over with. You've got things to do and I have a lady I don't want to keep waiting."

As Blackwell went to re-lock the door, Keaton called out, "Hey Leon, don't worry about that. Cleaners will be here soon, anyway. This won't take a minute."

Keaton had kept walking as he said this and stopped at the entrance that led through to the main office area. Blackwell looked at the front door, shrugged and then turned and came back towards Keaton. Keaton did a half bow and motioned Blackwell to go through to the office area first.

"Lead the way, Leon. I promise to make this quick."

As Blackwell passed Keaton on his way to his office, Keaton deftly removed his phone from a pocket in his jacket and pressed send on the text message to Franco. He pocketed the phone and then followed Blackwell. They had barely arrived in Blackwell's office before Keaton's phone rang. It was Franco calling as an arranged response to the text message.

Keaton answered the phone. "Hi, Richard. I've just arrived at Leon's office."

Keaton paused and pretended to be listening. He nodded his head occasionally and punctuated the silence with the occasional 'yes' during a ninety-second routine he and Franco had rehearsed earlier. They figured this was all the time Franco would need to get from the men's bathroom into Blackwell's office and up the spiral staircase to the first-floor conference room.

Blackwell could not see the reception area from his office and stayed behind his desk while he waited for Keaton to finish his conversation with Stelovak. Keaton muttered something that sounded like 'hang on', covered his phone with his free hand and looked at Blackwell with an apologetic face.

"Sorry Leon, Richard has asked me a question that, for your sake, I shouldn't answer in front of you. I'm just going to step back into the reception area, if you don't mind?"

Blackwell nodded. He didn't really have much choice. Keaton pretended to talk on the phone for another minute out in the reception area before he called out to Blackwell, "Hey Leon, Richard has a question for you."

Blackwell was over his suspicions and was now irritated, plain and simple. Walking out into the reception area, he found Keaton leaning against the spiral staircase that led to the conference room upstairs. Keaton was listening intently as Blackwell came and stood beside him and waited to be handed the phone. Keaton held one finger in the air to signal to Blackwell to wait a minute. The finger in the air was also the signal to Franco to lower a rope, complete with a noose, from the balcony above to a position just above Blackwell's head.

Keaton and Franco had spent some time rehearsing the next part of the plan. It required both men to have their timing synchronized in order for it to succeed. It had been Franco's idea and his ingenuity in being able to devise a hit to look like a suicide at such short notice had impressed Keaton.

Keaton dropped his finger and said, "Richard, here's Leon."

Keaton handed Leon the phone. As Blackwell took the phone, Franco dropped the noose down even further, so that it was now level to Blackwell's shoulders. Franco had chosen a thick nylon rope and had spent some time working the end knot formation, so it held a relatively round shape, slightly larger than the average size head. Franco had then adjusted the tension in the knot to allow the noose to close quickly and re-tighten properly when weight or tension was reapplied to the knot.

Keaton appreciated Franco's talent. Now it was time to see if it would all work. As Blackwell took the phone, Keaton seized the rope and quickly dropped it over the surprised Blackwell's head.

Before Blackwell could react, Franco pulled the rope tight, and it instantly knotted tightly around Blackwell's

The Catalin Code

throat and prevented him from screaming. Franco then wrapped the other end of the rope around one of the main support poles for the spiral staircase. For a man the size of Franco, it took little effort to pull Blackwell up several feet off the ground.

Keaton watched as Franco tied off the rope. As soon as Franco gave him the thumbs up signal, Keaton quickly moved across and locked the front door and fully closed all the blinds.

Meanwhile, Blackwell had his hands up around his neck, desperately trying to loosen the knot hold of the rope that was now buried deep in his flesh. He tried to yell for help, but with his airway cut off, he barely made a sound. As his face turned crimson and he realized his doom, Blackwell panicked and began kicking wildly to break the rope.

Franco came down the staircase and stood beside Keaton and watched as Blackwell jerked on the end of the rope. As Blackwell's tongue protruded and his eyes rolled back in his head, Franco said, "Good job, Randolph."

Blackwell's thrashing lasted only for a few more seconds. Franco took one last look. He turned to Keaton and said, "He'll pass out any second now, but he won't be clinically dead for another minute or two. I'm going back to get the car. There's nothing more I need to do here."

Franco unlocked the front door and opened it a fraction to check the lobby was clear before leaving. He called back over his shoulder as he walked out, "Don't forget the chair."

Keaton re-locked the front door. He would not need long, but he did not want to take any chances. He went back and looked up at Blackwell. He had stopped struggling and slowly turned on the rope like a hanging ornament in a slight breeze. Reaching out, Keaton gently grasped the sleeve of Blackwell's shirt to stop him from spinning. Blackwell's eyes were now almost fully closed. If he was not actually dead, he was very close.

Keaton whispered, "Hey Leon, no hard feelings," and then withdrew cotton gloves from his coat pocket. Apart from knocking on the door with a finger knuckle, he had touched nothing but the rope. Franco had chosen a special nylon that resisted fingerprints, so until now he had not needed the gloves. After putting the gloves on, he opened up the document wallet and withdrew copies of the photographs Eugene Brennan had taken of Blackwell and his secretary.

Keaton carefully took each photograph and placed them in Blackwell's hand and pressed his thumb and fingers against them to leave fingerprints. Satisfied with the results, Keaton half slid the photos into a plain manila envelope and walked back into Blackwell's office. He left the envelope in plain sight on the middle of Blackwell's desk and walked back out into the reception area.

He went behind the reception desk and retrieved the receptionist's chair and wheeled it over to where Blackwell was hanging. He flipped the chair on its side and engaged the wheel lock button on each wheel. He figured if he was getting ready to put a noose around his neck, he would want the chair as stable as possible before he knocked it over.

Keaton took one last look around. Satisfied that everything had been taken care of, he unlocked and partially opened the front door and checked that the building foyer was still clear. Satisfied that no one was outside, he engaged the door lock and pulled it closed behind him as he left. As he hurried back toward the rear building entrance, his phone rang. It was Franco. He kept walking as he pressed the call answer button.

He rounded the corner to the short walkway that led to

the rear exit and froze in his tracks as he saw the figure of a man looking into the building through the rear glass door. Keaton stared, almost in disbelief, as he locked eyes with the plain-clothes cop who had been stationed out front to watch Blackwell.

Chapter Thirty-Eight

Robbie stood behind Laura's chair and looked over her shoulder as she read the new message from Codos.

"I know Aaron is dead. How do I know you're Robbie Mayne?"

Laura looked up. "We didn't use your last name in the message we sent. How does he know your last name?"

Robbie thought for a moment. "Laura, would you mind typing back for me?"

She kept her gaze on the screen for fear of losing their tenuous connection to Codos. "What do you want to say?"

"Codos, I don't know who you are, but you appear to be a friend. I'm not sure how I can convince you by email. Can I call you?"

Laura keyed in the words almost as fast as Robbie could say them and clicked send. "Hopefully we will get a response as quick as last time."

Robbie put his hands gently on Laura's shoulders. "Here's hoping."

Laura liked the feel of Robbie's touch. It was intimate

and reassuring at the same time. They waited only a few seconds for the response. The inbox refreshed and showed one new message. Laura opened the email and frowned as she read the message.

"What is my sister's name?"

Robbie came around and sat next to Laura. "What kind of question is that?"

Before they thought about it any further, another message arrived in the inbox from Codos. Laura opened the message. It was two words: 'Think hard.'

Robbie repeated the question. "What is my sister's name? It's as if he thinks I know him."

Laura looked at Robbie. "Maybe you do? He knows your last name, and that wasn't in the email."

Robbie thought for a moment. "We assumed Codos was from Bulgaria because he, or she, has a Bulgarian email provider. I don't know anyone in Bulgaria—I've never been there."

"But you have recently met with people from other parts of Eastern Europe?"

Robbie thought for a moment and said, "Yes. I met many people in Eastern Europe as I did research for my latest set of articles."

"Did you meet anyone that was introduced to you as someone's sister?"

"Not that I recall."

Robbie got up and paced again. Laura noticed he seemed to do his best thinking on his feet.

"What are you thinking, Robbie?"

"Whoever Codos is, I must know them, but under a different name. I'm racking my brain to think of someone in Europe that I know, that Mac knew. But no one is coming to mind."

Laura thought for a moment. "Try focusing on the word sister. Do you think Codos means sister in the normal sense, or perhaps he's referring to a friend, or maybe even someone in a religious sense?"

Robbie continued his slow walk back and forth across the motel room. He walked over to the window and looked out at the freeway. It was almost dark now, but Robbie didn't seem to notice.

Laura waited at the laptop. She could not add any value by pacing around as well and let him be.

Without turning around from the window, Robbie murmured, "Afina. A - F - I - N - A."

Without asking who Afina was, Laura typed the one-word reply and clicked send. Moments later, a reply came back from Codos.

Laura frowned. "Robbie, this question is as strange as the last one."

'What's my mode of transport?'

Still looking out the window, Robbie replied softly, "Wheelchair."

Laura keyed in the one-word response and hit send. "I'm really confused, Robbie. What is this all about?"

Robbie continued to stare out the window. "Short answer is, Mac was killed trying to protect me."

Chapter Thirty-Nine

Franco sat in the driver's seat of the car, waiting for Keaton to emerge from the building. He was pleased with how well the job had gone. They were not home free yet, but the worst was over.

Franco checked the rear-view mirror. Everything in the laneway behind him looked quiet. He switched his gaze forward and looked through the windscreen to the laneway in front of him. It was quiet as well.

Keaton had done well, he thought. Very cool under pressure. He was a natural at this kind of work.

As Franco continued to scan front and back, he kept returning his gaze to the car parked directly in front of him. Something bothered him about the car, but he had not figured out what. It was a current model gray Ford sedan. There were thousands of them on the road here in Vancouver alone and nothing special about this make or model, yet he remained uneasy.

As he focused on the car, he realized the car had not been parked there when he and Keaton had arrived earlier.

Maybe it was simply that, he thought? Looking at his watch, he figured Keaton should be out any minute. Franco put the key in the ignition. Instinct was telling him to leave as soon as possible. As he went to start the car, he realized what troubled him. The car in front was almost identical to the car the plain-clothes cop was stationed in out front of Blackwell's building.

Franco got out of his car and sidled up alongside the vehicle and stared in through the window. He swore softly as his gaze settled on an in-car computer and 2-way radio. He had been in enough police cars to know what he was looking at. Franco returned to his car and started the engine. Keaton needed to get back here now. Reaching for his phone, he looked up the laneway and saw the plain-clothes cop from out front making his way up the laneway. The cop was looking up at the top of each building as he walked.

Franco knew the cop was looking for the building Blackwell was in. Blackwell was housed in a building that was three floors taller than the other buildings that surrounded it. It would be easy to spot when looking up at the skyline like the cop was.

As he pressed speed dial on his phone, Franco watched as the cop reached the back of the Blackwell building and placed his face up against the rear glass door to look inside. His call was answered moments later. In a low, calm voice, Franco gave Keaton instructions. "Stay put and don't come to the back door. You've got company."

Franco dropped the phone into his lap, pulled his cap even lower and eased out of the parking spot. He drove slowly past the cop, who still had his face pressed to the glass. He would worry about Keaton shortly. Right now, he needed to get out of the laneway. This was no place to be identified by a cop. It could quickly turn ugly in such a confined space if he was spotted.

Franco drove for three blocks and then pulled into a side street. Keeping his eyes focused on his rear-view mirror, he waited for several minutes with the engine running before calling Keaton back. Satisfied he had not been followed, Franco switched the engine off and hit speed dial.

Keaton answered on the second ring. "What's going on, Vince? I almost get to the rear door and the cop that was out front is eyeballing me."

Franco sensed this was going to turn bad. Self-preservation kicked in. "Where are you now?"

"Holed up in the men's room. I haven't moved. I've been waiting for your call. Is the cop still there?"

"I think we had a shift change. I got back to the car to find a plain Ford parked directly in front of us and the cop walking back up the laneway. I think whoever took over from him parked there and walked around to the front rather than trying to swap cars over out front in all that traffic."

"Fine, Vince, we can talk about that later. All I want to know right now is, has the cop left? Is it safe to leave?"

Franco looked in the rear-view mirror. "I'm not sure. I couldn't afford to hang around in case they identified me. I'm parked three blocks away."

Franco could hear Keaton curse under his breath before he added, "I'm going to check the rear door. Hopefully, he's gone. Hang on a minute."

Franco waited a moment before Keaton added, "It looks clear. I'm going to check outside. Hang on."

Keaton peered up and down the laneway. It appeared empty and the gray Ford was nowhere to be seen. Taking this as a good sign, he opened the rear door and half stepped outside. As soon as the door closed, he knew it would self-lock. As a precaution, he kept a foot in the door just in case he needed to get back inside.

"It looks clear, Vince. The gray Ford has gone."

Keaton waited for Franco's response, but the phone was silent. He looked down at the screen and realized he had been disconnected. Keaton quickly hit speed dial and waited for Franco to answer. But after the preset number of rings, the call went through to voice mail.

Keaton cursed under his breath as he hurriedly made his way towards the end of the laneway. He needed to get out of here fast, just in case the cop was going for backup. He dialed Franco's number twice more, but got the message service both times. Keaton shook his head and smiled grimly to himself. He was on his own, plain and simple. Franco had abandoned him.

As he reached the end of the laneway, Keaton put the phone back in his jacket pocket. He had no idea where he would go right now, but he figured walking in the opposite direction to the main road where the cop car had been parked was a good start.

He needed time to think. Stelovak would not tolerate any more excuses. He needed to plan an exit strategy, and fast. He had not gone very far when his phone buzzed. He pulled it out of his pocket and looked at the caller ID, hoping it was Franco finally calling back. The day just went from bad to worse for Keaton. It was Richard Stelovak.

Chapter Forty

Laura looked down at the laptop screen. "Robbie, there's another message from Codos. It's longer. You should probably come here and read it."

Robbie left the window and came and sat beside Laura. They read the message together.

To: catalin1989@cybamail.com From: codos9009@proteja.bg
  Subject: re: Help?

Robbie, I was very sorry to hear about Aaron. He was a good man. You should know it's bad here as well. Nicolai was found yesterday, floating in a river with a bullet hole in the back of his head. They have come for me as well, but I managed to escape.

  I'm sleeping in a warehouse at present and keeping away from my friends for fear I will get them killed too. I'm currently piggy backing a Wi-Fi connection but won't be able to communicate much longer as my battery is almost dead.

  You need to be very careful. The list is what they are after.
  Petru

Robbie quickly typed and sent another reply.

*To: codos9009@proteja.bg From: catalin1989@cybamail.com
Subject: re: re: Help?*

P I'm really sorry to hear about Nicolai. Let's hope we can get through this alive. Let me know when we can talk in person. Do you need money? If so send me your bank details. R

Laura and Robbie received a brief reply from Petru with bank account details, a thank you and a promise to communicate again tomorrow.

Robbie looked at Laura. "His real name is Petru. Codos must be some sort of code name or alias he's using to protect his identity. He's in a wheelchair. I'll explain all that later. He's from Romania and is, or I should say was, one of the best computer hackers in Eastern Europe. When I went on the last research trip to Europe, I was originally trying to gather information on cyber crime for the feature article I was writing. I asked Mac if he knew anyone over there that could help. He put me in touch with two guys in Romania. Petru and Nicolai. They were both very good computer hackers and had both been heavily involved in organized crime."

"Okay, this is all making sense," said Laura with a nod.

"Petru had a sister called Afina. She disappeared not long after her seventeenth birthday. Petru searched for months but could not find her. Eventually, he got word that she was being sold as a sex slave, ironically by members of the same organization he worked for."

"Wow!"

"He went looking for her, but he was four days too late. They had her addicted to drugs and she was shot trying to escape. Petru confronted the head guy in the syndicate and a gunfight broke out. Petru was shot in the spine and almost died. He spent months in the hospital and had several operations to try to get him walking again. But they weren't successful."

"Hence the wheelchair."

Robbie let out a long breath. "Petru never went back to the syndicate. Normally, you can't leave—they simply track you down and kill you. When I met up with him, he said the wheelchair kept him alive. Word soon got around after he got out of hospital that he would never walk again, and they lost interest in pursuing him. Nicolai also hated the syndicate for what happened. His sister also got caught up in the organization and he vowed to do whatever they could to bring it down. He worked at their bank and pretended to still be a loyal, but he was secretly working as an informer for Interpol."

Laura frowned. "The organized crime gang has their own bank?"

"Yes, the Roma Bank. This is where the list comes in. The list that I'm positive Mac wanted to warn me about that got him killed." Robbie leaned back and stretched. "I need a break. Are you hungry? I could do with some fresh air and some food as soon as I've transferred some money to Petru."

Laura half smiled. "Sounds great, Robbie. We could both do with a break. I'll grab a quick shower and be ready in five."

Laura and Robbie discovered they both had a love for authentic Mexican food as they searched through the local restaurant guide provided by the motel for a suitable place to eat. The closest Mexican restaurant was twelve blocks away and hardly local, but they were both keen for a walk and some fresh air; so Mexican, it was. They walked the first block hand in hand, enjoying the reprieve from the confines of the motel room.

As they walked, Robbie said, "I'm not sure where to start. This is definitely all connected to my last trip to East Europe. Mac and I talked on the phone before I left. He had developed a number of contacts over there in computer security and told me about Petru. Mac and Petru had become good friends online, so much so that he was trying to get Petru out of Romania for good. Mac said who better for me to talk to about international credit card scams than someone who used to make a very good living from it."

"No one could have imagined it turning out like this, Robbie."

Robbie shook his head. "When I met up with Petru and Nicolai, Nicolai told me he mostly worked on the bank's security systems. He was using his elevated access to compile a list for Interpol of organized crime groups and individuals who were using the bank to launder money. The list wasn't complete yet, but he gave me a copy of what he had. It was mostly groups and some individuals who were using the bank to launder money. Some of them are even located here in Canada."

Laura's eyes widened. "Have you been through the list yet?"

"I looked at it briefly back at the hotel after the meeting. It made little sense. Bank account numbers, mainly for holding companies and their transaction records. There are huge sums of money being moved illegally between the two countries. Nicolai was working on the inside, slowly gathering information on the real client identities. This is what Interpol needed to act on. He had gotten as far as providing some aliases on the list he gave me, but figured he needed several more months of patient and careful investigation before he could really name names."

"Several months he never got."

Robbie grimaced. "Before I flew home, I spoke to a colleague back here who specializes in financial analysis about helping me make sense of the list. I emailed him the raw data, and he was confident we had enough to go on. He warned me then that it was potentially dangerous having this kind of information in my possession, but I thought little of it. I planned to look at it more closely when I got back, but… I got the call about Mac as soon as I got off the plane and haven't had a chance to take it further yet."

Robbie stopped walking and added, "This has to be more than just Nick. There are people here who have to be very nervous about being exposed. They are obviously prepared to go to extreme lengths to protect their identity, but I'm not stopping."

As Laura's gaze focused on him, Robbie momentarily lost concentration. She was wearing her hair, still slightly damp from her shower, pulled back off her face in a simple ponytail. With tiny wisps of her hair moving gently in the evening breeze, she still looked amazing in a pair of plain Levi jeans and a windbreaker. It wasn't just her physical beauty or the chemistry between them that attracted him. Robbie already knew that what they had was a far deeper bond—a bond being built on trust and shared experience. It was the same bond that he found he had formed with Annie after only knowing her for a few days.

Robbie paused for a moment. He was not sure how to

say what he felt he needed to say next. "Laura, a lot has happened these past few days... most of it is a nightmare."

Laura said, "Most?" with a half smile.

"When I lost Annie, I... never imagined I would find anyone else. Someone special like that is a once in a lifetime gift."

Robbie paused again before continuing, "I think I was wrong. I'm now thinking maybe it can happen twice?"

Laura bit down on her lip and then put her arms around Robbie and her face to his chest. "Robbie, I put mascara on a few minutes ago. If you expect me to respond to that now and tell you how I feel, it's going to run everywhere. If it's okay with you, I'd like to take a rain check at least until after we've left the restaurant. Then my mascara won't matter. Deal?"

Robbie smiled, and then gently kissed her. "Deal."

As they continued walking, Robbie added, "I'm going to confront Nick tomorrow. He gets one chance to explain himself and one chance only. I would more than understand if you wanted out, Laura."

"I'm not a quitter, Robbie. We're in this together. To be honest, I think it may be the only way we survive."

Laura was quiet for a moment and then said, "We need a plan. If Nick has tried to have you killed once, he won't stop. Take it from someone with experience; he survived the scandal at the OCTF not because he was clean, but because he was cunning and ruthless. He will use every situation and every opportunity to his advantage until you're dead."

Robbie grimaced. "You're right. We need a plan."

Chapter Forty-One

Keaton walked four blocks, thinking through his next move before he hailed a cab to take him home. Richard Stelovak had called once more, but he had ignored that call as well. Keaton had hoped Franco would call back to come and pick him up, but the further he had walked, the more he realized that would not happen.

The walking gave him time to think, and he decided tonight would be his last night in Vancouver. After being seen by the cop as he was about to leave Blackwell's building, he realized the game was up. Eventually, he would be questioned and then most likely charged in connection with Blackwell's death. Right now, Vancouver Metro was the least of his problems. His immediate concern was the repercussions from Richard Stelovak.

After the botched attempt on Mayne and now being seen by a cop in Blackwell's building, Keaton knew Stelovak would not tolerate any more excuses. He knew he needed to stay one step ahead of him to stay alive.

When the cab got within a block of the complex where

he lived, Keaton instructed the driver to cruise by slowly. He did not expect to see Franco or any other welcoming committee yet, but it always paid to be cautious. After circling the block twice, he was satisfied that everything was clear for the moment.

It was after eight p.m. by the time he keyed his PIN number into the security panel for his apartment to disengage the alarm. He would have liked nothing better than a hot shower; some smooth jazz and a few single malt whiskeys to take the edge off the day, but that was just a pipe dream.

Keaton had a sophisticated alarm system and pressed a button on the control pad to view the last ten entries in the system's security log. He breathed a sigh of relief as the log showed no one had been in his apartment since he had left early that morning.

Keaton hesitated as he went to turn on the internal lights to his apartment. He stood in the foyer in the darkness, thinking what to do next. He clearly needed to pack and leave in a hurry. After ignoring two of Stelovak's calls, he was fairly sure Stelovak would have contacted Franco by now. He was also fairly sure Franco would have ratted him out. Stelovak would by now be in the first throes of planning a retirement package for him. He had seen Stelovak's idea of retirement up close and personal. It generally involved a bullet to the head and a hole in the ground—things he was keen to avoid.

He decided not to use the lights. He figured he had a couple of hours at most before Stelovak got a crew organized and maybe not even that long. He would pack several changes of clothes, but the main thing he needed was his money. During his tenure with Richard Stelovak, he had managed to save or graft close to a quarter of a million dollars in cash, which he kept in a safe in the apartment. It was risky keeping this much money close by, but it allowed him to walk away permanently at a moment's notice. It turned out to be a risk worth taking.

As he stood in the foyer and let his eyes adjust to the dimness, he mapped out where he needed to go in his apartment before he moved. Leaving the lights off might just save his life. If Stelovak had moved quickly and a crew was already close by observing, lights coming on would be the signal he had arrived home.

Keaton walked silently through his apartment to the main bedroom. There was just enough light to navigate without bumping into furniture. He quickly located an overnight bag and packed a few essentials. At the back of his walk-in-robe was a set of floor to ceiling drawers for socks and underwear. Keaton removed the third drawer from the bottom to reveal a small safe built into the rear wall of his apartment. He turned on his mobile phone and shone the light into the cavity to give him the light required. It put a glow throughout the robe, but Keaton had closed the door to the main bedroom area to avoid telegraphing to anyone watching outside that someone was home.

The safe had an old-fashioned rotation dial and, with a practiced hand, he had it open in a matter of seconds. Keaton pulled out a plastic box and removed the lid. He quickly counted the money more out of habit than anything else. It was all there. He allowed himself a brief smile. This was his ticket out.

Keaton closed the safe and put the drawer back. He put the money in his overnight bag and zipped it tightly shut. He walked back into the living room and fully opened every curtain before heading to the foyer. He paused as he passed his heavy mahogany coffee table and picked up a small custom-made remote control, which he planned to use in a few minutes. He did not reset the alarm as he opened the front door. It was important to give the appearance that he was at home. Keaton was not at all sentimental and locked the front door and made his way to the elevator without looking back.

Using the side entrance to leave his apartment complex, he hurried away from the lit area around the building and stood for a few moments under some shade trees in a landscaped garden area at the side of the complex.

Keaton's car was still in the underground parking lot at Stelecom headquarters. He decided he would use a taxi for now and figure out tomorrow what to do about transport in the longer term. While he had unfinished business at Stelecom, picking up his car was not on the list. Even if his security access had not been revoked yet, it was too risky driving around in his own car, just in case an alert cop spotted him.

Looking at his watch, Keaton made a quick calculation. He knew it was not smart to stay here for long. What he needed to do at Stelecom, he could not do before eight in the morning, which was still eleven hours away. He needed to get away from the complex now to avoid any risk of being seen by the retirement committee he felt sure Stelovak would send.

Keaton looked across the street at the apartment complex that was directly opposite to where he lived. Both complexes were very upmarket and sat at the end of a street that backed onto the Fraser River. The complex across the road was mainly glass and steel. Keaton didn't like it much. Its official title was the 'Glass House', but Keaton had always thought it looked more like a fancy five story fish bowl, rather than an elegant residential complex that people would want to live in. Tonight, however, the building held some attraction for him as he thought about how he might use it to his advantage.

Taking the custom remote control from his pocket, Keaton walked briskly around to the front of his complex. Rather than calling a cab right now, he crossed the street. As he reached the curb, he paused momentarily and pointed the remote towards his apartment and pressed one of the four buttons on the control panel. Keaton's top-floor apartment was on the front left side of the complex with views across the street and the river. In an instant, the dark apartment transformed, as all main living area lights came on.

Keaton smiled to himself. With the lights on and the curtains open, he was doing his best to signal to anyone watching that he was now home. He quickly crossed the road and then strolled along the footpath out front of the Glass House complex. A jogger appeared moments later and appeared to be slowing down and moving towards the front doors.

Turning as casually as he could, Keaton made his way to the front entrance and timed his walk so that he arrived just after the jogger did. The jogger swiped his security card to open the front glass doors to the building and then held his hand out, beckoning Keaton to go first. So much for building security, Keaton thought as he took the jogger up on his offer and walked into the building.

Keaton immediately walked across the foyer to the front internal stairwell. Even though the complex had four elevators, the stairwell was what he needed tonight. The stairwell, like the rest of the building, was a large ostentatious construction of glass and steel. In Keaton's mind, it had one redeeming feature only; an uninterrupted view across the street to his apartment. He slowly made his way up the stairs, watching the entire time for any signs of activity in his apartment.

When he reached the fifth floor, he settled into a small alcove next to the stairs. The alcove was filled with plants and shielded him reasonably well from anyone using the elevators, while providing him with a clear view across the street.

Keaton watched his apartment for well over an hour and was starting to cramp up. He did not have the patience of some of the hit men he had worked with. They would occasionally brag about spending days in one cramped location waiting for their target and the right opportunity. He looked at his watch and decided to give it one more hour. More than anything, he wanted to see how quickly Richard Stelovak would react and what that reaction would be. Understanding this would be helpful to him as he figured out his strategy for tomorrow.

He only had to wait another fifteen minutes before he had his answer.

Chapter Forty-Two

Delray looked at his watch. It was almost nine thirty p.m. Westcott would return momentarily; he thought. He watched as the forensic photographer took his final shots of Leon Blackwell, whose lifeless body still hung from the rope. The photos would be far from pretty. Blackwell's head had swollen considerably from the strangulation. His face had turned a purple-blue color through lack of oxygen and was spotted with red marks from burst blood capillaries. All this combined with a distended tongue made him difficult to recognize. It was a grisly scene and Blackwell was long past, being photogenic.

The photographer gave a nod to Delray. "Finished here for now. We'll get the rest of the shots we need during the autopsy."

Delray thanked the photographer and returned his gaze to Blackwell. He grimaced and murmured, "What a mess."

He could not remember a time in his career where so many murders had happened in such a short space of time. He cursed himself for not putting more of his already stretched resources into minding Blackwell. Delray was officially counting Aaron MacDonald as a murder now, and with the Brennan and now Blackwell murders, his stretched team had added three cases to its load this week alone. Having McKenzie in the hospital didn't help matters, either. It had been a rough week and was not about to get any easier.

Delray had dismissed the idea of Leon Blackwell's death being a suicide soon after arriving at the crime scene. It had been Blackwell's wife, who had called in Blackwell's murder to Vancouver Metro at close to seven p.m. Delray and his team were getting ready to call it a day after another grueling twelve-hour shift when the call came through. Blackwell had been under his authorized surveillance, and he and Westcott had responded immediately.

Westcott was currently finishing up taking Blackwell's wife's statement. Delray had sat in on the first ten minutes of the interview and had found her to be refreshingly candid. She knew what her husband did as an accountant was 'not entirely legal' and they both had become increasingly worried about his long-term safety. They had been planning their departure from Vancouver for several months and everything was in readiness to leave at the end of the month. Blackwell had not told his wife exactly what the catalyst was for leaving tonight, but she did not care. She was just relieved it was all coming to an end.

When Blackwell had failed to show in the laneway behind his office building at six thirty as arranged, she had tried calling both his mobile and office phone numbers without success.

Delray and Westcott had felt very sorry for her as she explained how she had parked her car and gone to his office to find out what was taking him so long. She broke down and sobbed uncontrollably as she recounted walking in with her two children to find him hanging from a rope.

It was clear to Delray that someone did not want him leaving. Delray and Westcott had fast tracked Richard Stelovak to the top of the list of suspects. Because most of his work was illegal and highly specialized, Blackwell only had a small, exclusive group of clients. The research Westcott had done since Brennan's murder showed a number of companies Stelovak had an interest in, all appearing on Blackwell's client list. While there was no direct connection back to Eugene Brennan's murder yet, it was too coincidental that both the photographer and the subject of his blackmail photo shoot were now both dead.

Delray shook his head as he looked at Blackwell hanging lifelessly on the rope. "You should have taken the deal, Leon. You'd still be alive if you had."

"Boss."

Delray turned to see his detective coming back into the reception area.

"How did it go?"

Westcott pursed his lips and shook his head.

"Not great. I feel so sorry for her. She had no idea about the photos or any association with Eugene Brennan. I asked her about Richard Stelovak and she immediately became very agitated. She wouldn't say much. I think she has fears for her and her kid's safety right now. She did, however, reluctantly confirm that he was a client of Blackwell and was not to be trusted. She also said that Randolph Keaton was the primary contact Blackwell had with Stelovak's company. Keaton, in his capacity as Stelovak's principal legal advisor, does most of the work on behalf of Stelovak and, to quote Mrs. Blackwell, 'He's another A grade creep just like his boss'."

Delray nodded and let out a long sigh. He pointed to Blackwell's office before continuing. "So, what's it like in there?"

"A lot of files have already been shredded, but there are still about three boxes he hadn't done before he was interrupted. I've got two analysts on it now, but it may be days before we really know if we've got anything solid from it. Most of the files relate to shelf companies. Notes and notations seem to be written in code. Leon was very particular not to leave a paper trail. I think our best chance is a witness or crime scene DNA."

Delray nodded and looked Westcott up and down. He had pulled a lot of hours this week already. "Danny, I don't want you to be here all night, okay? As soon as the crime scene techs have finished the preliminary examination and the coroner has collected the body, wrap it up for the night and go home. You need sleep and this will still all be here in the morning."

"Thanks, boss. There's only one other loose end I want to tie off tonight."

"And what's that?"

"Coleman. Toward the end of his surveillance shift today, he got a little curious. All Blackwell's employees left the underground parking lot at five p.m. He did a shift change with Simpson at six. Simpson parked out back in the laneway and as Coleman came up the laneway to get the car, he was still curious about why everyone left right on five. He came to the rear entrance to do a spot check, but it was locked. He looked in through the window before going to his car and saw a guy walking out of an office. The guy spotted Coleman and ducked into the men's bathroom, almost as if to avoid being seen."

Delray scratched his chin. "You might be onto something there."

"We haven't got an accurate time of death yet, but it has to be somewhere after five and before six thirty. Coleman comes up the lane way just after six, so the timing is good. Coleman didn't think too much of it until Simpson called half an hour ago to let him know what happened. He's coming back in. He didn't recognize the guy but got a very good look at his face. I've got file photos in the car of all the known suspects to show him."

"You never know, Danny."

"Coleman was confident, boss. He said if we have the guy on file, he'll recognize him."

Delray allowed himself half a smile. "With a little luck, things might start to unravel for Richard Stelovak."

Chapter Forty-Three

Keaton watched from his vantage point as two men walked casually up the street and stopped out front of his apartment complex. Even though he was five floors up, he recognized one of the two men immediately.

The metal bridge supporting Vincent Franco's broken nose stood out like a neon sign. With Henning in jail, Franco had moved quickly to organize another partner. Keaton did not recognize the other man, but he knew he could also be a cold-blooded killer if the price was right.

As the two men stood together smoking, they pretended to be just engaged in casual conservation, but it was clear to Keaton they were scoping his apartment complex for entry and exit points. He almost laughed as he thought of the irony. Hours ago, he and Franco had been partners and now he was the target.

After several minutes, Franco extinguished his cigarette and disappeared down the driveway to the side entrance of the complex. The man Keaton did not recognize stayed out front and continued smoking and doing his best to look casual and relaxed.

Franco emerged several minutes later and strolled back to his partner. They both lit fresh cigarettes and continued their conversation. Occasionally, they would turn and casually glance up at Keaton's apartment. After several more minutes, the two men split up again. Franco headed back down the driveway to the side entrance again, while the other man walked a short distance before stopping and lighting a third cigarette.

Keaton could tell from his position that the other man now had a full view of both the front and side entrances. Keaton assumed the rear section of the complex, which opened onto a visitor parking lot, was intentionally left unguarded. A high security fence surrounded the building and there was no exit via the driveway that was now covered. Good plan, thought Keaton. Franco had you covered if you got out of the apartment alive and tried to escape by car or on foot.

The unknown man held his position and did not move except to light, smoke, and extinguish cigarettes. Keaton quickly became bored watching him and returned his gaze to his apartment. He did not have to wait long before the familiar face of Vincent Franco appeared, cautiously moving through his living room. He watched with amusement as Franco moved around the apartment with what looked like a Heckler and Koch pistol fitted with a silencer in his right hand. No attempt to feign a suicide here, he thought.

Franco disappeared from his view as he searched the rest of the apartment. After almost five minutes, Franco returned to the living room. A mobile phone, which he was currently using, had replaced the pistol. Keaton looked down at the unknown man in front of the complex. He still had a cigarette in one hand but was now holding a mobile phone in the other and also involved in deep conversation.

Keaton laughed softly. "The cupboard is bare gentlemen. What are we going to do now?"

He watched with amusement as Franco paced backwards and forwards across his living room for several minutes, in deep conversation with the man downstairs. Keaton switched his gaze to Franco's associate. He was not pacing, but he was still smoking while he talked to Franco. He figured the man was now on his sixth or seventh cigarette.

It was time to leave, Keaton thought. He had the information he needed, and nothing could be gained by staying here any longer. He was not surprised that Stelovak had acted quickly and decisively. Stelovak now considered him expendable, and that was fine with him. What he had observed tonight was useful information for what he had planned for tomorrow.

Franco and his partner continued their conversation as Franco came and stood at the front window of Keaton's living room and looked down at his associate. Franco continued talking as his gaze moved up from the street to the complex Keaton was now observing them from. Keaton could not be sure, but he had an uneasy feeling that he may have been spotted by Franco as he moved away from the window and went back to pacing and talking on the phone. Franco had paused momentarily as his gaze had focused on the floor he now occupied. He had the information he needed. There was no sense hanging around, just in case.

Keaton decided he should use the rear exit to avoid Franco's associate. He took one more look down at the street, but the man was no longer there. Keaton cursed as he looked back at his apartment to see Franco rushing toward his front door.

It was too much of a coincidence. Keaton cursed as he realized he had been spotted. As he quickly headed for the rear stairs, he pressed the elevator call button as he passed the elevators. The seconds that passed while he waited for the elevator to arrive seemed like an eternity. Keaton forced himself to breathe deeply and slowly to avoid panic setting in. Panic would get him killed for sure.

Breathing a sigh of relief as the elevator bell sounded and the elevator doors opened, Keaton reached in and pressed the button for the second floor. As the elevator closed and headed for the second floor, Keaton headed for the rear stairs. He concentrated on being as quiet as possible. Speed down the stairs was important, but silence was more important. He quickly descended to floor three and waited before proceeding down further. He hoped the ruse would work.

As the elevator stopped and opened on floor two, Keaton heard the heavy fall of footsteps coming up the rear stairwell. It looked like the man had fallen for his deception. Keaton held his breath as he saw the man, gun drawn, exit the stairwell on the level below him at speed. He figured he had a minute at most to get down and out of the building while the man checked level two for possible places where he could be hiding.

Quickly descending the remaining stairs, Keaton was gambling on Franco, taking longer than he had to get down and out of his apartment complex and then across the street. Keaton paused briefly at the bottom of the rear stairwell and looked toward the front foyer area for any sign of the hit-man. It was clear for the moment, which made him uneasy. He would have preferred to know exactly where

Franco was before he left the building, but he could not afford to wait. Franco's associate would soon realize he had been duped and would be back down momentarily.

Keaton partially opened the heavy steel door that served as the rear exit to the building before exiting. Unlike the front of the Glass House complex, the rest of the building was constructed with concrete and steel and afforded no view outside. He could not see Franco and decided it was now or never.

Slipping out the rear door, he turned left and made his way quickly along the rear wall of the building. As he reached the corner of the building, he slowed down to check that Franco was not waiting around the corner. As he paused, he heard a low staccato thud from behind him as the rear wall of the complex exploded in a shower of concrete shards near his right shoulder.

Time seemed to slow down for Keaton. The time it took for his brain to register that Franco was behind him and not waiting around the corner of the building could be measured in microseconds. Keaton's reaction time was quick, but not quick enough. As adrenaline coursed through his body and his brain transmitted signals to his legs to flee, he felt a searing pain high on his right bicep as a second bullet sheared more concrete shards from the rear wall.

Keaton was around the corner of the building and halfway to the street, running faster than he could ever recall in his life before he fully realized he had been hit. Without a weapon of his own, he had no option but to run. As he reached the street, he thought he heard another thud from Franco's silenced pistol, but he could not be sure.

Having no time to think through his options, Keaton started running up the street away from the river and towards the neighboring residential complex. This complex was smaller and less elaborate than the Glass House and he hoped offered a path through the rear section of the property to the adjoining street.

Keaton ran up the driveway and around to the back of the complex at full speed. He cursed as the rear security fence of the complex came into view. It was close to ten feet in height and fully surrounded the rear of the property. There was no way out. As he heard the heavy footfall of Franco running up the driveway, he realized he was trapped.

With one brief one eighty-degree scan of the area, he knew he only had one option. Parked next to the rear security fence were three vehicles, the closest of which was a Ford F350 pickup truck. It had an open cargo area and was backed up next to the rear fence. Keaton hoped his deception would work. With his good arm, he tossed his overnight bag at the fence next to the rear of the vehicle and then quickly ran for cover behind a Toyota van parked up against the rear wall of the building.

The pain in his bicep was now intense, but Keaton blocked it out of his mind as he eased himself under the vehicle and out of sight. Franco's footsteps grew louder and closer until they stopped next to the van he lay under. Keaton had a perfect view of Franco's feet from his vantage point. He could have almost reached out and grabbed Franco's leg. He did his best to control his breathing. While he did regular workouts in the gym, he did little running and was still gasping for air. He could hear Franco's labored breathing above his own and realized Franco was in the same position, if not worse.

He knew the next sixty seconds would probably determine whether he lived or died. If Franco started checking under cars, he was as good as dead. Franco remained in the same spot for almost thirty seconds. Keaton could see Franco's feet slowly moving in a three sixty-degree arc as he did a full scan of the rear area of the complex.

Franco then stopped moving all together. Keaton was not sure what he was doing. Franco may have been getting ready to bend over and plug him full of holes, or may have simply been listening for a clue as to where his quarry might be. Keaton had to admire the man. Franco never panicked.

Keaton focused his energy on the bag. He didn't believe in telepathy but willed his thoughts to be picked up by Franco; 'Look for the bag, Vince. Look at the fence.'

He knew the longer Franco remained by the van, the more likely it was that he would be discovered. If Franco's associate showed up, it would be much easier to do a systematic search of the area, and he knew it would be over.

Franco's feet shuffled two steps away from the van towards the car parked in the adjacent parking space before stopping. To Keaton's dismay, Franco bent down and started looking under that car. The Adrenalin coursed rapidly through Keaton's system and he thought his heart was going to explode through his chest. Keaton could see Franco shuffling backward and forward just a few feet from him as he checked under the other car for signs of his presence.

Franco muttered softly to himself. Keaton could not discern exactly what he said, but he appeared to be struggling with the dim light. Franco straightened up again. Now or never, thought Keaton.

Keaton held his breath as he waited for Franco's next move. He saw Franco's feet move again. He began breathing again as he watched Franco move away from the van and towards the F350. He knew he was a long way from being safe, but he allowed himself to feel a glimmer of hope as Franco closed in on his overnight bag.

The Catalin Code

He watched as Franco leaned down and picked up the bag. He could only see the bottom half of Franco's body from his position under the van and watched as the hit-man walked around to the front of the F350 and stopped. The feet shuffled momentarily, and Keaton heard a soft clunk of metal on metal. Franco has placed his gun on the bonnet of the F350 to make it easier to search his bag, he thought.

Keaton heard the unmistakable sound of the zip as his bag was opened. Everything went quiet for a moment before Franco let out a low whistle. Keaton had not heard Franco whistle before, but it had a low satisfying tone. He's found my money, he thought. He silently cursed himself for not splitting his money up and carrying at least some of it on his person.

He waited and watched. There was little movement in Franco's legs or feet for over a minute. Keaton knew he was counting his money. Franco then broke the stillness by talking on his phone again.

"Where are you?"

A silence followed before Franco continued. "I'm in the apartment block next to the Glass House. Around the back in the parking lot. He's used a truck near the fence to get over the wall. Left his bag behind."

Another silence followed.

"No, we call it off. We can't afford to be running around the streets after him. We'll call Stelovak when we're in the car and keep it simple. We checked his apartment. He's been and gone. No clues as to where he went. We don't mention what happened here, end of story."

More silence followed. Franco then barked, "Look, you still get your money. Keaton was a bonus, nothing more. You put me up tonight and get me out to Tyson's by six-tomorrow night as planned and you get your money. Nothing's changed and you know I'm good for it. Now get the car and meet me out front. Last thing we need is some nosy resident calling this in."

Silence descended on the parking lot again. Keaton watched Franco as best he could to see what he would do next and flinched as his overnight bag was dropped to the ground next to the F350. He watched as Franco walked quickly away from the vehicle, and to his relief, back up the driveway to the front of the complex.

Keaton remained motionless under the car. Franco was not beyond deception of his own, and he decided he would wait a while before he got out from under the car. His whole arm and shoulder were on fire from the pain of the bullet wound. He reached out with his good arm and touched the bad shoulder. It was wet and sticky with congealing blood. It did not appear to him to be still bleeding, at least not badly, and he hoped it was not much more than a flesh wound that would heal itself.

His self-examination was interrupted by the sound of a car pulling up out front and a door being opened. Keaton thought he heard two male voices as the car door closed and the car sped away. Keaton let out a long sigh. Maybe, just maybe, he was going to survive. He waited another five minutes before crawling out from under the car. He scanned the parking lot but did not see anyone. He was reasonably confident that he was alone now, but still moved cautiously across the lot to retrieve his bag.

After picking up the bag, Keaton opened it up and checked the contents. The plastic box he had his money in was still there, but the money was gone. Keaton felt numb as he realized he was now down to a few hundred dollars in cash he carried in his wallet. He quickly checked the rest of the bag's contents. His clothes and the other essentials he had packed all appeared to be there, which was at least one positive. He would certainly need a fresh change of clothes before tomorrow.

Keaton slung the bag over his good shoulder and headed towards the street. He needed money and lots of it before he could leave town. He was philosophical about losing a quarter of a million dollars in cash tonight. If the bag had simply contained clothes, he was positive Franco would not have given up so easily. The money made the decision to call the hunt off easy. Franco was a 'quit while you're ahead' kind of guy, and he knew when he was ahead.

Keaton's thoughts returned to Richard Stelovak. He was not surprised this day had come. He counted it a minor victory that he was still alive. For now, Keaton was content to find a motel, tend to his shoulder and get some rest. Tomorrow was a new day and presented a whole new set of opportunities. He had unfinished business with Richard Stelovak and planned to make tomorrow a day Stelovak would never forget.

Chapter Forty-Four

Robbie and Laura both had a restless night's sleep. After finishing one of the best Mexican meals they could both ever remember, they had returned to the motel to plan how they would confront Nick Carney. It had been a long and involved process, but shortly after two a.m. they were satisfied with the plan they had developed.

The plan required a second hire car, another mobile phone and a specialist piece of electronic equipment, so they had risen early for a shopping trip to get what they needed. Before returning to their motel, they stopped for breakfast at a cafe in a quiet backstreet away from the main freeway.

They had spent close to two hours on preparations for the encounter with Nick and were both starved by the time they got to sit down and eat breakfast together. After bacon and eggs for both of them, a pot of Russian Caravan tea for Laura and two black coffees for Robbie, they both felt much better and enjoyed the quiet peaceful surrounds of the cafe for a few minutes.

In silence they both contemplated the day ahead. They had discussed taking what they already knew to Vancouver Metro, but it was all circumstantial. There was nothing in the Catalin emails or Mac's diary that would stand up in court. Robbie and Laura both knew they needed more hard evidence. What they had planned for today was potentially high risk for Robbie, but he felt it needed to be done and Laura had backed his judgment.

"Ready?"

Laura looked at Robbie with a pensive smile. She was worried for the safety of the man she was falling for but put on a brave face.

"As I'll ever be, Robbie."

They paid the bill and walked out to the street and got into Laura's Bronco. After they were settled, Robbie picked up his phone and said, "Here we go."

Robbie dialed the publicly listed number for the Director of the OCTF. After several rings, the phone was answered. "OCTF Executive, Renate speaking."

"Good morning, Renate. I'm Robbie Mayne and I used to be in the same class as Nick Carney at high school. I need to talk to him about an important, private matter, please."

"Just one moment, Mr. Mayne."

Robbie was placed on hold and listened to tedious elevator music while he waited. When Renate came back on the line, her tone had become noticeably frostier. "The Director is currently unavailable."

"Okay, when will he be available?"

"I'm sorry, Mr. Mayne. The Director is very busy and has no appointments available until the middle of next week."

"Can I please speak with him by phone at least?"

"That won't be possible. He's in a very important meeting right now."

Robbie looked at Laura and rolled his eyes. As a journalist, he was quite used to secretaries stonewalling.

"I see. Let me level with you Renate. Not only am I an old school acquaintance of Nick, I'm also a journalist. Your boss has exactly ten minutes to call me back and not a second more. If he doesn't, I publish with the tag line, 'the Director of the OCTF refused to comment'. I'm not about to discuss the details with you, so do your boss a favor and get him to call me. I'm assuming you have a pen and paper, Renate, so write this down and give it to him."

Robbie paused briefly and then said, "C - A - T - A - L - I - N - 1989. He will know it's me then, and trust me Renate, he'll want to talk. Are you there, Renate?"

After a begrudging mumbled response, Robbie then gave her his phone number before finalizing the call.

"You have ten minutes, Renate. Not a second longer."

Robbie disconnected and looked at Laura. "What do you think?"

"I'm thinking Renate won't have a job tomorrow if she doesn't pass that on. As for Nick, we wait, Robbie. You've done all you can for now."

Robbie and Laura waited in the car for close to fifteen minutes before Robbie's phone rang. Laura crossed her fingers as Robbie answered.

"Hello."

"Mr. Mayne, I passed on your message. The Director told me to pass on details of any discussion you would like to have with him to his lawyer. Do you have a pen and paper handy, Mr. Mayne?"

Robbie grimaced and shook his head. "I'm terribly sorry Renate, it's too late. I've already forwarded the information on to my publisher. I can provide your director with their details if you like?"

The phone went dead. Robbie shook his head. "She hung up on me."

Moments later, Robbie's phone buzzed again.

"Hello."

The unmistakable deep voice of Nick Carney responded. "You've got one minute, so you'd better make it good."

Robbie's anger surfaced immediately he heard Nick's voice. He took a deep breath to calm himself before he spoke.

"And hello to you too, Nick."

"I hope you've got more than that, Robbie."

"I do, Nick. To cut to the chase, Mac was murdered. The hit and run was no accident. I can't prove that conclusively yet, but I will in time. I also have documentary evidence of an appointment you had with Mac shortly before his murder and an eyewitness. I know about your laptop, Nick, and I know Mac was trying to protect me."

"I'm bored, Robbie. You and Mac bored me twenty-five years ago with your petty causes and nothing's changed."

"I have the list, Nick. Are you bored now?"

There was a pause before Nick responded. It was barely noticeable in his fluid delivery of responses. Laura had moved across as close as she could to Robbie's seat and had her head next to Robbie's phone. She had listened in silence to the exchange. She had also detected the pause and gave Robbie the thumbs up sign. Robbie had clearly struck a blow.

"I have no idea what you're talking about."

"Well, I think you do, Nick. I think you're using your position and your resources to help someone big. Of course,

I could be wrong, so you get one chance to explain yourself and one chance only."

There was silence at the end of the phone as they waited for Nick to respond. "Nice try, Robbie, but I'm not buying it. In fact, you publish any of that rubbish and I'll sue your ass for every cent you've got. I've got the best lawyers in town. It will be a lot of fun."

"Suit yourself, Nick, but make no mistake, I won't stop until either I'm dead or someone's in jail for Mac's murder. I get syndicated coverage now. So once the story is out, you and whoever you work for won't stand a chance of containing it."

The line went dead. Nick had hung up on him. Laura and Robbie sat and looked at one another as they thought about what had just happened.

Laura grimaced. "He'll be on the phone now. Circling the wagons."

"Do you think he'll call back?"

"Yes… when he thinks he's got enough to control you."

Chapter Forty-Five

Keaton had the taxi driver pull over out front of the Stelecom building on the opposite side of the street. With his sunglasses on, he did not feel too conspicuous and felt it was low risk sitting here for a minute or two. He watched as people entered and exited the building. Keaton's focus was on the front security desk and, in particular, who was manning it.

He smiled as he observed Lennie Fowler sitting at the front desk pulling security detail today. Fowler had been working night shift several months ago and had fallen asleep at his desk. Keaton had been working late and had woken him on his way out. Rather than having him sacked on the spot as he should have done, Keaton had let Fowler off with a warning.

Fowler had taken extra special care of Keaton ever since. As Keaton dialed Fowler's number he murmured, "Today's the day you get to pay me back in full, Lennie."

Keaton waited for Fowler to answer the phone. "Security Desk."

"Hey, Lennie, it's Randolph Keaton here. How are you doing?"

There was a short pause before Fowler responded in a low voice, barely above a whisper.

"Mr. Keaton, I'm not supposed to be talking to you. Your building access has been revoked and you've been black-listed. I could lose my job."

Keaton refrained from pointing out to Fowler that if it weren't for him, Fowler would be the one who was unemployed. Instead, in a jovial upbeat manner, he continued.

"Don't worry about that, Lennie. All a misunderstanding, really. I'll get it sorted in the next couple of days. I just wanted to know had anything official been said about my departure yet? You know an email, for instance?"

"Nothing that I've seen, Mr. Keaton. All I know is the security manager was in about seven this morning and said they have revoked your building access. If we see you, we have to report it to him immediately. I'm sure glad I haven't seen you."

Keaton laughed to try and lighten the moment. "I don't want to get you into any trouble, Lennie. You have a good day now, and I'll speak to you soon."

"Good bye, Mr. Keaton."

"Bye, Lennie."

Keaton disconnected and said to the cab driver. "Just keep the meter running."

The call to Lennie Fowler had been brief, but he got the information he needed. No official news had been issued about his departure yet, but as expected, he no longer had building access.

He had no choice but to go with Plan B. It was a long shot, but it was all he had. If Richard Stelovak and most of the executive were already at the City Planning building getting ready for the final presentations and contract signing, he had a chance.

Keaton checked his watch. It was almost nine a.m. and time to call Richard Stelovak's personal secretary. Stelovak had hired Stephanie Crayton several years ago more on her looks than ability. Although she was still quite young, she had proven reliable and loyal and was the only person other than Keaton himself, who Stelovak trusted with the combination to his outer safe.

Keaton drew a deep breath before making the call. It was vital that he appear relaxed and normal if he was to pull this off. He pressed speed dial and waited for her to answer.

"Richard Stelovak's office, Stephanie speaking."

Keaton let out the breath and put on a relaxed smile. "Hi, Steph, it's Randolph. How goes the office?"

"Hi, Mr. Keaton. It's all quiet here. The top floor is almost deserted. I assume they're all with you getting ready for the contract signing this afternoon."

Keaton's smile turned from fake to real. Stephanie Crayton had not been informed yet that he had been fired. He was not overly surprised. Richard Stelovak would normally make announcements about senior staff departures himself. He had, as Keaton figured, bypassed the office and gone straight to the City Planning building this morning. This might just work, he thought.

"Steph, it's totally mad over there at present. You're lucky to be back there holding the fort. It's the best place to be."

"So you're not there, Mr. Keaton?"

"I was, Steph, but right now, I'm in a cab on the way back to the office. Richard and I got our wires crossed. There's a document in his safe that we need. He thought I was bringing it and I thought he was bringing it. In the end, nobody brought it and I'm on my way back to pick it up."

"Okay."

Keaton did his best to control his breathing. It all came down to how he delivered the next few lines. He had planned and rehearsed them in his motel room early that morning until he felt he had them right.

"So, Steph, I'm a bit under the pump. Richard needs those documents for a legal presentation in about thirty minutes. I didn't expect traffic to be this bad. Would you mind getting the documents from the safe and bringing them downstairs to the cab for me? I might just make it back in time if you could?"

"No problem, Mr. Keaton. You might have to tell me what they look like. It's a big safe."

"Are you on your wireless phone?"

"Sure am. I'm already in Mr. Stelovak's office. If you give me a minute, I'll get the safe open."

Keaton waited patiently. It all appeared to be going so well he was contemplating whether he should push it further.

"Okay, Mr. Keaton. It's open. What am I looking for?"

"Well, Steph, it's a large white envelope which Richard has written my name on."

There was a silence and some paper shuffling. Come on Stephanie, Keaton thought. Half a million dollars will make life so much easier.

"Got it, Mr. Keaton. It was third from the top."

Keaton fist pumped the air in the back of the cab. Trying to contain himself, he said, "That's great, Steph, thanks so much."

Keaton weighed up whether he should push his luck. Every minute he delayed getting the envelope with the money bonds out of the building was a minute closer to discovery that he had been fired. As soon as Stephanie Crayton was made aware of his situation, the game would be up, and the money would be gone. The new security manager that Lennie Fowler reported to had only been on the job for several months. He would be around shortly, full of self-importance, advising everyone of what happened ahead of the official email from Stelovak himself.

Keaton decided to risk it. "Steph, you've been super helpful. I'm wondering if I could ask one more favor, seeing as how you're using the wireless phone?"

"Okay. If I can?"

"Richard gave me some photos to look at yesterday of some land the company might be buying. It's all on the hush-hush right now and he asked me to put them back in his safe when I had finished with them. To be honest, we're not technically supposed to have them yet, hence why Richard likes to keep them in his safe. Anyway, with everything that was going on last night getting ready for today, I forgot to put the photos back. Needless to say, Richard's going to be…"

"It's okay, Mr. Keaton. I'm on my way to your office now."

Keaton's office was two down from Stelovak's. Even though Keaton had been a top floor senior executive in the company, Stelovak made sure everyone knew their place. Keaton's office was nowhere near as large, nor did it have the commanding view of Vancouver that Stelovak's office had. It also did not have a safe. Stelovak micro managed information and made sure everyone knew who was in control.

"Okay, I'm here, Mr. Keaton. Where do I look?"

Keaton did not allow himself to smile. Too much could still go wrong.

"Steph, if you go around behind my desk, you will see I have a suspension file drawer on the left-hand side. It's currently locked."

"Okay."

"Now, in the top left-hand drawer of my desk, you will find a small brown vitamin bottle with a plastic safety cap on it. Inside that bottle, you'll find the key to the file drawer."

"Just one moment, Mr. Keaton."

Keaton waited while Stephanie got the key. "Okay, I have the drawer open. Where should I be looking?"

"We'll, Steph, if memory serves, it's in the first partition. You're looking for an olive colored heavy legal-size envelope. It has one of those old-fashioned string fasteners on the back that you wind to hold the flap down."

Keaton waited a moment while he heard Stephanie searching the drawer.

"I think I have its, Mr. Keaton. It says, 'Blackwell Originals' on the front."

Keaton now allowed himself a small smile. "That's it, Steph, that's the one."

"I'm just walking it back to the safe now."

"Thanks, Steph, I really appreciate this."

Keaton waited while the secretary walked back into Stelovak's office.

"Okay, Mr. Keaton. I'll put the photos on the bottom shelf. That way, it won't look like they've just been put back."

Keaton let out a short laugh. "Our little secret, Steph. Thanks."

Stephanie Crayton laughed as well. Keaton had long

suspected she secretly had a crush on him. Ordinarily, he would have asked her out and then entertained her back in his bed long before now, but Crayton was Stelovak's property and off limits.

He needed to milk the goodwill just a little longer. Getting the envelope downstairs was one thing, but convincing Stephanie not to leave it with the guards was another. Keaton would need all his charm to get the envelope personally delivered. If it was left at the front security desk, it may as well still be in the safe. Lennie Fowler may have owed him, but he knew his every move on the front desk was recorded on security cameras and would not jeopardize his job for Keaton.

"So, Steph, I'm about four blocks from the office. I'm looking at my watch and I'm really running short on time here. Would you mind meeting me out front? It would save me valuable time not having to get out of the cab?"

Keaton was half expecting some resistance and was pleasantly surprised by the response.

"No problem, Mr. Keaton. I'll be out front in two minutes. You can just swing by and I'll hand you the envelope."

"Thanks, Steph. I owe you big time!"

Keaton then turned to the cab driver. "Okay, pull a U turn and we'll wait out front of the building. Should be only two minutes and we'll be on our way."

The cab driver did as he was instructed and made the U turn and pulled up in a no standing zone as instructed by Keaton. He did not look particularly happy about it, but Keaton wanted a good view of the front of the building and did not want Stephanie Crayton to have to come looking for his cab. There was always a danger she would miss him and return to the building.

"We won't be here long, pal. Just one more minute and we'll be out of here."

The one-minute wait quickly turned into two minutes and then three. Keaton was starting to get worried. 'Where is she?' he thought? Keaton looked at his watch. It was now close to five minutes since he had ended the phone call. He was now worried. If the security director or someone else had tipped her off, there was a good chance Stelecom Security had either called the cops or were making their own plans for his capture. Staying directly out front of the building any longer could be extremely risky.

Keaton looked at his watch again. Six minutes had elapsed. He decided to give it one more minute and then he would need to leave. Keaton stared closely at the front of the building, trying to get a glimpse inside as the automatic glass doors opened to allow people in and out of the building. Still no sign of Crayton. Keaton looked at his watch again. Seven minutes had elapsed. Keaton pursed his lips and shook his head. Money or no money, it was time to leave. As he opened his mouth to instruct the cab driver to drive off, the front glass doors opened again, and Stephanie Crayton emerged with the white envelope, rushing towards his cab.

Keaton had mixed feelings. He was both elated to see her and wary at the same time. There were no security guards walking with her or behind her, which he took as a good sign. He glanced out the front and back windows of the cab to see if there were any signs of cops. It all looked clear.

Keaton wound down the window and put on his best smile as Stephanie Crayton approached the cab.

"Hey, Steph, I was getting a little worried there. Everything okay?"

The Catalin Code

Stephanie Crayton looked clearly flustered. "Sorry, Mr. Keaton, I got caught up. The new security director came to see me about some important security matter just as I was getting in the elevator. I told him I had to get these documents downstairs ASAP for a special delivery to Mr. Stelovak."

Keaton kept the smile on his face and tried to remain calm. "So, what did our security director say to that?"

Stephanie Crayton passed the envelope through the open window of the cab to Keaton. "He said he'd wait. He's sitting in the visitor's chair at my desk as we speak." She smiled as she added, "He wasn't happy either."

Not nearly as unhappy as he will be in a few minutes when he figures out what has just happened, Keaton thought. He resisted the urge to open the envelope there and then. Instead, he said, "Thanks, Steph, you've been a big help. I owe you one."

"My pleasure, Mr. Keaton. I hope you get back in time."

Keaton smiled. "Me too."

Keaton watched for a moment as Stephanie Crayton walked back into the building. He would had loved to have been a fly on the wall when the pompous new security director realized he had let Randolph Keaton slip through his fingers and take half a million dollars with him in the process. The ensuing conversation with Stelovak would be short. He knew the security director's title would change to 'unemployed' before the day was through.

Keaton instructed the cab driver to head downtown. As the cab driver moved off into traffic, he asked Keaton where he specifically wanted to go. Keaton ignored the question. He had to check the contents of the envelope to make sure Stelovak had not double-crossed him one last time. Keaton opened the flap of the envelope and slowly withdrew five heavy bond paper documents. As he turned them over, he breathed a sigh of relief as he realized he now held half a million dollars' worth of Roma Bank's money bonds.

"Let's head for the Roma Bank on Market Street, driver."

Keaton sat back in the cab and grinned. It was turning into quite a good day. After almost being killed last night and losing a quarter of a million dollars, it was good to still be alive and half a million dollars richer. There was only one thing that could make it better, and that was a little personal payback to Richard Stelovak.

Keaton closed his eyes and smiled. His arm still hurt like hell from the bullet wound, but what he had just pulled off was a far better medication than any painkiller he could take. He had one last task to take care of after his visit to the bank before leaving Vancouver for good. Richard Stelovak was about to realize he had severely underestimated his protege. If it all went to plan, Stelovak would have a lot more than just a two billion-dollar contract to remember the day by.

Chapter Forty-Six

Robbie and Laura waited another twenty minutes before the phone rang again. As Laura predicted, Nick Carney came out swinging and attempted to control the conversation from the outset. "We meet today at four p.m. in my office. I'll have my lawyer with me. You can bring whoever you want."

Robbie's anger surfaced again the moment he heard Nick's voice. He did his best to calm down before he replied. "Nick, you don't hold all the cards anymore. In fact, in this game you've got a lousy hand. I'm not meeting you in your office or anywhere else of your choosing, for that matter. I was almost murdered two nights ago, so when we meet, it's just you and me, no one else. And it will be somewhere I feel safe."

Nick laughed. "Robbie, I'm the director of the OCTF. You don't get to talk to me on your own, not now, not ever."

"Fine by me, Nick. I'm happy to forgo the professional courtesy and publish without your spin. But make no mistake, the list is going public. You tell whoever the hell it is you're working for that you're all on borrowed time. You can't go around killing people any longer to make it disappear. Killing Mac was a huge mistake. You have…"

Nick interrupted. His shouting was so loud that Laura did not need to lean in towards the phone. She could hear everything, word for word, from the passenger seat. "I haven't killed anyone! So, get that crazy idea out of your head, Robbie. I'm a highly respected and decorated senior law enforcement officer and your way out of your depth."

"You better have a good lawyer, Nick. Round one hasn't even begun yet."

Robbie disconnected and let out a deep breath. It had not gone according to plan, but he was beyond caring. "If he doesn't call back, I get together with my analyst friend and we go through what we have with a fine-tooth comb. If they're prepared to kill, the information has to be there somewhere."

Laura touched Robbie on the arm. "He will call back Robbie. You're a loose end and Nick hates loose ends."

Before Robbie responded, his phone buzzed again. As he answered, he noticed Nick Carney was more controlled this time. "Where and when?"

"Today. One o'clock at the Shell Gas Station, just before the entrance to the northbound freeway. You call me at one p.m., and I will tell you where to go. And Nick, I will be watching, so no tricks."

Chapter Forty-Seven

Richard Stelovak had very little of substance to do at the City Planning building that morning. The lawyers and accountants had officially concluded the legal negotiations for both sides days before. Today's official Southwest development contract signing at four P.M. was as much ceremonial as anything else and allowed the city's politicians another opportunity for self-promotion to the media. Unless something extremely controversial broke today in the media or was otherwise leaked to City Planning, the deal was as good as done. As he sat in the auditorium listening to another presentation, he discretely looked at his watch and smiled to himself. Just a few more hours to negotiate, he thought.

The final presentations today were all joint exercises between Stelecom Industries executives and Vancouver City Planning. The goal was to keep the media and other senior stakeholders informed and promote the development as an exciting new growth opportunity for Vancouver. Stelovak was big on self-promotion and planned to attend every presentation. So far, he had smiled a lot and shaken hands with a lot of people he didn't know who wanted to congratulate him. He was used to people falling all over him to gain personal favors, but today it was fever pitch.

When his phone rang, it was normally with a sense of relief that he excused himself and went to the back of the auditorium to answer. Stelovak looked at the caller ID as his phone rang yet again. This was one phone call that could derail everything he had worked for. He needed to take this call in private.

He made his apologies to the group he was currently with and answered the call with an 'I'll call you back' response and hung up.

What he had to discuss with Nick Carney was not something that could be done in public. Stelovak made his way out of the auditorium and into an isolated section of the lobby before returning the call.

Carney answered on the second ring. Neither man had a propensity for more words than was required and they covered a lot of ground in a brief space of time.

"I'm meeting with Mayne today. He's confirmed he has the list."

Stelovak looked around to make sure he wasn't being observed before he responded.

"OK. What's the plan? This should have been taken care of two nights ago, and yet he's still walking around."

"He got lucky. That won't happen twice."

"So, how are you taking care of it? Is it going to be an OCTF matter?"

"No. I'm meeting with him today. I'll be taking care of this personally. He'll be dead by sundown and I'll have the list."

"That's all I wanted to hear, Nick. You realize my

release of your remuneration is not just conditional on contract signing today, but also having Mayne and that list out of the picture permanently?"

"Yes."

"I'm glad we have an understanding. Call me when it's done, and I'll arrange the release."

Stelovak disconnected the call and reflected for a moment on the profitable three-year association he had with Nick Carney. To date, he had proven to be a very useful asset. His contacts and influence inside Vancouver Police had proven useful, but the intelligence he could glean and pass on from the OCTF had been gold.

Stelovak still had some active links with organized crime in Eastern Europe. Being able to monitor the police intelligence on this had helped him stay one step ahead of the law, and in some cases, he had used the information to bring down some of his enemies and competitors.

The one and a half million dollars he was about to pay Nick Carney was looking like an excellent investment. He would know for certain by this time tomorrow.

Chapter Forty-Eight

The rest of the morning had been frantic for Robbie and Laura as they prepared for the one o'clock meeting. While the conversation between the two of them had been strained, it was the uncertainty of what might happen rather than their relationship that was causing the tension.

Laura watched as Robbie drove the second rental car into the multi-story parking lot and parked next to her Bronco. They had decided on the parking lot they had been using near their motel. It was close to both the gas station and the freeway and it was as good a place as any for the first part of the meeting with Nick, which Laura would manage.

Robbie got out of the car and came around to where Laura was standing. "You got everything?"

Laura nodded. She had a bad feeling today would not go as planned. As she looked at Robbie, she realized without a doubt that she had fallen for him. Now was not the time to be dropping the 'L' word on him, she thought. He has enough to worry about without further distractions.

Instead, she wrapped her arms tightly around him and held him. Robbie sensed what the hug meant and held Laura tight as well. "I promise to come back, Laura."

"You better Robbie. I'm going to be damn mad at you if you don't."

They held each other for another minute before Robbie let go. "I'll call you as soon as it's over. I promise."

Laura watched as Robbie got into his first rental car and drove off. He had ten minutes to get into position to be ready for Nick's call.

Robbie had been in position only four minutes when his phone rang. He checked his watch. It showed Nick was ringing in a good five minutes early. Robbie debated whether to answer the call or leave it until one p.m. as arranged. He knew Nick would do his best to throw him off and take control and this was one example of many to come; he thought.

Robbie muttered, "Let's get this over with," as he answered the call. "Hello."

The unmistakable deep gravelly voice of Nick Carney responded. "I'm at the gas station and ready to play your little game, Robbie."

Robbie ignored the jibe. "There's a large green dumpster over near the rear brick fence. You see it."

"Yes."

"I've written something on the back of it. Tell me what it says."

The phone line stayed open and Robbie could hear Nick walking across to the bin. "Not very original. It says 'Mac'."

"Just wanted to remind you why we're here. Now look toward the freeway. Do you see a multi-story parking lot?"

"I see it."

"Drive your car up to the fourth floor. Someone will be there to show you where to park. Also, you will get a new phone when you get there, so throw this phone in the dumpster, but don't hang up."

"What is this, Mayne? You've been watching way too many spy movies."

"Your call, Nick. I'm trying to avoid getting killed, so do it my way or not at all. I don't care either way. I'll just publish the list."

Robbie heard the phone clunk as though it had been dropped. The connection remained active. It seemed like Nick was going to play ball, Robbie thought. Robbie waited a few seconds longer. When the phone connection continued to stay active but silent, Robbie was reasonably sure Nick had dropped the phone in the dumpster as instructed.

Robbie disconnected and then sent Laura a text message. It simply said, 'He's coming.'

Laura stood by the second rental car and watched as Nick Carney drove his car up onto the fourth level and parked opposite her Bronco. She did not fear for her safety, but was wary and eager to get this over with.

She had never trusted him. Even before the OCTF scandal, there was something about him that made her wary around him. The scandal had proven her intuition to be correct. Nick had shown his true colors and had twisted and manipulated every situation to his advantage. She knew of at least two OCTF officers who were still in jail based on lies Nick had fabricated to protect himself.

Nick got out of his car and closed the door. He stared at Laura for a moment and then shook his head in a disapproving manner as he sauntered across to meet her.

Laura removed an electronic scanning wand from the back of her Bronco. "I need you to empty your pockets of all weapons and communication devices before we go any further."

Nick extended his arms as if preparing to be searched and then swiftly grabbed Laura firmly by the jaw. As Laura attempted to scream, Nick pushed her backwards and down onto the hood of the Bronco and held her there. With a menacing smile, he leaned in close to Laura. "It's been quite a while, Laura. I must say I'm disappointed. I thought you would have had more sense than to get mixed up with someone like Robbie Mayne."

In a muffled but defiant tone, Laura spoke as best she could through Nick's vice like grip. "You were a pig when I worked for you and nothing's changed. Robbie is expecting my call, so you need to decide what's more important."

Without releasing his grip on her jaw, Nick responded, "I could snap your neck like a twig. Kill you or paralyze you for life. How does that sound?"

Laura's head was ready to explode with pain. Still defiant, she managed, "I'm the least of your problems. You have far more to worry about than me."

Nick gave Laura a final shove as he let go and silently began emptying his pockets onto the hood of the Bronco. As Laura massaged her jaw, she watched as Nick placed a phone on her car. He then reached into a jacket pocket and pulled out a SIG Sauer pistol and aimed it at her forehead.

Laura stood defiantly. Nick laughed before lowering the pistol and placing it on the hood as well.

Although physically shaken, Laura had experienced worse while working for the OCTF. She quickly recovered and said, "You can lock all of that in your car. You won't be needing it."

In silence, Nick made his way back to his car. He opened the passenger door and deposited the phone and gun in the glove compartment and then re-locked the car.

When he returned, Laura moved the electronic wand over him from head to toe to identify any other metal and electronic devices Nick might be carrying. The wand's alarm only went off once when placed against Nick's left arm. After he removed his watch, the rest of the search process was uneventful.

Satisfied that he was no longer carrying any weapons, Laura held up a set of keys to the second rental car. "This is your new ride. Take the back exit and head for the freeway. I'll call Robbie and tell him you're on your way. You only have a set time to get to the next destination. You stop at a pay phone, we'll know, and the meeting is off. There's a phone on the passenger seat. Robbie will call you shortly with further instructions. And by the way, Nick, the phone is only good for receiving calls. You can't call out on it."

Nick grabbed the keys and called back over his shoulder as he walked towards the rental. "Be seeing you soon."

Laura watched as Nick Carney started the car and drove off. She massaged her jaw again for a moment as she thought about what had just happened. If they lived beyond today, she knew she and Robbie would need to sit down and develop a longer-term plan for their survival.

Laura opened her phone and hit speed dial. For now, it was time to call Robbie and tell him Nick was on his way.

Chapter Forty-Nine

Westcott had made good progress in the Leon Blackwell murder. Coleman had given Westcott what he wanted most when he had returned to the crime scene the previous evening. Coleman only had to look at eight photographs from Westcott's file of suspects for the investigation to get a positive ID for Randolph Keaton, Richard Stelovak's senior company lawyer, no less.

Coleman had been positive, 'that's the guy I saw ducking off into the bathroom, no doubt about it.'

It had not taken long to discover Keaton's home address. Westcott had moved quickly to interview and arrest Keaton. After calling and getting the okay from Felix Delray, Westcott had taken Coleman with him to interview Keaton late in the evening. Neither man was surprised that Keaton wasn't home. Westcott had been given approval for a twenty-four-hour surveillance detail to observe the residence in the hope Keaton would return home, but no one was confident that would work.

Westcott currently sat in Delray's office talking strategy

and planning what to do next. It was time to interview Rudy Henning again. This time, they had a lot more leverage. Randolph Keaton had been positively identified at the Blackwell crime scene at the time of the murder. Henning would be aware that Keaton was the kind of guy who would sell out his own grandmother to get a lighter jail sentence if arrested. They would use this as a wedge and pressure Henning to cut a deal while there was still time.

Delray looked almost as weary as Westcott. "You know, Danny, we have one guy in jail and now two guys on the run, all with close ties to Richard Stelovak. All we need is for one of them to finger Stelovak and we have a whole new game that Stelovak will be forced to play."

Westcott yawned. "I need more coffee. You want me to get you a cup, boss?"

Delray was momentarily distracted by his computer screen.

"Boss, do you want coffee?"

Delray's gaze became transfixed on his computer screen. "I'll be damned", he mumbled quietly.

"What is it?"

Delray swung his computer screen around so that Westcott could see it as well.

"Randolph Keaton has just sent you and me an email message with what looks like a video attachment. The message subject line is entitled 'A Gift'."

Westcott moved his chair to get a better view of the screen. "I wonder what he means by the term 'a gift'?"

Delray clicked on the video attachment in the email message. As the computer's video player launched, he said, "Only one way to find out."

Westcott and Delray watched as the face of Randolph

The Catalin Code

Keaton appeared on Delray's computer screen. It looked to Westcott like it was a self-recording taken on a smart phone.

Keaton was looking at them through the video with that same self-serving smile Westcott remembered from his recent court appearance with Richard Stelovak. Westcott hoped this was more than just a video message to brag and gloat.

"Good morning, gentlemen. Sadly, today is my last day in Vancouver. Richard Stelovak has chosen to terminate my employment with his organization, and I use the term 'terminate' literally. Now, while you're more than capable of doing the detective work yourselves, I thought I'd give you a head start by providing you with this video confession. The reason is twofold, gentlemen."

Delray hit pause on his computer media player and looked at Westcott. "You got a copy of this, right?"

Westcott replied, "I saw my name included in the email, so I assume so. You want me to check?"

Delray thought for a moment. Before he could answer the question, Westcott got up and moved towards the door. "I'll go check. We need to be sure."

Delray stared back at the frozen figure of Randolph Keaton on his computer screen. This was fast turning into the most memorable week of his career. If Keaton's confession had substance, it might solve several open cases. The anticipation was palpable; he could hardly wait for Westcott to return.

After an agonizingly long minute, Westcott walked back into the room and nodded at Delray as he sat back in his chair. "I got it, boss. I made a back-up copy as well. We're good to go."

Delray used his computer mouse to click the play button on the video. Keaton came to life on the screen again.

"Richard Stelovak wants to retire me permanently and sent a hit squad to my apartment last night. I was lucky to escape with my life and took a bullet in the arm in the process. I must confess I am the vindictive sort, so this is payback. Also, I figure if Stelovak is in jail, my chances of survival improve substantially."

Keaton paused and smiled at the camera. Westcott had always found Keaton to be cold and calculating and nothing he had heard so far made him want to change his mind.

Keaton continued, "So here it is. You have two new murders to deal with this week. Photographer, Eugene Brennan and Accountant, Leon Blackwell. Stelovak orchestrated both murders. In the case of Brennan, the man was engaged to take photos of Leon Blackwell in a compromising position suitable for blackmail. Alas for Eugene, he got too greedy and wanted more money than what was originally agreed. Suffice to say; he learned the hard way about crossing Richard Stelovak."

Westcott and Delray exchanged glances as Keaton continued. "Now our friend Leon Blackwell was a harmless accountant with a wonderful flair for laundering money. Unfortunately for Leon, he decided he wanted to start a new life and neglected to tell Stelovak or negotiate a way out. Stelovak is neurotic when it comes to protecting information about himself and poor Leon knew too much for his own good. When you good folk from Vancouver Metro interviewed him in relation to the Brennan murder, he panicked and made plans to leave, triggering Stelovak's decision to have him murdered."

Westcott paused the video. "He's really spilling the beans."

Delray nodded. "That he is. Let's keep watching."

Westcott hit play again. "So, gentlemen, Richard

Stelovak is the man who ordered the murders of both Blackwell and Brennan. In both cases, he of course had associates help him. Rudy Henning was the man who threw Eugene Brennan off his balcony, and Vincent Franco was responsible for Blackwell's hanging. I understand Henning is already in custody. Vincent Franco is planning his departure tonight from a small, and some would say dubious, private plane charter company, owned and operated by Max Tyson. The departure is scheduled for six o'clock tonight, so that should give you plenty of time to organize a reception committee at the airport for him. Besides being involved in the Brennan and Blackwell murders, Stelovak asked Franco to take out a journalist this week by the name of Robbie Mayne. Mayne is currently investigating Stelovak's connections to international organized crime and making some inroads. Franco was unsuccessful and got his nose broken in the bargain, so he'll be easy to spot."

Delray clicked on pause again, "Notice how he didn't mention his involvement in any of this?"

Westcott nodded in agreement. "It's hardly surprising. He's doing this for pay back, not because he's suddenly become a good corporate citizen and wants to unburden his soul. Even so, the confession looks solid. I think we can use this."

Delray clicked the play button on the video again. Keaton continued his confession.

"And so, gentlemen, time is pressing, and I have a plane to catch. By the time you get to play this video, I will be long gone from Vancouver. In closing, I have one final gift for you. Stelovak will no doubt hire the best lawyer's money can buy and will do his utmost to discredit my testimony. However, as a lawyer myself, I know there is no better evidence than physical evidence itself."

Keaton paused for effect and smiled at the camera. "If you hurry, gentlemen, I believe you will find a copy of the Leon Blackwell pictures taken by Eugene Brennan in Richard Stelovak's office safe. Stelovak has handled these photographs and they will bear his fingerprints. Now, this testimony should be enough to get you the relevant approval to get a search warrant, but you'll need to hurry. As soon as he discovers the photos, he'll do what I didn't and burn them. Well, that's it. I bid you good day, gentlemen, and wish you well with your apprehension."

The screen went blank as the video ended.

Delray shook his head. "That's the most bizarre thing I think I've ever heard in my life."

Westcott nodded. "We need to get a search warrant for Stelovak's office."

"Indeed, we do, Danny. I'll get started on the warrant while you round up all available detectives to meet in the muster room. Let's make it in fifteen minutes. We need teams for both the Stelovak office search and to intercept Franco at Tyson's plane charter, wherever the hell that is."

Westcott was already out of his chair and moving toward the door when he responded, "See you in fifteen, boss.'

Delray sat behind his desk for a moment and contemplated what had just happened. If they made the right moves today, they would finally have Richard Stelovak playing their game rather than the other way around. He looked at his watch as he picked up his desk phone to dial Vancouver Metro's legal team. He had a lot to do in the next fourteen minutes.

Chapter Fifty

After receiving the call from Laura that Nick was on his way, Robbie checked his watch. He had driven the entire trip very early that morning and knew this leg would take Nick about eleven minutes in traffic.

Robbie hit speed dial and waited for Nick to answer.

"I've just come onto the freeway and I'm heading north, as instructed by your girlfriend."

Robbie ignored the small jibe about Laura. "You should see the first major welcome sign to Cypress Falls on the freeway in about nine minutes. Pull over when you get there and call me. If you hit bad traffic that's going to delay you, call me. If I think you're not on the level, I'll call off the meeting immediately and publish without your comments."

Robbie disconnected and checked the time on his watch. He had no desire to talk to Nick Carney any more than he had to. Robbie looked up at the back of the first major welcome sign to Cypress Falls. Satisfied with the word he had scrawled in chalk for Nick to read, Robbie got back in his rental and moved back into traffic and continued heading north.

As Robbie pulled off the freeway to take the next call, he checked his watch. Ten minutes had elapsed since his last call to Nick.

"You should have called by now," Robbie muttered.

As Robbie debated what to do, his phone rang.

"You're late."

Nick's response was brief. "Cool your jets. It was only a minute."

"Last chance, Nick. I mean it."

"It says 'Robbie', but it's spelled backwards. Seriously Robbie, do we need all this boy scout nonsense? Tell me where to meet and I'll be there."

"I'm just trying to stay alive, Nick. Call me when you get to the Catalin Mountain lookout turnoff and tell me what's written on the turnoff sign. Traffic is light from here on, so you've got twenty-eight minutes, no more."

Robbie disconnected. He would need every bit of the twenty-eight minutes to be in position for Nick's last call.

Robbie made good time in the light traffic and arrived at the Catalin lookout turnoff with several minutes to spare. After getting out of his car, he went and stood beside the turnoff sign to the lookout. Putting his hand to his brow to shield his eyes from the sun, Robbie looked up the mountain and could just make out the viewing platform in the distance. He decided not to worry about chalking a word on the back of the sign this time. He figured he should be able to make out Nick's car from the viewing platform.

After getting back in his car, Robbie drove the rest of

the way to the lookout and was relieved to see no other cars as he pulled up in the small parking lot. The meeting place needed to be private if his plan to get Nick to open up was to work.

After checking his watch, Robbie realized he had made better time than expected. He figured he still had a few minutes before Nick would reach the turnoff. He wound down the car window to let in some fresh air as he sat and thought about what would happen next.

He was positive Nick would give away as little as possible while trying to find out as much as he could about the list. They were as confident as they could be that the precautions they had taken would ensure Nick would arrive unarmed.

They had also done the best they could to make sure a support team didn't follow Nick by making him dump his mobile phone, switch vehicles, and leave the parking lot by a rear exit. Robbie reflected on the precautions they had taken. There were no guarantees. At least from the vantage point of the lookout platform, he could see the turnoff from the highway and some sections of the road leading up to the parking lot. Not ideal, he thought, but hopefully he could see enough to know whether Nick had somehow brought support with him.

Robbie tried to dismiss the risks from his mind as he went through the questions he wanted to ask. He knew Nick would never give him a straight answer or a confession. Robbie went through the questions one last time in his mind. His questions were designed to differentiate lies from the truth based on body language and what was not said, more than what was said. He would start by asking Nick why he had killed Mac, hoping to get him angry. In his experience as a journalist, angry people lost control and were far more likely to be truthful than those who remained in control.

After checking his watch again, Robbie decided it was time to get into position. Letting out a deep breath, he got out of the car and walked across the parking lot and out onto the viewing platform. As he leaned on the railing, Robbie watched the second rental car come into view.

Chapter Fifty-One

Felix Delray could not remember a busier day in his entire career in Vancouver Police. At times, he had literally run between offices as he coordinated the planning for the two teams required for the afternoon's planned arrests of Vincent Franco and Richard Stelovak.

Sitting in his office, with his phone wedged tightly in the crook of his neck, Delray was currently on hold and waiting for the legal department to confirm the search warrant for Richard Stelovak's office had been approved and duly authorized. As he devoured a ham, cheese and tomato sandwich, Westcott appeared at his office door and gently knocked.

Delray swallowed an only slightly chewed chunk of his sandwich and put his hand over the phone mouthpiece. "I'm on hold. What have you got?"

"We're good to go, boss. McKenzie wants to lead the Franco team on account of what happened to Jamieson. I've got the second team organized for the search and, hopefully, the arrest of Richard Stelovak."

With the phone still wedged against his neck, Delray nodded. "Good work, Danny. Your the lead on the Stelovak search. Make sure the team knows that. I'll ride shotgun and smooth out any issues we may have with his lawyers. I can take them offline to another room to argue while the team gets on with the job if need be."

"Thanks, boss. Appreciate your confidence in me."

Delray watched a piece of sandwich sail out of his mouth and land on the other side of his desk as he tried to chew and say "No problem," at the same time. He held up an index finger to signal to Westcott that he was no longer on hold. Delray listened intently for a few moments and then broke out in a broad smile.

"I'll be right down."

Still beaming as he hung up the phone, Delray turned to Westcott. "We have a warrant. Let's get the troops assembled for a quick final briefing and then it's time to pay Mr. Richard Stelovak a long overdue visit."

Chapter Fifty-Two

Robbie watched the steady stream of freeway traffic moving north from the viewing platform. While the cars and trucks appeared small in the distance, they were large enough for him to be able to distinguish both car shape and color. Robbie's focus narrowed to a silver Toyota as it came up over the small rise on the southern end of the visible section of the freeway. He tracked the vehicle as it continued north and was positive it was Nick as it began to slow on approach to the lookout turnoff.

He expected Nick to stop the vehicle at the sign as instructed, but the vehicle exited the freeway and started the long steep climb up to the lookout without stopping. Robbie suppressed his anger. He needed to keep his head clear for the meeting. It was typical Nick, he thought, ignoring instructions and always trying to get the upper hand.

Robbie watched as best he could as the car wound its way up the road to the lookout. The car regularly disappeared from Robbie's view as trees or ridges obscured much of the road. The car seemed to keep up a consistent pace and within a few minutes; it rounded the last bend in the road before reaching the parking lot.

Robbie walked off the platform and back to the edge of the parking lot as the Toyota pulled up and parked alongside Robbie's rental car. Nick got out of the car and quietly closed the door without looking in Robbie's direction. As if totally immune to Robbie's presence, Nick started walking around the parking lot. His focus was on the trees and thick vegetation that surrounded all but the viewing platform and road leading into the parking lot.

He watched Nick with a mixture of caution and curiosity. Nick's steps were slow and deliberate as he walked and checked the entire perimeter of the parking lot. He did not seem in a hurry to talk to Robbie and the parking lot was silent for several minutes except for the soft sounds of Nick's shoes crunching on the gravel.

Without looking at Robbie, Nick called out over his shoulder, "Just checking you're not setting me up with hidden cameras or microphones." He glanced at Robbie before continuing his search. "I don't trust you either, Robbie."

"There's no one else here, Nick. It's just you and me, like I promised."

Nick walked slowly towards Robbie as he continued to scan the area. When he was satisfied they were alone, he stopped and locked eyes on Robbie. "You're just a glorified journalist writing for glossy magazines. Your promise means nothing to me."

Robbie let the insult go. He was not interested in petty arguments and decided to go on the front foot from the start.

"I need the keys for the rental before we start."

Nick stared at Robbie and made no move to hands the

The Catalin Code

keys over. "I don't think so, Robbie. I'm not walking back from here."

Robbie held out his hand for the keys. "You won't need to. After the meeting, I'll leave first and drop the keys on the road down the hill where you can find them. You get a nice ten-minute walk and I get a ten-minute head start so you can't follow me."

Robbie kept his hand out. "I'm not going to beg, Nick. It's this way or no way. You suit yourself."

Nick shook his head slightly before reaching into his pants pocket to get the keys. As he handed the keys over to Robbie, he asked, "Now what?"

Robbie took the keys and pointed to the viewing platform. "Now we talk."

"We can talk right here, Robbie. We don't need a view."

Robbie kept his hand extended towards the platform. He was already tired of Nick's little power plays, but he knew he could not give in to even one of them or he would lose control of the meeting.

Robbie fought to keep his anger in check. "I insist."

Nick rolled his eyes and walked out onto the platform without a word. Robbie followed as far as the walkway to the platform and stopped.

Nick looked out at the view down the mountain before turning around to face Robbie. Leaning back against the railing, Nick continued. "You afraid I'm going to bite you, Robbie?"

Robbie responded, "No, just cautious and I have a desire to go on living for some time to come."

"So why am I here, Robbie? What's this mysterious list you keep referring to?"

"Before we get to that, Nick, tell me. Did you kill Mac yourself, or did you get someone to do your dirty work?"

Nick became visibly angry and started to move across the platform back to where Robbie was standing.

Robbie could no longer contain himself and began shouting. "Why, Nick? Why did you have to kill him? Mac was never a threat to you. He was just looking out for me."

Nick stopped short of the platform walkway. Raising his hand and pointing a finger at Robbie, Nick barked, "I'm the Director of the OCTF! You don't get to accuse me without proof and all I've heard so far Robbie is noise. Again, I ask, why am I here?'

Robbie regained control of his anger and changed tack again. In a quieter voice, he said, "Did you kill Stewart Wilson?"

Nick stopped pointing and lowered his hand as he stared back at Robbie. Robbie could not decide whether Nick was confused or angered further by the question, or both.

Nick screwed up his face and shook his head. "What?"

Robbie responded, "You heard me, Nick. Did you kill Stewart Wilson?"

"What kind of fool question is that?"

"I thought we should start at the beginning, Nick. That's always a good place to start. I just want to know how old you were when you started killing people. Was Wilson your first?"

Nick stared back at Robbie with a mixture of loathing and contempt. "You're crazy, Robbie. I haven't killed anyone except in the line of duty."

Robbie walked out onto the platform past Nick and stood at the railing. As he looked down the mountain, he continued.

"One day in my mid-twenties, I was doing research for an article I was writing about murder victims. I found out a lot about rigor mortis that day. Turns out the process starts about three hours after death and takes another six to nine hours to reach its peak. I remembered back to when I held Wilson's hand to check for a pulse. Based on how cold and stiff he was and what I'd learned, he'd been dead for five or six hours. We hadn't been out there long enough to kill him. But that's not to say…"

"I killed him, Robbie."

Robbie felt a chill run down his spine as he realized he had underestimated Nick. They were no longer alone. He recognized the other voice immediately and at that same instant understood why Mac had chosen the phrase 'catalin1989' for the email account. Turning around, he saw Nick had moved well away from the edge of the platform, and was no longer looking at Robbie, but at the man who stood between the two cars in the parking lot.

At dinner the other night, it had been a jovial Jerry, the face that Vancouver had voted for as mayor that he had dined with. Today, holding a pistol pointed at the middle of his chest, it was hard for Robbie to reconcile that this was the same man.

As Robbie focused on the gun, he felt a rush of adrenaline hammer through his body as his heart raced. Now was no time for panic, even though that's exactly what he wanted to do.

Jerry shook his head and in a grim and menacing tone said, "You just couldn't stay out of it, could you, Robbie? You and Mac are both cut from the same cloth. Prying into things that don't concern you. Now it's going to get you both killed."

Robbie quickly scanned the area for a way to escape. The platform was too high off the ground to jump from without breaking a leg, at least. The only way off the platform was past both Nick and the gun, which was rock steady in Jerry's hand.

To buy time so he could think, and in as calm a voice as he could muster, Robbie replied, "It didn't have to be this way, Jerry. You always have choices."

"Not always, Robbie. When Wilson got out of jail, he started coming around our house, trying to scare my sister. It terrified her, and we were afraid it would tip her over the edge. The cops were no help. You really think I had choices?"

Robbie looked at Nick. "So, you were in on it? You had to be. It was your idea to use the mine shaft?"

Jerry responded instead, "No Robbie. I shot him with my bow down at his cabin, wrapped him in plastic, and took him up Catalin on my dirt bike. I didn't know exactly where the mine shaft was, so I left him where I knew we would find him later."

Robbie frantically went through his options for getting out of this situation alive. It appeared hopeless. The best he could hope for was putting a wedge between Jerry and Nick in the hope they would turn on one another.

"So why involve all of us if you only needed, Nick?"

"Safety in numbers, Robbie. I figured if Wilson were ever discovered, it would be harder to prove against me personally if there were four of us involved. Of course, I took a risk that you or Mac might not go along with disposing of Wilson. But I figured if you thought it may have been you that shot him, you would come around."

Robbie turned to Nick. "You didn't know about any of this?"

Nick looked at Jerry and chuckled softly, as if they were sharing a private joke. Looking back at Robbie, he said, "I figured it out in the first year of my criminology degree.

You're not the only one that studied rigor mortis, Robbie. I confronted Jerry, and he confessed the whole thing. I couldn't very well take what I knew to the police without having to answer some tough questions myself, so I agreed to keep it a secret. Years later, that decision paid off in spades. When everything was coming apart at the OCTF, Jerry happily provided me with some wonderful alibis that kept me out of jail. The public perception is we don't get on, which suits us both fine. But, over the years as Mayor and director of the OCTF, we have formed a very… shall we say, lucrative partnership."

Robbie looked back at Jerry, desperate to keep the conversation alive. "How did you know we would be here, Jerry? It can't have been a wild guess?"

"We've had a private detective and an electronic tracker on your car since you arrived here. It was most inconvenient when the Vancouver Police discovered the tracker after you survived your stint in jail. Our private detective followed you to your little hideaway motel, and we put another one in place."

Nick snarled, "Enough of the chitchat, Robbie. Tell us about the list."

Robbie could sense the mood changing. There was nowhere to run. Robbie was considering rushing Nick and using him as a shield against Jerry. It was bound to fail, Robbie thought, but at least he would go down swinging.

As if reading his mind, Nick produced a thick plastic shiv that had been finely sharpened at one end. "Don't get any ideas, Robbie. Your girlfriend's little wand is good for metal, but not industrial plastic."

As Nick advanced on Robbie, Jerry said, "Robbie, we can do this the easy way or the hard way. Tell us about the list."

Before Robbie could respond, Nick was at his side and grabbed his head. As Robbie felt the sting of the shiv being pressed it into his neck, Nick added, "We know about the list, Robbie. Yesterday, we would have happily just killed you, but with your threats this morning that you've passed it on, we need more information. You tell us who and I'll make it quick. You don't…"

Nick leaned in close to Robbie's ear and whispered, "I'll take my time. I know what I'm doing Robbie and…"

Swinging his right fist hard into Nick's solar plexus, Robbie tried to pull away from Nick. As Nick clutched at his stomach with his free hand and began gasping for breath, Robbie felt a burning sensation on the left side of his neck as Nick attempted to drive the shiv deep. Robbie twisted and punched Nick again.

As Robbie and Nick wrestled, a gunshot reverberated across the parking lot. With his face covered in blood, Robbie collapsed onto the platform.

Chapter Fifty-Three

Westcott listened as his boss gave some final instructions over the phone to McKenzie, who was leading the team for the Franco take down and arrest. Delray was very specific. 'No unnecessary risks, no heroes. Everyone works as a team and everyone gets to go home alive.'

Under normal circumstances, Delray would have led the operation himself. But these were not ordinary circumstances, and Delray could not be in two places at once. Westcott understood Delray's concerns. Franco had shot and almost killed one of his men, and he did not want a repeat of what happened at Henning's arrest, or worse.

Westcott's boss seemed as happy as he could be. The team was in place a full two hours before Franco's scheduled arrival time at the airfield. Max Tyson, the owner, was cooperating, but he wasn't happy about the Vancouver Police chaperon he now had who accompanied him everywhere he went at the airfield. McKenzie had volunteered for this role himself to ensure everything possible was being done to make sure Franco was not tipped off.

Delray finished his phone call with the closing line. "Stay safe and keep me posted."

After disconnecting, Delray turned to Westcott and asked, "Where are we at?"

Westcott's team had been forced to split in two when they learned that Richard Stelovak was spending the day at Vancouver City Planning Office signing off the Southwest land development deal. Two detectives were currently waiting outside the Stelecom building with the search warrant that they would execute on instructions from Delray or Westcott, and the rest of the original team were at City Planning with Westcott.

"We're good to go," said Westcott. "Forbes and Rainbow are in place at Stelecom, awaiting our instructions. Lamont and Knight were covering the rear exit of the auditorium. We go in through the front and we have it covered."

"I'm not expecting he'll run, Danny, but no other exits?"

"That's it, boss. Front and back entry and exit points only. There's a balcony, but it goes nowhere unless you want to jump three stories."

Delray extended his hand toward the main auditorium. "Lead the way, Danny."

Delray and Westcott walked in through the front doors of the auditorium. There was a large conference table set-up in the middle for all the key officials from Stelecom and City Planning. The surrounding area was occupied by a mixture of media and what Westcott figured were minders and aids to both parties. It looked more like a United Nations gathering than a meeting to sign contracts, he thought.

Richard Stelovak sat front and center in the middle of the conference table alongside Brice Stanley, the Director for City Planning. Stanley was close to sixty, overweight and wore what was left of his hair, too long in a comb-over to hide his balding dome. His hair, beak nose and baggy suit gave him a slightly disheveled appearance, but the looks belied the man. Stanley's reputation preceded him. He was highly intelligent, did not tolerate fools lightly, and had ended the career of more than one aspiring public official who had crossed him.

Before Delray and Westcott had taken a dozen steps into the room, Stanley had observed them. Westcott watched as Stanley rose from his chair, made discrete apologies to those gathered, and quickly made his way over to where they were now standing. As he approached, Westcott could see he was clearly annoyed at the interruption to the proceedings and his moment in the spotlight.

As Stanley waddled towards them, Westcott locked eyes with Richard Stelovak. Stelovak showed no emotion as he stared at Westcott, seemingly oblivious to the conversation and activity that surrounded him.

Stanley stopped directly in front of Delray and Westcott and used his considerable frame as a barrier to stop them from moving forward. With his back to meeting participants and media, he hissed, "You two better have a lot more than a parking ticket to come barging in here unannounced. You've got one minute and then I call the mayor and your chief of police."

Westcott took the threat in his stride. "No parking ticket today. We're here to see Richard Stelovak—arrest him, in fact."

Stanley's face immediately turned red. In the same hushed tones as before, Stanley spoke again, only this time the urgency in his voice made it sound more like a hiss.

"Outside now, both of you!"

Delray rolled his eyes and gave Westcott a 'let's play the game' look as Stanley held the door open and they walked back out into the foyer. Before Stanley could demand an explanation, Westcott had his badge out and up in Stanley's face. "Detective Westcott and Inspector Delray from Vancouver Police. We're here to arrest Richard Stelovak."

Stanley's face remained red. Westcott noted the veins in his neck had popped. "Are you two out of your mind? We have media here and we're just about to sign a two-billion-dollar land development deal with his company.

Delray responded, "Three people have been murdered this week alone that Stelovak is connected to. No amount of money buys immunity or special privilege. You've got five minutes and not a second longer. Then we walk in and arrest him in front of the cameras. Is that what you want?"

Stanley's rage was clearly visible as he turned to leave. "Wait here."

As an afterthought, Delray added, "I'll write our names and badge numbers down for you if you like? I would be more than happy to continue this discussion with senior representatives of Vancouver Police."

Westcott and Delray watched as Stanley went back into the auditorium and closed the door firmly behind him. Delray said, "What do you think, Danny?"

"I think he'll be back out shortly with a message from Stelovak himself."

Two minutes later, Westcott was proved right as the doors opened again and a young professionally dressed woman appeared and walked towards them. Westcott thought she looked about as happy as Stanley had if her icy stare was anything to go by.

"Detectives, my name is Bridget Cummins and I am Mr.

The Catalin Code

Stanley's personal assistant. The contract signing is occurring now, which will be followed by several minutes of photos and brief answers to questions by the media. Mr. Stelovak will see you briefly after this concludes before we reassemble downstairs for the formal press conference."

Delray let Westcott take the lead. "Ms. Cummins, I'm not sure you fully appreciate the situation. We're not here to have a cozy chat with Richard Stelovak at his convenience. We're here to arrest him. He will leave with us in our squad car in handcuffs. Now we can do this the easy way and embarrass just him, or we can do it the hard way. It's your choice!"

For several seconds, Cummins stood seething in silence as she struggled to find an appropriate comeback line for Westcott. When nothing came to mind, she turned her back to Westcott and Delray and hurried back towards the auditorium.

Westcott called after her as she approached the door. "Ms. Cummins."

Bridget Cummins stopped at the door and looked back in Westcott's direction.

"Just so we're perfectly clear. The next person out of those doors is Richard Stelovak. If it's anyone else, even the janitor, we're coming in. Also, there are two other detectives at the other exit."

Westcott watched as Bridget Cummins walked back into the auditorium and closed the doors. He figured he had conveyed the message loud and clear, which was confirmed by Delray, who squeezed his shoulder and gave him the thumbs up signal, while he speed dialed Lamont and Knight to update them on what was happening out front.

Westcott and Delray kept a close eye on the time. Ten

minutes had come and gone and there was still no sign of Richard Stelovak.

Delray shook his head as he looked at his watch again. "Looks like everyone wants to do this the hard way."

As Delray was about to tell Westcott, the time for waiting was over. The doors to the auditorium opened and Richard Stelovak emerged.

Westcott had to admit he looked an imposing figure. Elegantly dressed in a tailored Italian business suit that probably cost half of Westcott's monthly salary, Stelovak walked confidently towards the two detectives, stopping halfway between the auditorium doors and where they both stood. Mind games, thought Westcott; 'never go to them, always let them come to you'.

Unlike Stanley and Cummins, who both openly showed their emotion, Stelovak was a closed book. As Westcott and Delray walked toward him, Westcott studied Stelovak's face. Stelovak's face and steel-blue eyes were void of all expression.

But when he spoke, it became obvious they had clearly irritated him. "You two better have an extraordinarily good reason for delaying a press conference, otherwise I'm going to see that you both lose your badges and your pensions."

Westcott quickly moved behind Stelovak to cuff his hands. "Richard Stelovak, you are under arrest on the suspicion of being involved in three murders. Inspector Delray will formally read you your rights in a moment, but right now you are being detained to accompany us back to your office to witness the execution of a search warrant. You're not required to say anything, and we will give you the opportunity when we are in the squad car to ring an attorney."

Stelovak made no move to resist Westcott and smiled at

Delray as he formally read him his rights. When Delray finished, he asked, "Do you have any questions?"

Stelovak snarled, "Just one. Are you two clowns any good at cleaning toilets?" He looked from Delray to Westcott and then added, "Because when I decide I'm through with you, that's the only job you'll be able to get."

Chapter Fifty-Four

Robbie opened his eyes and did his best to focus through a hazy sea of pale blue. It was hard for him to take in a breath, and the throbbing sensation in the back of his head made it even worse. He realized he was lying on his back, staring skywards as his head cleared. He glanced to his right and gasped as he stared at the blood-covered face of Nick Carney, who was slumped across his chest. When Robbie's focus returned to normal, his gaze shifted from Nick's lifeless eyes to the bullet hole above his left eyebrow.

He remembered everything that had just happened and quickly rolled Nick's body off him and tried to stand up. The ground started spinning and Robbie only got as far as a sitting position before the nausea made him stop. Robbie felt the back of his head where he had hit the platform. He checked his hand for blood and was relieved there were no detectable signs of bleeding or damage.

Robbie slowly stood and turned around to face Jerry in the parking lot. He was in no condition to run and expected to see Jerry advancing towards him to get close enough to make sure he did not miss a second time. To Robbie's surprise, Jerry was not looking at Robbie at all, but was crouched between the two rental cars, with his gun pointed toward the dense vegetation on the opposite side of the parking lot.

As Robbie watched Jerry and tried to make sense of what had just happened, a second gunshot rang out across the parking lot. Robbie flinched and watched as the back of Jerry's white shirt turned red as he fell backward onto the ground.

As quietness returned to the lookout, Robbie tried to comprehend what was happening. The ringing in his ears had almost stopped, and he heard the familiar sound of gravel being compressed as someone walked across the parking lot. A lone figure carrying a high-power rifle came into view and walked up to Jerry Marsden's body. The man momentarily looked down to pick up Jerry's gun and grab one of his hands to check for a pulse. Satisfied Jerry was dead, the man returned his gaze to Robbie before rising to his full height.

As he pointed the rifle at Robbie's chest, Robbie estimated the man was about six feet four. The man had a shaved head, a pale complexion, and was unusually thin. It was easy to see why so many had nicknamed him the undertaker. Robbie said, "You're Peter Trelor."

Peter Trelor continued to point the rifle at Robbie's chest. He looked agitated and impatient. Robbie did not think his anxiety had anything to do with remorse over the two people he had just killed and figured he was no better off now than he had been two minutes ago when Jerry had a gun pointed at him and Nick had a shiv pressed against his neck.

"I'm pleased to hear my reputation precedes me. Hopefully, it will help make our meeting here short and productive."

Trelor motioned Robbie to move back out to the lookout railing with his rifle and continued; "Now, unless you want to start our meeting by me putting a hole in your chest to match your friend Jerry's, I suggest you move back out onto the viewing platform. That way, I can lower this rifle for a few minutes without risking you making a run for it."

Robbie was in no position to argue and made his way back out onto the platform and leaned against the railing. He was still feeling slightly nauseous and giddy and did not have the energy to argue with Trelor. He figured he would find out soon enough what he was after. Trelor only walked as far as the platform walkway and stopped. Cradling the rifle in one arm, Trelor deftly withdrew a cigarette and lighter with the other hand. When he had the cigarette well alight, he returned the lighter to his pocket and took several deep drawers on the cigarette before continuing.

"I heard some of the conversation that you had with your friends. It seems like there is a lot of history between you. Normally, I would love to discuss that in more detail; however, I am pressed for time, so we need to get to the here and now."

Robbie did not know how to respond and stayed silent. As he felt the fog clearing and his strength returning, he realized he would need to figure out quickly what Trelor wanted and how he could best use it as a bargaining chip to save his life.

Trelor took another long draft on his cigarette and blew a plume of smoke skyward. As he watched it dissipate, he returned his attention to Robbie.

"So, here's the deal. You give me what I need, I walk

away, and you get to live. You don't give me what I want—I walk away a frustrated man and you get to join your two friends in the life hereafter. Am I making myself clear?"

Robbie was still not sure where the conversation was going and simply said, "Perfectly."

Trelor tossed his cigarette butt to the ground and continued. "So, to put it into context for you, I've run a successful security company ever since being shafted by the recently deceased Nick Carney when we both worked at the OCTF. MacDonald has worked with me on and off and we kept in touch, although I'm sure that's not news to you. Your new girlfriend will already have filled in the blanks on that by now."

Robbie interrupted. "How do you know about Laura?"

Trelor sighed. "You've been the most followed man in Vancouver this week."

Robbie went to ask another question, but Trelor held up his free hand to cut him off.

"I'm short on time. Your two dead friends here had a nice partnership going with Richard Stelovak. Jerry Marsden used his considerable influence and a few well-placed bribes to get the Southwest development deal across the line with City Planning for Stelovak. Carney has been using his law enforcement contacts locally and internationally to provide intelligence to Stelovak any time one of his companies or people came under the radar for investigation. A pleasant arrangement for everyone—Carney and Marsden both stood to make one point five million in bonuses today when the Vancouver planning deal goes through."

Robbie felt his strength returning. Being trapped out on the viewing platform made it impossible to make a run for it. I need to stall for time in the hope I can negotiate my way out of this, he thought. "So how do I fit in to all of this?"

"I'll get to that in a minute. Stelovak was a client of mine for a while and ended up buying six state-of-the art listening devices from my company. They have a transmitter not much bigger than an aspirin and are undetectable in basic bug sweeps. Unbeknownst to him, while I was in his office one day, I planted one of these same devices, thinking it would help me understand the man and his company more so that I would know how to pitch for extra work. But the more I monitored his conversations, the more I realized what a nasty piece of work he really was. I was contemplating having it removed and then in the space of an afternoon, three things changed my mind."

Trelor grinned. "First is a call Stelovak makes to a bank in Romania where the bribe money is being held for Heckle and Jeckle here. The money is already in accounts for them, but such is the paranoia of Stelovak, he had the bank set it up with a special voice activated release key. Stelovak must give the verbal clearance by phone to the bank's computer system in order for the funds to be released. The second is a call I get from MacDonald. He's worried because you've been poking your nose into Stelovak's business interests in Romania for some article your writing. Carney was alerted by his contacts over there and told Stelovak. And so this week you have become top of the hit-list to prevent you publishing anything damaging."

Trelor shook his head. "Of all the crooked banks in Eastern Europe, you had to pick the one Stelovak uses. MacDonald knows, or should I say knew, the Stelovak account numbers. He and his wheelchair friend in Romania had become quite close and shared a lot of information."

It all made sense to Robbie. "That's why you met with

Mac at Irish's on the night they killed him. You were after the account numbers."

"He confided in me what he'd found hidden on Nick Carney's laptop, so I even offered to cut him in. But MacDonald wasn't interested. I couldn't pressure him anymore in such a public place without arousing suspicion and before I had another opportunity, he'd met with his untimely accident, courtesy of Stelovak. It was then that I decided I needed to disappear. I knew Stelovak will figure this out before long, and I would wind up on the same dispatch list."

Trelor stopped talking and stared intensely at Robbie. Robbie knew before the question came what he was after. He also knew his life expectancy was less than a minute if he didn't come up with the right answer. He needed more time to come up with a strategy.

"What was the third thing?"

"The bug I planted has recorded all the words in Stelovak's own voice that I need. I now have a digital copy of the magic sentence; 'Funds release authorized, Richard Stelovak.'" Trelor touched his top pocket and continued, "In fact, I have a digital copy right here, ready to use." Speaking softly, he continued, "I just need the account numbers and the thee million will be mine."

Robbie recalled the emails Mac had exchanged with Petru using the catalin1989 account. The account numbers had been referred to, but if they had been exchanged, they would have been sent to one of Mac's regular email addresses prior to the switch to the special purpose address. He thinks I know the numbers too, Robbie thought. He chose his words carefully. "How do I know you won't shoot me as soon as I hand them over?"

Trelor laughed softly. "I'm not convinced you have

them, Robbie. I took a gamble that you might, which is why I tracked Jerry Marsden here today. I've been through your motel room and through your girlfriend's place and found nothing."

Robbie was genuinely confused. "Why didn't you get the details off Nick and Jerry before you shot them?"

"Obviously you don't know Nick Carney like I do. He survived the OCTF scandal and actually prospered when all around him were falling. I couldn't take the risk that he didn't have another concealed weapon. Last thing I want is to be shot at close quarters. He got the better of me once. It wasn't going to happen again."

Trelor glanced back towards the parking lot before continuing, "Our friend Jerry should have taken one in the shoulder and lived at least long enough to tell me what I needed to know. But he pivoted at the wrong moment and took the bullet in the chest instead. So, you're all I have left."

Trelor carefully removed his backpack with one hand while he continued to cradle the rifle. As he placed it gently on the ground in front of him, he said, "In there is my laptop and a satellite phone. I can connect to the Internet in seconds from almost any location in the world, including here."

Robbie went numb as he watched Trelor slowly raise the rifle into the firing position. With the barrel pointed at the middle if Robbie's chest, Trelor said a second time.

"I need those account numbers."

Robbie lied, "I can't give them to you right now. They're on a memory stick I hid at the farm the other day."

Trelor looked up from the telescopic sight. "Try again. You're a seasoned traveler used to storing information in email and cyberspace. I want an email address and password or a cyber storage account ID and password right now or I shoot."

Robbie swallowed. "I told you, I don't have them here."

Trelor's face contorted, and his mood turned dark. He lowered the rifle from Robbie's chest to Robbie's knee. "We'll soon find out if you're telling the truth."

Robbie closed his eyes and braced for the gunshot and excruciating pain that would follow as his kneecap shattered. The gun shot was as loud as the previous shots, but the pain he expected didn't follow. Robbie opened his eyes and saw Peter Trelor staggering forward as his eyes rolled into the back of his head. Trelor let go the rifle and stood unsteady for a moment before collapsing face down in front of him. Robbie watched as Trelor lay perfectly still, his back slowly turning red as he bled out.

Robbie heard a sound in the parking lot and looked up. He stared in disbelief as Laura dropped what appeared to be a gun to the ground. She appeared in shock as she stepped over the body of Jerry Marsden and staggered toward him.

Chapter Fifty-Five

The car trip from City Planning to the Stelecom building went without incident for Westcott and Delray. They had placed Stelovak in the back seat and handcuffed him to a special purpose restraint to prevent escape. He still had one hand free and used it to make a phone call to his lawyer, Michael Phipps. The crux of the phone call had simply been a demand by Stelovak for Phipps to meet him at his office and see what they could do to shut down the search before it started.

Delray and Westcott rolled their eyes in amusement as Stelovak instructed Michael Phipps to have his legal team draw up lawsuits against Vancouver Metro, as well as Delray and Westcott personally.

Detectives Forbes and Rainbow were both waiting in front of the Stelecom building when they arrived. Westcott knew Delray was proud that his workforce was diversifying and two female detectives could now be assigned to a team together.

After parking the car, Westcott got Stelovak out of the back seat and had him stand beside the car while he was re-handcuffed.

Stelovak pulled his free hand away and said, "You're not seriously putting these things back on me to walk me into my own building?"

Westcott grabbed his hand and said, "It's standard procedure, and I am."

Stelovak shook his head. "Do you have any idea how demeaning this is? Frogmarching the CEO into his own building in front of five hundred employees?"

Westcott replied evenly, "No, I don't and let's not make this any worse than it has to be."

Stelovak fumed and in a measured voice responded, "You will regret this day. I don't forgive and I don't forget."

As Westcott led Stelovak toward the building, Delray fell in and walked several paces behind. When he was sure the situation was under control, he turned to Forbes and said, "Where are we at?"

As they continued to walk, Forbes provided an update. "Top floor of the building is sealed off as instructed, boss. We have two uniformed officers stationed outside Stelovak's office. Stelovak's lawyer, a Michael Phipps, is already up there and raising hell because we won't let him in the office. We have been polite but firm, sir."

"Has he seen the warrant yet?"

Forbes smiled. "No, boss, we were waiting for you as instructed. Besides, this is something you should enjoy personally. We'll just watch."

Delray took the warrant from Forbes and said, "Showtime, detective. Lead the way."

When the elevator opened on the top floor, Michael

Phipps and two other lawyers in dark suits from his law firm were waiting in the lobby to meet them.

Phipps flew into a rage upon seeing Stelovak in handcuffs and demanded he be un-handcuffed immediately.

Westcott looked at Delray as he weighed up what to do. They had stationed uniformed officers at both ends of the floor. It was highly unlikely Stelovak would run. His major weapons of self-defense were always attorneys, courtrooms, and well-placed bribes.

Delray nodded to Westcott, who undid the handcuffs.

Delray turned to Phipps and said, "We placed your client under arrest for the purposes of being here to witness and answer questions in relation to this search warrant."

Phipps snatched the warrant out of Delray's hand and began reading. As he read the specifics of the warrant, he roared, laughing. "This isn't valid and certainly isn't legal. The basis of your search is on the testimony of a former sacked and disgruntled Stelecom employee who, as I understand it, is currently wanted by authorities in connection to several criminal matters."

Delray had been expecting this and hit speed dial on his phone. "You can sort this out with Judge May yourself. She signed off on it, so your fight is with her, not me."

Delray had pre-planned the call with Judge Harriet May. Judge May had a reputation for being fair and reasonable but loathed anyone who tried to step on a proper judicial process or usurp her authority. Judge May and Phipps did not get on and he had been slapped with contempt of court charges on several occasions when he had abused his position in her courtroom.

Delray waited and when the call was answered, he exchanged a few brief words before handing the phone to

Phipps. "Cindy is Judge May's personal assistant. She will pass you on to Judge May momentarily."

Phipps rolled his eyes before snatching the phone from Delray. He motioned Stelovak to join him as they retreated to the other end of the hallway to speak with the judge in private. Westcott and Delray watched for several minutes as Phipps talked on the phone. From the body language and the animated gestures being displayed between Phipps and Stelovak, it did not appear to be going well.

Finally, Phipps stormed back, holding the phone at arm's length as if he might catch a disease from it. When he reached Delray, he thrust it under his nose. "She wants to speak to you."

Delray took the phone and waited for Phipps to retreat out of earshot before he spoke. "Judge May?"

"Very briefly, Inspector Delray, I want to remind you that your search only covers the safe and nothing else. You find anything, you stop immediately like we discussed and formally arrest Stelovak. I will then issue a wider search warrant for his office and we take it from there. Are we clear?"

"Perfectly, judge."

"Alright, one last piece of advice. Keep everyone from Vancouver Metro out of Stelovak's office until the search of the safe is over and you have been issued with a wider search warrant. If one of your team so much as lifts a ballpoint pen off Stelovak's desk or brushes up against a file and moves it, Michael Phipps will claim the search went beyond its lawful boundary and he will have a solid case for having all evidence collected declared invalid. I suggest just you and Detective Westcott only conduct the search. The only other team member to be present should be whoever is in charge of the video recorder. Are we clear?"

"Crystal clear, judge."

"Good luck, inspector."

Delray disconnected and turned to Westcott. "We have the green light. The judge is adamant we keep the crew for the initial search to a minimum. How good is Forbes with the camera?"

"Better than me."

"Okay, Forbes is on the camera, Rainbow at the door, which we leave open. Everybody else outside. You take the lead and I'll be your backup and monitor Phipps. No other lawyers inside either."

Westcott nodded. "I'll go get Stelovak and Phipps."

Westcott walked over to where Stelovak and Phipps were standing.

Before he could tell them the search was about to begin, Stelovak interrupted. "You like promises, detective?"

Westcott ignored the question and motioned Phipps and Stelovak towards Stelovak's office. "Time to start the search, gentlemen. Just the two of you, the other lawyers can observe from outside."

Stelovak paused on the way past Westcott. He held Westcott's gaze easily with his cold steel-blue eyes and a practiced chilling smile. In a voice barely above a whisper he said, "You're making a huge mistake on so many levels, detective. I promise you, you'll regret this day personally and professionally for the rest of your life, no matter how long or short that might be."

Westcott ignored the threat and followed the two men into the office. When Forbes had the video camera setup and recording, she gave the thumbs up to Delray.

Westcott watched Stelovak closely while Delray re-read the search warrant for the benefit of the video recording.

He noticed Stelovak's anger and aggressive body language had disappeared. Stelovak now appeared calm and in complete control. He's playing for the camera now, Westcott thought. Stelovak wants to look the model citizen if this ever gets to court.

When Delray had finished, he gave a brief nod to Westcott, who stepped forward in front of the picture that covered the safe.

"In accordance with the search warrant, Richard Stelovak, you are now requested to open this safe for the purpose of a police search in relation to several legal matters we are investigating. Can you confirm this is the only safe in this office?"

Stelovak nodded.

Westcott responded, "I'll need a yes or no answer."

Westcott could see the body language changing. Stelovak clearly wants to rip my throat out he thought.

In a stifled reply, Stelovak said, "Yes."

Westcott asked Stelovak to open the safe and stood back to give him room. Stelovak looked at Phipps, who nodded. Stelovak stepped forward and slid the painting covering the safe back on its rails. The safe was far bigger than Westcott had expected and was almost the size of a three-drawer filing cabinet.

Stelovak used his body to shield the safe from view as he entered the combination. When the safe was unlocked, Westcott motioned Stelovak to return to his position next to Phipps while the search was conducted.

Westcott put on rubber gloves to begin the search. He noticed the top shelf was split in two. The right side appeared to be another safe within the main safe and would also need to be examined. Westcott quickly shuffled through the envelopes and documents. He was relieved when he found an olive-green envelope with the name 'Blackwell' written on the front, as Keaton had described. There was always a chance that Keaton was leading them on a merry dance just to embarrass them and inconvenience Stelovak.

As Westcott removed the envelope from the safe, both he and Delray closely watched Stelovak's response. Stelovak did his best to remain impassive as he got a good look at the envelope. Phipps whispered to Stelovak, who then nodded. Neither man said anything as Westcott carefully opened the envelope.

"Let the recording reflect, I have removed an olive-green envelope from the safe in Richard Stelovak's office. The envelope has a label on the front entitled 'Blackwell.' I am now opening the envelope."

Stelovak swore under his breath but said nothing more.

Michael Phipps entered the conversation. "Let the record also reflect that my client has advised me he has no recollection of ever seeing that envelope."

Westcott was not sure what Phipps was up to and ignored him. Westcott slid his hand into the envelope and took a deep breath. Slowly, he withdrew several high quality eight by ten glossy photographs. They were all of Leon Blackwell, semi naked with a woman in various compromising sexual positions. The blackmail pictures as promised by Randolph Keaton.

Westcott provided a short and discrete summary of the pictures for the video recording. Throughout the process, Westcott never took his eyes off Stelovak.

When he finished, he gave the nod to Delray. Delray stepped forward and stood in front of Stelovak.

"We're suspending the search while we wait for a second warrant to be issued to expand the search to the entire office. Do you have any questions before I formally arrest you?"

Phipps stepped forward. "You have made a grave mistake here. My client is clearly being framed. This fiasco will never get to court, and your careers with Vancouver Metro will be over within the month."

Chapter Fifty-Six

Robbie bent down and grabbed Trelor's left hand to check for a pulse.

"He's dead, isn't he?"

Robbie looked up at Laura, who had stopped walking. She looked pale and was clearly in distress as she stood and stared down at the body.

"Yes, he's dead."

Robbie walked across to where Laura stood. She was shivering and had her arms wrapped around herself as if she was cold. Robbie placed an arm gently around Laura and then held her tight. "You saved my life, Laura."

"I didn't want to kill him, Robbie, but I had no choice."

"You did the right thing. As soon as Trelor realized I didn't have what he wanted, there was only one way this was going to end."

Laura gently pulled away and looked at Nick Carney, who lay on his back, his lifeless eyes staring at the sky.

Laura then turned and looked back at Jerry Marsden, who lay in a contorted heap between the two rental cars.

"The Director of the OCTF, the mayor of Vancouver and Peter Trelor all dead in the one incident. The media storm from this is going to make what happened in the OCTF seem like a kindergarten outing by comparison."

"I'm not sure I can do this again, Robbie. It nearly killed me last time, but I'll try…"

Robbie let out a long breath. Even though they were innocent in the deaths of Nick and Jerry, and had acted in self-defense against Peter Trelor, he knew the media would be relentless. The murders of the Vancouver Mayor and the OCTF Director would be front-page news and examined from every angle for months. He studied Laura for a moment. She looked overwhelmed and extremely vulnerable. He knew any hope of a lasting recovery and normal life for her would be gone once the police and media became involved. In an instant, he knew what needed to be done. He walked the few steps that separated them and gently placed his arms around Laura and then held her tightly.

In a quiet but determined voice, he said, "I love you and I'm going to fix this."

Robbie felt Laura relax a little as she said, "Thank you, Robbie, although I'm not sure how you can fix this mess."

As Robbie held Laura, he looked at the three bodies before asking, "Where did you park your truck?"

"It's back down on the fire trail where we parked the other day. Why?"

"Do you have a tarp in the back?"

"Yes."

Robbie pulled the keys for his rental out of his pocket.

"Where are we going with this, Robbie?"

"We'll talk about it on the way. We need to get these three out of the parking lot before anyone comes up here. Your Bronco is the easiest way to transport them all at once without raising too much suspicion. Are you okay with that?"

Laura looked to still be in shock, but was recovering. "I'm not thinking clearly yet, Robbie, but I trust you."

As they made their way down off the lookout to the fire trail in Robbie's rental, he asked, "I didn't tell you where I was going to meet Nick, so how did you know where I would be?"

"From where we organized Nick to exchange cars, I figured it had to be somewhere south of the city. Somewhere out of Nick's comfort zone, and I thought here, Cypress Falls, or your house on the farm. If it was me, Cypress Falls was too public, the house too personal, so that left here."

Robbie held Laura's gaze. "You saved my life, Laura. I'm not sure I can ever repay you."

Laura smiled briefly and said softly, "You told me you love me Robbie, I don't need anything else."

As they approached the fire trail, Robbie asked, "Why? Why did you come?"

"You have Nick Carney to thank for that. When he arrived in the parking lot, he pushed me down on the hood and roughed me up a little."

Robbie protested, but Laura continued. "I'm okay, Robbie, he didn't really hurt me. But, before he let me do the search, he placed a SIG Sauer pistol, not an OCTF issued gun, on the hood of the Bronco. It was then that I got really worried. I made him lock the pistol in his own car before he left in the rental. I waited a couple of minutes, debating what to do. In the end, I couldn't take the chance that Nick hadn't arranged some other way to have you killed after what he did to me, so I smashed his car window and took his gun. By the time I got out of the parking lot, Nick was well on his way and too far ahead to follow."

Robbie smiled as he shook his head. "You find new ways to amaze me on a daily basis."

Laura continued, "I was pretty sure you would come to the lookout, so I planned to park on the fire trail and quickly walk up the rest of the way to observe, but not let on I was there unless I had to. I knew Nick couldn't be far ahead and thought I would have time. I figured Nick would play along to get as much information as possible before he did anything."

Robbie swung the rental onto the fire trail and parked behind Laura's Bronco. He looked further up the trail from Laura's Bronco and saw another parked car.

Laura continued, "But when I pulled in here, I saw this black Lexus."

Robbie recognized the car immediately. "That's Jerry's car. He gave me a ride back to the hotel in it the other night."

"I didn't know who owned the car, and I had no idea what was going on, or what to expect, so I ran up the hill as fast as I could. I was close to the parking lot when I heard the first gunshot. I wanted to scream and fall in a heap, but I kept going. I got to the edge of the parking lot and could see just enough through the trees and vegetation to see you and Nick in a heap on the ground and Jerry crouching between the two cars."

Laura paused for a moment to compose herself. As tears welled in her eyes, she stammered, "I thought you were dead, Robbie. I thought I'd lost you."

Robbie switched off the engine and reached across and squeezed Laura's hand. "I'm still here, Laura."

"And then I saw you rolling Nick's body off you. I

wanted to scream. And then the second shot. I remember closing my eyes and crying 'no'. I wanted to be sick, thinking I had come this far and got so close and then you had been shot after all. I said a quick prayer and then opened my eyes to see you trying to get up. When I saw Trelor crossing the parking lot, I realized he had shot Jerry instead."

Laura shook her head. "I wasn't sure whether Trelor was a friend or an enemy at first, but it soon became clear."

Laura paused again and breathed deeply for several seconds. Robbie understood the next part would be difficult for her to recount. "When he raised the rifle to your chest and then threatened to start at your knees, I knew I had no choice…"

"It was Nick's gun?"

Laura nodded. Robbie reached across and held Laura. "Thank you. I'd be dead now if it wasn't for you."

"I'm okay now, Robbie. We need to keep moving."

"You sure? I don't want to push you."

Laura opened her door. "No, I'm good."

Robbie thought for a moment. "I think the priority has to be the bodies. We worry about the cars later."

"Okay."

After switching cars, they drove back to the lookout in silence. Robbie marveled at Laura's resilience. But after what had happened today, he knew she would need support in the coming months to get through this ordeal properly. That was fine with him. He intended on being that support person she could lean on.

As they drove into the parking lot, Robbie was relieved to see no one else had come up to the lookout yet. He wanted to get this over with as quickly as possible and said,

"I'll get the bodies and bring them over while you lay out the tarp. No sense us both getting covered in blood."

Before Laura could protest, Robbie got out of the truck. He pulled Jerry up into a sitting position and picked up his body using a fireman's carry. After carrying his body to the back of the Bronco, he gently laid it on the tarpaulin that Laura had spread out on the cargo tray.

Robbie then quickly checked through Jerry's pockets. He said, "Keys to the Lexus," as held up a set of keys. "We can't leave it up here."

Laura watched in silence while Robbie retrieved the other two bodies. When he had finished laying all three in the back of the Bronco, she simply said, "Thank you."

Robbie went back to each of the locations where the men had fallen and moved gravel and dirt around as much as he could to cover up the blood staining. As he walked back to the Bronco he said, "Not great, but if we get rain in the next day or so, anything short of a forensic team will never work out what happened here."

Laura pointed at his shirt and said, "You're covered in blood." She reached under the front seat of the Bronco and pulled out an old heavy-duty raincoat. She said, "This used to be my Dads," as she handed it to Robbie. "Hopefully, if we're careful, you won't leave any blood stains behind."

Robbie thanked her for the coat. As they got into the Bronco, he asked, "Do you know where we are going?"

Laura nodded. "Yes Robbie, I do."

Chapter Fifty-Seven

Vincent Franco checked his watch as his associate turned off the highway and headed down the narrow tar road that lead to Tyson's airport. Traffic out of Vancouver had been slow, and they were ten minutes behind schedule. Franco was not concerned about missing his flight. He was the only passenger and still had the ten thousand in cash the flight was going to cost him in his carry-on bag.

Franco was cautious by nature. He had not survived this long without being careful and thorough. As they approached the small regional airport, Franco could see it was little more than a runway with an aircraft hangar and adjoining low-set white two-story building in need of repairs.

As they reached the entrance, Franco said to his driver, "Slow down, but don't go in the front gate. We'll drive around and check things out first."

The airport was surrounded by a high, rusting chain link mesh fence that separated it from the service road for the semi-rural community that surrounded it. As Franco's associate slowly drove around the airport, Franco scanned the airport from every angle, looking for anything unusual or out of place that would signal trouble.

"You expecting trouble, Vince?"

Franco ignored the question and continued his reconnaissance as they drove around the service road. As they approached the front entrance again, Franco finally answered the question.

"I'm not expecting trouble, but it's had a habit of finding me this week. I'm jumpy and just want to get the hell out of here."

As they drove in through the front gate to the airport, Franco could see only two other cars in the parking lot. One was a beat up and aging blue Ford, which he remembered belonged to Max Tyson. The other car was a large brown Nissan van.

Franco was suspicious and said to his associate, "Park next to the van, but leave the engine running."

Franco pulled a pistol from his jacket pocket and held it close to his leg as he got out of the car. He walked around the van looking in through the windows and checking for high-tech radio equipment and anything else that would identify it as an undercover police vehicle, or worse still, a sign that a Stelovak farewell committee might be close by.

Franco saw nothing suspicious. The rear cargo area was empty and the front driver compartment only had very standard appointments, which did not even extend to air conditioning. Franco was reasonably satisfied the vehicle was no threat. He removed a brown envelope from his jacket and returned to the car to knock on the driver's side window.

As his associate wound down his window, Franco handed him the envelope. "Here's your money. Pop the trunk and I'll get my bag. Wait here for two minutes before you leave. If I'm not back by then, I've found Tyson and I'm good to go."

Without a word of thanks or a goodbye, Franco retrieved his bag and walked across the parking lot and into the white building.

The office space and reception area were sparsely furnished with furniture and fittings that would have been modern back in the early seventies. If business was good, Tyson was not spending it on improvements, Franco thought. Max Tyson stood behind the reception counter, writing on a form attached to a clipboard. He was in his early fifties, slightly overweight and wore his long graying hair in a ponytail. He had grown a goatee since Franco had seen him last, but nothing else about him had changed, including the fact that Franco still did not trust him.

Without looking up, Tyson said, "Been a while, Vince."

Franco responded, "Quite a while, Max," as he kept scanning the interior of the building. Tyson appeared to be on his own, which was the way Franco wanted it.

Tyson detected a nasal twang in Franco's voice and looked up. He momentarily stared at the metal bridge supporting Franco's broken nose. "What the hell happened to you?" Realizing this was not the question you ask someone like Vincent Franco, the man quickly added, "Never mind, I don't need to know."

Franco kept looking around as Tyson went back to completing his paperwork. In a soothing voice, Tyson added, "Won't be long, Vince. I have another job tonight after yours that requires paper work."

Franco nodded, but said nothing more.

"You want to use the bathroom before we go? Flight time is ninety minutes."

Franco said, "No, I'm good," as he walked towards a set of stairs that led up to the upper level of the building. "Who owns the brown van?"

Tyson frowned. "Van?"

"In the parking lot."

"Oh, that. Just a guy I flew out-of-town yesterday. I pick him up tomorrow. Problem?"

Franco said, "No," as he stopped at the set of stairs. He pointed and asked, "What's up there?"

Tyson glanced up at the stairs before returning to his clipboard. "Storage area and my apartment. I moved in about six months ago. Been doing a lot of night work and get back at all hours, so now I don't need to drive home. Also, keeps my costs down."

Glancing up from his clipboard again, Tyson added, "You want a tour?"

Franco continued to look up the stairs. "No. We need to leave."

Tyson picked up a set of keys from the counter along with his clipboard. "You got the ten grand?"

Franco nodded. "You get it when we arrive."

Tyson motioned Franco to a doorway that led from the office building to the runway. "The plane is full of fuel and ready to go."

Franco followed Tyson out of the building and across the tarmac to the small Cessna four-seater plane.

Tyson said to Franco, "Hop in around the other side while I do my last checks."

Tyson spent a few moments on a visual inspection of the plane, before giving Franco the thumbs up. "We're good to go."

Franco watched Tyson as he opened the door to the pilot seat of the plane. As he went to get in, Tyson looked back at the hangar and cursed. "My mechanic didn't lock the roller door again. I swear he'd leave his head here if it wasn't attached."

Tyson glanced at Franco. "Sit tight, I'll only be a minute."

Franco watched as Tyson hurried back to the hangar. He could clearly see the door was slightly ajar and only became suspicious when Tyson disappeared inside instead of locking it. Six heavily armed Vancouver Metro police officers in black combat gear and bulletproof vests burst from the hangar, confirming Franco's worst suspicions.

Franco pulled his gun out of his jacket pocket and cursed as he watched the police quickly spread out into a semi-circle formation on the hangar side of the plane. He quickly weighed up his options. He was not sure exactly who had sold him out or how, but he knew instantly his situation was bad. Being unable to fly a plane or even know how to start the engine meant he needed to get out of the Cessna quickly.

He looked to the fence on the opposite side of the runway to the hangar as his only potential escape route. He was confident he had enough of a head start on the cops that if he made a run for it, he could reach the fence before they did, but quickly dismissed the idea. After shooting a cop, they would not bother chasing him down. He knew he would be lucky if he got halfway to the fence before he had a dozen bullets in his back.

As the police formation continued to spread out and surround the plane, time seemed to stand still for Franco.

He reflected on the week that had just gone by. It had been busy, even by his standards. Apart from shooting the cop, his jobs for Stelovak in running down the security geek, the Brennan job and hanging Blackwell had all been highlights. Allowing Robbie Mayne to get the better of him had not. At forty-seven, he realized the life he had known for twenty-five years was over.

As the police formation tightened around the plane, Franco realized these were probably the last seconds of freedom he would ever have. As he looked at each police officer, he could clearly see the grim and determined look on the face of each man as they stopped advancing and assumed firing positions with their rifles and pistols.

He zoned in on the face of the police officer he recognized from outside Henning's apartment when he had shot his partner. Franco could see the hatred in the man's eyes as they stared at one another. He thought about shooting him through the Plexi glass window of the Cessna. It would be nice to take out one more before it was all over, he thought. He realized the other five cops would never let that happen. He would be dead the moment he raised his gun.

As he continued to stare down the cop, he realized he was out of options. Spending the rest of his life in jail would never happen, nor would he allow them the satisfaction of killing him.

As he weighed up what to do, the cop who he was staring down said, "It's over, Franco. Put your hands in the air where I can see them, and you won't get hurt."

In an instant, Franco knew what needed to be done. As he continued to hold the cop's stare, Franco gripped his gun tightly before raising it to his mouth and pulling the trigger.

Chapter Fifty-Eight

Robbie and Laura were silent for the drive from the lookout back down to the fire trail. Neither of them felt comfortable talking with three dead bodies in the back of Laura's Bronco. When they reached the fire trail, Robbie broke the silence.

"Might be best if you pullover just before the turnoff. There won't be room to squeeze past, so I'll back Jerry's car out first."

Laura reached across and grabbed Robbie's hand to stop him from getting out. "Robbie, we can call the police if you think it's the right thing to do. I don't want you living with regrets about today."

Robbie shook his head. "No. No regrets. The three of them would have killed us in a heartbeat. We did nothing wrong, and it's some sort of justice for Mac, at least."

Robbie held Laura's gaze. He could see it was important to her he agreed with what they were doing. He added, "I really am okay with this," and then got out of the Bronco.

Robbie backed the Lexus out from the fire trail and onto

the main road leading down from the lookout. He parked the car off the roadway as best he could before returning.

As he got back in the vehicle, he said to Laura, "Are you okay with driving?"

She replied, "Yes," as she put the Bronco into gear.

They turned onto the fire trail and drove at a slow and steady pace, both understanding that getting the Bronco as close as they could would make the task ahead of them easier.

After about ten minutes of cautiously driving up the fire trail, they approached a small clearing. Robbie said, "I think this is as far as we can go. We can turn around here as well to save us having to back all the way out."

Laura turned the vehicle around with a precision three-point turn. In silence, they got out and opened up the cargo area. They both stared at the three bodies wrapped in the tarpaulin. Robbie turned and looked up the ridge-line to the mine shaft he and Laura had visited the other day.

"Do you have any gloves in your truck?"

Laura frowned. "Gloves?"

She then realized why Robbie was asking. "Oh… No gloves."

Laura went around to the front driver's seat and reached underneath and produced what looked like a small prospector's pick. "When I first got my driving license, my father gave me this to keep under my front seat for protection. Just in case I was ever attacked while in my car alone. I've kept it ever since, but never had to use it."

Robbie gave a brief smile. "Remind me never to make you angry while we're out and about in your truck."

Laura gave half a smile in return. "Hopefully, it will help clear away the thorns and brambles."

Robbie half pulled; half slid the tarpaulin containing

the bodies off the cargo tray. It landed on the ground with a heavy thud.

Robbie studied the bodies for a moment and said, "I'll have to make three separate trips," as he began undoing the tarpaulin. He added as an afterthought, "I'll take Nick first. He's the heaviest."

"Robbie, please let me help."

"You can. You can take the rifle, the guns and Trelor's backpack up for me. When we get there, I'll leave you to clear away the mine shaft while I get the other two."

Robbie finished opening the tarpaulin and dragged the body of Nick Carney into the sitting position, before hoisting him onto his shoulders in a fireman's carry.

Laura followed him up the ridge-line and insisted on helping Robbie each time he had to stop to rest, but he refused. When they finally reached the mine shaft, Robbie unceremoniously dropped the body of Nick Carney on the ground and stretched out his back.

After resting for a moment, he said, "I'm going to head back now. Will you be okay here alone?"

Laura held up her small coal miner's pick. "I have plenty to do."

Robbie turned and started back down the slope to where they had parked the Bronco.

"Be back in twenty."

Laura watched as Robbie disappeared down the slope. It was time for her to turn her attention to clearing away the mine shaft. The brambles and thorns that had overgrown the shaft entrance were thick and looked almost impenetrable. No wonder this had never been discovered, she thought. After circling the bramble bush twice, Laura decided on a plan of attack.

Patiently and carefully, she separated the outer brambles

with her pick and then carefully pulled them back away from the main body of the bush and placed rocks on them to prevent them from springing back into place.

It was a slow process, but after almost twenty minutes Laura could finally see a glimpse of the dark opening to the mine shaft. As she stepped forward for a better look, she heard heavy footsteps behind her and turned around to see Robbie trudging the last few paces carrying the body of Peter Trelor in a fireman's carry.

As he laid the body of Peter Trelor next to Nick Carney, Robbie said in a breathless voice, "You've made good progress."

"So, have you. You must be exhausted, Robbie."

Robbie drew in a couple of deep breaths. "I've felt better and felt worse."

Looking at the two corpses and then at the sky, he continued, "At least I'm still alive. I need to keep going."

"Shouldn't you rest?"

Robbie looked at the sky. "It gets dark early here. I need to keep moving."

Laura walked across to where she had dropped Peter Trelor's backpack and rifle.

"Wait."

Laura opened the backpack and sifted through the contents. She pulled out Trelor's laptop and satellite phone before pulling out a MAG-LITE flashlight. She switched it on to make sure it worked before holding it up in triumph.

"Will this do, Robbie?"

"That's great, Laura. We should be able to get back down to the Bronco in the dark without breaking a leg now."

Laura put the satellite phone and laptop back in the

laptop bag. As Robbie watched Laura, he suddenly had an idea. "We'll keep the phone."

Robbie bent down and began searching the top pockets of Peter Trelor's shirt. He quickly found and removed a USB memory stick.

After putting the memory stick in his pocket, he added, "A satellite phone may come in handy."

Before Laura could ask Robbie what he meant, he called out over his shoulder, "See you soon," as he started his walk back down the trail to get the body of Jerry Marsden.

Laura watched Robbie until he disappeared out of sight. Their last conversation had been confusing, but she felt sure all would be explained on his return.

Laura picked up her small prospectors' pick and returned her concentration to the bramble bush. In less than ten minutes, she cleared a good size opening and could get close enough to peer down the shaft.

The shaft was just a wide, dark black hole. The closer she got, the more she could smell the chilled and stagnant air coming up from deep within the shaft. She shuddered as she realized this was also a man's grave.

Laura moved back from the edge. She was keen for Robbie's return and suddenly uncomfortable with all the death that surrounded her.

Laura continued her work, pulling back the vines with the prospector's pick. Twenty minutes later, she was satisfied she had made a big enough opening to allow access to dispose of the bodies.

Laura looked at her watch with alarm as she realized Robbie had been gone for well over half an hour. He's at least ten minutes late, she thought. Laura looked down the trail and decided she shouldn't wait. If Robbie had fallen and hurt himself, time could be critical.

Grabbing the flashlight and Nick's pistol, Laura started back down the trail. After a minute of walking, Laura could hear heavy footsteps coming up the trail. She stopped and waited patiently for Robbie to appear.

It took several more minutes before Robbie finally emerged, making his way slowly up the trail carrying the body of Jerry Marsden. Robbie looked exhausted as he trudged the final short distance toward the mine shaft.

As he approached Laura, she said, "Robbie, you looked exhausted. Please stop and rest."

"If I stop now, I'll never start again."

Laura followed Robbie as he walked the rest of the way. The last part of the trip took Robbie ten minutes as he neared total exhaustion. When they finally reached the mine shaft again, Robbie dumped Jerry's body on the ground and collapsed in a heap.

Laura came and sat beside him and placed a hand on his shoulder. It was getting dark, but she knew Robbie needed to rest. They still had work to do here and then they had to get Robbie's two rental cars, the Lexus and Laura's Bronco, down off the mountain. It was going to be a long night.

After resting for ten minutes, Robbie sat up and looked at Laura and then at the opening she had made through the brambles and thorns to the mine shaft. "You've done a good job. How are your hands?"

Laura held up her hands and examined them. "Not too bad. I took my time. The pick really helped."

"You ready for the last part?"

Laura nodded.

Robbie stood up and dragged the body of Nick Carney

through the opening Laura had cleared to the mine shaft. Just as they had done all those years ago with the body of Stewart Wilson, Robbie maneuvered Nick's body until his legs were hanging over the edge of the mine shaft hole. As Robbie prepared to lower Nick's body vertically into the shaft by his arms, Robbie turned to Laura and asked, "Do you want to say anything?"

Laura shook her head. "I have nothing nice to say, so no."

Robbie nodded and then let the body go. Laura winced as she heard the thud of Nick's body coming to a stop at the bottom shaft. Robbie quickly moved to get the body of Peter Trelor.

After several minutes of working in silence, Robbie had all three bodies disposed of down the mine shaft. Laura threw the backpack, guns, and rifle down the shaft as well. Robbie came and stood alongside Laura and removed his shirt.

After wrapping the garment around a large rock, Robbie tossed the blood-covered shirt down the mine shaft. "I'll put your father's coat on when we get back to the Bronco."

"You won't be cold in the meantime?"

"No, I'm still trying to cool down. Going shirtless for a while will help."

Laura and Robbie stood staring down into the blackness of the mine shaft. Neither of them spoke for a moment as they reflected on what had happened that day.

"What are you thinking, Robbie?"

Robbie was silent for a moment before responding.

"I was thinking about the last time I stood here like this back in nineteen eighty-nine. I felt guilty... conflicted. I felt pressured by Jerry and Nick into hiding Wilson's body and walked away with a lot of regret. I don't feel like that this time. How about you?"

"It doesn't feel real to me yet, Robbie. I'm still trying to process the fact that there are another three men at the bottom of that shaft now... all who wanted to kill you... but I don't have any regrets."

Laura paused and then said, "Thank you for doing this, Robbie. I really appreciate it. I know this must be playing on your conscience."

Robbie wanted to change the subject. He was happy with the decision he and Laura had made and did not want her to feel indebted to him.

"I understand now why Mac chose the term catalin1989 for the email address. It had nothing to do with Stewart Wilson's death, as I first thought. It was simply code for something all four of us were involved in, just like in nineteen eighty-nine."

"Except, this time round, you weren't all friends."

They were both silent again as they relived what had happened today and how so much had changed. Finally, Robbie picked up Peter Trelor's aging satellite phone, which looked more like an old walkie-talkie than a modern communication device.

"I don't have reception up here with my phone, but this satellite phone is an entirely different matter."

Laura watched as Robbie keyed in an international number from memory and waited to be connected. He whispered 'voicemail' to her before continuing in a normal voice.

"Hi Petru, it's Robbie. I'm sending you a digital voice file by email in about twenty minutes. It has a recording of Richard Stelovak's voice command that is required to authorize the release of funds from the two accounts with the three million dollars of bribe money. If you know the account numbers, and I believe you do from Mac's emails, the money is yours. Nick and Jerry are both dead, so they won't be needing it. I'll explain it all later, but you need to act fast. When Stelovak finds out they're dead, he'll move the money and the opportunity will be gone. I'll call you tomorrow. Take care."

Robbie disconnected and then dropped the phone down the shaft.

Turning to Laura, he said, "We still have a lot to do. After we put the vines back and get back to the Bronco, we need to get all these cars down off the mountain. We don't have time to find Trelor's vehicle, but if it's the only one hidden up here somewhere, that won't matter as much."

"And you have an email to send."

"I'll stop and send it from my laptop when we get down to the highway. I'll have reception then."

"Okay."

"Then, there's just one more loose end we need to make sure is taken care of for Mac."

"Richard Stelovak?"

"Yes… Richard Stelovak."

Chapter Fifty-Nine

It had taken almost two hours for Robbie and Laura to ferry the two rental cars down off the mountain and back to Robbie's farm. The last task was to abandon Jerry's Lexus somewhere in Cypress Falls. It was almost nine p.m. as Robbie followed Laura's Bronco into Cypress Falls in the Lexus. He was looking forward to a shower, something to eat, and sleep.

They were both exhausted, and neither of them wanted to travel back to Vancouver that night. Robbie had suggested they stay at the farm. There was very little in the way of furniture in the house beyond a mattress and a sofa, but the power and water were still connected for use by the tenants who leased the stables.

Robbie smiled as he recalled Laura's response when he had suggested, 'After the day we've had Robbie, sleeping under a tree and eating pizza will seem five star.'

As they drove through the outskirts of Cypress Falls, Robbie saw the indicator lights of the Bronco come on as Laura pulled off the road in front of a small row of shops.

Robbie smiled and murmured, "She's found pizza," as he parked the Lexus behind the Bronco. Robbie got out and walked to the Bronco and climbed into the passenger side.

"Hey, stranger."

Laura looked out the window at the neon lights of the late-night pizza shop she had found.

"They're still open Robbie. I'm scared to drive any further into Cypress Falls, just in case everything else is closed, and this place shuts before we get back."

Robbie stared at Laura. He was glad Laura was excited about finding a pizza shop. If she was thinking about food, and had an appetite, hopefully what had happened today would not have any lasting detrimental impact on her. The early signs were good, he thought.

"Robbie, you're staring."

Robbie smiled. "Sorry, you better get used to it. I'm not going anywhere."

Laura suddenly became very serious. "Robbie, when we were up on Catalin Mountain today, you told me you loved me and wanted to take care of me. I know I didn't respond then, but it made me feel very special. I'll never forget that moment... I love you too."

Robbie reached across and kissed Laura. The kiss was long, soft, and gentle. He sighed as he eventually pulled away. "I need to get rid of the Lexus and you need to order pizza."

Laura smiled. "There's always something..."

As Robbie opened the door, Laura asked, "So, where are you going to park it?"

"I was thinking about that on the drive in. There's an upmarket tourist cafe and gift shop on the other side of the river. It has its own parking lot. The Lexus won't look out of place there, and it may be a couple of days before it's noticed and reported."

"I was also thinking on the way in. Should we be wiping it down to avoid leaving fingerprints or DNA?"

"No need to. Jerry gave me a ride home the other night after our meal at the restaurant. If anything comes of it, I had a legitimate reason to be in the car."

"Good. You want me to swing by and pick you up when the pizza is ready?"

"Hopefully, I'll be back by then. There's an elevated footbridge across the river near to the cafe's parking lot. It's only a ten-minute walk back across from there. I think I'll almost be back before you have a chance to eat my pizza."

A smile spread across Laura's face. "Maybe, Robbie. No guarantees, though. I'm starving." Laura tilted her head slightly and added, "So, Robbie, tell me something I don't know about you already. What's your favorite pizza?"

"Supreme with extra cheese. And you?"

"Meat lovers with double pepperoni."

Robbie kissed Laura again and added, "I'm happy with either or both." As he opened the car door, he said, "Back soon."

"Promise?"

"Promise."

Laura watched Robbie through the rear-view mirror as he went back to the Lexus, got in, and drove away.

Chapter Sixty

Robbie drove to the tourist cafe without incident and parked in the empty parking lot. The cafe and gift shop had long since closed for the night and he was glad to be alone. As he got out of the car, he noticed Jerry had left a lightweight jacket on the rear car seat. He was still wearing the large overcoat Laura had given him. While it was less conspicuous than going shirtless, it was cumbersome and overly warm for such a mild night.

Retrieving the jacket, Robbie got out and locked the car. As he was about to change coats for the walk back across the footbridge, Robbie decided a wash first would be a good idea. He carefully made his way down to the river's edge and took off the heavy coat. Finding a small rocky outcrop to stand on, he reached down and cupped his hands in the water. The cool water felt refreshing as he splashed his face and washed the blood, dirt, and grime from his upper body.

After several minutes, Robbie felt clean again and walked back up the bank to put Jerry's coat on. His phone rang. He thought it would be Laura ringing to tell him the pizzas were already ready, but as he pulled the phone from the pocket of his jeans and looked at the caller ID, the name Will Sherlock appeared.

After such a grueling day, the only person Robbie wanted to talk to was Laura. Robbie debated letting the call go through to voice mail, but decided he should answer it. He had used his publisher's financial analyst in the past and knew Will Sherlock never called without good reason.

"Hi, Will."

"Hi, Robbie. How's your week been?"

Robbie smiled, "Will, it would take me a week to tell you about my week."

"Well, I don't have time for that, Robbie. I'm still at work, just about to leave, in fact. But I have news for you. Good news, in fact."

"Don't leave me hanging."

"Well, to cut a long story short, the Roma bank data you gave me checks out. I've spent sixty hours on it this week and it's all paid off. We've made solid connections from the bank back to several corporations here, all involved in organized crime activities from credit card fraud right through to large-scale money laundering. I've run it by the corporate lawyer here and she's very excited. We're talking major jail time for several CEOs of well-respected companies previously thought to be legitimate. The evidence is solid, Robbie, you've done a great job."

"Tell me, Will, was the name Richard Stelovak on the list?"

"At the very top, Robbie. He set up an incredibly complex web of intermediary companies to separate his Stelecom Development Company from what he had going on in Eastern Europe. The guy is seriously wealthy but will probably wind up in jail inside twelve months."

Robbie smiled again. "Thanks, Will. I appreciate your hard work."

"No problem, we're a team. Hey, I've got another call coming in. I'll call you tomorrow to arrange a phone conference on Monday. You're going to get syndicated coverage again, my friend."

After they disconnected, Robbie put on Jerry's jacket and started his walk across the elevated footbridge back to Laura. The footbridge over the river was part of a tourist feature walk and provided a good view of the township of Cypress Falls. As Robbie looked out across the township while he walked, he reflected on some of the happy moments he and Mac had shared here as young boys growing up.

As he neared the halfway point, he stopped for a moment to enjoy the view and look down at the water below. The river current here was almost non-existent, which made it a popular fishing spot for locals. Robbie remembered how he and Mac used to fish in this part of the river before they constructed the footbridge. He smiled as he remembered the first time Mac had actually caught a fish. The look on his face had been priceless.

As the memories of Mac and their childhood came flooding back, Robbie decided he needed to keep walking. Tonight was not a night to be somber, but a night to celebrate still being alive. As he started walking again, he felt sure that's what Mac would have wanted.

Robbie had only taken a few steps when the sound of a mobile phone interrupted his thoughts. The ring tone differed from his own phone, and it was only then he realized the sound was coming from the top pocket of Jerry's jacket, which he was now wearing. Robbie had no interest in answering it and decided to drop the phone in the river.

As Robbie pulled the phone out of the jacket pocket, he checked caller ID out of habit.

As the phone continued ringing, the caller ID on the phone's screen showed only two letters: 'RS'.

Robbie murmured, 'It couldn't be', as he hit the answer button and listened to an angry male voice.

"We had a deal, Jerry. You get your money only when the deal was done to my satisfaction and that included being there today for contract signing. Your no-show stunt today is going to cost you big time. You and Carney have no idea..."

As the voice rose in volume, Robbie cut him off. "This isn't Jerry Marsden, Stelovak!"

The phone was silent for a moment before Richard Stelovak demanded, "Who is this?"

"I'll give you a clue. You had my best friend murdered a week ago and tried to do the same to me on Wednesday night, but failed."

There was a slight pause before Stelovak responded. "I don't know who you are or what you're talking about. Put Marsden on now."

"Jerry Marsden is dead, and so is your other goon, Nick Carney. Peter Trelor shot them both this afternoon."

There was silence for a moment on the other end of the phone before Stelovak said, "And how do I know I can believe you?"

"I don't care if you do or you don't. Why don't you wait a couple of weeks? That should be proof enough when they haven't surfaced."

"You have no idea who you're dealing with, Mayne. This is a very dangerous game you're playing."

"You're wrong Stelovak. I know exactly who I'm dealing with. A murderous scumbag who lives off organized crime. I know all about your links to the Roma bank. We've made the connection through all your dirty little shelf companies right back to the mother ship—Stelecom Industries itself. You may have been able to get your hit men to do your dirty work and hide behind your alibis and bribes and clever lawyers and crooked judges in the past, but that's all over now. You've overplayed your hand and as CEO of Stelecom, you're going to—"

"I'm going to kill you myself, Mayne, and that's a promise!"

"No Stelovak. You can't shut this down any more. It's gone too far. My publishing agency knows. Their lawyers know. And one of the best corporate fraud investigators in the country is documenting it all. I'm going to make this syndicated front-page news within days and you're going to need an army of lawyers to keep your jail time to under twenty years."

"You're bluffing!"

"It's over, Stelovak. You can't kill everyone. You played the game too long and now you're going to pay."

Stelovak flew into a rage in response, but Robbie was no longer listening as he dropped the phone over the side railing. Robbie watched the phone as it fell to the river below and disappeared with barely a splash.

Satisfied, Robbie whispered, "It's not over, Mac", and then continued his journey across the footbridge and back to Laura.

Chapter Sixty-One

Delray and Westcott sipped their coffees from paper cups as they stood in the hallway outside Stelovak's office. Apart from the photographs of Blackwell, the search, so far, had not been productive. Both Delray and Westcott figured Stelovak would only spend one night in jail before making bail unless they could find other evidence that would reveal he was a threat to society and should not be released.

Westcott looked at his watch. "It's nine p.m. and we still have a long way to go, boss. I'd be happier if we had found some other evidence."

Delray scowled. "I'm not surprised, Danny. Guys like him don't get this far without learning how to cover their tracks properly. We just need to be patient and thorough."

"I think we need to re-interview Rudy Henning again, first thing tomorrow before Stelovak makes bail. I think we can get his confession if we play him Keaton's video and tell him Stelovak is in custody."

"Good plan. He's more likely to take the deal if he thinks his time is running out. We'll offer him protection as well and keep him out of the general prison population to make it a simple decision."

"We should also schedule the interview with Stelovak at the same time, boss. That way, Henning will only get one of Michael Phipps' underlings providing legal representation. Phipps won't be letting Stelovak out of his sight. That should make it easier to convince Henning that he's not overly important when he only gets the second fiddle lawyer. I'm confident we can convince him he needs to look after himself."

Delray shook his head as he smiled. "Danny, sometimes you scare me." Delray nodded towards Stelovak's executive conference room door, outside of which a uniformed police officer stood guard, and added, "It's awfully quiet in there?"

"I stuck my head in ten minutes ago to let Stelovak know the search would take a couple more hours at least. He wasn't happy and Phipps went off his dial. Called it an outrage and promised me he would have my badge, but that was more for Stelovak's benefit than mine."

"How did Stelovak look?"

"He's unraveling. I asked him about the contents of the inner safe, particularly the bank bonds from the Roma bank. He clammed right up and Phipps refused to answer questions until we have an itemized list of the contents and we conduct the interview formally. They're hiding something, boss. I'm sure if we dig hard enough, we'll find what it is."

"They're also buying time to get their story straight. I'd love to know what the two of them are talking about right now."

Michael Phipps was satisfied with the progress he had made with Stelovak in the two hours they had been alone in the conference room. While he had expressed outrage at Westcott and Delray for his client being detained, the time had been a bonus and allowed them to get their story straight before the formal interview.

Richard Stelovak looked satisfied. "Only one night in jail?"

"It will just be a holding cell, Richard. We go before a judge tomorrow and get you bail and then work on getting the whole thing thrown out. We can easily discredit Keaton as a disgruntled employee who used nefarious means to plant photographs in your safe. Your secretary's testimony will back that up."

"I'm still not sure about the fingerprints?"

"We stick to the story, Richard. Keaton showed the photographs to you after claiming they had arrived in the mail. You thumbed through them, gave them back, and told him to report it to the police. We keep it simple, no elaboration beyond that."

Stelovak nodded. "That's good Michael, I like it."

Stelovak picked up his phone. "I need to make a call while those two buffoons finish their search."

"I can wait outside if you like, Richard."

"Michael, you and I have no secrets, except the upper limit of how much I'm prepared to pay you an hour."

Stelovak hit speed dial on his phone and mumbled why he waited to be connected, "This better be good, Jerry."

A moment later, Stelovak started shouting into his phone. Phipps tried to counsel Stelovak to keep his voice down, but he was in another world.

"We had a deal, Jerry! You get your money only when the deal is done to my satisfaction and that included being there today for contract signing. Your no show stunt today is going to cost you big time. You and Carney have…"

Pretending to busy himself with some of his legal pad notes, Phipps listened intently as Stelovak turned white and demanded, "Who is this?"

Phipps watched as Stelovak's body language changed from confident to uncertain as he listened intently to whoever it was on the other end of the phone. It could not be Jerry, he thought. Although Jerry Marsden was the mayor of Vancouver, in Stelovak's organization, they gave him little more than lip service.

Phipps' observation was confirmed when Stelovak responded, "I don't know who you are or what you're talking about. Put Marsden on now."

He listened with astonishment as the exchange continued. He had known Richard Stelovak for many years, and no one had ever spoken to him like this that he could recall, at least no one who was still living.

"I'm going to kill you myself, Mayne. That's a promise."

Phipps watched as Stelovak flew into a rage and yelled a volley of threats and obscenities into his phone. Before he could get to Stelovak to calm him down, the conference room door opened.

As Westcott stood in the doorway looking from Phipps to Stelovak, the room went quiet again. "Everything alright in here?"

Phipps and Westcott both looked to Stelovak for an answer. As Stelovak stared into space, oblivious to the question and his surroundings, a single bead of sweat formed on his brow and slowly trickled down the side of his face.

Westcott stared at Stelovak for a moment before he closed the door. Phipps knew Westcott had his answer.

Epilogue

Robbie put the paintbrush down as he heard the unmistakable sound of Laura's Bronco coming up the gravel driveway to the farmhouse.

It had been three months since 'that day' on Catalin Mountain. Robbie had spent every moment he could with Laura since the incident. They had talked at length about what had happened, and he was now confident she was making a full recovery.

Robbie had decided early in those weeks that he would move back to Vancouver permanently. His base for his work as a freelance journalist could be anywhere that had a phone and Internet connection. Laura had become his priority as their relationship continued to develop.

Much of the past four weeks had been busy painting the farmhouse inside and out. Laura had insisted that if Robbie was going to move back to the family farm, that it needed some repairs and a fresh coat of paint. It had been great therapy for them both.

Laura was not afraid of hard work and, after choosing

the color themes, had done most of the interior painting herself and always arrived early and dressed for painting and renovating.

After parking the Bronco, Robbie's mouth fell open as Laura stepped out to greet him in a pair of new tight-fitting burgundy jeans, a black top and matching high heel shoes. Today's outfit was quite a contrast to what Laura normally wore to the farm. After a long and lingering hello kiss, Laura said with a pretend frown, "Mayne, you're staring again."

Robbie's lopsided grin was back. "You can't wear clothes like that and not have people stare, particularly me."

Picking up a cloth, Robbie began cleaning paint from his hands as he stepped down off the porch to admire his morning's handy work. The house looked better now than at any time he could remember from his childhood. He was sure his father would be proud if he were still alive.

"One more day, Laura, and we'll be done."

As Laura came and stood alongside Robbie, she said, "I'm glad you moved back, Robbie. This is so much nicer than a long-distance relationship."

"I can't imagine wanting to live anywhere else now," said Robbie with a smile. "This is home."

"So, where are we going on this mysterious date?"

Robbie had arranged to take Laura on a picnic to a remote spot called Tangmere Lake. It was a secluded, picturesque location, twenty minutes north of Cypress Falls. He wanted to keep the details a secret and grinned as he responded, "Well… It wouldn't be a mystery if I told you, now would it?"

"Am I'm dressed appropriately?"

Robbie laughed. "On so many levels."

"Can you at least give me a clue?"

"A picnic. By a lake. I've packed everything already. We even have champagne, the de-alcoholized kind, of course."

A huge smile spread across Laura's face, which she did her best to hide. "Champagne? Are we celebrating something?"

Robbie and Laura had already talked about their future. They were not only in love, but deeply committed to one another. Marriage was the obvious next step and something they both wanted.

"I sure hope so."

Before Laura could respond, Robbie changed the subject. He wanted his formal proposal to happen in the special setting as he had planned. "I got a call from Detective Westcott this morning. Stelovak is going to trial for the murder of Mac and the two other guys connected with his company in three weeks. One of his former hit men has confessed everything and will testify at the trial. You'll never guess who they have lined up as the other key witness."

"Give me a clue?"

"He's now very rich."

"Petru?"

The day after the Catalin incident, Petru and Robbie had a very long phone call. Now three million dollars richer, Petru was planning to leave Romania and his past life behind for good. Robbie had asked him if he would be prepared to cooperate with Vancouver Police by providing evidence about Stelovak's business associates and dealings in Romania. Petru had readily agreed and Robbie had provided his contact details to Westcott.

"Yes. Westcott is arranging a visa for him as we speak. There's even an offer of citizenship on the table if he wants."

"Petru really is turning his life around."

"I'm not sure we will get to see him, though. He's still in hiding. The syndicate is still after him in Romania and Westcott thinks Stelovak will try his best to see he's taken out here before he gets a chance to testify."

"So that means witness protection?"

"For a while, at least. Once Stelovak is behind bars, the threat will probably be over if he stays here."

"So… did the detective mention anything else?"

Robbie and Laura had both been initially concerned that they may have been suspects in the disappearances of Nick Carney and Jerry Marsden. The disappearances of Vancouver's mayor and director of the OCTF had made front-page news for weeks and were now being treated as murders.

They had only interviewed Robbie once since then to complete the statement he had made on his attempted murder in the holding cell.

"No, but I asked how the investigation was going. Westcott said, off the record, that they discovered both Nick and Jerry had accumulated sizable sums of money in secret bank accounts that could not be explained. He suspects they were both dirty, and it finally caught up with them. But, with all the media hype around this, he's not saying so publicly."

"Seeing as you're a journalist, I'm surprised he said that much to you?"

Robbie thought for a moment before he responded. "He trusts me. I introduced him to Petru and gave him everything I had on Stelovak for my story on organized crime. And, almost winding up another one of Stelovak's murder victims must have helped as well."

In a quieter voice, Laura asked, "Do you really think it's over, Robbie?"

Robbie didn't think it would be really over until they stripped Stelovak of his power and fortune, but now was not the time to be worrying Laura about that. She was making a great recovery, and he wanted to keep it that way.

"We've done as much as we can, Laura. Everyone connected with Mac's death is either dead, behind bars, or soon will be. It's time for us to move on. I know that's what Mac would have wanted."

"Good. I want to look forward, not back."

"I better go take a shower before I change. You smell way better than me."

"And I will visit my friends while I wait."

With a pretend frown, Robbie said, "You didn't bring sugar again, did you?"

As she started walking back to her Bronco, Laura replied, "I might have..."

Feigning being cross as he watched her retrieve a small brown paper bag from the vehicle, Robbie protested, "Their teeth are going to fall out..."

Laura waved him off with a laugh and kept walking.

Robbie walked back onto the porch and opened the front door. Before going inside, he paused and looked back at Laura, who was now standing at the front fence feeding sugar cubes to the horses. Life was good again, he thought, and turned to walk inside.

Next in The Catalin Series

vinci-books.com/catalin-crossing

His testimony could destroy an empire. If they don't kill him first...

Former hacker Petru Janco is ready to present evidence against a notorious crime boss and vanish into witness protection. Instead, he's brutally ambushed and forced to run for his life. His only hope of escape is a young midwife caught in the crossfire. Pursued by relentless hitmen through the unforgiving Catalin Mountains, Petru must forge a desperate alliance to survive.

Turn the page for a free preview...

The Catalin Crossing: Chapter One

Petru Janco's world narrowed to a single line of parked cars as he sprinted in a zigzag pattern through the shadows. Desperately seeking refuge from the gunman, the narrow alley in Bucharest offered no hiding place; the shooter's steady hand tracking his every movement. There was no hesitation, only the silent promise of retribution as the gunman squeezed the trigger. The 9mm Glock discharged with lethal purpose, its bullet tearing through the air at a blistering 1,200 feet per second. The physics were mercilessly efficient—speed and momentum carrying the projectile on a path that outpaced sound itself.

The Glock's boom was barely perceptible to Petru as he felt a sharp sting just above his hip while darting between two parked cars. His legs gave way, and he crumpled to the ground—his escape brutally thwarted by a small copper projectile that left him paralyzed from the waist down...

The Catalin Code

Petru's gasp cut through the silence of his hotel room as his eyes snapped open. The remnants of the recurring nightmare clung to him like his sweat-drenched cotton shirt. He exhaled slowly, his heart rate gradually returning to normal. Now awake, he turned his head, his gaze landing on the wheelchair parked beside his bed. The sight no longer shocked him, nor did it stir resentment. Instead, it offered an odd comfort—a silent acknowledgment of the battle he had endured and the scars—both visible and hidden—that it had left behind.

The chair had begun to appear in his recent dreams, an unassuming participant amidst the turmoil of his subconscious. Once he had sprinted through dreamscapes with able legs; now the wheels often whispered along unseen paths, integrating themselves into his dream world as they had into his waking life. Perhaps it was acceptance, or maybe resignation, of his new reality as a paraplegic. The boundary between his two worlds was blurring, the chair becoming as much a part of him as the blood coursing through his veins.

With the night's terror behind him, Petru prepared to face the day anew. After combing back his dark wavy hair off his face with his fingers, he glanced at his phone on the nightstand—it was just after 6 a.m. His uncle would arrive in two hours to take him to the airport. It had been almost twelve months since that fateful day in Bucharest when he'd been shot in the alley while fleeing Richard Stelovak's henchmen.

Stelovak, a notorious crime boss with an empire spanning Europe and North America, had orchestrated a string of murders, including that of Petru's sister, Elena. She had been killed while trying to escape Stelovak's Romanian gang, who were hunting for young girls to abduct and sell as sex slaves.

Initially, Petru had been rash—his rage overtaking any clear thinking as he sought revenge. But he had quickly realized he was no match for Stelovak's men after they hunted him down, shot him, and left him for dead. But Petru had survived and Stelovak had come after him again.

With a fortune rumored to be worth half a billion dollars, Stelovak had seemed untouchable and above the law. But the authorities had finally caught up with him, and he was set to stand trial for the murder of an associate in Vancouver. Petru had readily agreed to testify—if he could survive long enough. What he had failed to do, he hoped the Canadian police could accomplish in bringing justice for Elena and Stelovak's many other victims.

Despite his disability, he had successfully evaded Stelovak's grasp in Romania, constantly moving every two or three days to a new cheap hotel and staying entirely off the grid. But he knew things would be different in Canada on Stelovak's home turf. Petru's stomach churned as he contemplated his decision to enter the Canadian witness protection program. He knew it was the only way to escape Stelovak's powerful hold, but at what cost?

Petru sighed as he looked at a spot of peeling wallpaper on the wall of his hotel room. It would be what it would be —he was on a collision course with Stelovak and no obstacle would stand in his way of seeking justice for his sister, even if it cost him his life. After folding back the bed sheets, he used his forearms to maneuver himself to the edge of the bed. He reached for his wheelchair and easily transferred to it to begin his daily routine. As someone who was paralyzed from the waist down, he had perfected the skills needed for showering, getting dressed, and taking care of his medical needs independently. It usually took him about an hour, leaving him plenty of time for a final pack before his uncle arrived.

Richard Stelovak stared out through his corner office window at the Vancouver skyline as day turned to night. Despite the breathtaking vista, he couldn't quell the rage simmering within him as he thought about the impending trial—a ticking time bomb threatening to shatter his carefully constructed world.

He reached for a Mont Blanc pen on his imposing oak desk and twirled it absently between his fingers as Leon Blackwell's face flashed in his memory. It had been a necessary evil, he told himself—a loose end that needed tying up. Blackwell's attempt to flee, to escape from the money laundering operation they were ensnared in, had sealed his fate. Stelovak's lip curled in derision. In this game, there were no resignations, no early retirements. Only loose ends—and those who tied them up.

His mind wandered back to the moment it had all unraveled: the blackmail photographs, the hit gone wrong, and then the ultimate betrayal—Randolph Keaton, his own in-house counsel, turning on him. The rage that had simmered now threatened to boil over. Revenge would be his. But he just needed to weather this storm first.

A sharp rap at the door jolted Stelovak from his brooding. "Enter," he barked, not trying to hide his mood.

The door swung open, revealing the lean, imposing figure of Michael Phipps. Stelovak narrowed his eyes as he took in his defense lawyer's immaculate appearance—the perfectly pressed suit, the meticulously groomed silver hair.

Phipps's hawkish appearance seemed to slice through the tension in the room as he strode forward with an aura of icy competence.

Without preamble, Phipps lowered himself into the chair opposite Stelovak. His piercing gaze locked onto his client. "We have much to discuss, Richard," Phipps stated, his tone clipped and businesslike.

Stelovak leaned forward, his eyes glinting with barely contained fury. "Indeed we do. And we can start by you explaining to me why this is going to trial. As I recall, you promised me it wouldn't get this far—"

"I never promised that," Phipps interrupted. "I said I was confident the murder trial would never get to the point where a jury would decide your fate." He paused, then added in a more measured tone, "And I am still confident."

"I pay for results, not words, Michael."

"And results you shall have, Richard. But it will take time. Those photos found in your safe are the key to the prosecution's case. Once I discredit them, their case will collapse like a house of cards."

Stelovak brooded over the photos of Leon Blackwell. Eight pictures taken with a telescopic lens by a photographer staked out in a building across the street from Blackwell's office. The photographer had been patient and had finally captured Blackwell with his pants down and in the throes of infidelity with his temp secretary on his office desk. Stelovak had thumbed through the originals provided by Keaton before ordering copies to be sent to Blackwell as a threat. Usually, this tactic provided the loyalty he demanded from his associates, but Blackwell panicked and chose to run instead. Then, there was the ultimate betrayal by Keaton, who had planted the photographs with his

The Catalin Code

fingerprints on them in his own safe just before a police raid.

He pushed the incident to the back of his mind. "And how do you plan on discrediting the photographs?"

"We know they were planted to frame you," said Phipps calmly.

Stelovak listened without interruption as Phipps laid out his strategy and then nodded his approval. "Let me know if there is anything I can do to assist."

Phipps said, "It's all under control. This is what you pay me for, and I won't let you down."

An amused smile spread across Stelovak's face. "I will end up paying you a king's ransom before this is over, Michael. But I'm confident you will make this all... go away."

Phipps ignored the compliment as he pressed on. "There's been one more development that we need to discuss."

"What kind of development?" snapped Stelovak.

"Petru Janco," said Phipps flatly.

Stelovak clenched his jaw. "What the hell has he got to do with this?"

"They're flying him in from Romania as a witness. He will—"

"A witness? He knows nothing about Blackwell!" snarled Stelovak.

"The prosecution is going to use him as a character witness," said Phipps calmly. "They say he knows about your supposed international organized crime syndicate and that you have had people killed before."

Stelovak barked, "This is totally unacceptable! I won't have my reputation dragged through the mud by some juvenile upstart."

"That may be a little harder to achieve than you or I would like, Richard."

"And why is that?" snapped Stelovak.

"He's being placed in witness protection when he flies in. The first time we will see him is in court." Phipps outlined his strategy for dealing with Janco at the trial, but Stelovak heard none of it. The meeting ended shortly after, with Phipps again assuring Stelovak he would get the outcome he sought.

After Phipps's exit, Stelovak stewed alone in his office, his thoughts fixed on Petru Janco. He had never met the Romanian and was reasonably sure Janco had stolen three million dollars in bribe money from one of his offshore accounts through the tiresome Randolph Keaton. He still had staff tracing the money trail, and when he confirmed who it was, his retribution would be swift and lethal. But the prospect of Janco coming to Canada for the trial presented him with a unique opportunity he intended to leverage—witness protection program or not.

He removed a burner phone from the middle drawer of his oak desk and dialed a number from memory. After the call connected and he was greeted by a dispassionate silicon voice, Stelovak said, "I have a job for you."

The caller listened without interruption as Stelovak laid out what he wanted. When he finished the call, Stelovak pocketed the phone and murmured, "You just made a huge mistake, Janco."

The Catalin Crossing: Chapter Two

The doughy scent of fresh bread lingered as Petru maneuvered his wheelchair toward the passenger side of his uncle's aging bakery truck. After being helped into the vehicle by his uncle, Petru took one last look at the rundown hotel that had been his temporary home for the past three nights on the outskirts of Bucharest. Now a millionaire, he could afford to stay wherever he pleased, but he preferred small, unassuming hotels that accepted cash and didn't ask too many questions. As his uncle settled into the driver's seat, he wondered if he would ever spend another night in Romania. His uncle's voice cut through the creaking of the truck's suspension as it shifted under his weight, "Are you sure about this?"

Petru looked out through the truck's windshield at the dark clouds that were forming over Bucharest. The forecast had been for storms and almost felt like an omen for him. "I've never been more certain about anything in my life."

Stefan shook his head as he started the engine. They

were quiet for a moment as his uncle navigated his way through the back streets of the city to avoid morning traffic. "You know Stelovak's construction empire in Vancouver… it's a facade."

Petru nodded. "An empire built on blood and deceit…" His eyes remained fixed on the street ahead of them, but his mind was tracing through the intricate web of digital accounts he'd once hacked, accounts that told stories of Richard Stelovak's criminal reach. "I can't let him get away with what he's done."

"Your courage is commendable, but you need to remember he plays a ruthless game." Stefan's voice dropped to a whisper, almost drowned out by the hum of the engine. "And he doesn't lose."

The bakery truck's engine rumbled, starkly contrasting the silence that had settled between them like frost. Petru used the strength in his hands and arms to shift in his seat. He felt the vibrations travel up his arms—the same arms that had grown stronger as his legs refused to heal. With each pothole and bump on the road to Bucharest airport, memories jostled within him.

Petru broke the silence. "Why did you give up the life?"

Stefan glanced at him, his expression unreadable for a moment. He returned his attention to the road and said, "I was young and stupid. Richard was my older cousin, and I was easily influenced. One night, we broke into a house in Bucharest. The owner was supposed to be at the theater with his wife, but they came home early because she was sick. Richard fired shots as we made our escape, and the man's wife was killed…"

After a long silence, Stefan continued. "I couldn't make peace with it. She was a young mother and innocent. When

Richard brushed it off as nothing, I knew I wasn't cut out for that life and returned to the family bakery. It was a long time ago, but I still think about it every day."

Petru nodded as he thought about his sister, Elena. Just a year ago, she was a lively and energetic young woman. But then she became addicted to drugs, and her life quickly spiraled out of control and she found herself immersed in a dangerous underworld run by a distant relative on the other side of the world.

"What you are doing is noble, Petru, but it is not without its risks."

"I know the risks. I live with them every day."

"He knows, Petru," said Stefan, his eyes dark pools of concern. "Richard is aware that you're testifying, and he'll do anything to stop it."

Petru's fingers curled into a fist, the memory of the bullet that severed his spinal cord igniting a familiar anger. "What else can he take from me?"

"Being in a wheelchair is better than being dead." Stefan's voice was blunt, a stark warning that echoed the fear lurking in the periphery of Petru's resolve.

Petru gritted his teeth. He knew the path ahead was fraught with danger, yet he owed it to Elena's memory to face the man who had taken everything from him.

Stefan killed the engine after the bakery truck rattled to a halt in a side street near Bucharest airport. They both stared at the late-model black Mercedes van in front of them.

"Is that them?" asked Stefan.

"I assume so. They will take me in through a side entrance and directly to the plane, just in case Stelovak has someone hidden in the airport to take me out."

Stefan's weathered face creased with concern. "I'm sure this witness protection team is very competent..." Stefan paused, pulled out a crumpled slip of paper from his shirt pocket, and pressed it into Petru's palm.

"Listen," his uncle added in a low and earnest voice, "I have a contact in North America. I haven't seen him in a long time, but he is someone I trust and a man of considerable resources. If you get into trouble and the police can't help, call him."

Petru felt the paper's edges dig into his skin as he closed his fingers around it. He nodded, tucking the note safely inside his jacket. His heart hammered against his rib cage, not from fear but from an unwavering sense of duty that propelled him towards the unknown.

After taking a deep breath, Petru pulled out his cell phone and dialed a number from memory. He waited for his call to be answered and said, "I'm in the bread van behind you."

Petru disconnected, and they both watched as a side door of the black van opened and a man and a woman dressed in business suits emerged. After making a three-hundred-and-sixty-degree sweep of the street, they nodded to one another and opened the rear cargo door of the van.

As Petru stared into a space set up for a wheelchair in the back of the Mercedes, he sighed and said, "This is it."

Stefan nodded. "You will be in my prayers each night."

"I'm going to need them," murmured Petru as he watched the officers approach.

The Catalin Code

The sleek Mercedes van glided away from the airport, its tinted windows concealing the cargo within. Inside, Petru's wheelchair was securely fastened, the young man's eyes darting nervously between his two silent companions from the Royal Canadian Mounted Police. The transition from his uncle's humble bakery van to the government vehicle had been swift, almost too swift, leaving Petru with a creeping sense of unease.

Petru's voice cut through the tension as the Romanian countryside blurred past. "We're not flying today?" The words tumbled out, tinged with a mixture of confusion and trepidation.

Agent Jim Charlton, his weathered face a mask of calm professionalism, turned to Petru with a smile that didn't quite reach his eyes. "We're flying out tomorrow," he explained, his tone measured. "Tonight, we're staying in a safe house not far from here while we get final clearances."

Petru nodded slowly, his mind racing. "So why collect me today and why so early?" he challenged, his voice steadier than he felt.

Charlton's response came smoothly, almost rehearsed. "There's paperwork we need to complete here in Romania and in Canada to take you out of the country." He launched into a detailed explanation about Canada's witness protection program and pre-departure briefings, but Petru was only half-listening.

The gnawing doubt in his stomach was transforming into a leaden weight. Petru had been free all his life, even after losing the use of his legs. But now, he felt trapped in this speeding van with strangers—the walls of an invisible cage closing in on him. His uncle's parting words echoed as a haunting refrain: *"Are you sure about this, Petru?"*

As the van continued its journey, he desperately hoped he had made the right decision as the shadows of doubt lengthened in his mind.

Grab your copy...
vinci-books.com/catalin-crossing

About the Author

Trevor Douglas is a multi-award winning author and the recipient of the gold medal for the Best Crime Fiction Novel, and the gold medal for the Best Overall Novel in the 2024 Global Book Awards.

Trevor is married with two adult sons and when he is not writing, enjoys bushwalking, watching AFL and discovering the best coffee shops in Brisbane with his wife.

After a long and successful career as an IT consultant, Trevor now writes full time.

www.ingramcontent.com/pod-product-compliance
Ingram Content Group UK Ltd.
Pitfield, Milton Keynes, MK11 3LW, UK
UKHW040249230426
470297UK00004B/50